THE CURSE OF A FAEBLOOD

MK LORBER

Three Pom Press

The Curse of a Faeblood
By MK Lorber

Copyright © 2022 by MK Lorber

Published by Three Pom Press

ISBN e-book: 978-1-7359717-2-8
ISBN Paperback: 978-1-7359717-3-5

Cover Design by Bianca Bordianu at Moonpress/moonpress.co

DEDICATION

To Hershey Almond—
Wishing you all the plot bunnies in the next life

CONTENTS

Chapter 1   1

Chapter 2   9

Chapter 3   23

Chapter 4   35

Chapter 5   47

Chapter 6   65

Chapter 7   73

Chapter 8   85

Chapter 9   97

Chapter 10   111

Chapter 11   125

Chapter 12   139

Chapter 13   151

Chapter 14   163

Chapter 15   177

Chapter 16   191

Chapter 17   203

Chapter 18   217

Chapter 19   231

Chapter 20   243

Chapter 21   259

Chapter 22   273

Chapter 23   285

Chapter 24   297

Chapter 25   311

Chapter 26   325

Chapter 27   341

Chapter 28   357

Chapter 29   371

Chapter 30   383

Chapter 31   395

Chapter 32   411

Chapter 33   423
Epilogue   435

Acknowledgments   445

CHAPTER ONE

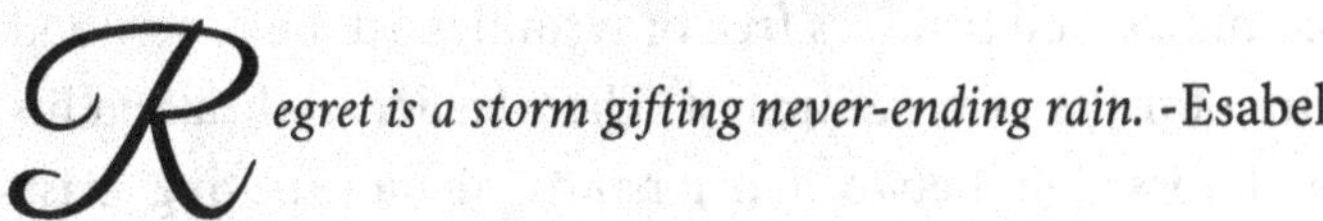

egret is a storm gifting never-ending rain. -Esabel

Midpointe, the Mining Territory
Present day...

Mother claimed the Red Guard were only good for two things: protecting the Faeblood Lords and terrorizing the human populace.

While the same cursed magic ran through Ember's veins, it didn't prevent her from becoming their next target.

Sweat pooled on her brow and trailed down her cheek. It rolled along her skin as easily as her composure threatened to climb up her throat. Behind her, the rough stone wall dug into her thin tunic, reminding Ember the only way out of this pile of rubbish was the way she crawled in.

A self-inflicted snare.

She knew better than to steal bread during daylight.

The barkeep spotted had her and alerted the nearest Red Guard patrol.

She counted six pairs of legs marching past the stack of barrels concealing her hiding spot in the alley between the tavern and bakery. Afternoon sun glinted off polished armor plates, an unnecessary signal for her to stay put.

The leader of the group halted a mere twenty paces away, rested his hand on the hilt of a dagger looped in his belt, and let out a shrill whistle. Five men fell into line behind him like ducklings waddling after their mother.

Except these weren't fuzzy, innocent creatures.

Despite spending most of last night's patrol drinking with the locals, the men appeared alert. They sported clear eyes, clean red tunics, and trousers free of wrinkles. All but one stood tall waiting for the next command. Their leader unsheathed his blade and tossed it between his hands, demonstrating crisp reflexes.

"Find the girl." He waved his arm in dismissal.

She grasped the fraying strap of her small satchel. A gift for her mother while pregnant with Ember, it served as a constant companion on their brief forays into society these past twenty-one years. Too bad the relic was heavy with memories and tears but light on anything she could use as a weapon. It twisted around her torso, hindering her movements and drawing attention to her profile.

But her escape wasn't worth the price of abandoning it. She'd rather rot in the Castle dungeons than part with a piece of her mother.

The men drifted apart.

Two squeezed behind the bakery on the right, turning sideways to fit through the narrow passage. Another pair marched straight ahead, their long strides carrying them to the main square. The leader rummaged through a pile of crates across the alley, flipping over the larger ones and peering underneath.

The last one, the pock-marked soldier with a slight slouch, kicked at the spoiled fish bones in front of the stack of barrels, calling out in a sing-song voice, "Here, kitty-kitty."

Keep moving at the first sign of a threat. It was her mother's adage.

The slightest perception of trouble meant a different farming village. A new home. Another chance to start over while hiding in the territory that supplied crops for the realm. The two of them had perfected their guise over the years — a lonely healer and her fatherless child trading a valuable commodity for shelter and provisions.

It was easy. Safe. But with only her mother to share her day, she'd become listless — from the endless isolation and predictable routine and lack of companionship — yearning for the life of a common villager instead of the snippets of time stolen with others her age.

The leader grunted.

He kicked a pebble, and the tip of his unmarred leather boot sent up a plume of dust. His dagger flew in a high arc, landing with a thud on the closest barrel. She resisted the urge to flinch.

"She can't have gone far."

When Ember had arrived in the village two days prior, she noted the fine homes and neat shop windows lining cobble-stone roads arranged in a square. There was a central grassy hill, surrounded by benches and rows of cultivated wildflowers. A well at the top boasted a stacked stone surround and a constant supply of water.

But the longer she stayed, the more she recognized the freshly thatched roofs and the cheerily painted shutters were an illusion — a sleight of hand to tempt an unobservant eye from the less than idyllic living conditions.

All was not as it seemed in the mining village.

Those quaint homes and fancy shops concealed a dark

underworld of back alleys, shady trade, and broken family dynamics.

Children always followed a half pace behind their parents. Never speaking. Never playing. The absence of giggles was more deafening than squeals from an intense game of tag.

Those strategically placed benches sat empty of gatherings and harmless gossip. And the women, clothed in finery with nary a hair out of place, wore poorly concealed bruises, the colors clashing with the deep hues of the latest fashion trends.

It was clean, polished even, different from the farming communities where her mother raised her. But not a safe place to linger.

Not a safe place to ask for help.

When she glanced up, a man's shadow covered her. He was close, near enough to hear the rheumatic wheeze of his breathing as he exerted himself searching the debris. Close enough to smell the alcohol weeping from his pores despite his neat appearance.

Dear gods, she needed to find a way out.

Not that she minded waiting amidst the rot until darkness covered her movements, but it was only a matter of time before the guard discovered her hiding spot. Unfortunately, her instincts chose a terrible location, and they screamed for Ember to put distance between her and the six predators.

Perhaps she should stop following her gut and instead listen to her mind. But an empty stomach and a barren satchel screamed louder than logic.

"You drunken cur. Find her, or it will be your head displayed on a pike," the leader said as he stepped forward and jabbed a finger in the guard's chest. After a scathing look, he pivoted on his heel and marched south, opposite the main square, muttering under his breath.

She waited until the leader was out of sight and edged to her left, shimmying between two barrels, using an opening so narrow, there was doubt she would have fit only a month prior. Weeks of inconsistent meals and surviving on scraps had a way of whittling away the spirit, not to mention the body.

The odds swung in her favor.

All she had to do was sneak past one soldier. One measly hungover man instead of six. But her blood continued to pound in her ears even with her improved situation. She rubbed the scar on her palm, willing her hands to stop trembling.

Aim for the soft spots.

A simple question, a plausible *what if*, had prompted her mother to distill the lesson in self defense down to five simple words.

As a healer-in-training, Ember didn't require additional details. *Eyes. Throat. Groin. Feet,* she repeated. But her mother left out the most crucial piece of advice — when to strike.

She crouched down. A broken slat rested at her feet. She picked up the curved piece of timber with both hands, careful to avoid the large splinters sticking out from the edges.

Just like chopping wood.

Her knuckles turned white. She waited until the guard turned his back, then popped up.

Ember summoned what little strength she had left and raised the board above her head.

Crack.

The slat split in two on the back of the man's neck. Vibrations radiated the length of her make-shift weapon, and she glanced down, surprised to find the bottom half still in her grip.

The man rubbed the back of his head and slowly turned around.

Stunned, she didn't have time to recover before she raised the jagged wood and rammed it into his throat.

Blood splattered her chest.

The man clutched his neck and staggered forward. His mouth gaped open and closed, but no words came out. He lurched to the right, then stumbled to the left. An outstretched hand grazed the hem of her tunic but fell limp at his side, failing to grasp the garment.

What had she done?

Ember stood over his unmoving form as life leaked out of the gash, staining the alley. A fountain of red pooled at her feet.

"I'm sorry," she whispered as she knelt down and clamped her hand over the wound. It was fatal. Her magic thrummed through her. She closed her eyes, and the syrupy sweet taste of a cast filled her mouth as his skin knitted together. "Forgive me."

The guard would suffer a headache upon wakening, but he would live.

Ember swayed and caught herself before falling to the unforgiving ground. Casting for mortal wounds drained her energy.

She must run — put distance between her and the patrol — but her powers anchored her to the spot. The magic wasn't satisfied with mending the injury to his neck. It wouldn't allow her to leave until she healed his cough, too. Her eyelids closed once more, and she waited until the last bit of fluid burned off his lungs.

Her hands shook, and the din of the main square roared to life in her ears.

Iron horseshoes clopped in the distance, reminding Ember she wasn't alone. A door banged against its frame. She flinched, and a wave of fear washed over her.

And pooled in her bones.

The guards would return to the alley any second. Five to her one. They were probably on their way, frustrated by their lack of success, and now she'd given them a more pressing reason to apprehend her.

She allowed herself one shuddering breath while she scouted the alley.

We'll head to the tip of the peninsula, her mother had said. *If*

*they discover your powers, we will follow the river through the moun-
tains and catch a ship sailing across the Strait of Vian.*

It was a last resort — seeking safety in the Northern Isles.
When her mother first mentioned the plan, Ember didn't worry
about the details. How to find sustenance. How to find shelter.
How to avoid the Red Guard, the Castle.

She'd never expected to travel alone.

The way behind her wasn't an option. She couldn't blend in
with the crowds in the main square covered in blood. South
took her closer to their leader. The other two goons took the
passage on the right — the one she had mapped last night.

It was out, too.

She must circle the mining village. The route would take her
to the borderlands of Midpointe and into the territory responsible for training the militia, where the fighters didn't carry the
same tarnished reputation as the Red Guard.

Still, she had hoped to avoid them all the same.

The strap of her satchel dug into her shoulder.

Ember popped up and dusted her hands on her trousers. She
slipped between the tavern and the fishmonger's shop. Her
small stature lent an advantage in the claustrophobic space,
allowing her shoulders to remain square in the passage.

When the path opened up, she didn't look back over her
shoulder. Didn't check to see if anyone pursued her. Didn't let
gnawing hunger, growing fatigue, or crippling doubt slow her
down. In the safety of the forest, she bent over and rested her
hands on her knees, struggling to catch her breath.

Ember had once yearned for the life of a common villager.
To stay in one place long enough to form friendships. To share
her day with a family.

To connect with other casters, a dark voice purred.

Now, she wanted the impossible — she wanted her mother.

CHAPTER TWO

K indness weaves a charm and warms the soul. -Esabel

BORDERLANDS OF MIDPOINTE, THE MILITIA TERRITORY
One week later...

GAVYN LEANED AGAINST THE SEAMSTRESS'S SHOP AND SIGHED.

His early morning errand just became more complicated; he planned to meet with his reluctant informant, not apprehend a thief.

Shapeless clothing provided little details as to her identity.

While the utilitarian britches blended in with the gritty color of the shop's exterior, their dull hue stuck out against the vibrant hues and high-quality dress of the locals. The brown fabric was consistent with the miners to the east. Or the farmers to the south.

They were all the same. Thin. Hungry.

Desperate.

The thief crept along the outskirts of the market. She moved with a bumbling inefficiency, suggesting a more recent recruitment to her *occupation.*

He clenched his jaw.

An increase in the annual tithing by the Castle and its greedy ruling class forced more and more families out of their homes. His village housed various wanderers over the years — kind-hearted locals opened their doors to those who fate did not favor.

While not immune to drifters' plight, he must balance the safety of the community against its inhabitants' desire to lend a hand.

Three days had passed since this thief showed up in the marketplace.

She stayed on the outskirts of the main road and had yet to contact any local. Unusual. Most drifters held out a hand on their arrival. More than one inhabitant bent his ear to her presence.

Confident this waif posed little harm, his curiosity allowed her unfettered movements.

The market stirred from slumber.

The butcher opened his door for business. Farther down, the farmer unhitched his cart full of today's harvest. To his right, his sister Jade emerged from her quaint home, carrying a wicker basket laden with food. He sampled the breeze. Pheasant.

Right on time, families clattered down the road.

The thief made the next move. She stayed low to the ground, darting between carts, and crouched in the bakery's shadows.

His path opened up, leaving Gavyn with little to hide behind. Three long strides carried him closer, and years of hunting venison quieted his footsteps. The lack of cover didn't bother him. His prey focused too intently on her next meal, disregarding the surroundings.

Smart, this thief.

She had chosen her mark with care — Jade's cart always bustled with crowds. A well liked owner, his sister often flitted around, talking to every customer. The village emptied the shelves of her savory pastries most days before the sun melted the last drops of dew off the fields. It would be easy to squeeze in between groups and swipe a loaf from the corner.

Or a pie from the bottom shelf.

Jade turned her back, greeting her first customer.

"I wouldn't do that if I were you," Gavyn said as he encircled the thief's wrist the moment she reached for a pastry.

The thief tilted her head to meet his glare, and a range of emotions fluttered across her arresting features. He glimpsed surprise, followed closely by a note of unease. Once the initial shock subsided, a hint of defiance ringed their hazel depths.

As he expected, a veritable novice — lifelong crooks learned to control their facial expressions early in their life.

Up close, it was difficult not to catalog their disparities.

Dark to his light. Her hair was the inky black of a starless eve, and her skin, tanned from the summer sun, boasted a warm olive undertone two shades darker than his pale complexion devoid of any color except for the occasional freckle.

The gods blessed her with unblemished high cheekbones, framing a wide mouth with full lips almost too big for her heart-shaped face. He loosened his hold. His leather cuffs, with their intricate inlay, looked out of place next to the sleeve of her grubby tunic.

Gorgeous was too simple a word; she was breath-taking.

"I was going to pay for it." She fidgeted in his grip.

"Sure you were. With all that coin you have rattling around in your sack." The hair on the back of his neck stood up. He wanted to look over his shoulder but couldn't tear his eyes away from his captive.

"Gavyn, let her go," Jade said as she circled the cart. She wrinkled her nose and chose a thick slice of brown, crusty bread from the nearest shelf. "Are you hungry? Pay him no head."

"A little." The thief's stomach chose that moment to protest its discomfort, and she tilted her chin. A refreshing bit of stubbornness. She tried to wrench her arm free but twisted and fell into his chest.

He knew what she would see.

A scar under one eye marred half of his cheek. Stiff lips formed a well-rehearsed frown. His childhood was hard — his work was physical — and the looking glass reflected it, something he often used to his advantage. But she seemed more afraid of losing her next meal than his intimidation, a truth he wasn't ready to think about.

He relaxed his grip and took a step back. Fury simmered in his chest at her situation and the depths she fought for her fare, but he had responsibilities with no capacity for softness.

"Jade, you can't keep feeding every person who wanders to your cart. You know the rules. No more drifters. This one will rob you blind like the rest."

Jade waved him off.

"Thank you," the thief murmured as she tore off small pieces.

"Tsk, don't thank me." Jade pointed to the last piece hanging in front of her mouth. "You'll pay for the meal."

"But I don't carry coin." Blush bloomed across the thief's cheeks.

"I know, but you have two hands, don't you? Once I finish with the morning rush, I'm going to put you in my kitchen." Jade examined the thief's nails and asked, "Know your way around pots and pans?"

"Washing, sure. But I can help cook, too."

"Forgive me if I don't give you a paring blade right away. Let's start with the scrubbing, and then we'll see. It's a full-time job keeping the village fed, and I could use the help. Relax. Eat. Plenty of work awaits this afternoon."

"Thank you." She polished off the last bite as her gaze strayed to the cart. "It's been a while."

"You good?" he asked Jade. Gavyn ground his teeth, torn between staying nearby and completing his original task. He lingered, but it was clear his presence halted their conversation. "I need to pay Pigeon a visit."

"Of course. Now get out of here. I'll see you later tonight."

He gave the thief one last hard stare before jogging around the corner. Still preoccupied with her arrival, the punch took him by surprise.

Wiry hair, gray from a combination of age and lack of regular bathing, streaked by him.

Gavyn pivoted, and the blow grazed his upper arm. Its momentum carried the man forward.

One minute, Pigeon was lunging. The next, he lay face-first on the ground, with Gavyn's knee digging into his shoulder blades, the offending fist tucked deftly behind his lower back.

A regrettable necessity.

Pigeon hatched a crazy plan every other week, sold ill-gotten goods to gullible villagers, and nicked the wrong items from the wrong people. If he wasn't so efficient at ferreting out information, they would have booted him long ago.

"Enjoy your vacation?" Gavyn wrenched Pigeon's arm higher and brought the wily informant to his feet. He pressed him against the brick wall of the dressmaker's shop.

"What— Ow... ow... Ouch." Pigeon's face smashed against the rough surface and spittle dribbled down his chin. "I was off to... to see a sick relative. 'Tis not a crime."

Gavyn chuckled darkly.

"It is, if you poisoned them first and stole their belongings. Give it up, old man. I don't have all day." Gavyn applied more pressure. "What news do you bring?"

"None for an upstart such as yourself." Droplets flung in the air with each word, and Pigeon rose higher on his tiptoes. "All right." He clenched his jaw and ground out, "All right."

Gavyn released his grip and took a step back.

"I got wind of a chance to barter. Me brother—" Pigeon shook out his arms and righted his tunic.

"Your brother?"

"As I was saying..." Pigeon glared at him. "Me brother sent word of an *opportunity* to trade some of my stock."

"Where?" Gavyn stepped forward.

"Out east," Pigeon said too quickly, his eyes shifting to the side.

This was their dance. Gavyn grew frustrated with the circular questioning. His size did not intimidate Pigeon, but the informant respected his authority. Well, as much respect as a crook could muster.

He took another step forward. and asked, "Where?"

"On the edge of the mining territory." Pigeon fidgeted. He held up a hand, warding off the question on Gavyn's lips. "It never pops up in the same place."

"What kind of *market*?"

"The usual sort." He rubbed his side and tapped his fingertips on the pocket of his pant leg. "You know... buying and selling... trading wares."

Gavyn rolled his eyes. "What did you trade? What did you *see*?"

"Rings." *Tap. Tap. Tap.* "Some leather." *Tap.* "Maybe some necklaces."

"Who was there?" Gavyn ran his hand over his mouth and narrowed his brows, focusing on Pigeon's nervous fidgeting.

"Well... there was me brother. And his friend. And a lady I never met—"

"Pigeon..."

Thunk.

A leather sheath fell to the ground next to Pigeon's shabby

boot. His pant leg obscured the handle. Gavyn thrust his forearm across Pigeon's neck, earning a half-strangled cry.

"What do you have?"

"That's not mine. I can ex—"

"Enough." He eased some of the pressure across Pigeon's throat. Gavyn bent down, picked up the contraband, and turned it over in his palm. His eyes snapped forward and in a voice barely above a whisper he said, "Tell me you didn't nick this off a Red Guard. That you didn't bring trouble back to the village. Tell me you don't dare flaunt the decree against commoners possessing blades of warfare."

"No. No. No." Pigeon held out his hands, palms up. "I swear it on me brother's grave."

"Your brother?" Gavyn cocked his head.

"Erm… my mother's grave, then. I took it off a fella for a song. He seemed relieved to be rid of it, methinks, for how little fight he showed."

"Who?"

"Dunno."

"Where was he from?" Gavyn grabbed the front of Pigeon's collar. "What did he look like?"

"I dunno." He shrugged. "Never seen 'im before."

Gavyn sighed. "What *do* you remember?"

"Not much." Pigeon shuffled his boots and scratched his mangy beard. "He wore a fine cloak. Kept his hood up so I dinna see nothing. Nice boots. Would'a liked them boots. Tried to follow him, but he gave me the slip."

"Just the one?"

"No. No, I remember he had a pair."

Gavyn forced a bark of laughter.

"No, old man. Not the boots. Did you come across any more blades?"

"No. He only had one." Pigeon rubbed his hands together. "Is that all? I have someplace to be."

Typical. He'll find trouble again by nightfall. Still, Gavyn couldn't send him off without a warning, so he lowered his voice and said, "You take a swing at me again, and I'll let the fighters at you. Get out of here before I change my mind."

"Just… ah… just a misunderstanding. Won't happen again." Pigeon stumbled backward. He darted around the shop, slinking to the alleyway in the back.

Gavyn tucked the dagger inside his boot. He made one last sweep of the market.

What were the chances the blade belonged to a Red Guard? Few in the fortress were aware Pigeon received refuge in the village. Was he a dupe and the blade meant to find its way to the compound? Or was the appearance of the illegal weapon plain bad luck?

Gavyn shook his head, wishing he had the luxury of staying in the barn and overseeing morning sparring. He craved the simple life of a fighter, a trainer. Not navigating the bloodier politics of the peninsula.

And what of the thief?

He trusted Jade, but he would stop by later this evening to ensure her safety. To check on her pretty guest. Just in case.

The trail from the market opened up, and he set off for the compound, consumed by thoughts of the early morning errand that just became more complicated.

ERIK SWUNG HIS LEG OVER THE THICK TREE BRANCH OF THE OLD oak and located Gavyn.

A whiff of baking bread hit his nose — the smell, a glorious, light scent of flour and yeast, with a sprinkle of cinnamon — was thick in the morning air.

He shifted his weight, easing back against the trunk, and

wished he could start his day with half a dozen warm rolls instead of scouting on an empty stomach. He peered through an opening in the lower limbs, watching Gavyn apprehend the pretty thief.

His target worked fast.

The massive fighter prowled with a lightness at odds with his size, hiding in shadows when available and blending in with the shop's facade when not. The whole encounter had only taken moments. And in the end, instead of being carted off to a holding cell, the thief who tried to steal from Jade was being... *fed?*

He rubbed his eyes with the back of his hands.

Hope, Erik's father had said.

These fighters were creating hope and goodwill, spinning a web of the most fragile ideals and linking territories. Was this it — the source of their power and influence in the peninsula? Could it be as simple as *acts of kindness?* Or did they employ stronger methods of coercion?

Crumbles of bark stuck to his sweaty palms, coating his hands in an earthy layer of debris. He wiped them on his leathers and popped to his feet. The branch wavered, and he ignored the tinge in his legs, a constant ache since arriving in the territory. He massaged the top of his thigh, his eyes never straying from their mark.

Gavyn was on the move.

Dammit. Erik debated between returning to the training compound before anyone noticed his absence or following the fighter.

In the end, orders from his father won out.

He leaped off his perch and grabbed a limb halfway down the tree. Two swings of his legs propelled him to the baker's roof.

He wrapped an arm around the chimney and braced for landing. The impact jarred his teeth, but he held on. New beads of sweat rolled down his back, and he wiped his brow with his free hand.

Hope, Erik's father had hissed. *Such a human emotion. It starts as a small spark, a single flicker of a candle, and is easily blown out.*

This spring, his father had ordered him to spy on the militia. Despite the letters he sent back home noting a lack of illegal activities, Erik had yet to convince him of these fighters' innocence.

At first, his reports were easy to write. He kept them brief, outlining everyone's roles.

When prompted for more information, he penned succinct descriptions of their daily routine. The fighters' habits. But months passed, hours Erik spent alongside these men, and the letters became more difficult to craft.

His father's last correspondence was full of displeasure and threats.

It was the neat handwriting of the one he loved — the woman who replaced an absent mother — smeared by salty tears long since dried, which convinced him to betray this band of brothers.

It was why Erik crouched on a tile rooftop, straining to hear the conversation below and wishing for some evidence of subterfuge to report back to his father. He resisted the urge to check his enchantment — to ensure magic camouflaged his heritage.

At eight summers, his first visit outside the protective walls of his home was a lesson. Surrounded by his father's personal Red Guard, he stole glimpses of daily life in the human village. Men held their tongue in his presence. Women closed window shutters and scurried back into their cottages on his approach.

It was the children, with their lack of fear — the ones who dared to gesture at his pointed ears and then rub their own — who taught him about the differences between being born in the Castle and being raised outside the shackles of nobility.

Faeblood, they whispered.

Amongst the Lords, it was a term of superiority. Arguments broke out in the dining hall over percentages of *pure blood*. Duels fought over perceived slights to family lineage. Parents arranged matches for their bairns before they left the crib, securing the continuation of the purest lines in the next generation.

Ironic, considering those with the strongest powers often had the audacity to sprout from unsanctioned matings with humans.

Beyond the Castle walls, under the cloak of nightfall and outside the watchful eye of the guards, Erik heard a different tone.

Faeblood, they whispered, but instead of reverence, spoken with a healthy dose of derision.

He saw the punch before Gavyn and leaned forward to determine its owner. Erik's lips curled up at the edges. *Pigeon.*

They gave the sly crook a fair amount of leeway in the village. He enjoyed a sort of amnesty in the territories — nothing as respectable as an emissary — but they granted him an allowance for coming and going as he pleased. An unwitting *carrier*. He delivered messages and told tales village leaders wanted spread throughout the mountain realm.

Useful, if they could control him.

A thud on the ground drew his attention back to the pair. He squinted, trying to identify the object. Sunlight reflected off the metal dagger, the ray hitting him in the chest.

This was something to pen in his next missive. This was the incriminating evidence his father sought. After months and months, this might be the key to freeing her.

Hope, Erik's father had emphasized, *skillfully destroyed by snuffing out their weaknesses.*

He understood his father's demands. There was no honor in spying. But his sire wasn't interested in his morals, and the only allegiance Erik owed was to the woman who raised him. Sheltered him in the pit of vipers. The woman who now suffered every moment he delayed.

He cast one last look at the Red Guard's dagger, and for the first time in a long time, Erik had *hope*.

CHAPTER THREE

*T**he folly of youth matures with the foolishness of experience.* -Esabel

THE FAMILIAR SCENT OF STRAW, SWEAT, AND SAWDUST GREETED Gavyn as he crossed the threshold of the training barn.

A half-a-mile hike from the village, perched on the highest part of the terrain, the building was a sign of prosperity reaped from years of grueling work.

Several fighters nodded in greeting as he walked a lap around the elevated sparring ring. He ran his hand along the lower of three levels of rope. They wound around four oak barrels and defined the platform.

The tension drained out of his shoulders.

They had finished construction on the open two-story structure five years ago, but he'd felt more at home here than in his small childhood cottage in the mining territory. Destined to work the mountain as his family had done for generations, circumstances had propelled him in another direction.

A decade passed since he escaped his fate. Barely eighteen years old, an accident created many instantaneous orphans.

A single moment — one sliver of time — cleaved the last strands of youth and forced adulthood down their throats. Not wanting to repeat history, Gavyn and his friends bucked the trappings of spirit-breaking labor in the mines and set out on their own.

Growing up in a harsh community groomed them for two things — fighting the land for her treasures and sparring in dark alleys with other youths for their place in the community. Since their former village provided the Castle with all the stone required, they leveraged another skill set — training the militia in hand-to-hand combat.

Shared grief had strengthened their bond. Blood and sweat built the compound. Results grew their reputation.

Youthful ideals had grown an empire.

Per usual for this time of day, fighters occupied all corners of the barn. He stopped to observe a group of younger men. They lost the softness that clung to them their first day in the training barn. A couple of years of moving boulders in the valley, plus steady rations from the mess hall, would add to their size.

Old fabric wrapped several times around their hands, marking their inexperience. Closer inspection revealed dried blood staining the strips of off-white fabric, confirming they had been at each other for a while.

They never kept a healer long at the compound, so he learned years ago to protect the knuckles of the more zealous beginners.

"Take a break." He grabbed the hand of the nearest fighter. "Make sure you soak these in the springs before ground work this afternoon."

Gavyn didn't wait for an acknowledgement.

He pivoted and strode toward the grappling area.

Thick logs outlined a pit filled with coarse sand excavated

from the banks of the nearby stream. A group of older fighters circled two men wrestling on the ground and shouted encouragement.

Gavyn spotted the broad shoulders and dark hair of his brother, Rowan. He shouldered his way into the crowd and nodded toward the center. "Rematch from yesterday?"

"The cub wanted another lesson." Rowan chuckled. "Getting his face ground into the dirt last time wasn't enough. He convinced Mikel to join him for another round."

"Some learn the hard way." Gavyn shook his head and shifted his stance, settling in for the match. The noise increased, and Mikel, a seasoned fighter, pinned the first-year trainee with an arm across his neck, a grin splitting his face as he applied more pressure.

"Just tap already." Rowan massaged his temples. "The cubs take forever to figure it out. I don't know how you do it."

"That's why Xavier sticks you in the cellar, my friend." Gavyn slapped Rowan on the shoulder and dismissed the idea of speaking with the trainee in private.

Rowan was right. Some learned the hard way.

"Enough," Gavyn barked at the crowd and pointed at the defeated fighter. The younger man hung his head. Color crept up his face. "Here amongst your brothers, know when to tap."

Mikel rolled to his feet and made his way over to Gavyn. A tiny bead of sweat trickled down the side of his jaw. Clean clothes hinted at the lopsidedness of the match. He ran a hand through his shoulder-length hair, and the mark on his neck drew Gavyn's gaze.

It was the size of a silver coin and blacker than a smudge of soot. His pulse had yet to slow, the beat lending movement to the circular pattern. A small cross filled the middle, identical to the design on his and Rowan's neck.

"Morning. You headed for tea?" Gavyn held out a fist.

"Might as well." Mikel scoffed at the taunt and bumped his

knuckles. "Barely broke a sweat with that one."

"Appreciate it all the same."

"He'll come around tomorrow for more." Mikel strode to the entrance doors and shrugged. "Maybe I'll feel like rearranging his nose then. Maybe not."

Rowan nudged Gavyn and pointed to the center ring.

Empty on his arrival, it now held two fresh occupants. Fighters gathered around the new entertainment. Unlike the earlier matches, no one cheered or spurred on the action.

Xavier, his leader and best friend, leaned against the top rope and barked directions. Dark chestnut hair curled at his temples and sweat stained the back of his tunic, a testament to his hands-on style of command.

Gavyn didn't miss the subtle clench of his jaw. He ran a hand over his mouth, not looking forward to delivering two pieces of bad news when Xavier already simmered.

"Xav, a word. It's about Jade."

"Let me guess." Xavier didn't bother to take his eyes off the two men trading blows. "Did she leave the village again or take in another charity case?"

Family by circumstance, not by blood, Jade wore her compassion on the finely embroidered edges of her tunic. She took too many risks, finding every stranger shelter and arranging work for anyone who desired a more permanent residence. Every sad soul was a friend. She even left out gold, hoping the drifters would pocket it when her back turned. Her logic was exasperating.

I have more than I dreamed, she had told him once. *If it buys the strong ones another day...*

Still, Gavyn would rather spar with ten men at once than suffer her displeasure.

"She has another waif in the kitchen as we speak. This one is paper thin just like the others and looking for handouts."

The thief may have the face of an angel, but she still posed a threat. Jade wouldn't listen to Gavyn, but Xavier still held some sway. Though not as much as he used to… and not nearly as much as the girls. If anyone had a chance of convincing her to reconsider her latest acquisition, it was his leader.

But his stomach churned at the idea of casting her out of the village.

"Anyone we can train?" Xavier asked.

"No. Too soft." His thoughts drifted back to the thief, recalling a long mane of thick black hair framing a mesmerizing face and sensuous curves pressed against baggy clothes dusted with the grime of travel. "Maybe a summer or two older than twenty."

"Alright. I'll have another word with Jade. What about Pigeon? What news does he bring from the other territories?"

"A roving black market sprouted to the east."

"A proper paradise for our fickle friend." Xavier smirked.

Fickle was right. Gavyn wasn't entirely sure where Pigeon's loyalties lay. And he didn't know what was more troubling — a large gathering bold enough to trade suspect goods in the middle of the day or Pigeon stumbling across an illegal weapon.

Both threatened the careful balance of power the territories shared with the Castle.

Gavyn placed his hand on Xavier's shoulder, leaned in, and whispered, "He ran into a blade."

"How many?" Xavier whirled to face him.

"Just the one. A small dagger." Gavyn dropped his arm and rubbed the back of his neck. "And that's not the worst of it."

"Our stamp?" Xavier asked, his focus back on the ring.

"No. It had the Red Guard's crest."

"Keep your left up. You've taken three in a row because you keep dropping it." Xavier paused, then said, "Someone is either desperate or has a death wish. Not sure yet, but I don't want the attention on us. Throw it on my desk."

"Yes, sir."

~

Ember followed Jade as she pushed through the front door of a small cottage.

Midday sun poured through a pair of windows and brought warmth to the one-room structure.

Despite its coziness, Gavyn's frigid accusations sent a chill down her arms. Even lacking a layer of chain mail, he had the look of a soldier — formidable, with a thick body sculpted from training and a wicked scar hinting at a bit of danger. There was no kindness to his demeanor, but he seemed to respect Jade.

Still, it would be smart to steer clear of him the brief time she stayed in the village.

A large stone hearth dominated one wall.

Above the mantel, a tapestry depicted three children huddled together with their arms around each other. From the wheat-colored hair on the girl in the middle, she guessed it was Jade and her brothers.

Not wanting to get caught staring, she scanned the room, taking in the other contents. On the opposite wall, a tawny fur covered an inviting bed. The solitary pillow at the head show-cased the same fine needlework as the tapestry.

A dangerous intimacy.

She picked her mark well.

With a ready smile and outstretched hands, Jade was easy. During the short time she spent on the run, Ember learned a few truths the hard way. One could always count on good people to make the right choice and bad people to make the wrong ones. Unfortunately, most lived ambiguously somewhere in the middle. Morally gray.

Unpredictable.

While this morning's outcome didn't justify her methods, she was relieved her punishment consisted of scullery work instead of languishing in a damp jail with no one to rescue her.

Jade emptied the contents of her basket at a sideboard in the back. Trenchers and various pots, likely from this morning's work, filled a large copper basin at one end. Bundles of drying herbs hung from the rafters. She identified many of the same ones she gathered in the meadows back home.

"The water should be warm enough by now." Jade gestured to the large black kettle hanging above the smoldering fire. "Come. I'll help you lift it to fill the tub."

Together, they carried the heavy pot to the copper basin and emptied it over the dirty dishes. As they were returning it to its rightful place in the hearth, a face, pink with eagerness and sparkling amber eyes, popped in the open doorway. The woman's long mahogany hair tumbled down her back and swayed as she bounded into the room.

"Ada." Jade chuckled. "You're here sooner than expected.

The newcomer took her words as an invitation. She stole a quick glance at Ember, plopped on a stool, and said, "I was in the barn this morning and overheard Xav and Gavyn."

"And what were you doing in the training barn before the nooning meal?" Jade's nose twitched.

"I was in the loft working on my numbers for tonight." Ada splayed a hand across her chest and a blush crawled up her neck. "I was working on my parchment, but *maybe* I noticed the training. Consider it study for the fights. Or at least that's what I tell Xav when he catches me."

"Mmm, hmm. And how are the fighters? Or did your *observation* only include one in particular?"

"I'm pleased to report that Mikel appeared to be in dominant form. He should do well tonight." Ada kept a straight face for half a second before a giggle bubbled free.

Jade sighed and said, "This impish creature who barged into my home without invitation is Ada. Ada, meet…"

"Ember," she said, nodding to the newcomer. "It's nice to make your acquaintance."

Ember turned back to the mountain of dishes and rubbed her palm. After an hour, the pile dwindled so she could see the bottom of the tub, but the water grew cooler, making it difficult to scrub the heavily sullied trays. She risked a glance over her shoulder and verified the two women were still in discussion.

Ada's arms flailed with a story, while Jade rested her head in a propped hand. Neither paid her a speck of consideration.

She turned back to the copper tub and cupped the bottom. Bubbles floated to the waterline. The sour tang of her magic coated the back of her mouth.

Too much time had passed since her last cast, leaving a nasty film instead of its normal, syrupy taste.

She brushed her tongue against the back of her teeth, unable to scrape off the flavor. Satisfied with the warmer temperature, Ember leveraged the scrubbing brush's wooden handle, but her stomach chose that moment to release another rumble.

"That'll do. Go on ahead and wash up and make yourself a plate." Jade flicked her wrist in her direction.

"But I still—"

"They will be there when you finish." Jade shooed her again. "Go on and eat."

Ember grabbed a leftover slice of bread from the basket and joined both women.

"Are you looking to stick around?" Ada asked as soon as Ember bit into the loaf. "Or merely passing through?"

"Hush, let her be. Besides, I haven't heard her story." Jade placed her elbows on the table's surface and clasped her hands in front of her lips.

"I'm unsure," she lied.

Ember hadn't spoken with another since fleeing home.

Her throat was scratchy, but it was nice to use it again. Surely that was the reason she didn't voice her intentions to travel to Northern Isles.

"Where are you from? Why are you on the road by yourself?

And what on earth are you wearing?" The questions burst from Ada's mouth in rapid fire. She vibrated on her stool, and her eyes darted between them.

"Dresses are..." She tilted her head to the side and searched for the right word. "Impractical."

"I hope you choose to stay. We would all do well with more women around here." Ada smiled mischievously. "If you consider the compound as a part of the village proper, the men outnumber Jade and I at least a baker's dozen to one."

"Don't listen to her complaints, the odds favor our resident flirt." Jade winked at Ada and handed Ember a hunk of cheese. "Still, another lady in the village would be a wonderful addition. We host a new crop of fighters every spring but rarely gain new residents. Well, if you decide to leave tonight, at least you will sport a full belly. If you are going to stay a little longer, I could really use the help to prepare for the fights."

"The fights?" Ember placed the small morsel in her mouth, and the bold flavor exploded on her tongue. She stifled a groan.

"They announce the matchups Monday. The men square off in the ring every Friday. It's a chance for the men to blow off some steam. The competition gives Gavyn and Xavier an opportunity to evaluate the new guys, and it provides a chance for those from other villages who completed their training at the compound to return and test their skills."

"Does everybody go?"

"Most of our village comes and watches the first few rounds." Ada bit her lip. "Outsiders stay for the entire evening. It's a chance for everyone to catch up on gossip and interact with those beyond their territory."

"And a chance for *some* to ogle their favorite fighter." Jade slung an arm around Ada's shoulders. "When *one* fixates on the match, older brothers don't accuse them of staring."

"Too bad Xav keeps me from watching ringside." Ada

stretched out her lean frame, bumping the table with the tops of her thighs.

"Somebody has to run the numbers. Miss Ada is our resident bookkeeper. She takes wagers on the fights. Keeps things interesting." Jade stood and wiped her skirts. "Stay for a spell and see for yourself next week. I must abandon you to serve the hungry spectators, but the cottage is yours if you so desire."

A rare offer.

Ember searched Jade's face for signs of malice, unable to find the tiniest bit of cruelty. She weighed the risk of staying in one place for too long against the thought of battling the elements another night.

Exhaustion crept into her limbs.

It was the type of fatigue that clings to a person like sludge coating the bottom of boots from traipsing through the semi-dried marshes in summer. More difficult to shed its gloomy weight with each passing day.

She was tired. Tired of hiding. Tired of scrounging for food and of fighting against the swell of loneliness.

Keep moving. Never stay in one place for too long. Don't form bonds — it's too risky. Our kind does not exist outside the Castle. The worst will covet your gifts, ensnaring you for their pleasures. Her mother's words countered Jade's generous promise.

Today, with her belly full and the warmth of the cottage wrapping around her like a favorite shawl, she shoved the voice down and locked it deep in her mind.

"Okay. I can stay for one more night. To help you out."

"Wonderful. It's settled then." Jade gathered up the remaining scraps and placed them in her basket. She hooked it over her arm and slid on her slippers. "Now, if you will excuse me, I'm going to feed the chickens."

The front door opened with a soft snick, and her heart dropped through the freshly polished floor.

CHAPTER FOUR

*N*ever *burn the hand who feeds your hunger.* -Esabel

A MAN, RIVALING GAVYN'S SIZE, LEANED AGAINST THE DOORFRAME and greeted them with a scowl.

Cuffs wrapped around his thick forearms, the luxury of the leather drawing her attention in a way his simple linen tunic and black pants could not. Sunlight poked through the threshold behind him, highlighting the tips of his chestnut hair and casting a long shadow in the room.

This is it. He must be here to lock her up. Of course she got off too easily this morning.

He pointed at Ada and said, "You're a thorn in my side today."

"Relax, Xav." Ada rose and placed a chaste kiss on his cheek. "I'll have the numbers before supper."

His expression softened, and he tilted his head a fraction of an inch to meet the affection.

"Gavyn's waiting for you at the barn. There are some last minute changes for tonight. I'll return shortly."

"I want all the tales, so toss the idea of scampering off into the night without so much as a word of farewell," Ada said to Ember. "I want... no, I *need* all the gossip from the other territories that the fighters keep from my ears. Who's who and what's what. And where I can find riveting drama to spice up my mundane life. Jade. Dear brother."

She grinned, and after an informal curtsy, Ada skipped out of the cottage with the same level of enthusiasm she entered.

"Jade." Xavier uncrossed his arms and waved in Ember's direction. "You know why *this* can't keep happening."

This shoved another bite of cheese in her mouth and bristled at his tone.

"I should have known Gavyn wouldn't let it be." Jade sighed and dropped the basket on the sideboard. "Go on then, let's hear it. My birds wait."

"I have an obligation." He walked toward Jade with his palms extended. "To my men. To this village. To *you*."

"Don't lump me in—"

"Whether you like it or not, it's my responsibility to protect this territory." Xavier prowled the length of the cottage and stood next to Jade, his body close enough that his chest brushed against her arm. "That includes you."

The argument unfolded in front of her, near enough she caught Jade's sharp inhale. Yet, far enough her contribution was unwelcome. There was anger, certainly on Jade's part, but the sexual tension between them was palpable. It was wrong to witness such an intimate moment but she failed to avert her gaze.

"—she's harmless and weighs about a stone soaking wet," Jade said, her chest heaving.

Ember wanted to crawl into herself at the discomfort of being the center of discussion while not participating in the conversation. She was uncertain whether to speak up. Jade didn't deserve this censure, but her stomach tumbled at the idea of drawing Xavier's focus.

"Desperate people do desperate things. You know this." He pressed his body more firmly against Jade's. "We found a dagger today. It showed up around the same time your new friend did."

Ember gasped.

"It has nothing to do with her, and you know it."

"It seems unlikely, yes. But I don't have the luxury of not considering the possibility. I'm not kicking her out of the village. She can stay." He hesitated, then said, "But not with you."

Xavier leaned forward. Instead of retreating, Jade stood her ground, forcing him to reach out and steady her from tumbling backwards.

"I'm not your soldier. Not your minion." Jade poked him in the chest. "Consider yourself relieved of any *duty* you feel toward me."

Ember rubbed her palm.

"Why?" He sighed. "Why must she stay with you when an alternative exists? Hell, she can have the new home at the end of the market, if she chooses. It's vacant until harvest."

Ember raised her hand to accept the generous offer, but neither one of them paid her notice.

"Gift me this, Xav. I don't ask for much." Jade paused. "She doesn't deserve the emptiness of a strange home."

"You." Xavier pointed to Ember. "You can stay as a guest of Jade's, but if I find out you deceived her in any manner, there is not a territory far enough where you can hide from my vengeance." He pressed his forehead against Jade's. "Just watch her. Be smart."

Xavier's hands fell to his side. He took a step back.

"Alright," Jade exhaled and repeated, "Alright."

Xavier looked as if he wanted to say something more, but he tucked a tendril of hair behind Jade's ear, his hand lingering longer than the task required. He kissed her temple and left the cottage through the back door.

"I'll tend my birds, then let's finish stuffing the pies." Jade's smile failed to reach her eyes. She used the top of her skirts to wipe invisible crumbs from her hands, a fine tremor overwhelming her graceful fingers. "If we hurry, there may be time to pick some berries along the farmer's fence line. I'd like to make some tarts later."

They worked in silence for the next few hours, finding a simple rhythm. The tasks went faster with two sets of hands. Ember could hasten the progress, but she hesitated to use her powers in front of Jade.

Her mother filled her head with childhood stories of powerful casters, but no one back in the farming community shared her ability for spell work.

Ember's travels these last weeks took her through various villages. Some prosperous, with tranquil cottages and kind owners. Others dilapidated, housing families scratching out an existence with no extras to spare for a drifter. Despite their outward differences, the villages shared a commonality — no evidence of magic.

Faeblood don't exist in the territories, mother had cautioned.

It was a warning.

A warning to never look. Never seek others. Never bring attention to herself by asking too many questions. She heard the rhetoric often enough, and when Ember was ten or eleven summers, she stopped asking for stories of others like her.

But she never stopped searching.

Ember shook her head and continued to work shoulder-to-shoulder with Jade in the small space, rolling dough on the floured surface and arranging the savory filling in the center. A stiffness from years of relying on magic for household chores slowed her fingers. But there was no way she could cast in the confined space without the other woman noticing.

Still, dull kitchen work was better than crouching in the shadows, stealing her next meal.

"That should do." Jade dried her hands and arranged loaves into cloth-lined baskets, tucking containers of jams and spreads around the edges. "We have plenty for tonight, plus I can sell any leftovers at a discount in the market tomorrow morning."

Ember's mouth gaped at the evidence of their afternoon. Plates and trenchers buried the surface of the table and sideboard. They had enough food to feed an entire legion of soldiers.

"Let's get you washed and changed."

"Changed?"

"Yes, changed. Unless you want to wear lad's britches to bed." Jade clucked her tongue and bent over a large chest in the corner. Her head disappeared inside the compartment, her backside wiggling in the air.

"'Tis all I own." Ember's eyes flicked to her downtrodden satchel. Heat rushed up the column of her throat, curling around her ears. She rubbed the back of her neck and said, "I don't mind."

"I have a nightgown that will work with your coloring. It fit Ada last summer, so it should be near your size." Jade rummaged around in the trunk. She held up a long thin shirt, the color of new spring grass, and shooed Ember around the screen separating the bed from the rest of the room. "Go on and get out of those rags."

Jade flung the nightgown over the top. Its neckline scooped low, and small tulips, stitched by talented fingers, sprung up around the collar. The lighter material would lend itself to comfort.

She peeled off her drab, dusty clothes and pulled the clean garment over her head. The length of the nightshirt was perfect. However, its fit ran snug at the top and loose around the middle. She trailed her hands along the soft fabric until magic warmed her palms.

The gown molded to her shape, allowing Ember to catch her breath. The bitter taste of a cast filled her mouth. She smoothed out the fabric at her waist, and after the flutter of her heart slowed, she stepped around the screen, letting her arms dangle at her sides.

"It's beautiful. Thank you for lending it."

"Ah, that fits better than expected. I'm glad you enjoy it." Jade gave her a once over, pausing at Ember's middle. Her forehead wrinkled. "Mind the hearth, would you, while I change?"

Ember crossed the room and added another log to the fire. She stoked it until the flames picked up. The aroma of the roasting meat swirled around her. Ember wrapped a swath of thick linen twice around her hands and moved the remaining pot away from the heat.

She lifted the lid and wafted her hand above the mixture. The scent — a greasy mixture of pork and fresh garlic and dried rosemary — teased the back of her mind.

She shut her eyes, but not before a single small tear escaped and rolled down her cheek. Ember swiped it away and cleared her throat.

She had yet to cry.

Survival whispered for her to bury the grief.

There was no place in this new world for melancholy, but it didn't disappear. Most days it was a dull ache, barely registering through the weight of external needs. Tonight, when she was full of food and kindness and surrounded by scents of her past, it bubbled to the surface and spilled over like an unattended cauldron.

"What do you think?" Jade stepped out from behind the screen.

Ember returned the lid, prolonging the movement to steady her hands, and surveyed the dress. It was a deep forest green, a shade darker than Jade's namesake. She'd left her hair loose around her shoulders, and the golden strands contrasted with the deep hue, highlighting her rich green eyes. The material was luxurious, a plush velvet that would feel foreign if she ran her travel worn hands down its length.

"'Tis lovely."

"Let's see if I can wrangle some of the younger villagers to assist us with all this food." Jade floated across the room and opened the front entry. She leaned forward and cupped the sides of her mouth. "Lads. Spare a moment for me?"

Jade swung the door wider and stepped to the side, allowing two young men to spill across the threshold. They stumbled in their haste but quickly righted themselves upon setting eyes to Ember. Both surprised her with small bows and ready grins.

"At your service, milady." The taller of the two swept his arm wide and asked, "What beast shall we slay for you this day?"

"Ah, I require help with the beast of burden." Jade gestured to the baskets of food. Her eyes twinkled with their game. "Please run these up to the training barn and set them behind my cart, and I shall forever be in your debt. If anyone inquires, I will follow in a moment."

They looped baskets on their arms and carried platters above their heads. They shimmied through the open front door, chatting merrily along the way.

"For this eve…" Jade closed the door behind her and laid a hand on Ember's shoulder. "Please make yourself at home. I will not return for several hours, at which time, I expect you to be asleep. Take my bed. 'Tis wide enough to share, and help yourself to food and drink. I left a pitcher of water on the sideboard and extra logs near the hearth."

"You do too much." Ember rubbed her palm and kept her gaze downcast. "I cannot repay your kindness."

"Nonsense. You need a place to stay and I… I could use some

company." Jade clutched her wrist. "Please. I am satisfied with this arrangement."

"If you insist. But it's for tonight only. I must continue my journey tomorrow."

"Yes, of course," Jade said quickly. The last basket swung from the crook in her elbow. She opened the cottage's front door and sent a small wave in her direction. "I *understand*."

Ember raised her hand in protest.

"No, I must resume my travels." She crossed the room and leaned out into the evening. The sticky air coiled around her outstretched arm. Clouds gathered overhead, knitting together to block out the last rays of sun and curtaining off its exit from the day's stage. "Jade…"

"I didn't catch the last." Jade grinned and grabbed the hem of her skirt. A small skip appeared in her step as she sauntered down the main road. She cupped a hand to her ear and mouthed, "I can't hear you."

Ember shook her head, unable to prevent the corners of her mouth from turning upward. Despite the chilly breeze swirling around her ankles, warmth spread through her core and down her fingertips. She stepped back into the quaint cottage, and the door shut behind her, cutting off the rest of the world.

A night wouldn't hurt. Plus, it was rude to refuse the gesture.

A small tea kettle sat next to the pitcher of water in the back. On the kitchen windowsill, glass jars cocooned a variety of dried leaves.

She padded over to the sideboard, poured a generous amount of water into the teapot, and wrapped her hands around its middle. The kettle warmed beneath her palms, steam rising from the spout.

Aye. It was smart, prudent even, to hide in Jade's quaint cottage, plotting her travels. Avoiding Gavyn.

She grabbed a small vessel from the drying rack and plucked a jar of what she recognized as dried chamomile from the window's ledge. After pinching a few petals between her fingers, she confirmed the spicy, woodsy scent. She pushed up on her tiptoes and grasped the edge of the shelves above the counter, moving small containers and bowls aside.

"Now, where would Jade keep her sachet bags?"

Ember pulled two small jars off the lowest shelf and placed them on the counter. She pushed off one foot and craned her neck, searching behind some of the larger platters. No luck.

A sharp knock echoed in the room.

She snapped her head to the front of the cottage a moment before the door swung open.

Gavyn ducked under the frame.

"Looking for something." He crossed his arms over his chest. Rain droplets ran down his forearm and clung to his elbow, before splashing onto the floor. His lips pinched together, and he leveled her with his gaze. "Please continue. Don't cease your thieving on my account."

He took another step forward, cocking his head to the side. *Thud.*

Howling wind caught the door, and its handle banged against the plaster wall. The draft snuffed out the candle flames in the front half of the room, and uninvited rain poured in at an angle, coalescing in a puddle on the floor. The fire from the hearth cast shadows around the cottage and under his handsome cheekbones.

She wanted to take a step back, but an unwelcome urge drew her to him. A bark of thunder boomed off of the walls.

Ember flinched. "I wasn't—"

"You weren't what? Helping yourself? Taking advantage of your circumstances?" Gavyn shut the door and whirled to face her. "Preying on Jade's generosity?"

"Tea. I wanted tea. And… and I couldn't find the cloth for steeping the leaves." Her voice shook, but she raised her chin higher. "What brings you to Jade's home?"

Gavyn narrowed his eyes at the steaming kettle and empty cup. He marched over to where she leaned against the sideboard. The wet sleeve of his sodden tunic brushed her forearm as he grabbed a stack of small square cloths from the highest shelf.

Thin pink ribbon bundled them together. It looked out of place in his large palm.

Heat radiated from his body and blanketed her, creating an unpleasant mix of sensations. She took a step back, putting breathing room between herself, Gavyn, and his ire.

"Thank you," she said to the floor. "I didn't know where to look."

"Watch yourself," Gavyn said as he closed the distance between them with one long stride. He bent at the waist and angled his head, capturing her attention. "Jade is neither friendless nor lacking family. We take care of our own. She may show favor to your plight, but pretty smiles and soft words do not sway me."

"Tis only tea." Ember's back stiffened. She gripped the side of the counter, bracing herself on its sturdy surface. "Jade invited me into her home. I apologized for my earlier transgression in the marketplace and worked in her kitchen this afternoon to correct my offense. Besides, you're too late. Xavier already threatened to hunt me to the ends of the realm if I so much as breathe wrong in Jade's direction. "

His nostrils flared, but he took a step back. Then another. At the edge of the sideboard, he turned on his heel and stalked toward the front door.

He rested a hand on the lever and tilted his head to the rafters. To the ceiling he said, "Don't hurt her, and you and I won't have a problem."

Gavyn gripped the handle, and with the final warning, he stepped out into the night.

It was difficult to summon anger at his accusations, as his measure was not wholly incorrect.

Her satchel rested in the corner next to Jade's trunk. The bag could conceal a dozen pies, with room at the top to roll up Jade's heavy cloak. The fine garment enticed her from the hook next to the front door. Three pairs of stockings could wrap around the bag's frayed strap, snug during transportation until winter beckoned.

Various spices could tuck in the nooks and crannies of the pouch. Dried, they would weigh nothing but could yield enough coin to feed her through a dozen moon cycles.

A smart thief wouldn't linger. A smart thief would seize the opportunity before her.

Too bad she wasn't a smart thief.

A treacherous longing bloomed in her chest.

No matter how many times her mother uprooted her life, she always glommed onto any affection thrown her way.

It's prudent not to form attachments to the community. Her mother's voice was like a talon scrapping its sharp tip down Ember's deepest wishes.

For the night, she had a soft bed. A roof protecting her from the rain and warm blankets to snuggle under.

It was foolish to hope for more.

"Oh, mama. I miss you," Ember said to the room as she rubbed the locket nestled in the hollow of her throat. The copper chain, once a warm reddish brown color, now carried splashes of cool blues and greens from sleeping under the night sky. "Tomorrow. I'll stay for one more day and ponder my path forward. One more night."

CHAPTER FIVE

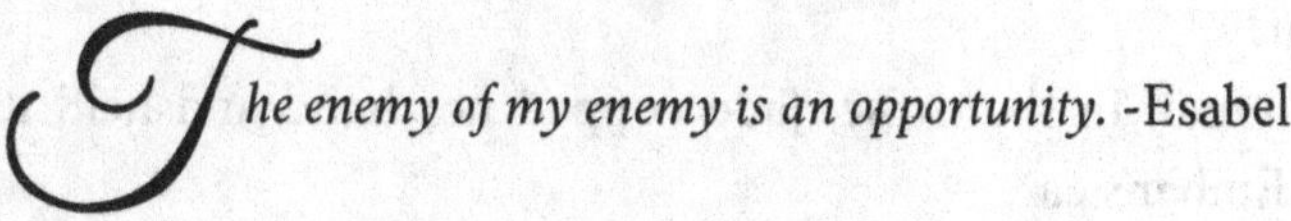 *he enemy of my enemy is an opportunity.* -Esabel

SOMEHOW, ONE DAY TURNED INTO TWO.

Those two days melded into a week. She fell asleep next to Jade each eve, planning to depart in the morning, but an abundant amount of work greeted her at sunrise, and her friend needed Ember's help.

A fabrication, as Jade had managed on her own before her arrival, but her full belly — similar to her ravenous stomach — didn't listen to logic.

Noise floated down the hill, and the dark outline of the training barn rose before them. Light from the two enormous front doors spilled out, illuminating the end of the path. Ember couldn't decide if the rays were a beacon in the night or a warning to all those who entered.

'Twas fight night. The excitement was palatable.

Villagers fanned out in all directions, shouting and cheering the two men trading blows inside the center ring. In many spots, spectators crammed five deep, pushing on the back of those in front, craning to see the action.

She couldn't think, let alone hear, anything.

Jade gestured for Ember to head toward the cart in the back corner.

Earlier, she had commanded one cub, if you could call a grown man a cub, to carry their wares to the training barn.

Pies and breads and jars of jam covered the surface.

Next to their station, a smiling woman pulled taps and filled patrons' glasses two at a time. Amber liquid flowed from a spout on a barrel in the lower row. Mead.

The bar top had to be twenty paces long, and with spectators crowding around two deep, it was as hectic as the entertainment.

At a break in the noise, Jade cupped her hand and held it close to Ember's ear.

"Let's head over to lighten this crowd of their gold." She hooked an arm through Ember's elbow and steered them over to her cart in the corner.

The next hour passed in a blur, and they found a rhythm, packing fare and collecting coin. Men, women, and children of all ages swung by for their supper.

She delighted in the tidbits of conversation offered between the rise and fall of the crowd noise. More than once, her eyes drifted to Gavyn, who stood ringside.

He wore a clean white shirt with the sleeves rolled to his elbows. Fawn-colored leathers fit snugly on his lower half, straining when he ducked under the ropes between rounds.

Warmth fanned across her cheeks and distracted her from the next customer in line.

"I'm heading over to grab a drink from Zoie," Jade said, startling Ember. She pointed to the woman working behind the bar. "I'll be right back."

A large body blocked the view of Jade's departure.

She tilted her head back and couldn't prevent her mouth from gaping open.

The warm candlelight highlighted the deep luster of gold in the newcomer's light brown skin. A firm jaw and sharp cheekbones anchored a classically perfect face. His strong features were sensual, a type of beauty from which many would find it difficult to tear their gaze away, regardless of their preferences.

"I'll take some pheasant, if there is any left." He rocked back on his heels.

"Mmm, hmm." She gathered the pie and avoided his gaze.

"Relax. I trust Jade. If she's comfortable having you around, it's nothing to me." He smiled, reading her reaction incorrectly. A solitary dimple formed on his cheek, and a curl of raven black hair fell forward as he leaned on the front of the cart.

Ember grinned back.

"I'm not here to steal from Jade. I mean, I was initially, but—"

"Hey, I understand. But it can't happen again." A subtle edge laced his flirtatious tone. "I'm Rowan. It's my good fortune to meet you."

"Ember." She answered as she moved the remaining slices of bread from the upper shelf down to nestle in with the pastries.

Rowan brought the pie to his nose, closing his eyes, and inhaled.

"Don't tell Jade, but—"

"Are you here to heckle my new apprentice?" Jade returned with her drink and the bartender. She raised her cup to her lips, one eyebrow shooting up as she peered over its edge.

"No, no." Rowan raised a hand in surrender. "I'm just here for some supper. I'll leave all the heckling to Gavyn."

At the sound of his name, Ember turned toward the center ring. Slowly. Ever so slowly, his eyes raked over her. The heat from his gaze stripped her bare.

From another man, there would be little doubt as to his intentions.

From another man, she would be all a flutter at the prospects of fulfilling the unspoken promise. But Gavyn was not another man, and there would be no passionate meeting. From him, she suspected it was a warning.

"What's he doing ringside?"

"He's cornering." The newcomer handed her a cup with clear liquid. She wore her ash blonde hair in a severe knot to the side. Her peach skin carried a faint flush. "It's water. Jade thought you might be thirsty. I'm Zoie, by the way. Ada already spilled the story of your arrival."

"Thank you." Ember took a deep sip of the cool liquid and studied the barkeep. "What do you mean 'cornering'?"

"Coaching. Giving instructions. Acting as an extra set of eyes for the fighter in the ring." Zoie sent Ember an indulging smile. "Do you see the other man on the far side?"

"Aye." Ember stood on her tiptoes to see over the crowd. "I see him."

"He's the other fighter's cornerman. They hop the ropes in between rounds, tend any cuts, and give advice on what the fighter is doing wrong." Zoie shrugged. "What they need to fix."

"Or go back over the original strategy." Rowan slid his arm around Zoie's midsection and tugged her against his side. He placed a small peck on the top of her head. "Did you bring me something to drink, too?"

"You're not a guest." Zoie ducked under his arm, spinning out of his embrace.

Rowan tilted his head back and let out a hearty laugh.

"Alright, beautiful. Message received. I'll leave you ladies in search of my own." He bent at the hips, kissed the back of Ember's hand, and winked. "It is my sincerest wish that you remain with us. It would be a pleasure to regularly rest my eyes on such beauty."

Rowan extended two fingers in a jaunty salute and strolled to the bar.

Zoie straightened, and a smirk split Jade's face. Ember looked back and forth between the two women. What just happened?

"Rowan is our resident charmer. He will flirt with anyone with a pulse," Jade said.

Ember glanced back to the bar to find Rowan surrounded by several ladies and a few gentlemen. They pressed close and vied for his attention. Their mouths moved in rapid succession. He opened both arms, and a couple squeezed nearer, snuggling into his embrace.

Beside her, Zoie haphazardly rearranged items on the cart.

"Miss Zoie, here, is not impervious to jealousy." Jade swatted Zoie's hand and fixed the mess she made of her display.

"Psst. I'm nothing of the sort." Zoie tucked an errant lock of hair behind her ears. "He rubs me the wrong way."

"Born an old lady, Zoie has little time for those who don't cater solely to life's demands." Jade arched her brow.

"I prefer the term 'old soul'." Zoie elbowed Jade and sighed. "He should take his training more seriously. Every time I slip into the loft with Ada, he's never around. I'm not sure why Gavyn puts up with it."

"We all can't be like Gavyn or Xavier or even you." Jade smiled. "Some of us need our brief breaks of pleasure. Speaking of fun, let's get this cleaned up. I want a better spot to watch Gavyn's fight."

Rowan strolled to the far side of the barn, snuggling his companions from the bar. Beside her, Zoie clenched her jaw.

Ember agreed with Jade; it wasn't exasperation clouding Zoie's features.

Gavyn's first strike landed with a satisfying thud, but he didn't have the heart to put all of his might into the second.

His opponent, a mercenary, fell to his knees from the blow, a fast hook meant to stun not to knock out.

He preferred the stand up game, driving opponents to the ground was Rowan's specialty, so he patiently waited as the man staggered to his feet and gave him a few extra counts to catch his breath.

Gavyn shook out his hands, failing to dispel the tension humming through his body.

She'd stayed. One night at Jade's turned into a week. The little thief ignored his warnings… and stayed.

He was in a mood — strung tight, like the strings on a fiddle. No amount of extra pad work had dulled the edges of his temper enough for him not to sharpen his tongue on everyone at the compound.

Gavyn needed more — a match in front of a thirsty audience was certain to lighten his worries and focus his errant thoughts — which is why he told Xavier he was taking the last spot on the card at this week's fight night.

Unfortunately, this fighter wasn't the answer either.

"That's all you have, pretty boy?" His opponent sneered.

Gavyn locked on to the mercenary's breast bone, ignoring the overactive hands. Typical. The idiot was so busy moving his fists he forgot to protect his face.

Gavyn split the middle. One quick jab through his guard, and his opponent's head snapped back.

Another shot to the ribs had him doubling over.

Gavyn hadn't even learned to pen his name before an older neighbor dragged him into his first brawl. The lad needed backup to settle a score, to teach a lesson to the bully terrorizing his younger sister. Big for his age but lacking experience, Gavyn served more as a punching bag in his first backyard scrap than a help. He left with two swollen eyes, a bloody lip plus a cracked rib.

And a sense of direction. A purpose.

He didn't know it then, but the beating was the start of his lifelong friendship with Xavier. And a lifelong obsession with the art of fighting.

Gavyn switched stances. A knee to the head would put this opponent out of his misery.

Too bad it would make for a complicated night for everyone involved. Gavyn didn't want to strain relations with the mercenary group more than they already were. Knocking out their best fighter in under a minute was a quick way to sour the tenuous friendship Xavier counted on for information from the other territories.

A fact he had to keep reminding himself, as these weren't honorable men.

Strength-for-hire.

Their communities tossed every one of them out as a punishment for various misdeeds, or they left on their own from an inability to follow society's dictates. While Gavyn could understand severing bonds to masters who supplied a system designed to work them until their last breath, he didn't respect their lack of training. Their lax moral code.

They sold their allegiance to the highest bidder.

With a finite division of labor in the territories, earning a living meant getting creative. Or often bartering your conscience to the master with the most gold. Manual labor was honest. Extra security was a boring and simple assignment.

Kidnapping and murder paid the most.

Not that Xavier could link this group of mercenaries to any unsavory jobs, but their presence in his home rankled Gavyn all the same.

At least, that's what Gavyn told himself for his foul mood this eve.

His opponent spit blood at his feet and wiped the back of his mouth with his hand. Flat-footed, he sauntered back to the center of the ring and held his fists in front of his face. "That all you got?"

About time the fighter fixed his guard.

Now, Gavyn wouldn't feel so bad for laying him out. He exploded, throwing a jab for misdirection. A half step to the right allowed his cross to land. He finished the quick combo with a left uppercut, dropping the man once again.

This time, the fool would stay down.

"Tap out before I put you to sleep." Too fast to be satisfying, but Gavyn would not waste any more energy on the fighter. He crouched down. "Do it."

This one was either smart enough to recognize defeat or fearful enough to yield to self-preservation. He couldn't bring himself to care either way. The mercenary pounded the floor twice and rolled over on his back.

Gavyn's chest heaved, empty from the usual pride of winning a match. He crossed the ring and accepted a small linen towel and cup of water from Xavier.

Nothing was simple this eve.

Instead of the normal matchups with neighboring villages, Gavyn had to play nice. He wanted to celebrate the night's victories with his fighters, but they continued to pace a wide arc around him. Even cornering the younger men had failed to pull him to the present — strategy not enough to corral his thoughts.

He wiped the back of his neck and took a long pull of water.

"You finished chewing off the fighters' heads, or you need another challenge?" Xavier asked.

An offer of peace.

Xavier preferred exchanging punches instead of words. If needed, his friend would drag him down to the stream and let him punch out his frustrations. But the longer this unease continued, the more Gavyn reckoned physical exertion would not snap him out of it.

"I'm good." He tipped his chin.

The lie sounded half-hearted even to his own ears. Xavier let it land between them.

"Tonight was a wash. I doubt Ada made a quarter of her normal purse." He set the water down and leaned against the corner barrel.

The crowd thinned out, the first years herding them through the open front doors, their faces alight more from the mead than the lopsided entertainment.

Gavyn finished unwrapping his hands, letting the long fabric gather at his feet.

Xavier grunted.

He didn't expect an opinion. Despite their years together, his leader rarely shared counsel. It never bothered him. Gavyn owned his strengths. His place. Xavier may not say it in words, but he showed his gratitude by allowing him to lead the training at the compound.

"Enjoy your twirl in the ring?" Rowan's voice grated. He slipped his big body between the ropes and slapped Gavyn on the back. "I thought you fell asleep there for a minute."

Rowan picked up Gavyn's cup and emptied the contents, the curve of his mouth hinting from behind the wide rim.

That was the difference between the compound's resident jester and their taciturn leader. Gavyn could always count on a round of sparring with Xavier. Rowan never disappointed with his jokes.

"Or maybe your focus runs in another direction these days." Rowan tilted his head to the far corner, where Jade served the spectator's more basic appetites.

Gavyn knew what he would find. Not because things were as usual — Jade busying herself serving patrons, fighters lining the outer wall running crowd control, villagers lingering for a bit of gossip — because he couldn't keep himself from watching her. The thief.

A week's worth of meals and coddling had improved

Ember's coloring. He wasn't sure how it was possible, but she grew more enchanting each time he set eyes to her.

Still, he was surprised she stuck around, busying herself in Jade's skirts.

Gavyn was certain of her measure — so sure of her flight after that first day. But he underestimated the spell of Jade's generosity. Or the thief's desire for a warm bed and easy friendship.

Tonight, Jade had trussed her up in a frilly skirt more suited to formal dances than an evening in the utilitarian training barn. She reached on tiptoes toward the top shelf, exposing a sliver of skin at her waist.

Gavyn ground his teeth.

It would be easier if she was sneaky. Calculating, ready to take advantage of Jade and bolting at the next available opportunity. Then, he would have reason to observe her so closely. To allow his attention to linger over the simplest of gestures.

But she moved in time with Jade, an effortless grace and confidence expected after years of companionship, not a mere week in the same cottage.

Simple gestures of affection passed between them. Knowing smiles. Gentle squeezes. If pressed, he couldn't explain his fascination with her.

"Your thief looks right at home, doesn't she? I can't tell who owns your displeasure — Jade for keeping her, the girl for staying, or you... for your own impossible standards." Rowan slung an arm around him, letting his weight sag on Gavyn's frame. He heard the smile in his brother's tone without the necessity of looking at his mouth.

"You talk too much."

"You tell yourself those lies, but I possess the courage to lend voice to what stews behind your frowns." Rowan's bark of laughter drew curious looks from the lingering spectators, the last few waiting for a chance to speak with their favorite fighters.

"Go on then." Gavyn sighed. "Speak. I know you didn't postpone your time with your admirers to chat about my match. Unless, you seek pointers on footwork. The gods and everyone else knows you need the help."

"Harsh." Rowan pulled him in for a one-arm hug and muttered, "Stubborn brute. I won't waste my words on you. Your back is wide enough to carry all the responsibilities of the compound but you aren't ready to shoulder the truths in front of you."

Gavyn snatched the empty cup.

"Your thief has made herself at home. Stolen Jade's devotion. Watch. She'll pay it back with friendship, and then Jade will go on 'n keep her. Might as well accept it."

Gavyn nodded to the bar and nudged Rowan's boot, not ready to consider the possibility of her actually staying. "And what of your secrets — the ones you don't face yourself?"

Rowan patted his cheek and declared, "I never said I was any better."

For the last four hours, Ember didn't know where to look.

Oh, she told herself scanning for lingering patrons was a part of her responsibilities while helping Jade pack up her cart for the night, but she doubted staring at every fighter who wandered by was truly necessary.

What did they put in the food here?

Farming was hard work, and the bodies of the sons who plowed the fields grew to meet the demand. But these men were twice the size of the lads back home. And half of them wandered around shirtless. It was difficult not to gape.

Harder not to search the crowd for one man in particular.

"You're staring again," Jade teased.

Heat spread across her cheeks, and she hastily turned back to her task. Ember arranged the unsold pastries in the smaller baskets. The monotonous work grounded her. She was grateful for something to occupy her time.

The barn was bathed in light even at this late hour.

Candelabras lined the wall every few paces, their clear glass surrounds amplified the flickering candles inside.

Three enormous chandeliers hung from two-story rafters, the multi-tiered rings were wide enough to fit a round hay bale in the middle. A chain, with links as thick as Gavyn's wrists, suspended the fixtures from the central timber down to hooks mounted on the outer wall. Everything here was... big.

She rubbed the tip of her nose.

The first hour of fighting passed before she could place the faint smell of pine. There was a heady mixture of floral perfume from the families who visited the cart.

Once they paid for their fare and returned to the entertainment, the fragrance of woodland forests wafted down to replace the sweeter notes, reminding her of cold days playing hide-n-seek in the forest with only the squirrels for mates.

It was the candles.

Not only was their illumination practical but their perfume masked the scents the summer breeze carried through the open doors. And when combined with the brutality of the fights, the overwhelming sensations had her on edge for most of the matches.

Despite Ember's best intentions, her eyes strayed toward the center ring.

Dear gods, why did he have to be here? She had managed to avoid Gavyn the week she stayed with Jade, but his appearance at the fights, while expected, unsettled her tonight.

He was... hypnotic.

It was easy to admit observing from a safe distance, one out of reach of his constant frowns.

Gavyn was agile, and Ember found it difficult to keep up with his quick movements. A fine sheen of sweat coated his bare chest, and the candle light reflecting off his skin created an ethereal glow.

She scoffed. More like a fallen angel than one who retained his divinity.

"What do you think of your first fight night?" Jade wiped the top shelf with a damp linen and rested her hip against the side of the cart.

"T'was… intense." It was clear, even to her inexperienced eye, the fighters at the compound were more skilled than the bunch of visiting mercenaries.

"Why don't you take a break and splash some water on your face. There is a stream around back. The path will lead you right to the banks." Jade gestured toward a door behind the cart. "I'm going to help clean up the bar and will wait for your return."

"Thank you," she said. "I'll hasten my step."

Ember slipped through the back door and leaned against the barn's stone foundation. The din of the fights faded away but the rush of the evening continued to throb between her ears. Her eyes adjusted to the darkness, and her breathing deepened in the crisp, fresh air.

Her magic hummed in her fingertips.

Surrounded by so many injuries, her powers awakened.

Busted lips. Swollen eyes. Shoulders sagging from sprains or bruises. They called to her — a siren song meant to lure her away from her good senses — loud enough it almost drained her resolve to remain in the fringe of the crowd.

It took every ounce of concentration to ignore the over-whelming sights and sounds. To dampen her instincts and tune out the force thrumming though her blood. She slid down the wall, letting her head rest on her knees.

"You received my message?" an unfamiliar voice asked. It was far enough away that there was a slim chance of its owner spotting her, but Ember crouched lower all the same.

"Aye. Subtlety is not your strength."

Her head snapped up. *Xavier.*

They stood under the branches of a small maple tree planted at the edge of a courtyard.

She was torn between shrinking farther down into herself or parting the tall grasses at her feet to steal a glimpse of the men. In the end, her interest won out, and she leaned forward, propping herself on her hands and knees.

"I wanted your attention." The stranger shrugged.

He was Xavier's height, but the shadows from the tree's canopy concealed his features. The stranger leaned against the trunk, one ankle crossed over the other. A surprisingly casual stance given Xavier's clenched fists.

"You have two minutes before Gavyn starts looking."

"Ever the loyal dog." The words were raspy as if he seldom commanded them.

"Hold your tongue," Xavier said. He pulled out a small pocket watch and held up a finger. "One minute."

"And I should need but half. The Castle watches. Interest grows in your alliance with other territories. Your absences from the compound, in particular, cause concern. I suggest you ask your *brothers* to provide lessons in covering your tracks."

He pushed off from the tree.

"What of Jade?" Xavier asked as he grabbed his arm. "Do they still suspect who she is to me?"

"Still no concern for yourself, then?" The stranger yanked his arm free. He cocked his head and regarded Xavier over his shoulder. "They'll never forget. You need to stay away from her. Make them think you lost interest. Their fickle hearts won't question a wandering eye. Hell, find another and parade her around the village. The whispers will travel back to the Castle."

"Not a chance. I may not be able to claim her, but I won't tarnish our bond." Xavier flicked his wrist. The hilt of a dagger swayed in the air, its tip lodged in the ground at the stranger's feet.

Ember covered her mouth, stifling a gasp.

"Don't forget your blade. You never know when you may need to stab someone in their back." Xavier turned on his heel and slipped around the corner.

The stranger bent down and retrieved the dagger. He wiped it on the hem of his tunic. After several methodical passes, he sheathed it in his belt, sent one last look in the direction Xavier disappeared, and sprinted out of sight.

She took a shaky breath.

Nothing was simple this eve.

Instead of enjoying the easy camaraderie with Jade and her customers, Ember spent most of it keeping her emotions under guard. She wanted a chance to observe the normalcy of the compound. But these were not simple fighters — men who scratched out an existence, fitting neatly inside the societal constructs created by the Castle.

She pushed off the wall behind her and steadied her feet.

No, they were something more dangerous — men who fought on their own terms, who thumbed their nose at the Lords while delivering their heavy tithe. Who courted Red Guard spies in the night.

These fighters were family, with all the messy trappings expected of a large brood.

And yet, they drew her in.

She was fascinated by their fierce protection of one another. The complicated affection they displayed, the haven they created. But she needed to keep her wits.

It was one thing to house a drifter. To lend a hand to an unassuming stranger on the wrong side of lady luck. But how quickly would the bonds of brotherhood snap tight, if they found out she shared a kinship with their enemy — not if, but when they discovered she harnessed the same vein of power as their oppressors in the Castle.

Her magic required an outlet.

After tonight, she doubted her abilities to dampen it indefinitely. She may not be able to stay in control next time.

Faeblood, she'd heard whispered on her journeys.

Dirty blood.

While she enjoyed the ease of friendship and the tantalizing glimmer of new beginnings, Ember would do well to remember her survival — the life her mother died to protect — pointed in another direction, away from human strangers and the welcoming spell they wove.

CHAPTER SIX

All men possess darkness, wanting what belongs to another, coveting beyond their reach. -Esabel

THE PIGS WERE LOOSE.

Not one. Not a couple. The farmer's sow and her entire litter of piglets escaped from their pen. A day after the fights, they wedged open their gate and went on a stroll in the market.

Well… if one considered upending crates, darting between the legs of patrons, and snagging food… a stroll.

Ember hugged the tree trunk with one arm.

Her ladder lay flat on the ground below, the sow's first casualty.

Earlier, she'd volunteered to climb to the upper branches, where the sun ripened the plum's skins, and pick enough of the juicy fruit for an afternoon of jam making.

Her mouth watered as the sticky sweet scent wafted up from the full basket resting on her hip.

Despite her clumsiness on solid ground, she was a fair climber, born from years of observing life at an acceptable distance. Trees were safe, according to her mother, a refuge even, for a young girl forbidden from interacting with others.

In every new farming village, she'd found a sturdy vantage to observe the locals.

As a child, she scrambled up towering oaks and majestic birches after her morning chores, often hiding in the canopy long after the nooning meal and ignoring the pinpricks in her limbs from staying in one position for too long. The neighbors sent curious glances in her direction, but after a few days, they either forgot her existence or grew accustomed to the feral girl living above them.

She became invisible.

It was astounding what some would say in her presence. At her last home, she learned the laundress dallied with the baker. She overheard the blacksmith confessing to substituting crude iron in his horseshoes, a ploy to save the cost of purchasing sturdier materials. And Landon, the farmer's son, secretly courted the stable master's school-aged daughter.

She shuddered.

When she wasn't listening for secrets, she watched passersby, wondering about their life.

How would it feel to share a meal with others, devouring morsels of harmless gossip? How would it feel to wander through her day, never worrying about magic threatening to take over her thoughts and actions at any moment?

She climbed lower, careful not to jostle her harvest.

A few plums on lower branches fell to the ground and splattered on impact, a feast for the woodland creatures brave enough to venture near the market.

She wedged the basket against the trunk and swung both legs over a lower branch.

How would it feel to fall in love? a dark voice asked. *To share covert glances across a meal? To sneak out, meeting under the moonlight?*

At eighteen summers, she experienced her first courtship. It was brief, unsatisfying. She knew her mother would discover her secret and sever ties to the village, but just once she wished to lay with another, wanted to feel their skin against hers.

A piglet dashed into the baker's shop. Jade chased another under the cart, her cheeks ruddy and her smile stretching from ear to ear.

Perhaps more than a lover, Ember wished for a friend — someone to share her day, someone to tug along on adventures, *someone to whom she could confide her dreams.*

Her fingertips picked at a piece of loose bark. Bits crumbled and lodged under her nails.

Today, like many days in Ember's childhood, she was close enough to witness the excitement, but the distance from the market highlighted how little she belonged.

She must move on, but Ember was torn.

Duty pulled her to the Northern Isles. Longing held her firmly in Jade's cottage. Impractical childhood dreams demanded she abandon both plans and head straight for the Castle, where it was certain other Faeblood lived.

None of the options were safe, but when had her life ever been safe?

Staying with Jade was selfish. Death, enslavement, and torture — her fate and the fate of those she loved, if her mother was to be believed. Her stomach churned as if she'd eaten spoiled meat. If only she could—

Gah. A snare wrapped around Ember's ankle, startling her.

The pressure increased and prevented her from tumbling backwards.

Gavyn.

His grip eased, and his thumb wrapped around her calf. Displeasure radiated off him in waves.

"Why are you in the tree? Spying?" He ran both hands up her legs and cupped the back of her knees.

"What?" she asked. Focused on regaining her seat, the words reached her a heartbeat later than normal.

She braced one hand against the trunk. Her other hand found the only available anchor in this position — his hair. She tangled her fingers in the silky mass.

Time sucked sound and air out of the market.

What did he ask?

She struggled to control her breaths as the surrounding noise faded to nothing. Ember's entire world shrank to the two of them. Her eyes slowly traced a path from his leather cuff up his thick forearm, settling on his handsome profile.

A wicked scar marred his cheek. It was as if the gods knew he was too pretty for his personality and marked his face, easing its impact.

At last, she met his gaze, and her stomach fell to the ground even though her body stayed in the tree.

SHE WAS A DRIFTER. A THIEF. A GORGEOUS TREE NYMPH SENT TO tempt Gavyn from his wits, his responsibilities.

But her legs were so… puny. She seemed fragile under his palms. Though that couldn't be true. Despite her diminutive size, she must posses a will of steal to travel unprotected in the territories.

His thumbs continued to caress the back of her knees.

Perhaps he was wrong about her. If she meant Jade harm, wouldn't she have acted by now? He didn't want to admit it, but maybe she wasn't the menace he once imagined.

Still, he needed to stay alert.

Aye. Someone should check on her. Daily. Just in case. What was he doing? His tongue stuck to the top of his mouth. He must look silly, staring up at her.

She let go of his hair and grabbed onto his shoulders with both hands.

"You don't fool me." He resisted the urge to lean forward and said, "You enchanted Jade and half the village, but I will continue to monitor you."

Truth. He couldn't help but follow her every move. Whenever she was near, his eyes moved on their own. He kept telling himself it was for the safety of the compound, but his reasoning sounded hollow.

Her lips turned down in what he suspected was an attempt at frowning.

"Follow me all you want, but in the meantime, make yourself useful and grab this." She handed him a basket overflowing with fruit. "We plan to make jam this afternoon, and I don't want to feed the forest creatures my hard work."

He hesitated, not wanting to release her legs, worried she might tumble.

She shoved the bounty in his face.

He could either let her go or get hit with plums. When he was certain she wouldn't topple off the limb, he grabbed the basket and placed it next to the ladder.

He straightened, and his gaze snagged on her slippers.

"You need new shoes." Travel worn, the rockier paths connecting the territories thinned the soles to less than a fingernail's width. He wrapped a hand around her ankle before he thought better of it and brought her foot closer to his face. "Keep your sticky fingers off any pairs belonging to the villagers."

"Why you—"

He yanked her ankle, and she fell into his arms. Gavyn sucked in his breath, and his heart beat furiously in his chest. Two thumps. Three thumps. Four.

"I'll say it again." His hands settled on her waist. "You may hoodwink Jade, but I'm not convinced you won't bring trouble."

"I wouldn't." Her chest heaved, and her grip on his shoulders tightened as she slid down his body.

The sun blazed overhead.

Later, when he stared up at his chamber's ceiling trying to find sleep, he could admit the heat spreading though him had little to do with its intense rays.

He held in a groan.

Frustration — that was what this was. Was she aware of how much she rattled him? How long would she disrupt his schedule? His composure?

"I will not steal," she whispered. "Or hurt Jade."

Dear gods, she was so... soft. He resisted the urge to pull her tighter. Instead, he ground his teeth and released his hold.

Gavyn took a step back, gaining much needed space. It would be prudent to take another, lest he do something foolish like tuck that loose tendril behind her ear.

"Why are you here?" She cocked her head to the side as if she only just remembered something.

"I live here."

"No. Why are you *here*?" She gestured to the market.

A muddy piglet shot between his legs. One of the baker's boys gave chase. The escapee rooted under the tree, delighting in a fallen plum.

Gavyn scooped it up, scratched it behind the ears, and handed it to the boy.

"Thanks, Mister Gavyn." The lad smiled, revealing two missing front teeth.

"Welcome," he muttered.

Gavyn stared at her lips as if they held the answer to her question. He was stalling. But his head was fuzzy, like when Xav punched it too many times in the ring.

Think. What if...

He could blame his visit on his aching shoulder. Jade kept an array of tea leaves and tinctures in her kitchens for such ailments. Perhaps he should mention it to her and ask for a draught.

Or he could check the cottage. In spring, he and Rowan patched a leak in Jade's roof. Perhaps he should inspect the repair. He didn't wish for either of them to catch a cold if the weather threatened to come inside.

Or... sugar. That's it. Didn't Rowan mention the stores ran low at the compound? Perhaps Jade would share some until they received their quarterly shipment from the farming community. She always kept a surplus.

"I wanted to borrow some sugar from Jade," he blurted out. There. That sounded reasonable.

"You wanted some sugar?" she asked, using the same tone one often did for small children.

"Aye. Sugar for... a cobbler. I wanted some cobbler." Who wouldn't want a slice of the tasty treat? He needed to think quickly if she asked him what kind. Not plum. Apples ripened in the fall. Cherries would do. The fighters picked some yesterday.

"You plan to bake... a cobbler?" She rested her hands on her hips and tilted her head to the side. "And need some sugar?"

"Aye," he said loudly since her tone suggested she didn't believe him.

"Do you also require flour? Or butter? Or fruit for this... cobbler?" She smirked.

He required a great many things. None of them ingredients to a dish he had no plan to make.

He wanted answers. She likely wasn't a threat to his family, but he must be certain. How did she end up in his territory? What was her history? How long did she plan to stay?

How would her lips taste?

He didn't need to know the last, so he crossed his arms over his chest and said, "No. Only sugar."

CHAPTER SEVEN

The kernels of good and evil grow inside all men. -Esabel

They couldn't leave well enough alone.

It was the morning of their weekly fights, and word reached Gavyn of a contingent of Red Guard hassling Madam MaLota, a kind soul to all who favored a spot of afternoon tea or a compassionate ear to spill their troubles.

Instead of spending time preparing for this evening, his worry dragged him to the village to check on the hardworking seamstress.

While Gavyn and Xavier trained an army from the ranks of the populace — a militia not called upon to defend the realm since before their fathers' time — the Lords kept an additional force for their safety. One who terrorized citizens with impunity and guarded the ruling class from threats both outside the fortress walls and inside their nest of subterfuge.

Like flies buzzing near open wounds on abused horse hide,

they circled the territories and reported the affairs of the peninsula back to their masters.

Uninterested in the politics of the Castle, he never understood if the Faeblood's fear for their well-being arose more from internal backstabbing or simple awareness of the suffering they spread over a working class whose numbers exceeded their society over fifty to one.

Either way, he never cared.

He was content with his station. Aware he led a charmed life compared to many in the territories. Duties filled his days with gratifying labor and left his mind free to succumb to a deep, untroubled slumber at night. There was no need to clutter his consciousness with matters outside his expertise.

The bell of the shop rang above his head.

Gavyn ducked under the low door frame with Rowan a step behind. He looped his hands in his belt. A long looking glass, framed from pine harvested in the forest they hunted, mocked his attempt to portray a relaxed posture.

Rowan bumped into Gavyn's side, pushed in front of him, and stepped into Madam MaLota's enveloping embrace.

With his effortless charm and amiable smiles, Rowan put everyone at ease.

Instead of training in the mornings, as Gavyn demanded of all the fighters, he spent the start of his day making rounds with the merchants and shopkeepers, gathering gossip and keeping a finger on the pulse of the marketplace.

Madam was two heads shorter than Rowan, requiring him to stoop for a proper hug. A smacking kiss on her cheek earned a swat to his chest and an appreciative smile.

"Always the dandy," she said. "Two visits in one day. What a surprise. By the looks of your frowns, though, you do not grace my shop for another pair of leathers."

She was a beautiful matriarch.

Her skin was a rich sepia color with warm red undertones

more pronounced in the scarce sun of shorter winter days. With a melodious voice and velvety umber eyes, it was easy to be lulled into her confidence.

The corners of her plump lips were free from wrinkles. Tight silver curls were the only sign of her advancing age.

She wore a pincushion on one wrist. Bangles on the other. The various bands knocked together and drew the eye away from the thick scarring underneath — strips of poorly healed wounds spiraling from the edge of both palms.

An abhorrent declaration of status.

Born in the Castle, a beloved daughter of two servants, they had etched Madam MaLota's place in society on her skin the summer of her eighth year.

Identical marks wrapped around Mikel's wrists, a heritage he never claimed despite the proof of his origins.

Gavyn learned to conceal his rage every time he set eyes on the angry, raised flesh, and if given the opportunity, he would snuff out the life of the person responsible for the barbaric practice.

If he ever found out who to hold accountable.

Neither Madam nor Mikel spoke of the events, and as much as he wanted to push — wanted to force them to reveal their torturer for both the sake of avenging their honor and alleviating his discomfort — he respected their silence.

"News reached Xavier of the Red Guard in your establishment." A statement, intended as a question, but Gavyn failed to temper his tone.

"I don't want any trouble," Madam MaLota said as she shrugged out of Rowan's embrace, wagging her finger in his direction. She folded and refolded the stack of linens on her front counter.

"Marissa," Rowan cooed. "We do not come to stir up tales. Xav wants you protected."

She scoffed.

"I don't require protection from that bit of riff raff. They barged in here this morning after you left. Tossing my creations to the side and throwing around their reputation."

"Did they declare their intentions?" Gavyn asked without the same finesse as his honey-tongued brother.

While he waited for her response, his thoughts strayed to Ember. Was she the cause of the patrol's appearance in the marketplace?

The Red Guard spent a fair amount of time at the compound — the excitement of the fights beckoning them like fleas feasting on the underbelly of a hound — but rarely patronized the shops.

Gavyn's gut twisted at the idea of her presence being the reason for their visit to the dressmaker.

He rubbed his breastbone.

Today, instead of regarding Ember as a threat to the village, considerations for her safety sprang to the forefront of his mind. An unwelcome admission he would ponder later.

"'Twas odd. They never put forth any inquiries." Madam MaLota pointed to the wooden box in the middle of her piles and pulled a measuring rope from her waist. "Bring your colossal body over here."

Gavyn climbed on top of the crate, knowing she would feel more comfortable disclosing information if she fussed over him.

"No questions?" he repeated, hoping to loosen her memory. "Did they mention whence they journeyed? What village they visited most recently?"

"No gossip. And no mention of where they stayed last," she said while wrapping the well-worn twine around the thickest part of his thigh. "Humph. You grew half an inch. I'll need to let out your winter leathers. The material is too stiff and won't yield to the change in size."

"Did they let anything slip?" Gavyn rested his palm on top of her shoulder. "Even the tiniest detail may be important."

"No. Nary a mention of the weather. Nor even their fare from breakfast." She patted his hand and stood. "They seemed content on wrecking havoc in my store, but there was no discernible purpose in their actions. 'Twas chaotic, and after a spell, they left as they came — without so much as a glance in my direction."

"If you venture a guess, how long did they stay?"

Madam MaLota tilted her head, and her eyes flicked to the rafters. "Maybe a third of an hour, at most. Took me three times as long to right my displays."

A disturbing puzzle.

Each territory had a unique style of dress, attire often suited to the work undertaken to pay the annual tithe.

The fighters in the village favored supple leathers, a material which lasted through the rigors of days spent grappling on the ground and sparring in the ring.

Artisans deep within the mountain's caves worked in long flowing gowns, linen stained bright colors, both as an expression of their passions and a vibrant contrast to the darkness of their home.

The woodcutters wore sturdy britches the color of their towering cedars and hardy walnut trees. Gavyn suspected they enjoyed the garments' ability to disguise a fine layer of bark and sawdust from the long days of harvesting as much as the camouflage it provided in their forests.

Within the Castle, pure borne Faeblood influenced the current fashion trends for the Lords and the ladies and their offspring. The styles rarely trickled down into the territories, either from lack of resources, an impracticality of the dress, or a disdain for anything they favored. Perhaps a combination of all three.

And while the patterns and cuts of the nobility changed with the seasons and the whims of a few, the dress of the human servants remained the same.

Another authoritarian declaration of status.

The servant's uniform comprised dark grays.

Monochromatic tops and bottoms meant to hide the grime they fought and allow them to blend into the stone surround of the mountain fortress.

Little more than slaves. Little more than ghosts. They appeared out of thin air when conjured and slunk back to haunt their stations at the flick of the wrist.

If the servants were invisible, then the Red Guard were prominent.

Long-sleeved tunics the color of fresh kill drew the observer away from the shine of their ostentatious armor. A layer of chain mail covered their torsos — a sign of prestige as opposed to a vital necessity, since the decree against blades of warfare unarmed potential enemies. They were loud. Overbearing. Sure of their lofty rank.

And with an issued uniform, they had no business at Madam's.

"—when Jade and Ember left," she said.

"What?" Gavyn asked, caught not following the trail of conversation. The tips of his ears burned with the mention of the latter.

"Our Jade and her new shadow paid me a visit earlier. I can see why you are so smitten." Madam MaLota bent at the waist and gathered a reel of fabric in her arms. In a voice muffled by the layers of cloth escaping the spool, she said, "No one wonders why you spent this past week in Jade's kitchens instead of taking your nooning meals at the compound."

Rowan coughed.

"I wanted to ensure no harm came to Jade." A lie he repeated throughout the week. Several times a day, more recently, as his focus wandered and his routine suffered.

During morning sparring, he made resolutions for midday — take his meals with the cubs, confer with Ada on the upcoming matchups, help supervise the fighters out on patrol — but after his late morning dip in the stream, his legs carried him along the narrow path from the compound to the village, and with little regard to his earlier intentions, dumped him in front of Jade's cottage.

To spy on a thief he no longer regarded as a threat.

His retort didn't deserve acknowledgement.

Unsurprisingly, Madam ignored it and shooed them out of her establishment. "Go on. And send the cubs 'round with your winter wardrobe."

"If you insist, but they will stay as guards."

Expecting her rejection, he was astonished when she beamed a knowing smirk and simply said, "As you wish."

Idiots.

Sycophantic, blundering fools.

Erik rubbed his back against the hard column of the black-smith's workshop, faking a calm he didn't possess.

Unlike the solid front walls of the other establishments, four stacked-stone pillars framed an open front room and supported the steep slope of a tin roof. The design allowed heat from forging horseshoes and homewares and the occasional sculpture to dissipate.

The blast from the active furnace curled over his shoulders, adding to the boiling rage stirred up by the antics of his father's goons.

Where was the bloody blade?

Erik had failed to set eyes to the dagger since the morning of Pigeon's interrogation, the night he'd sent back damning words coded in a mundane inquiry about his family's farm. Nor had he heard a whisper of its existence breathed between the leadership.

He had searched Gavyn's rooms, Xavier's chambers, and the loose board covering the middle tread of three steps leading to the ring in the training barn, the worn plank they used to conceal several bottles of Zoie's special brew.

It was as if the pressure to conjure proof of the fighters' crimes led to him fabricating the entire exchange.

He could admit to an overwhelming amount of fatigue the morning he followed Gavyn. Erik had suffered from an intense pad session with his sparring partners plus a cumulative loss of sleep, the combination causing his days to join in one achy blur.

But he knew what he witnessed.

Of late, his responsibilities at the compound had left little time to track Xavier and Gavyn. There were several occasions where they slipped his notice. Times when his obligations in the training barn pulled him in another direction.

If they were smart, and he held little doubt as to the level of intelligence of these men, cunning would lead them to dispose of the blade at the first opportunity.

His father was... displeased.

A letter arrived containing evidence of *her* suffering.

It presented as a dismembered pinky finger neatly rolled in the center of another scathing reply. A jagged edge below the second knuckle suggested a non-magical method of removal.

Erik had made it two strides beyond the back door of the mess hall before he lost his supper in the dense summer grasses sewn around the perimeter.

The cool breeze, ushered by a recent thunderstorm, had kept the string of tears at bay and stiffened his resolve.

He needed to search harder. Find friendship among the smaller fighter groups who gathered together any spare moment of relaxation. Question more of the men whose tongues loosened after a second cup of mead.

He expected his father to increase the pressure. Add more oversight.

What he hadn't predicted, however, was interference so soon after this latest sadistic power play. Certainly not in the form of an incompetent Red Guard patrol.

A piss poor distraction.

Their timing was off. He had sent home detailed notes on the minutiae of his schedule. Instead of causing a disturbance when he could capitalize on the chaos, they had chosen the busiest part of his day.

The dressmaker's shop was an ineffective target.

Constructed at the end of the marketplace, patrons thinned out near its entrance, leaving few with the opportunity to form a distracting crowd. With no plausible business bringing them to the proprietor, he could only imagine what sort of tales they spun while ransacking her rooms.

And now, the morons attracted the notice of both Rowan and Gavyn. Overprotective of those under their sphere of influence, they would react in a manner that would make his task even more treacherous — increased security around the compound and added guards in the village.

More eyes on his movements.

"'Lo, Erik," Gavyn said, as he waved from the small wooden walkway in front of the dressmaker's display window. "A moment?"

Erik uncrossed his ankles and met them in the middle of the cobblestone road.

A gaggle of women sauntered by, smiling and waving at Rowan.

He didn't return the flirtation, a testament to the seriousness of his mood, and peeled off toward the woods, a rare haste in his step. Over his shoulder, the Rowan said, "Meet you back in the mess hall for supper."

Gavyn rested a hand on Erik's upper arm.

"We've another squad of Red Guard passing through. You know the drill. Increase the patrols around the compound. This time, arrange for the cubs to take turns standing sentry at Madam MaLota's."

"Any message I should relay?"

"A handful of those thugs toured her shop this afternoon. Ransacked her front room." Gavyn hesitated, then added, "She insists all is well, but had trouble meeting my inquiries. Have them post up outside. Xavier will know the best way to address this. Expect further directions from him tonight."

He rattled off more instructions. Numbers for the patrols. Length of the watch shifts. More words than he'd ever strung together in Erik's presence.

The tightness in his chest returned, and the rest of Gavyn's direction blended into the noise of the marketplace.

As a teenager, Erik had escaped constant censure, nausea-inducing expectations, and cruel tasks given to him — all under the guise of grooming for succession — by training in the bowels of the Castle with the former head of the Red Guard.

A reasonable, albeit harsh mentor, the commander had recognized Erik's potential and understood his need for control, a necessity denied in the fortress's heart. He'd directed his education, sculpting Erik's mind and body into a warrior feared among all levels of rank in the elite Red Guard.

But it was an accomplishment unfitting a future High Lord.

And when his father found out that his only son and heir spent his days toiling next to filthy humans, his mentor paid for the transgression with his life.

It was a debt he couldn't bear again.

There was a special place in hell for what he must accomplish. Nothing would absolve him of these sins, but if he could prevent more suffering — and save *her*, as she saved him in his youth — Erik would pave the path to the underworld himself and march to its front gates with his arms wide open.

CHAPTER EIGHT

The best of intentions grind the shards of hurt into fresh wounds. -Esabel

JADE'S ONE-ROOM COTTAGE FELT DANGEROUSLY LIKE... *HOME.*

Early afternoon sun filtered through the two small windows facing the market. Coals glowed in the hearth, remnants from the pre-dawn cooking. A small mug of tea sat abandoned on the center trestle table, steam no longer evaporating from its surface.

A cozy illusion.

If she stared long enough, Ember could almost imagine this was her real life.

They had developed a routine over the last couple of weeks.

Jade preferred to sell fresh pies and breads, so instead of assembling everything the night before, they woke up before the rooster announced the day. After arranging the items for display, Ember retreated to the kitchens to start the washing.

A borrowed dress, once loose around her curves, now fit snugly across her chest and hips.

Jade favored cooler hues in her wardrobe. The pale aqua color of the gown popped against the fading tan from her weeks on the road. Embroidered swirls of navy thread accented the keyhole neckline and reminded Ember of the brief time she and her mother had stayed in the fishing village.

Water had always called to her — a soothing balm, washing over her spirit and reinvigorating her body. Any chance she stumbled upon, Ember had snuck off to the local swimming hole for a clandestine dip.

It had beckoned her that fateful day.

She took a deep, shuddering breath and glanced in the looking glass.

Faint purple circles fanned out underneath her eyes, but for the first time since fleeing her home, she recognized the person staring back. And if she didn't dwell too long on her circumstances — a Faeblood hiding in plain sight — she could almost believe the face in the glass belonged to a common villager, admiring a new gown or daydreaming about a handsome lover.

Ada visited most afternoons, filling the cottage with light-hearted banter and scintillating gossip. Easy camaraderie. But she was not their only guest.

The chances were high *he* would call again this afternoon.

Gavyn's daily visits started last week, after he helped her out of the plum tree. She was certain he would arrive at what Jade now referred to as his usual time.

She smiled to herself. He would soon run out of excuses to stop by.

First, he asked for a cup of sugar as if he baked in the mess hall kitchens. Then, it was under the pretense of checking a roof repair from the spring. Though, according to Ada, he inspected the wrong corner. Yesterday, he required a sachet of tea and left with an herb Jade confessed gave him hives.

Gavyn was many things — grumpy and suspicious. Overbearing. But above all else, he was predictable.

And captivating. The admission slipped out. By gods, he was mesmerizing.

No longer surprised by her reaction to him, Ember convinced herself, for the third time this morning, he was not for her. Not the sort of man with whom she could twist the sheets for a few nights, then part ways when she eventually left the village. No matter how much her body yearned for him.

Gavyn was not a lover she could easily leave.

He was a man who planted roots and thrived in one place, wrapping protective vines around all he cared for. If she lost herself in his tangles, Ember might not be strong enough to break free when the moment demanded she move on.

She massaged the scar on her palm.

Thick calluses remained from tending the gardens in the back, but her hands no longer cracked from constant exposure to the outdoors. The soil under her nails cleaned out with ease every night. But a hum of pressure gathered in her fingertips, growing stronger each day.

She must take care.

Ember chose small moments to unleash her powers, times when she was alone in the cottage. Repetitive kitchen tasks and other household chores did nothing to blunt its rumblings. The few snippets of casting, instead of dulling the edge, had left her unsettled.

"Here, take this," Jade said as she thrust a small tin container at her. "The smell would put off the dogs, but it does the trick."

The pungent aroma — a mixture of boiled eggs and onion and sharp notes of garlic — wafted her way even with the lid closed.

"What is it?" She wrinkled her nose.

"A special salve for bone sickness. Take care. It will stain your gown and taint the food you touch," Jade said as she sliced the tops off of the next batch of carrots.

"I'm well," Ember protested and held the ointment away

from her body. The last thing she wanted to do was slather herself in the gunk, especially moments before Gavyn was due to stop by.

"Your hand bothers you. I can always tell when you rub your palm. Don't be stubborn—"

A strangled yelp cut off the rest of the admonishment.

Jade's lips twisted into a grimace. Blood welled up from a cut on her thumb. She snatched the nearest linen from the sideboard and wrapped it around the wound.

"Ow. Ow, ow."

Ember's powers crawled beneath her skin, and a steady ringing filled her ears. *No. No, no.* Her heart thudded against her chest. She couldn't prevent the small trickle of sweat from rolling down her back.

Jade glanced up. "Are you all right?"

Ember bit her lip and shook her head.

She had to get out. Get away from the coppery tang coating the back of her tongue.

The scent filled her nostrils and sang to her — a thundering chant, echoing above the now deafening ringing in her ears.

"You're white as a ghost. Is it the blood?" Jade took a step closer and extended her arm. "Hey, 'tis a paltry wound. Doesn't happen too often, but I've a cream for cuts, too." She nodded to the lower shelf of herbs and asked, "Would you grab the jar? It's the closest to the door."

Ember found the small bottle and uncorked the top. She focused on the spongy texture of the pliable stopper and the coolness of the hard glass in her hand. Small fringes of vapor formed around the tips of each finger and, to her horror, spread rapidly over the clear surface.

"Place it on the counter, and I'll bandage the wound. Go on, take a minute outside." Jade nodded toward the back door. "The cut is not too deep, but it's a bleeder."

The bottle clattered on the wooden surface.

It wobbled to the side but remained upright.

The tip of her foot caught on her ankle, and she stumbled forward. Ember caught her momentum and clutched the edge of the sideboard to steady herself.

She swallowed her words and scrambled through the back door.

Chickens scattered out of her way, squawking their displeasure at her less than graceful entrance into the garden. All but one left, an undersized hen Jade had named Lady Marmalade for her orange-gold plumage and sweet personality.

She often wished her powers included the ability to communicate with animals. Growing up without playmates her age, woodland creatures had filled the role of childhood friends. Today, as every day before, she settled for a one-sided conversation.

"Hey there, little lady. How's the wing?"

The hen pecked at the dirt, fluttering her tail feathers in response and ignoring Ember's attempt at distracting her racing heart. The chicken's wing hung loosely at her side, its tip dragging on the packed earth.

She inspected the shoulder wound.

Thick yellow pus coated its edges, and the center was a shiny red, as if recently reopened.

"Where's your bandage?" she asked, searching for the makeshift sling Jade fashioned yesterday.

Ember stole a peek at the kitchen window and turned back to her non-verbal patient. She closed her eyes and severed the last tether of control, unleashing her powers.

Warmth gathered in her palms and radiated throughout her limbs.

Too quickly, the sides of the injury knitted together The relief she enjoyed moments before vanished, leaving an increasingly familiar ache in the pit of her stomach.

"How's my favorite girl?" Jade asked as she crossed the path to where Ember crouched with the bird. She reached into her pocket and tossed a handful of crumbs on the ground. "She never keeps her sling long. The injury healed faster than I expected."

Ember wiped her clean palms on her skirts and stood, forcing a serene smile.

A thin strip of cloth wrapped around Jade's thumb.

She ignored the faint pink stain blooming in the middle and disregarded the nagging urge to grab her friend's hand and ease both their discomforts.

Instead, she muttered, "I believe it's time I moved on. You've been—"

"Poppycock. Don't finish the thought." Jade dismissed her declaration with a wave of her hand. "Come. Let's sit in the shade. We're both a bit peaked."

She led them to the old oak anchoring the far corner of her garden.

"Growing up surrounded by males — with Ada as my closest companion, her head filled with numbers and who knows what — I learned quickly how to bandage most bumps and scrapes."

Jade gathered her skirts in her good hand and lowered herself to the soft patch of grass.

"I don't know—"

"But what the men won't admit, even now they have grown into their egos, is that most wounds don't require bandaging. It's the spirit that needs a bit of tending; the body heals faster than the heart." She patted the ground next to her, waiting for Ember to accept her invitation, and asked, "What troubles you so?"

A sincere question, one for which she couldn't answer truthfully, despite Jade's openness.

She rubbed her palm and searched for a believable excuse. Ember studied the wrinkles in her gown and said, "All is well.

Merely time to move on. I don't want to trespass on your hospitality for longer than you intended."

Jade's drawn out sigh filled the entirety of the garden.

"I respect your need for privacy and — as much as I want to pry your secrets from your lips — I won't push."

"That's not—"

"Don't fabricate platitudes for my sensibilities," Jade said in a sterner voice. "It's clear you run from some kind of trouble. I wish you would share your burdens, not to appease my curiosity, but voicing them may provide the clarity you seek, and," she emphasized, "we could prepare for whatever causes your worry."

Jade held up a hand to ward off another round of feeble protests.

"Don't deny it. My offer still stands — stay in the cottage as long as it takes for you to figure out what path you must follow. But I will tell you one thing, after watching you this past fortnight, you are not ready to move on."

"Just the one thing, huh?" Ember choked out an incredulous laugh.

How would she ever repay Jade's kindness?

She wanted to bottle her time in the cottage and keep it for the dark journey ahead. Her first genuine friend. It was difficult to trust the bond. Difficult to ignore a lifetime of being told not to trust.

It was hard to see herself worthy of such a generous offer, so she hesitated, then whispered, "Why me?"

Jade knocked her leg against Ember's, the corners of her lips hinting in a smile.

"'Tis not for your skills in the kitchen." Jade chuckled at her own jest. "You show little more proficiency than Ada. But… you remind me a little of myself those first few years we struck out on our own. Oh, if you ask Xav or Gavyn, they will tell you fanciful tales of a grand journey. An enterprising endeavor."

Jade tipped her head back and shuttered her lids. When they opened, she confessed, "But we were terrified. We fled our home, running from the promise of being dragged back to the mines to work off a balance accrued during our grandparents' lifetimes. Despite the threats. Despite sleeping with one eye open and wondering about when our next meal would appear. We all held hope. A thirst for the unspoken potential of something *more* — opportunities for a better life — earned from grueling work and stubborn wills and naïve dreams."

Jade placed two fingers under her chin and tilted it to meet her next words.

"I see all of that in you. But you are all alone. Even with a ready-made family, our path was fraught with peril. I cannot fathom undertaking the journey on my own."

Jade released her hold and let the words fester.

It was easy to visualize a young Jade smiling at Ada's antics. Fussing over Xavier and Gavyn. Easy to romanticize all of them huddled together in make-shift shelters, wondering about the next obstacle in their path but secure in the knowledge they would face whatever fate threw at them. Together.

What would it feel like to stand beside someone as their equal? Not in front nor behind. Nor alone.

"—And selfishly, I adore your friendship. You are kind. And funny. It's invigorating to view our world through the filter of your interactions. Plus, you rattle our stoic Gavyn. I've never seen him so off balance. 'Tis a delight."

A rusty creak split the air, followed by a thud as the back gate banged closed against the fence post.

Gavyn rounded the corner of the small garden shed and stopped on the path in front. His eyes widened when they settled on Lady Marmalade.

"Heya, pretty girl. I see you are feeling better." He picked up the plump bird and buried his nose in her side.

The hen chirped in reply and held still as he nuzzled her soft feathers. He placed the chicken back on the ground, patted her head, and shooed her into the tall rows of cornstalks.

"Oy, Gavyn, over here," Jade called out.

Gavyn had always appeared out of place in Jade's feminine home, sitting down for tea on too-small stools and grunting out one-word answers to Ada's relentless probing. And longer responses to Jade's more practical inquisitions.

His presence had overwhelmed Ember's sensibility, and she'd stayed on guard the hours he spent in the cottage.

Gavyn's sheer size, for one, swallowed up the surrounding air, forcing shallow breaths. He refused to sit and tuck into the table. Instead, his legs sprawled out in front and his wide shoulders eclipsed the sides of the stools, engulfing more than his length of seating.

His surly demeanor, for another, bristled Ember's poise. He sent indulging smiles and ready praise over to Jade and Ada, but lobbed glowers in Ember's direction when she'd attempted to join in the conversation.

In the garden, 'twas the same.

He stalked toward them with intent more suited to battle than joining in a bit of afternoon relaxation.

A head taller than the mature sunflower blooms, he towered over the dense canopy of the tiny summer garden. Leggy herbs and fluffy pink peonies and sunset orange nasturtium vines jumbled together in a chaotic display of color.

The whimsical growth mocked his neatly tucked shirt, his razor-straight side part in ruthlessly combed hair, and his consummate frown.

Jade coughed.

"What brings you to the cottage?" *Now* was left unsaid.

Gavyn knelt down beside Jade, bracing himself with a fist on the grass.

"I wanted to check on Lady Marmalade." His gaze raked over Ember. The corner of his lips tugged down. "Her wing appears... better."

She'd had enough.

"To what do I owe your displeasure?" Ember leaned forward, resting her hands on her thighs. "Why do you frown at me?"

"You're mistaken. You see things that are not present."

She blinked and kept silent, but he failed to elaborate. The chords of his neck rose, rippling the intricate black marking on the side. Her eyes flicked to the design, and her lips parted.

Gavyn shifted his weight to his heels and cocked his head to the side. A challenge. One she was now bold enough to accept.

"A fortnight has passed. As you can see, Jade's forgiveness extended beyond our initial introductions. I've no plans to repay her kindness with sticky fingers."

"So you say..."

"If I may," Jade interrupted, cutting off the caustic retort on the tip of Ember's tongue. "She remains a guest in my home. At my insistence. While I appreciate your concern, it has no place here."

Gavyn grunted.

He grunted. Oh, the nerve of this man.

Had she not seen his softer side, how he cooed over Ada and Lady Marmalade, Ember could have reasoned his serious disposition was a consequence of his occupation. Nope. He was plain grumpy. Irritable, prickly, and cross.

She searched for a couple more disparaging descriptors but stopped at Jade's knowing smirk.

"We shall stay alert," Jade said as she tousled his hair. "Tell me about the card tonight. Who's on it? Anyone I can wager against?"

The fights. With Gavyn's arrival, Ember had forgotten their plans for the eve.

As they strolled to the back gate, she vaguely registered their chatter about the matchups. So, she would see him twice in one day. Ember tracked his retreating form and couldn't decide if the butterflies in her gut were from irritation or something worse.

Something akin to… longing.

CHAPTER NINE

Beware of wrapping yourself in a world full of deeds cloaked in bravery. –Esabel

GAVYN GRIPPED EIGEN'S SHOULDER. THE TRAINEE'S MATCH WAS next on the card.

"Watch his left. It's loose. He'll throw it out to test his range. He likes to change the timing later in the round to see if he can get in a quick jab or two. My guess, he won't want to stand and trade blows with you and will shoot for a takedown at the earliest opportunity."

"Yes, coach."

"Don't leave any sloppy kicks in the air. He'll step in and use them for a single-leg." Satisfied with the last-minute instructions, he patted Eigen's shoulder and observed the conclusion of the fight in the ring.

A mixture of chants and insults filled the barn.

Gavyn sighed.

Mikel danced in the center of the ropes, taunting his opponent.

The fighter pivoted to keep Mikel in his line of sight, but the sudden movement on a damaged leg put a grimace on his face. He dodged Mikel's next two lazy jabs but missed the last punch of the series — a powerful cross.

Mikel either grew bored with the match or found mercy. He put the fighter out of his misery with one last uppercut to the underside of the man's jaw.

The crowd exploded in cheers. A few shouts of anger carried over the rest, no doubt from the other village.

Xavier climbed down from the corner, smirking.

"That man will get us all killed one day," Xavier said and bumped Gavyn's fist. "He can single-handedly incite a mob with his theatrics."

"Quit putting him on the card then if you're so worried."

"No. He's too much fun to watch." Xavier's feral grin broadened across his entire face. "Plus, he brings me gold every time he fights."

At the mention of betting, both men turned their attention to the back wall of the training barn.

A narrow platform rose out of the space directly across from the entrance doors. Four of the younger fighters perched at the structure's corners. Mirror images of one another, they positioned themselves with feet apart and arms across their chests.

The message was clear — spectators were unwelcome.

Ada stood in the center of the platform. She held a leather-bound book in one hand, and a quill in the other. Next to her towering guards, she jotted notes when someone shouted their bet and then pointed to the next patron to record his.

Off to the side, Erik collected coin at the conclusion of Mikel's match. Or when one of the nearby villagers approached, he handed it out.

Gavyn grunted.

The locals knew not to bet against Mikel.

A flash of deep purple and forest green wove through the

crowd. Ember and Jade pushed their way to the edge of the betting floor. They put their heads together in conference, and Jade cupped her hand to Ember's ear. The little thief tilted her head back, and her shoulders shook with laughter.

Gavyn's breath caught in his chest.

"Your thief cleans up nice." Xavier nudged him with an elbow to his side.

Gavyn scowled, and his gaze fell to the creamy expanse of her neck. She had let her hair loose tonight. It looked… *nice*. He wasn't the only one who noticed.

"We still need to watch her. Never known a pretty face to fool you."

"Is that what you've been doing all night? Keeping an eye out?"

"Yes." Gavyn clenched his jaw. "Jade's heart is too big. Ada just wants a new friend, and Rowan is already trying to charm her."

He should warn Rowan to stay away.

"Uh, huh?" Xavier shot him another knowing look. "Well, you won't need to keep an eye out much longer. Your waif has turned the men's heads tonight. She might find herself under someone else's protection soon enough."

At Xavier's prediction, the four men closest to Ember turned their backs to the betting and started crowding her space. One stroked a hand along her arm.

She took a step to the side, bumping into Jade.

Gavyn's ears rang.

He inserted two fingers into the front of his lips and let out a piercing whistle.

Erik's head snapped up. Despite his short time in the compound, the fighter had excellent instincts. Gavyn gave a thrust of his chin toward the crowd, and Erik hopped down off the betting platform, gathering the ladies under his arms.

He escorted them to two open spaces at the bar, away from the rowdy admirers.

Gavyn could breathe again.

Xavier's booming laugh blasted his ears, the rare sound drawing looks from the fighters warming up ringside.

"I have no desire for skittish waifs," he muttered under his breath.

~

EMBER TOOK HER CUE FROM JADE'S RELAXED POSTURE AND allowed the hulking man to steer her to a new vantage.

Zoie sent a small wave in their direction before she shuffled toward the other end of her bar.

"Stay." Their escort gestured to the open stools.

"Thank you for the help, Erik." Jade reached up and patted the man's cheek.

"Stay." He backed into the crowd, raised his voice, and said, "I must return to my post, but Gavyn doesn't want you two ringside. He needs to concentrate."

"That's one cub I can't control."

"He's a cub?"

"Yes. He joined later than normal." Jade's brow furrowed. "The villages send most fighters in their eighteenth year. I'm uncertain about his age, but his maturity makes it harder to earn a rise."

"My mulled wine. I added the spices you lent," Zoie said as she slid a mug on the counter.

Jade swirled the contents and took a small sip.

"Delicious. It needs to be warmed, but the flavor is rich." Hints of sweet citrus and spicy cloves wafted from the vessel. "Gavyn needs to try this."

At the mention of his name, Ember looked back toward the ring.

Gavyn stood off to the side and rested his arm on the shoulder of a shirtless man. The fairness of his coloring stood out against the fighter's dark skin. He tilted his head and spoke into the younger man's ear. Both wore serious expressions as their discussion continued.

"Oh, I didn't know Eigen was fighting tonight." Jade wrapped one arm around Ember's shoulders and pointed to the fighter. "Eigen always puts on a show. Next to Gavyn, he's the only sure bet. Never lay odds against either of those two or your purse will be lighter in the morning."

The starting bell rang.

Eigen's opponent reached out to tap his fist. The same gesture, she noted, from all the matches of the evening. But instead of taking a small step back to set up for the round, the other fighter hinged at the waist and lunged forward.

His outstretched arms never made their way around Eigen's middle.

One minute he was in the air, the next he was out cold on the ground.

"What was *that?*" Ember hopped off her stool and went up on her tippy toes.

"Knee to the head." Zoie shrugged and started wiping the bar down. "That's what happens when you shoot on an experienced opponent."

"A fitting end for someone who is unsportsmanlike." Jade hopped off her stool and rubbed her palms together. "I'm going to collect my purse."

"It can't be that large." Zoie pulled a tap and filled another cup. "Who is foolish enough to bet against Eigen?"

"I didn't place on the win. Ada set up a side wager for me." Jade started walking away but over her shoulder she said, "I bet he would finish under a minute in the first round."

"Jade's a smart one. I guess she got the scoop on the other guy." Zoie chuckled. "Your Gavyn is up next."

"Mine?" Ember went completely still.

"Yes, yours. The one that's been watching you all night. Don't think I didn't notice."

She tapped her temple and refilled Ember's water.

"I'm knee-deep in brew, but I have eyes. Gavyn is fighting the leader of the village to the east. I've been waiting for this rematch since the spring. He always puts on a show. It's your lucky night."

Gavyn slipped in the ring.

Bare feet matched his bare chest, and a lock of his hair grazed his forehead as he bounced side-to-side in the corner.

She let herself *look*.

Ember indulged in a prolonged study of his broad chest and strong shoulders, the muscles rippling with the steady movement.

A large scar spanned the width of his upper back. It traveled from the top of one shoulder blade and stopped underneath the other, the coloring a shade lighter than the surrounding skin.

Ember rubbed the one on her palm, and her fingers itched to run them along his old injury.

Jade reappeared, jingling a small leather bag in front of her face. Ember fought to tear her gaze away from his rugged profile.

"Tomorrow, we shall visit the seamstress. The new fabric in her window display caught my eye the other day," Jade said. "She has a few pre-made dresses that should work well for you. It would be nice to have some choices."

"This one is plenty, Jade." Ember bit the inside of her cheek.

"Nonsense. A girl needs more than one dress." Jade snagged the stool next to her. "Besides, your help in my kitchen is worth two dresses. There is a particular garment I have in mind for you. The cut is like the one you are wearing, and the color is lovely."

"Thank you, but there is no—"

"I tried it on, but it made my skin look like the color of seasickness." Jade scrunched her nose.

"Don't try to talk her out of it." Zoie came around the other side of the bar and stood next to them. "It's no use when she's like this."

A ruckus at the front drew every head in the barn.

"There," Jade said, pointing to the entrance doors.

A small group of men moved in unison toward the ring.

In the middle of their circle, a fighter alternated between throwing punches in the air and shaking out his arms. Ladies fanned out around the edges of the posse. Some stopped and went up on their tiptoes to get a better look at the man in the center.

Others waved and shouted his way.

"Harin likes to make an entrance." Jade didn't hide the scowl on her face. "He's new in his role as the leader of the mining village and fancies himself as a trainer. He's delusional for thinking he's Gavyn's equal."

Ember slowly lowered herself to the stool. She closed her eyes and willed her hands to stop shaking. The scent of pond trout assaulted her memories, and a shiver ran down her spine.

What were the chances anyone from the mining village would track her here?

Harin vaulted into the ring and smacked the ground with both hands. He jogged a lap around the perimeter. The crowd went crazy, but the boos and hisses were louder than cheering.

"They fought for the first time a few months ago. It was a bloody mess. Gavyn had the upper hand the first two rounds," Zoie said. "At the end of the second, Harin struck Gavyn after the sound of the bell."

"What happened?" Ember asked.

"Gavyn finished him. Xavier banned fighters from their village for three months. It stirred up a lot of tension between the two territories." Zoie leaned against the bar. "Xavier took a lot of heat, but things cooled down after he promised the rematch."

The bell sounded, cutting off the rest of her story.

Gavyn commanded the center of the ring, both fighters forgoing the customary tap at the beginning. The men were equal in height, but Harin appeared to have more than a stone of pure muscle on him. Even to her inexperienced eyes, the added weight lent a sort of choppiness to his movements. Instead of matching Gavyn's nimble strides, the other man covered the ground in lumbering steps.

Harin made the first move.

Ember gripped the edge of her stool with both hands. The sight of Gavyn trading blows soured her stomach, but she couldn't bring herself to look away.

For the next series of exchanges, Gavyn turned the aggressor.

He threw two quick punches.

The first one grazed Harin's cheek, while the other one found its mark. He followed them with a low kick to the thigh.

Harin shuffled his feet and switched stances.

"Ah, low kicks don't look like much, but they can make the leg feel heavy." Zoie pointed to Harin's left side. "Do you see how he is favoring it a little?"

Painful or not, the blow acted as a trigger for the fighter. He exploded into the middle of the ring, and both men battled until the sound of the bell.

Harin shouted and spat in Gavyn's direction as his cornerman wrapped an arm around his waist, ushering him to the side.

"Mikel likes to mess around for entertainment. Eigen doesn't waste time or energy." Zoie hopped back behind the bar to serve her new customers. "And Gavyn is always calm. Precise. Fierce."

Ember rubbed her palm again and shifted on the stool.

"Are you okay with all this?" Jade gestured to the ring and spectators.

"It's all so... intense. I can't say that I'm enjoying it, at least not like you and Zoie, but it's getting easier as the night wears on."

Jade wrapped a hand around her forearm. "Gavyn's—"

A man crashed into Jade's stool. She toppled over backwards, landing hard on the ground.

Ember rushed to her side and cradled her head.

"Are you—"

Crash!

More stools flipped over and bounced around them.

Ember clasped Jade's hand and yanked her upright. She wrapped an arm around her waist, steering them to the opening at the end of the bar.

Both girls ducked down below the counter, crouching level with Zoie's supply of hard spirits and extra glasses.

Unable to resist curiosity, Ember's head popped up to survey the action.

Two men locked arms and slammed into the bar top, hurling insults.

The thicker man changed his grip and grabbed the other patron by his shirt. He seized on the newfound leverage — lifting his smaller opponent off his feet and onto the bar — and wiped the surface with him.

Curses and grunts filled the air.

Bottles and drinks flew in every direction.

Ember gasped.

The man on top pulled his elbow back, ready to deliver a blow, but a hand gripped his fist and halted the forward progress.

"Rowan," Ember exhaled.

He hefted the attacker and hauled him to the entrance doors.

Rowan flung the man down the path, sending him on his way with an angry gesture.

"Jade," Zoie said, with more than a hint of panic in her voice.

Ember's head whipped around.

Jade sunk down the side of the bar and held one hand over her arm.

Blood oozed between her fingers, dripping on the glass shards strewn across the floor.

Zoie grabbed a linen cloth from the countertop and rushed to her side. She wrapped the bandage around Jade's wound, squeezing out a small whimper.

"Here. Hold this." Zoie took Jade's other hand and placed it on the cloth. "Erik, give me your shirt."

Erik? Where did he — ? When did he — ?

The edges of her vision narrowed. Ember placed a palm on her stomach.

Someone thrust a bunched up piece of fabric into Zoie's hands, but all she could focus on was the steady pulse in Jade's neck. And the dark red bloom on the cloth wrapped around her arm. Too dark. Too red.

And spreading too fast.

"Jade," Zoie said. "I'm going to wrap this around the towel. We need to apply pressure and stop the bleeding."

Right. Jade is bleeding.

The familiar coppery tang coated her nostrils.

The color drained out of Jade's face. Small beads of sweat pooled at her hairline.

Zoie wrapped the shirt around her arm a few times, tying the ends in a knot, but the blood continued to flow down the inside of her wrist.

Ember searched Jade's face and gritted her teeth.

Finished with her task, Zoie dragged Jade into her lap and cradled her head against her shoulder.

"Please," Ember said, her own words sounding foreign to her

ears. There was no time to think. No time to questions her actions. No time to weigh the consequence of her choice. "Allow me."

She grabbed Jade's hand and placed her other palm on the dressing. Her power hummed beneath her touch, and the gash began to close. 'Twas deep, deeper than she'd realized.

Her chest heaved, and her breath came in short, choppy spurts.

She concentrated until the last edge of skin knitted together.

The tips of her fingers tingled, as if a seamstress poked the individual pads with dozens of tiny needles. A common sensation after a hard cast.

She welcomed the discomfort, leaning into its warmth.

This was different, though. More intense.

The sharp pricks lasted longer than she expected, and a bitter taste coated her throat, a sure sign of dampening her magic for too long. One she hadn't experienced since she'd learned of her gift as a child.

A chill ran through her body.

Half a dozen deep breaths transpired before she realized where she was. Large rafters suspended a vaulted, two-story ceiling. The scent of pine mixed with the metallic aroma of blood.

Training barn.

Despite the cavernous size of the building, the walls closed in.

I'm in Jade's village.

She leaned against the wooden counter.

I'm not at home.

The shouts and noise of the patrons ceased. A loud ringing filled her ears.

An unnatural stillness stole over the bar.

Gone was the smack of fist on flesh she associated with fight night. The thud of knuckles connecting with their target faded into the background.

In its place, she experienced something worse — the roar of dread as it filled her veins.

What have I done?

CHAPTER TEN

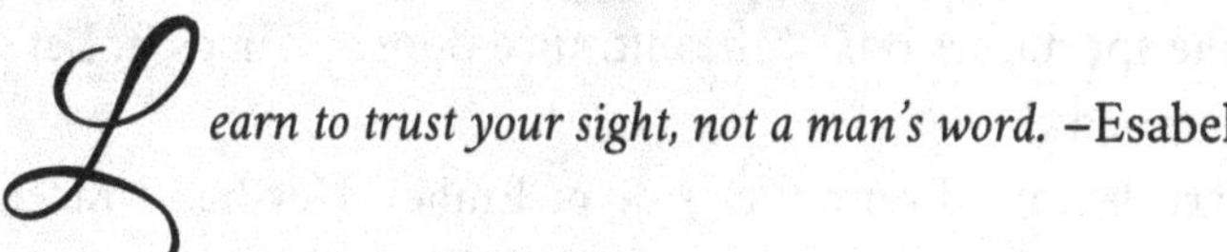

earn to trust your sight, not a man's word. –Esabel

THE TRAINING BARN BECAME A CAGE OF FEAR AND ALARM.

Heat from the press of bodies locked her in place, obscuring her vision beyond the walls of her captors.

Ember had worried about an uncontrolled release of her magic since she'd fled her home, and her premonition had dawned in the most unimaginable manner.

"Up." Erik spun behind Jade and hooked his arms around her middle. "We must move."

"What happened?" Rowan asked, his body still vibrating from the sprint back to the bar.

"Grab her," Erik snarled out of the side of his mouth.

The Faeblood was silent, but she heard the slur as if he shouted it from the treetops.

He kept his arm around Jade, whispering in her ear, and cut a path through the crowd. Where was Erik taking them?

Ember dimly registered a cheer from the mob.

"Just keep walking. That's it. One foot in front of the other." Rowan gently squeezed her waist. "Keep your eyes straight ahead. Go on now. Follow behind Jade."

"Xavier. Gavyn," Rowan bellowed as he jerked his head to the side. He grabbed the arm of a passing fighter. "Fight's over. Clear everyone out. Do it. *Quickly.*"

"Yes. Yes, of course." The young man stumbled, then turned sideways, and dove into the crowd. He flung his arms around a circle of fighters congregating along the back wall. Moments later, the group dispersed, and their collective voices rose over the din of the barn.

"Wrap it up, everyone. Tomorrow starts too early for most of us. Move along." The fighters held their arms wide and herded the spectators out of the entrance doors. "That's it. Let's all find our beds."

The crush flowed on either side of Ember. Her heart raced so fast it ached. It was as if the cavity of her chest shrank in proportion to the speed of the beats. She had risked too much lingering in the village this long.

But regret never came.

Had she judged wrongly? Maybe it no longer mattered. With her mother gone to the afterlife and no family left to miss Ember if she departed these lands, who would mourn her passing?

She struggled to level her breathing.

Jade would care.

Ember caught the side of her profile. A rosy flush returned to her friend's cheeks, and Jade's eyes were alert once again. Ember rested a hand on her stomach and thought more firmly, *Jade would care.*

Erik led them down a narrow hallway hidden from the main room behind a stack of hay bales. Torches illuminated the otherwise dark passage. Ember counted the warm flickers bathing the stone wall in alternating spheres of light and shadows.

Three, four, five…

Erik kept an arm around Jade and glanced over his shoulder, his expression unreadable. Rowan's faint touch rested at the small of Ember's back. An anchor, despite its near weightlessness.

She wouldn't mistake it for a lifeline, but 'twas more than a guide.

Six, Seven…

Ember shuffled her feet to keep up with their longer strides. Xavier and Gavyn, still shirtless, rounded the corner at a jog.

Eight, nine, ten…

Near the end of the passage, Xavier jostled Ember as he pushed forward and opened a door on the right. Shadows from the flames exaggerated his scowl. He ushered everyone inside.

Their group fanned out in a small study.

The room had a decidedly masculine feel with utilitarian furniture, sharp lines, and a musky scent — an appealing blend of pine and tobacco and leather that did little to calm her racing heart. The noise of the training barn didn't reach these walls, but as the number of bodies accumulated inside, her breathing failed to improve.

She traded one cage for another.

Gavyn cupped her elbow, angling his body between her and the rest of the group.

"Are you hurt? He ran his hands down her arms as if searching for a wound.

"Not me." She rubbed her palm and took a half step closer. For a moment, she said nothing. Are *you* hurt? she wanted to ask, not knowing the conclusion of his fight. So consumed with her own fears she was uncertain of his victory. Instead she whispered, "Jade suffered an injury. She—"

"What happened?" Xavier asked.

She blinked and shifted another half step closer to Gavyn.

Xavier stood behind a large wooden desk, its surface covered with stacks of parchment, and lit the oil lamp occupying the corner. He tossed the flintstone behind him.

Acrid smoke wafted her way.

"What happened?" Xavier repeated. He braced himself on the wooden top and leaned forward.

She flinched at the softness in his voice.

"There was a skirmish," Erik said, his voice cutting through the thick silence. He ran a hand through his spiked hair. His fingertips traced the tip of his ear.

"And…" Xavier pushed up the sleeves of his shirt. The muscles in his arms bulged, and his leather cuffs strained as he pressed harder on the desk.

"It got out of hand," Erik hedged.

"Go on." Xavier raised an eyebrow and cocked his head.

"Two idiots fought in front of the bar," Jade said, her voice steady. "I had my back to them. One minute I'm watching the fights, and the next I'm knocked off my stool."

Xavier's head snapped to the side, and he raked his eyes over Jade. He opened his mouth, but she stepped forward and cut off his retort.

"I'm fine, Xav." Jade's delicate fingers encircled the red bandage, and she tilted her chin higher. "I'll be a little sore tomorrow. That's all."

"And where were you this entire time?" Xavier asked Rowan without his focus ever leaving Jade.

"I was near the main doors when I saw…" Rowan ran a hand over his mouth and down the column of his neck.

"How did Jade end up covered in blood?" Gavyn gestured to the stained cloth.

"I slipped and fell." Jade forced a laugh, but it bubbled up as a partial sob. "When the morons cleaned the counter, they didn't put things back where Zoie likes them. I landed on a broken shard and lanced my arm."

"Come here," Xavier said.

Jade skirted the side of his desk.

Xavier gently untied the outer dressing and tossed the garment in the corner, a fine tremor prolonging the task. The smaller towel followed, and he caressed the length of her arm.

The rest of the room held their breath, but Ember knew what he would find. Smooth skin — a flat pink mark and thick trails of dried blood, leading to a wound which no longer existed.

After two complete passes, his eyes snapped to Ember. "Explain."

A chance. It was more than she expected. Perhaps more than she deserved.

"I didn't think," she said, her voice wavering. "There was so much blood, and I just didn't—"

Gavyn placed a hand under her chin.

"Relax. Just tell us what happened."

"I saw the bandage and knew it wasn't enough to stop the wound from bleeding." She preferred Gavyn's frown to Xavier's scowl, so she concentrated on his lips. "Her face... her face turned white."

"Go on," Gavyn coaxed.

"I grabbed Jade's hand, wishing to lend her strength. To convey everything would be alright," she said to the room, but silently she begged, *please let them understand.* "I... I didn't want to frighten her." She met Erik's stare and Jade's bewildered eyes. *Please, please, please....* "It's an old spell. A simple one my mother handed down. The wound was clean but deep. I... I mean no harm."

"You're *Faeblood.*"

A question? Or condemnation? Maybe it was a statement —

someone giving life to an unexpected truth. She wasn't sure who said it. Didn't matter, really, who voiced it aloud.

She took a step back. Gavyn's hand fell to his side.

"How long have you cast? Magic is foreign outside the Castle." Jade hugged herself with the uninjured arm."Your gift only exists among the nobility."

"I carry the line. Casting favors our family." She crossed her arms over the thumping of her heart against her ribs. To Jade she said, "Healing calls to me. It's under my command, but distressing circumstances… situations such as these, make it harder to control."

Wetness tracked down her cheek, and she resisted the urge to rock back and forth. Countless warnings. Endless tales of caution. Childhood lectures on the perils of summoning magic outside the privacy of home.

All for naught.

Fear tugged at the border of her mind, and thoughts of her mother's demise pulled to the surface. Did a similar fate await her? She clenched her fists as if to hold onto her powers despite their responsibility for her current predicament. If only… if only she left the first night. Still, she was glad, relieved even, she was nearby to heal Jade.

"You're the first of your kind here in the village." Xavier hesitated and said, "At least in this generation. There is no line. No one shares your gift. Barring the Faeblood in the Castle, magic doesn't exist outside of legends and lore."

A flicker of sadness lit inside her darkest fears.

She didn't expect the contrary. The chances of encountering her kinsmen beyond the fortress walls were always remote. But hearing the words… it was impossible to stop the familiar gut-wrenching disappointment from her childhood.

"Erik? Rowan? How many witnesses?" Xavier barked.

"Five. Ten at most." Rowan braced his legs and crossed his

arms over his chest. "I can't be certain. The bar shielded most of it."

"She stays with you." Xavier pointed to Gavyn. "Erik. Rowan. With me."

Ember closed her eyes and bit the inside of her cheek. Xavier's command looped in her mind. *She stays with you.*

Surely, he didn't mean…

She stopped trembling and searched their faces. Most wore varying degrees of shock, but Erik schooled his emotions, either he was better at controlling them or had more time to accept the truth of her powers since he witnessed the cast.

Relief — it came in waves. She was safe. They wouldn't kill her nor imprison her nor banish her from the territory.

Ember closed her eyes and for a moment the room vanished into nothing. The images of their faces burned behind her lids.

They won't kill me.

She took a deep breath and repeated, *They won't kill me.*

She must set off soon. When Xavier deemed it safe, she would continue her travels to the Northern Isles. In the mean time, she could gather provisions. Form a plan. Perhaps someone here knew the best route through the mountain.

"She's better served with another." Gavyn announced, an edge of panic in his tone.

Her eyes shot open.

"She can't bunk with the fighters." Xavier started toward the door. "And I won't risk her safety in the village."

"What? No." Jade grabbed Xavier's arm. The momentum of his stride carried her a few paces before he halted. "Xav, she can stay with me. You heard Rowan. Hardly anybody saw, and the men will make sure the villagers keep it quiet."

"Thank you for the offer, but I'm happy to stay at—"

"Jade." He dragged out her name, exasperation enunciating each letter. "Think with your head for one moment. Not your heart. The safety of this compound—"

"Enough with your twisted logic. No. One. Saw. She shall stay in my home, out of the path of prying eyes."

Xavier peered down his nose at her fingers. With his elbow bent, both of Jade's hands wrapped only halfway around the bulge in his sleeve. He twisted and gripped Jade's waist, earning her yelp of surprise.

"The Castle watches my every move. I cannot provide a reason for their interest to linger in the village. *Think,* Jade. How would they react if they discovered another with the gift? *Think.* The High Table does not welcome threats to their power with celebratory feasts." He rested his forehead on Jade's. "It's not only her safety at stake. Until we are certain this news is contained, she stays here."

"How would they possess such knowledge? What if she remained hidden in my cottage? What if—"

"I will not put you in danger. Don't ask this of me." Xavier brushed his hand over Jade's arm one more time and left. Echoes of Jade's pleas bounced down the corridor as she trailed after him. Rowan and Erik followed.

She was alone with Gavyn. Who was still shirtless and without boots.

"Let's get you settled." Gavyn pivoted on his heel and left her staring at the flame dancing in the blown glass.

By gods, why did it have to be him?

EMBER RAN AFTER HER RELUCTANT ROOMMATE.

Gavyn's long strides ate up the path winding around the training barn. More than once, the thin soles of her shoes caught on the uneven trail. Clouds hid the moon, making her progress difficult. Not wanting to prick his ire, she alternated between a quick shuffle and elongated strides to keep up.

The profile of the barracks jutted out from the tree line.

Longer than wide, several dozen small windows lined the front. Men stood at each corner, acknowledging Gavyn with a brief tilt of their chin. He stretched out an arm and gestured for her to enter the building first.

"This way," he said, brushing past, and marched down a wide center aisle.

On either side of the long room, beds lined the walls three high. Men of all ages prepared for sleep. Others sat up in their beds and chatted with their neighbors. A few sauntered around in various stages of undress.

She averted her eyes and concentrated on Gavyn's back.

He halted at the far end of the building, forcing her to grip his waist to prevent herself from falling forward.

"These are my quarters." He gestured to the open doorway. "And where you will stay until Xavier figures—"

"I'm sorry. I didn't mean—"

"It's done. I'll grant you privacy to get changed." He pointed to a large tub in the corner. "Would you like a bath tonight? I'll have the men fill it for you."

"Please. If it's not too much trouble." Ember ran her palms down the front of her skirts. "I... I just need one bucket."

"I thought you wanted to bathe." Gavyn rubbed the back of his neck.

"No. I do. But there's no need for them to bring more than one," she whispered to her feet. When she found the courage to look up, he was gone.

Not long after his departure, a knock on the door startled her from her worries.

"Come in."

A young fighter jaunted into the room, raising a bucket of water by its handle.

"Coach Gavyn said you needed some water to wash up. Where shall I leave this?"

"Would you dump it in the tub, please?" She smiled. His exuberance was infectious.

"Milady." He tossed the bucket's contents into the basin. An easy grin revealed a chipped front tooth. "If you'll give me a moment, I will have this filled for you in no time."

"Please… just the one." She smoothed her hands through her hair.

"Are you sure?" He cocked his head and paused at the doorway. "'Tis no trouble at all."

"Thank you," she said and dipped her chin. "One is all I require."

"Send word if you change your mind." He sent a wink in her direction before closing the heavy door behind him.

Ember let out a long sigh and padded over to the corner. She grasped the edge of the basin and closed her eyes.

The cast was easier this time. More natural. The small volume of water at the bottom expanded in size, and when it filled the tub shy of the brim, she removed her hands from its sides.

What was she doing? She should be running. Hiding. Not lingering for a bath. Her hands shook as she placed them in her lap. What if Jade was correct? What if nobody saw? Perhaps she could stay a few days until they were certain. At the very least, she needed to retrieve her satchel from the cottage before she left.

Her chest ached with Xavier's words. *No one shares your line.*

Another knock sounded at the door.

"It's me." Gavyn strode inside without waiting for her response. Water droplets fell from his hair to the wooden floor.

He changed into a cream linen shirt, the collar wet from the hair dripping down the back of his neck. Black britches molded to his powerful legs. The ends tucked into matching boots, and his footsteps echoed like cannon fire in the small space from their heavy soles.

"Here." He held out a misshapen bar of soap.

The familiar scent of pine wafted her way.

"Wait." She rotated at the waist and lifted her hair off the nape. "My buttons. I can't reach them. Jade helps… "

Gavyn stepped forward and wrapped her hair around his fist. He hesitated. The anticipation was almost unbearable.

Roughened knuckles brushed her sensitive skin as he made his way down to the last button. A shiver ran along her spine, a reaction to both his nearness and the chill in the room.

He dropped her makeshift ponytail and took a step away.

Cool air dusted her bare back.

"Thank you—"

"You have five minutes," Gavyn said over his shoulder and slammed the door behind him.

Ember's heart jolted, and her dress fell to the floor. She stepped out of the circle of fabric at her feet and immersed herself in the water. At least her head stopped spinning with his absence.

She vigorously scrubbed with the misshapen bar of soap, her skin turning pink with her rough ministrations. Ember massaged small circles in her scalp, careful not to create tangles. The last thing she needed tonight, on top of everything else, was a bunch of knots.

She rinsed and climbed out of the tub.

Ember spotted a primitive cloth on the chest near the foot of the bed. She dried herself and opened the heavy lid. Inside, there were color-coordinated stacks of linen tunics. She grabbed one from the pile and slipped it over her head.

The hem fell down to her knees and resembled a short, shapeless dress.

The lid of the trunk closed with a thud, revealing the bed.

There it was. The single bed in Gavyn's room. The one she refused to look at the entire time she bathed. Now, it mocked her. Where was she supposed to sleep? Surely, he didn't intend for her to bunk on the floor.

Her body moved on its own.

Two feet padded over to the side. An arm pulled the top cover back. Her lower half disappeared under the heavy blankets. It was comfortable and warm, chasing away the chill from her hasty bath.

Ember cradled her head in the crook of her elbow, and her eyelids grew heavy. In the last moments before she succumbed to sleep, she wished she found the courage to refuse Xavier's orders.

Because this was her new cage, and Gavyn held the key.

CHAPTER ELEVEN

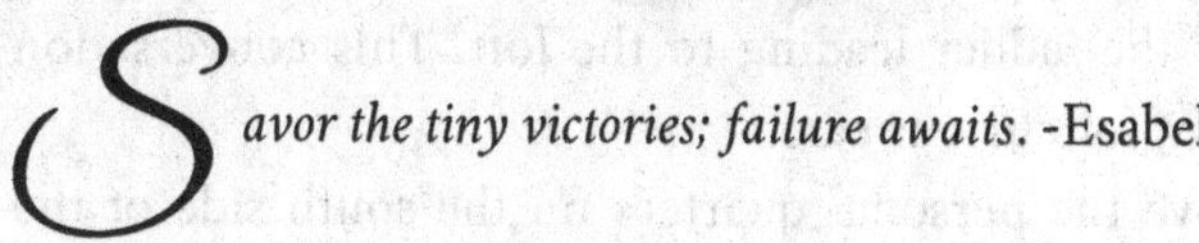

avor the tiny victories; failure awaits. -Esabel

GAVYN SECURED EMBER IN HIS CHAMBERS AND SET OFF FOR THE training barn.

His long strides carried him to the entrance doors in record time. Gone was the annoyance from her presence, it was replaced by a gnawing concern for her safety.

She was *Faeblood.*

A commoner with powers, though it didn't feel so magical in this moment. 'Twas a mark. A death sentence, if Xavier was correct in his assumptions, should the Lords discover her secret.

The light escaping the crack in the front doors meant he wasn't the first to arrive.

As a location for countless hours of sparring, a community center providing weekly entertainment, and a quiet spot for late-night meetings — the training barn was the hub of the compound. The heart of his entire family.

So it did not surprise him to find Xavier and Rowan huddled near the bar after an eventful night, even without discussing it first.

Erik, however, was a peculiar addition.

He suspected Xavier included him this evening because of his proximity to Ember's *incident* and subsequent clean-up with Rowan.

A fighter mature beyond his class.

Erik provided invaluable leadership to the entire group of first-year trainees. Gavyn relied on him a great deal over the past few months. Tonight, he was grateful for Erik's quick response to the girls' distress.

He raised a finger to his mouth, closed the entrance doors, and climbed the ladder leading to the loft. This conversation was not meant for curious ears.

Built above the personal quarters on the south side of the barn, the area tucked under the eves had originally been intended as bunk space for the men. For several years, it served as a make-shift dormitory for fighters, but with the construction of the larger, more permanent barracks, it now acted as the personal sitting room for Miss Ada.

A half-filled glass, likely from this morning's sparring session, perched on the edge of the wooden desk, an ornate monstrosity Mikel had hauled up last winter. Unlike the organized study of her sibling, pieces of parchment and dried ink bottles littered the surface in a haphazard manner.

Satisfied they were alone, Gavyn descended the ladder and joined the group at the bar.

"Get your new roommate all settled in." Rowan slapped him on the back.

"What did you find out?" He shook off the gesture.

"All the men were local villagers, except the two morons who started the fight," Erik answered, studying the upper row of barrels. "The crowd behind the stools was too far away to see over the counter."

"In the morning, pay Zoie's patrons a visit," Xavier said. "Take some of Jade's pies with you. Figure out what they saw. Let them know this doesn't get out."

"Yes, sir."

"And you…" He turned to Rowan. "Chase bedmates on your own time. Talk to Ada about the next card. If you're not on it, you pull taps with Zoie."

"What about the two men who smashed up the bar?" Erik took a hesitant step forward and tugged on his ear.

"Ask around. Let's see if anyone remembers anything about them. Hopefully, mead muddled their minds and anything they might have witnessed." Xavier ran his hands down the clean counter. His attention lingered on the upright stools.

Behind the bar, someone had swept the floor free of the earlier debris.

Xavier pointed a finger at Rowan and said, "Next time some fools bust up my place, keep them for questioning instead of throwing them out."

"How's Jade?" Gavyn straddled the nearest stool. "Was there any sign of Ember's powers during the weeks spent in her cottage?"

Xavier walked around to the serving side of the counter.

"A little rattled. And no, she was unaware, not even a hint. Zoie offered to stay the night with her." He shot Rowan a glare and unearthed a cup from under the counter. Dark amber liquid flowed out of the tap on the left. "Figured she shouldn't be alone."

"And the girl?" Gavyn took the first cup as Xavier filled another, aware of every eye on him, all wondering the same — how long was he required to endure her temptation? Surely, if Ada had not already done so, the entire compound would lay bets wagering on how many days it took for him to fall for her.

And it would be him falling first.

No one that beautiful would give someone with his appeal a second glance.

Gavyn was no monk. He had a handful of past relationships, but his partners made it clear they weren't with him for his looks. Or personality. Certainly not his cunning.

Heat flared in his cheeks, and he cupped the back of his neck.

They only wanted the prestige that came from being under the protection of a top-tier fighter. Most days, he didn't mind the arrangement, if he didn't dwell on it too long or too deeply. All parties were aware of their respective roles, and his were simple to fulfill.

"She stays with you until I figure out how far this has spread or when it's safe for her to return to Jade's." Xavier's eyes narrowed. "I don't want the Castle to know a Faeblood is under my nose. Let's not give them any more reason to look our way. The High Table lashes out at the slightest provocation and would twist my generosity into treasonous intents."

"Are you certain the High Table would look in our direction if we harbor a caster?" Gavyn asked as he turned on his stool. "Of all things, her gift is healing. She is no danger."

"Your thoughts run too narrow. It's not her abilities. It's what she represents."

Gavyn sighed and rested his cup on the bar.

Xavier played a different game than the rest of them — navigating the politics of the Lords and negotiating squabbles between territories. A day never passed where Gavyn wasn't glad about his responsibilities as head trainer, or more accurately, relieved at the ones not on his plate.

"First the blade. Now a Faeblood..." he said to no one in particular. "I never thought I'd miss the days of sparring in fields and sleeping in caves."

"I took care of the dagger." Xavier handed out drinks and

raised his in a toast. "To Gavyn, putting Harin out of his misery in the second round."

The clank of cups ended any further discussion. He bit back questions about the blade, despite his curiosity, trusting Xavier to handle the situation. One less thing to worry about.

"So it's true, a Faeblood. I'd never thought I'd see the day…" Rowan said, his voice trailing off. He had more reason than anyone to be stunned by this turn of events.

Erik placed his drink on the counter without taking a sip.

"Ah, the cub pulled patrol tonight." Rowan downed the contents of his cup in one swallow and reached for Erik's. He nudged Gavyn's side again. "Jade's going to be mad you kept her pet."

"I'll handle Jade." Xavier took a sip and knocked on the counter twice, rising to his feet. With a two-finger salute, he slipped around the stack of hay bales and disappeared down the hallway leading to his chambers.

"I'd rather come home to a caster in my bed than deal with our resident hellcat." Rowan flung an arm around Gavyn's shoulders. "Sorry I missed all the excitement at the end, old man. I guess Harin won't be coming back for another. It's a pity you didn't polish the floor of the ring with his pride. Head locks are effective in ending a fight but leave scant proof of the loss the next day."

"Who are you calling old?" Gavyn grabbed Rowan's arm and twisted it behind his back. He leveraged the larger man over the edge of the bar. "Not too old to take your goat. And I only have one summer on you."

Rowan tapped twice on the wooden top.

Gavyn released the hold, slapping him on the back.

"What about Harin's loss of control at the end of the first?" Rowan took a sip from his cup and nodded to Erik. "That's something I would expect from a cub. Not an experienced fighter."

Gavyn stared into the contents of his drink.

It was a good thing, too. His gut clenched at the memory of looking up at the sound of Rowan's whistle, finding Erik escorting a terrified Jade. Ember and Zoie trailing behind with pale faces, wide eyes.

"Come, let's finish one more before we find our beds," Rowan said as he poured two more rounds. "Erik, join us. I shall extend my kindness and consume your portion again."

Gavyn turned on his stool, searching for the fighter.

A crack in the entrance doors drew his gaze.

He rubbed the stubble along his jaw. Something scratched at the back of his mind, but the mead, combined with the long day, dulled his instincts. He finished his drink and rose to find his chambers.

"I expect you in the barn tomorrow afternoon. Don't be late." He nodded to Rowan.

The return trek to the barracks took half the time. Exhaustion and worry added haste to his steps, but if he was honest, they weren't the only reason his strides carried him so quickly to his bedroom door.

He lingered in the threshold, allowing his eyes to adjust to the dark.

A soft murmur from the blankets urged him forward.

He closed the world behind him with a soft snick as not to disturb her fitful slumber. Gavyn wetted his lips. It was impossible to ignore the whimper.

He removed his tunic and his boots. What was he going to do with her?

His initial measure of her was correct — Ember was a threat to his family — though, not in the manner in which he originally expected.

Her gift was a blessing, especially in a den of fighters, but the dark circles under her eyes made it seem more like a curse. Despite her considerable powers, in the dead of night she appeared almost fragile. It was difficult to see her as anything but someone to protect.

And after her cast to save Jade, *someone to cherish.*

"Mother," she said as she flung an arm over her eyes. *"Mama..."*

He lowered himself onto the mattress.

"Ember," he whispered as he tucked the covers around her and brushed a damp tendril from her brow. "Ember, wake up. 'Tis a dream."

She snuggled into his side, but never opened her eyes.

Dear gods, she was so beautiful. He melted into the covers, unable to stop running a hand up and down her side. Who knew how long he lay there, rubbing small circles on her lower back and trailing his fingers up and down her arm?

When his desire to kiss her became stronger than his body's demand for sleep, he flipped over on his back and let out a sigh.

It was going to be a long night.

ERIK'S HANDS SHOOK.

Faeblood. There is a caster outside the Castle walls.

Outside. The. Castle. Walls.

He cupped his hand over his mouth and ran it down the column of his throat.

The last he'd heard rumors of an individual with powers living in the territories... he'd been... maybe fifteen summers. A decade ago.

The memory was fuzzy, clouded by teenage angst and self-doubt. It was around the time he started training with the Red Guard, when his already tenuous relationship with his father strained beyond its usual capacity. What ever happened to the Faeblood?

She would remember. *She* would know how to proceed.

It was selfish — lamenting the loss of his confidant, the one person left in his life who listened as he confessed his sins. As the physical embodiment of his consciousness, she doled out advice when warranted and withheld it as often, forcing him to solve whatever puzzle circumstance had thrown his direction.

It was selfish—mourning their connection when she struggled to survive in the dank cells of the Castle, the dark rows of torture chambers that operated in the cloud of ignorance of the society hosting soirees floors above.

She would know, and hopefully soon, he would set eyes on her and ask for the tale himself.

Despite the lateness of the hour, the barracks buzzed with energy, a crackling hum usually reserved for the conclusion of a well-matched card. A few candles escaped curfew, betraying faces too distracted for sleep. Whispers swirled around him.

Erik bristled at the eyes tracking his every move.

A heavy hand grabbed the crook of his elbow. Mikel applied enough pressure to halt him in his tracks.

"What news do you bring?" A valued training partner, Mikel was seasoned, knowledgeable. Quick with advice and respectful to those who earned it. So it was with an ounce of regret Erik held his stare and said, "None."

Mikel's thoughts twisted his features, and the mark on his neck bobbed with a heavy swallow.

Erik traced the fighter's time at the compound back to its inaugural summer, but his origins remained a mystery. He didn't hail from the mining village and never spoke of his life prior to living at the compound.

A brother in every sense of the word, but he failed to rise in rank and attain a leadership position. He never showed animosity with his lot, happy to train with the others and trail after Ada in his spare time.

Mikel nodded and dropped his hand.

He wasn't long for conversation, either.

Erik held a sigh of relief and retrieved a short roll of parchment, a near empty bottle of ink, and a ragged quill from under his bottom bunk. His saddle bag hung from a hook at the head of the bed, and he grabbed it, tucking everything inside. Wordlessly, he strolled down the center aisle, ignoring the occasional wave and the sets of curious eyes, and snuck out the rear door.

They had constructed the barracks at the edge of the forest, where the growth was old — towering oak giants matured together, creating a canopy so dense he could not track his location using the northern star.

He kept to the well-trodden paths, curling around trunks at the faintest sounds.

The wildlife remained still, perhaps sensing an unknown predator prowling through their domain.

Erik avoided the patrols in the woods with ease, a benefit from commanding their shifts over these past two moon cycles. But his journey to the stream took three times longer than normal, and another half hour passed before he reached the cave on the western edge of the knoll.

At its entrance, he withdrew a small dagger from the inside of his boot. Another link to his heritage, one he judged worth the risk of exposure for the comfort it lent in his palm.

After months of disuse, its handle felt foreign.

He dragged his heavy boots over the carpet of fallen twigs and decomposing leaves, hoping to alert the cave's nocturnal inhabitants to his arrival.

The ensuing silence prickled the hair on his forearms, and Erik waited several heartbeats before he dared enter the forest den.

He'd discovered the refuge a month into his assignment at the compound. A simple shelter from the woods, the cave provided much needed solitude when Erik penned letters to his father or desired a respite from the crush of the ever hectic compound.

He ran his hand along the stone wall, searching for the small alcove where he hid a supply of candles nicked from the training barn.

His fingers wrapped around one of the thicker pillars, and the syrupy sweet taste of his magic coated his tongue.

The wick flamed to life, confirming Erik was alone in the cave's mouth.

He leaned back against the wall, its cool surface a balm against his heated back. His chest heaved, and Erik rested his head in his hands.

Faeblood.

A sorcerer raised beyond the ruthless society within the fortress. One with powers near his own. What were the chances of another healer in this generation?

The line had died out in the Castle, or so he was told. When Erik's powers had emerged, it had been a source of celebration amongst the nobility. The other Lords had called it a miracle, a gift from the gods themselves.

Another source of disappointment for his father.

While the rest of society considered it a blessing to have a skilled mender and herbalist at the Castle, his shape-shifting father belittled Erik for the softer powers and railed against him for the death of their paternal line of magic.

Hearing Ember confess in Xavier's office was akin to hearing the voice inside his head. The stark desperation. The rumbling crawl beneath his skin. The control he struggled to wrest every time he stepped foot in the training barn, surrounded by countless injuries.

He'd spent half a decade concealing his powers from his father, and those five years of dampening his magic served him well now.

Her presence in the village complicated matters, and the doubts swirling around Erik's mission grew in number, shrouding his next move.

The dagger was no longer in play. As he predicted, Xavier took care of the incriminating object and erased any evidence linking the compound to the illegal weapon. Erik wouldn't waste any more time searching for the blade.

The Faeblood, though, she was another story.

There was no doubt news of her whereabouts would escape Xavier's grasp, no matter how tightly he held the tongues of the villagers.

The truth wouldn't slip through his fingers out of disrespect... no... her mere existence was extraordinary. Gossip would spread in the territories like the summer fires plaguing the underbrush of the southern fruit groves.

He ran his fingertips over the tip of his ear.

Xavier was correct in his assumptions — his father would view her powers as a threat to his own. And if he ever found out Erik kept the information from him, their lives would be forfeited. Both *hers* and Embers.

How could he protect them both?

He paced the perimeter of the outer chamber.

Wind howled outside the cave, creating a miniature vortex of dust and leaves near the entrance.

Heat seared the inside of his thumb, and it took him a few heartbeats to trace the source to the near melted candle in his hand. The flame sputtered twice before snuffing out.

A chilly darkness blanketed the air, no longer held at bay by the warmth of light.

Erik lit another candle and emptied the contents of his saddlebag.

He would report the appearance of the Faeblood. No other way around it. But it was time he stopped acting as a pawn in his father's game and take control of his next moves.

Save them both.

Erik dipped his quill in the remaining ink, ignoring the fine tremor in his hands, and penned another missive to his father.

Unlike prior correspondence, his words were free of codes and secrecy. A challenge to his father's directives, one he counted on to filter through the Castle's numerous spies, and if he was lucky, those monitoring the channels of communication in the territories.

If there was one thing he learned in all his time at the compound, it was that *hope* was a precious human emotion, and once released into the world, it was difficult to control its spread.

He slung his saddlebag over his shoulder and blended in with the woods. Erik dodged two nearby patrols and joined the rear of the third.

No one questioned his sudden appearance in the middle of a shift. Nor his disappearance when he slipped away to enlist the services of his family's messenger falcon — the dappled blue-gray peregrine with a distinctive white marking on his chest.

CHAPTER TWELVE

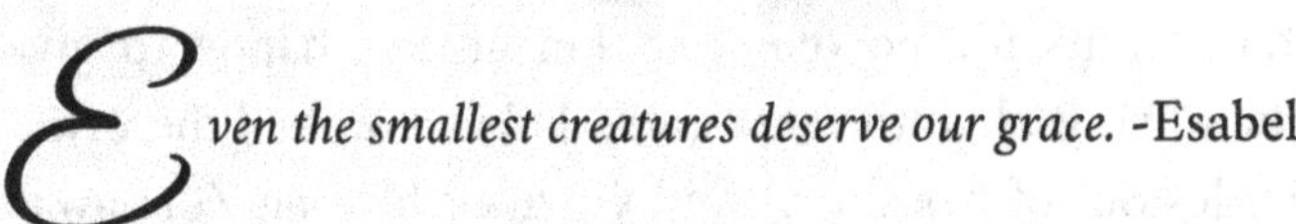

E ven the smallest creatures deserve our grace. -Esabel

THE FIRST RAYS OF SUN DANCED AT EMBER'S FEET.

She rubbed both eyes and waited for them to adjust to the light. The linens next to her were cool to the touch, but the covers wrinkled in a manner suggesting a large something or someone disturbed them in the night.

Gavyn.

She was wide awake now.

The details of the room came into sharp focus — a copper tub large enough to accommodate someone twice her size, a battered trunk at the end of the bed housing neat stacks of pressed trousers and tunics, and an overwhelming scent of pine. Opposite of the frilly atmosphere of Jade's cottage.

But not without its own comforting appeal.

Rested and alert, she swung a leg over the side of the bed and searched for her gown. Someone draped it across the back of a wooden chair. She tiptoed to the far end of the room, jerking Gavyn's shirt over her head as she went.

The borrowed dress was warm and plush and familiar. Her suit of armor for the day. Still, she stiffened at the knock on the door.

"Come in?" she answered, a question instead of a command.

"Wonderful, you're awake." Jade crossed the chamber and pulled her in for a long hug. "Turn around. I'll do up the buttons. The market opens soon, and I came to steal you away to assist with the morning rush. Afterwards, we can head to Madam MaLota's and play with gowns."

"I assume you grant me no choice?" Ember nibbled on her bottom lip. "Eager to spend your winnings from last night?"

"Fashion waits for no one, and I'm always happy to give chase when I stumble into extra gold." Jade smoothed the invisible wrinkles out of her skirt. "And we need to drag Zoie away from her cottage to join us at the dressmaker's. She left before dawn while I was busy in the kitchen and will stay in her lair until someone rescues her."

"Where does she go during the day?" Ember asked as she steadied herself with a hand on Jade's shoulder and tugged on her slippers.

"Rowan, with Xav' blessing, set her up in a little cottage in the woods outside the market. 'Tis a small home where she brews all of her ale and wine." Jade perched on the corner of Gavyn's bed. "I'll take you later, but first I want to know about last night."

"She makes all the mead in the kegs?"

"Nice try, but I'm not letting you change the conversation." Jade let out a chuckle. "Spill it."

"What do you want to know?"

"Everything." Jade clasped her hand and asked, "What can you do? How long have you been casting? Where did you learn? Are there others like you from your village?"

"I will never forget the first day I cast." Ember rubbed her palm. "It was the day that changed everything."

She closed her eyes.

"I often played in the meadow by our first home, gathering my mother's favorite purple flowers. That day, a whimper carried on the breeze. I knew I should stay in the clearing. Close to the cottage. My fondness for forest creatures led me astray on more than one occasion. But the cry pulled something inside of me. Something new. Different."

Her eyes opened on a drawn-out sigh.

"I found a small fox caught in a trap, his leg broken in the snare. Intuition guided the healing. It was clumsy. I remember running home and shouting for my mother. The story bubbling out of me. I didn't realize it at the time… what it all meant. Didn't realize why she crammed a hand over my mouth and slammed the shutters closed."

"She wasn't proud?" Jade asked, her voice barely a whisper. "How old were you?"

"Proud, yes, but she was also afraid." Ember said wistfully. "I was only six or seven summers by then, you see. It caught her unaware."

"I thought you said she was a healer?"

"Aye, she was a powerful one, but most in our line don't come into their gift until later, closer to their fifteenth or sixteenth year."

"Why was she scared?" Jade tilted her head.

"Magic shapes the mind and bends your thoughts, so it's better when you have more control of your body before it consumes you." Ember crossed her arms over her chest and hugged herself. "I was so young. There were so many times I couldn't control it… I couldn't keep from hurting myself… or someone else."

"Okay. Okay," Jade repeated, a lightness entering her tone. "Well, what can you do? Can you give someone warts? There's this man that comes to the market every morning and harasses farmer Whitby. Nothing serious, says he peddles spoiled vegetables and wilted salads. Trying to get lower prices."

She grabbed Ember's wrist and sent her a devilish smile.

"Just a couple of spots right on his nose, 'tis all I'm asking," Jade said, her eyes twinkling.

"My mother taught me to heal, not cause unsightly afflictions, even though he may deserve them." She nudged Jade with her shoulder.

The door cracked open. Ada leaned against the frame.

"Come in, come in. Ember was just telling me how she's going to give Barden a rash in his britches for heckling dear Mr. Whitby."

"I did nothing of the sort. Quit spreading falsehoods," Ember smacked Jade on the arm.

"Ooh, yes. He deserves one for vexing dear ole Whitby." Ada rubbed her hands together and waggled her eyebrows. "How did everything go last night? Any scintillating tidbits?"

"*Ada.*" Jade pinched the bridge of her nose. "She's under Gavyn's protection, not here to seduce him."

"What?" Ada grinned and batted her eyelashes. "I miss all the good stuff, plus the entire compound treats me like a little sister. No one tells me anything. All those big brothers dash my hope of ever stealing secret kisses. Let me share your good fortunes."

Warmth climbed the back of her neck.

"I'd prefer to stay out of his way. Gavyn's made it known that I'm unwelcome," Ember said as she nudged Jade's foot with her own. "First, I'm a thief. Now, I'm a Faeblood. His regard for me isn't very high at the moment. I'm a little nervous about sharing a room with him."

Despite her reservations, a spark of excitement ignited at the prospect.

Memories from her first and only coupling rose in Ember's mind. Two lonely souls, barely considered adults, rolling around in a haystack on a spring morning. The young man had panted with eagerness, the experience concluding before Ember had time to enjoy the bond.

Still, it had felt nice enough, the sensation of bare skin on skin. A headiness of being so desired.

They had planned to meet the next day, but Ember's mother, recognizing the budding romance, had packed their meager belongings and moved them in the dead of night. Again.

What would it feel like with Gavyn? A restless throb beat in Ember's core. What sensations would someone with his experience evoke? She licked her lips as the thought of lying under his powerful body took shape in her imagination.

"Gavyn's all bark," Jade said. "He has a lot on his shoulders with training and takes the safety of the entire village as his sole responsibility."

"He left before I woke up this morning." Ember hesitated. "My preference is to stay with you or not linger in the village at all. A relationship, however tempting, invites complications. I do not wish to be encumbered by the bonds of a romantic connection."

"As much as I complain about Xavier, he's right. Until we ensure word stays within the borders of the territory, there is no safer place you could be. That includes my home. While Xavier may have ulterior motives for keeping you around — having a healer in a compound of fighters is appealing — that's not who he is at the heart of it. He knows you fare better under his protection than scraping by in another village, especially if you draw the eye of the High Table." Jade bit her lower lip then whispered, "I fear your imprisonment if they discover your gifts."

"But no law or decree exists against magic outside of the Castle." Ada adjusted the bodice of her gown. "Why would the Lords concern themselves with one person?"

Jade stared at Ada until she stopped fidgeting.

"Magic serves as the division between our two peoples. Ember's mere existence outside the Castle walls is a threat to the advantage they lord over us." Jade paused, then said, "Alright ladies, enough of this gloomy talk. Ember, let's feed the townsfolk, and then we have a date with Madam MaLota. Unless you can conjure some new gowns out of thin air, I intend to keep it."

"I shall meet you there. An errand requires my attention, so I must bid thee farewell." Ada bounced on the balls of her feet, scurrying out of Gavyn's chamber.

Jade shook her head and sighed.

"It's a miracle gray hair does not cover Xavier's entire head."

"Stop dancing around and hit me," Gavyn taunted.

He squared up and threw a quick jab. For the better part of the morning's training session, he shared the ring with Erik who missed every chance to land a strike. Even the ones Gavyn left open, testing the younger fighter.

Dark circles formed half moon smudges under Erik's eyes, a testament to a late night on patrol. Fatigue still didn't explain his performance. If so, Gavyn would have landed more shots by now. It was uncommon for him to work so hard to set up combos on a first year trainee.

"Halt." Gavyn held a hand up. "Look at where you are. The pivot away from my cross puts you on my weak side. Shift on the balls of your feet without lifting your stance. Now drive your right behind my guard."

"Like this?" Erik extended the punch and grazed Gavyn's jaw.

"Yes, or you can drop your level and send a hook under my rib cage." He drew a small circle in the soft flesh on his flank.

Erik adjusted his stance and tested the new counter on Gavyn's side.

"Either blow will prevent me from squaring back up to you." He patted the back of his left thigh and said, "End with a leg kick to keep me from circling out."

Erik nodded his understanding and shadowed the movement. They went through the same sequence several times.

Satisfied with his progress, Gavyn dismissed the fighter to work with the others. He rubbed his jaw. What if Erik needed the rush of a match?

He crossed the platform and rested on the top ropes.

"Maybe ring his bell." Rowan greeted him with his customary grin. "It might jolt him enough to hit back."

"Why don't you hop in for a bit and volunteer in his stead?" Gavyn pushed off and opened his arms wide in invitation. "Make my morning."

"What's the matter, darling? Didn't get enough sleep?"

Gavyn stepped back from the edge and jogged a quick lap around the perimeter. "Slept fine, sweetheart."

Rowan ducked under the center ropes and jumped up and down a few times to get his blood flowing. His grin brought out the dimple in his cheek that the ladies and several of the older lads found so alluring.

"Remember, my admirers will be furious with you if you wreck my pretty face."

"Your face is fair game." Gavyn said as he shook out his fists. "Xavier only cares about your hands."

"Then, I'll make sure not to break them on your crooked nose." Rowan chuckled and squared up. Not one to stay up and trade blows, he liked to seize the first opportunity to take things to the ground.

The memories of old training sessions brought out Gavyn's grin.

Failed lesson after failed lesson later, he had accepted the scrappy style Rowan carried from his early years in another village. Born to a long line of crafters and smiths, he learned early on not to ruin his hands fighting. Swollen knuckles had meant no work. No wares meant a hard existence in any village.

They had spent many late nights practicing takedowns and ground work. It had taken them a long time to develop a successful fighting strategy.

Rowan may prefer the company of lovers over sharing a ring with fighters, but that didn't make him any less dangerous when he crossed under the ropes.

Gavyn wanted to try a new escape, so he goaded his friend into an early level change.

They slammed into the floor, a tangle of bodies and limbs.

"If you wanted me to put you flat on your back, all you had to do was ask." Rowan drove his shoulder into Gavyn's chest and attempted to swing his leg over him. "What's wrong? Did the beautiful thief not hold you tight enough last night?"

That was the other thing about Rowan. He never shut up. Years in the barn made it easier to ignore the banter. Still, it entertained Gavyn when the less seasoned fighters first grappled with his chatty friend.

He bridged his hips and drove a leg into the ground, hinging out from under the bigger man and scrambling to a sitting position.

The escape was short-lived.

Rowan lunged and pinned him again. He pressed his forehead against Gavyn's chest and said, "You've taken too many hits to the head if you think I'm going to let you up so soon."

Gavyn dug both palms into the ground and thrust backwards. As he moved inch by grueling inch back to the nearest corner barrel, Rowan stayed glued to his chest. His progress slowed every time he thwarted Rowan's attempts to pin his shoulders.

"Ember turned a few heads last night," Rowan's drawl rumbled against Gavyn's chest. "She's likely to catch the attention of a couple of seasoned fighters."

Finally, Gavyn's upper back bumped the cool slats of the oak barrel. He planted one foot and dug hard into the ground. Sweat poured down his face, and their combined weight proved difficult to lift. With every small amount of leverage gained, Rowan shifted and readjusted his pin.

"That one needs a keeper," Gavyn ground out.

"It's convenient then that Xavier already volunteered you for the position."

"I'm not in the market for a skittish colt, especially one that will scamper off at the first sign of trouble."

Rowan shifted his weight to the side and asked, "So you won't mind then if I court her? It would be nice to have someone around who could kiss all my pains away."

Like hell. He wouldn't allow Rowan anywhere near her.

Gavyn twisted to the side and bucked up. The force knocked Rowan just enough for him to scramble free. He sprung to his feet and eyed his brother's lazy move to stand.

"So you *do* mind then." Rowan chuckled.

"Rowan. Gavyn," Xavier called out. "Have either of you seen Ada today? I came back early this morning, and she wasn't in her room. I figured she stayed at Jade's, but I can't find her."

"I left Ember sleeping in my room. Maia's the only other female I set eyes to before dawn." Gavyn shook his arms out.

Maia stretched in the corner. A tunic clung to her chest, damp from the training session. At the mention of her name, her eyes met his, and she shook her head. "I didn't see Ada or Mikel in the loft, either."

"They are probably just at Jade's or in the market." Rowan frowned and followed Gavyn off the platform. They jumped down, landing next to the pile of garments removed earlier for sparring. "I found Zoie at her cottage early this morning. Alone, serenading her brews."

"Find them." Xavier crossed his arms. "I spoke plain enough last night about wandering around the territory until we determine if news of Ember's gift carries on venomous whispers. The Castle knows my weaknesses. If those cowards snatched my family out from beneath my protection…"

Xavier ran a hand through his hair.

"They would never be so bold to even entertain the thought," Gavyn said as he bent over to grab his boots off the ground. He leaned against the ring's platform and tugged them on. "To do so would anger the entire realm in our stead."

"You give them too much credit. The High Table operates in the shadows, outside the court of public opinion. They would capture Ada. Or Jade. Or anyone of us, and we would never feel the sun's warmth from the belly of that fortress. I do not relish the trappings of fear, but it will serve as my shepherd as I establish these rules. Bring them home."

CHAPTER THIRTEEN

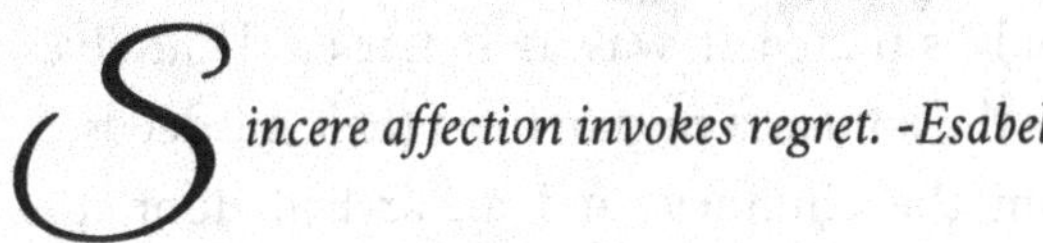

incere affection invokes regret. -Esabel

The midday sun blazed overhead.

Vendors and shoppers alike waved in Ember's direction. Gavyn might not welcome her into his village, but it seemed as if nobody else shared his concerns.

"Are you sure it goes against your morals?" Jade whispered as she bumped Ember's side and nodded to the young man approaching farmer Whitby's stand.

Ahh, the aforementioned, Barden.

"Yeessss," she hissed while nudging her back. Warmth spread through her cheeks at Jade's request. The sensation wasn't unpleasant, and considering the alternative reactions to her cast — imprisonment or death or worse, enslavement — she delighted in the mild teasing.

"Come. Let's rescue Zoie from her work," Jade said as she dusted off the empty shelves of her cart. "If allowed to keep to herself, she would never leave her brews."

She grabbed Ember's hand and steered them to a small cobblestone path. At the market's southern edge, the walkway was too narrow for a wagon but wide enough to beckon travelers on foot.

They strolled side-by-side, each lost in thought.

Deeper in the woods, the tightly arranged stones gave way to compacted dirt, its smooth surface occasionally disturbed by the roots of a nearby tree.

A quarter of an hour later, the trail opened up to a small glen — home to tall grasses and pops of color, benefactors of the light breaching the understory of the surrounding forest.

Water splashed to her left from a stream carving a course through the trees. A quaint cottage nestled into its sloping banks, so comfortably situated it was as if fairies themselves grew the home from the land as a respite from their misdeeds.

Smoke rose from the chimney, and an arched door, the cheerful color of dandelions, greeted woodland visitors. Flowers, denser in the front, surrounded all sides, their tight grouping suggesting someone planted their roots rather than nature scattering them about.

A home, by anyone's definition of the word. Welcome. Charming, with a personality of its own.

With their constant movement, a feeling she and her mother failed to invoke in all the places they rested their heads.

If given the opportunity to settle, what color would she paint her door?

The thought slipped in uninvited. Ember couldn't help but answer — blue. Nothing light or whimsical, with enough gray to be considered a serious hue in the hours between dusk and dawn. A grumpy shade not unlike the color of—

Busy gawking at the idyllic setting, she lost sight of Jade.

Ember picked up her skirts and shuffled to the front stoop, where her friend leaned against a wrought-iron railing.

"This is Zoie's?" Ember asked, slightly out of breath. "It's enchanting."

"Aye. Rowan and the cubs built it for her three, maybe four summers ago," Jade said as she knocked twice. "She needed more space for her brewing and wanted to branch out into wines."

Zoie answered the door, an apron adorning her front. Stains in various shades of red and violet overlapped on the linen.

"I told you I'm fine—"

"Good morning to you." Jade said as she brushed by her, heading straight for the hutch in the back.

"Oh, I thought you were someone else," Zoie admitted. She wiped her hands down her front. "Rowan swung by this morning before training."

"What do you have that's new?" Jade asked and clucked her tongue. She removed several jars and bottles from the shelf, inspecting their contents.

"I have a summer ale ready for the next fight night. I'm bottling wine now, but it needs a season to settle."

Ember ran her hands along a tall countertop commanding the center of the room. She paused, then picked up a glass bottle filled with clear liquid and several leaves of comfrey.

"That's a tincture for cleaning cuts." Zoie explained, pointing to the container. "The men go through a couple a week."

"And this one?" She asked and held up a smaller jar full to the cork with dark brown liquid.

"That's vanilla." Zoie took the container from her and pointed to the wrinkled husks. "Do you see the pods inside? The seeds provide the scent. The baker buys them for his sweeter treats, and I occasionally sell a bottle to a villager for soap making."

"My mother and I mixed them with lavender for our candles. When I was younger, I experimented with different combinations to find pairings that worked well together." Ember removed the small stopper and waved her hand over the mouth of the bottle. "Do Ceylon trees grow in your woods here? The inner bark yields a spice that blends well with your mulled wine."

"I'm not sure, but if you're interested, I'll take you with me next time I go foraging." Zoie gave her a welcoming grin.

A simple invitation.

And a layered offer. She'd never explored with another — visited the woods with anything more than her thoughts and daydreams. It was a chance, too. An opportunity to return a favor, give back in a manner that didn't involve her powers.

She was unfamiliar with the transactional nature of friendship, if such a ledger even existed, but this seemed like an easy way to keep the columns balanced.

"The traipsing around the forest will have to wait, ladies. Zoie, we came to steal you away for an afternoon of dress shopping," Jade said as she untied the ends of Zoie's apron and looped an arm around them both. "Come. I wish to lighten my coin before Xavier puts restrictions on my movements. Your bottles, jars, and barrels will wait for your return."

"Ooh, what about this one?" Jade flung another gown over the screen in Madam MaLota's shop. "Both the darker blue and heavier fabric will work for the coming season."

"Jade," Ember chided. She grabbed the beautiful dress and added it to the ones draped over her arm. "How many more do you want me to try on?"

"Just the one. Oh… maybe another." The screen's thick fabric lent an extra layer of concealment from the window shoppers in the market and muffled Jade's gleeful admission. "And we must look at skirts too…"

She was grateful for the light-hearted distraction — a chance to cast aside her fears of her future. Coupled with harmless gossip and a bonding ritual as old as time, it was easy to pretend all was well. Almost normal.

The dressmaker's backroom was a whirlwind of color and fabrics and giggles. A display for the senses.

Bolts of fabric slanted in one corner, their rich hues shouting against the bare white walls. No doubt a planned design, one which prominently featured the luxurious creations.

Madam MaLota staged seating for weary patrons in another corner. Sachets of lavender tucked in and around the plush cushions, the distinct fragrance a calming balm to the bustle of the main road. Light from the front window highlighted the intricate needlework on all the garments, reflecting Madam's talents and her penchant for shimmering silver and gold threads, pretty things.

"Bossy," Zoie whispered as she helped Ember button the newest dress.

"And don't think I forgot about that earlier comment, Zoie," Jade said in the stern tone she often summoned for Ada. "Pretty trappings shall not distract me."

A blush started at Zoie's neck and crept up her cheeks. Ember put her fist to her lips, unable to stifle the giggle.

"Rowan stopped by the cottage to check on me." Zoie shrugged. "You know how the fighters are after anything exciting happens, especially in the training barn."

The screen also provided a layer of privacy from Jade's interrogation. Blush continued its climb to the tips of Zoie's ears. While Ember enjoyed their banter, a ribbing she incorrectly assumed was reserved for blooded sisters, she sought mercy for Zoie.

"What do you think?" she asked, stepping out from behind the partition. A swish of her skirts cut off Jade's line of questioning.

"I knew it would work with your shape. Let's grab that one

plus the breezy white gown you tried on earlier." Jade bent down and gathered a handful of garments. "I want to—"

The bell on the front door chimed, announcing a new arrival.

"Apologies for my tardiness." Ada breezed in and gestured to Jade. "I'm happy you took advantage of the wager I set up for Eigen."

"Fools. All of them, but I'm delighted to take their gold. How did the fighters look today? I wouldn't mind lightening some purses again next week."

"Hmm. My books kept me from observing morning sparring," Ada said as if reciting her whereabouts from memory. She strolled across the room and ran her fingers along the hem of a light pink dress.

"The gown is not for your coloring, child." Madam waved her customer out the front door. She opened her arms wide, and Ada didn't hesitate to step into her embrace. "I've missed you."

Regal as a queen, but as welcoming as a familial matron, Madam MaLota hugged with her entire person. She was all soft curves over a strong work ethic. The perfect balance of gooey edges with a firm backbone.

It surprised Ember the first time Jade dragged her to the dressmaker's shop. Awkward when those strong arms wrapped around her. She didn't know where to place her hands. How to relax into the gesture. And in the end, Madam took pity, patting her on the back and offering a spot of tea and a sprig of sage advice.

There was never a time in her childhood when mother embraced her with such regard.

Sure, she doled out plenty of pats on the head, reassuring squeezes of the hand. Even one-arm clenches when distractions stole her away from her only child. But never the warm, all-encompassing hugs where she could sink into comfortable assurances and unburden her mind in a protective circle of arms.

There was no doubt mother had loved her. Cared for her. Sacrificed for her.

She'd shown it every day when they practiced casting. In her endless lectures of safety. As she tucked Ember in at night with stories of magic and blanketed her in tales of great sorcerers long since departed from the land.

Every time she uprooted their lives to keep her safe.

It may not have been the easy affection of Xavier's village, but it was theirs.

Madam's second hug was simpler to accept. The third, almost natural. And today's embrace... it was necessary — essential in a way Ember didn't know she needed until a little piece of her worries melted against the warm-hearted matron.

The bell rang out again.

Heavy footsteps echoed in the room suddenly devoid of its causal chatter. She stilled, and the fine hairs on her arms bristled in the silence — an increasingly common reaction this past fortnight; so much so, she needn't peek around the screen to determine the owner.

"Where's Ember?" Gavyn asked. It wasn't censure, but concern was absent all the same.

"I'm here." She held her chin high and emerged from around the screen.

It took great effort to pull her shoulders back and meet his grumpy scowl. She'd not forgotten how stormy his eyes turned. How unbending. The fragment of bravado rattling around in her chest splintered a little more.

"I'll make inquiries with Madam MaLota regarding these two." Jade gathered the dresses in her arms and scurried to the front of the shop. A relief — though Ember could use a friend — to not be the source of agitation between them.

"I'm going to look at... some fabric I saw in the window

earlier. Gavyn, swing by the cottage after supper. I bottled the whiskey you requested for Mikel's birthday." Zoie inclined her head and took off after Jade.

He grunted and to Ada, he said, "Xavier is looking for you. Mikel is out front and will escort you back."

Gavyn waited until the room was clear before taking in her dress and scattered gowns and proof of a fun afternoon away from her troubles. His demeanor was chiseled from stone, or something stronger, not harsh, but steady. Immovable.

"You left the compound." A tic appeared next to his scar.

A statement, not a question.

"Jade visited your chambers this morning." Her chin wanted to dip — to inspect the slippers commanding her sudden interest — but it stayed high. "I helped in the market, then we stopped by Zoie's."

She didn't add that Ada had planned on stealing her away for another errand this afternoon. Best not to irk him more.

"Are you finished here?" He asked, gesturing to the gowns hanging on the screen and the others folded on the small wooden chair in the corner. "I must return to the compound."

The intricate cuffs on his wrist snagged her attention.

She allowed herself to look at them, something she'd failed to do in all their prior interactions.

The crest was unfamiliar. Thick, dark lines contrasted with the lighter fawn-colored leather. One quadrant held the head of an animal, maybe a large cat. Another encompassed a cross of arms, the design matching the one at the base of Gavyn's neck.

The one she could have drawn from memory alone.

She licked her lips.

"Jade wants to purchase a couple more dresses for me, but I don't have a way to pay her," she confessed. They never spoke of currency or debt or payment her entire time in the village.

Her mother had always seen to such matters — communities welcomed healers with open arms, especially those who could mend near fatal wounds. A simple sleeping draught kept their powers hidden from patients, and joyous outcomes held additional questions at bay.

Miracles accepted with little thought.

Gavyn put two fingers under her chin and tilted her head higher to meet his gaze.

"I'll take care of it. Later," he muttered as his broad shoulders heaved with breath. His voice was thick. Perhaps filled with resignation of another responsibility added to his long list of duties.

She didn't want to become a burden to him. Another press upon his time. His nostrils flared, but she said nothing. Now was not the moment.

She closed her eyes. Frustration and yearning made it difficult to swallow. The pulse at the base of her neck swelled, and her question, now forgotten, lodged in her throat.

The fingers on her chin vanished, replaced by the pad of his thumb.

Her mouth parted in a soft *o*.

He slowly stroked a path along the underside of her jaw. Pressure wrapped around the back of her neck, his soft grip anchoring her as he traced the column of her throat. As if she would move. As if she wanted to be anywhere else. Ember would never voice this desire; he could never know of it.

Her eyes flew open.

She needed to stay away.

His was an intimacy she couldn't bear. Ember was no fool. Despite her sheltered existence, she knew tales of her powers would travel swiftly. Knew it would limit her time with him. It was dangerous to entertain this attraction, knowing fate would wrench her out of his arms.

She should step away, but she couldn't, could she? Therein was the problem; they were roommates. At least for the foreseeable future, and if she was unable to will her body in Madam's public dressing room, when his irritation alone should propel them apart, how would she ever resist him in private, when the softness of night lowered both their defenses?

"I'm needed at the barn," he said, though he left his hand on the base of her throat and made no move to leave. "Searching all over the village for you and Jade threw off my training schedule."

"I wasn't aware I needed to report my daily activities." Ember pushed into his hold. Her slippers aligned shy of touching his much larger boots. "I wasn't aware I was a prisoner here."

"You are not to leave the compound." He paused, then added, "Until we are certain of your safety. You're not a captive, but I can't protect you if you wander the village by yourself."

The scent of pine and sweat and sin howled at her good senses. Blowing them aside as if they were little more than dust in a windstorm. A powerful gust.

She wrapped her hand around his cuff, and ran her thumb along its edge.

"As you saw, I wasn't alone."

She didn't miss the sharp intake of his breath.

"Jade and Zoie don't count. And Ada needs a keeper almost as much as you do." He tightened the hand at her neck, not uncomfortable. Reassuring. His gaze slid down to the swell of her chest, and just as quickly, it snapped back up to her lips. "I'm busy the rest of the day, but I will find a safe way for you to explore the village, the territory."

He released his grip and took a step back.

"Madam," he called out, his voice rough, his eyes never leaving hers. "Add Ember's purchases to my account. Today's and any others she fancies in the future."

She didn't miss the heat in his directive. Or the implications.

He hesitated as if realizing the claim he staked.

"'Tis not proper," she said, choosing the words carefully and feeling the thread of conversation slip away. It was a half-hearted protest, even to her ears.

Gavyn leaned down.

His voice was soft — dangerously soft — as he whispered a hair's width from her lips, "Then it's fortunate I don't lend credence to propriety."

CHAPTER FOURTEEN

riendship begins with recognition of the same truths.
—Esabel

THEY WALKED SHOULDER-TO-SHOULDER DOWN THE VILLAGE'S main road.

Gavyn ran his hand through his hair and mourned the last semblance of his control, the fraying strand that stretched thinner every time he was near her.

He'd lost his mind.

Idiot. Big, dumb fool. What had possessed him to lay claim at the dressmaker's? He allowed Rowan's taunting to fill his mind and just… reacted.

Gavyn shook his head.

Thankfully, Ada had left by the time he lost all his sense and almost kissed Ember; otherwise, the imp would shorten the odds on his downfall.

His arm brushed against Ember's as she sidestepped another patron, and little bolts of energy zinged to his fingertips from the innocent, feather-light touch. Her cheeks were flushed from their walk. Or perhaps the embarrassment he caused her at Madam MaLota's.

While not as crowded as the morning rush, shoppers still clogged the main thoroughfare.

Small children played between carts as their parents exchanged conversation nearby. Doors and windows opened, beckoning the summer breeze. Men nodded as he passed, and a group of fighters flicked a two-fingered salute on their journey to the village's outskirts.

Unattached women sent small smiles his way.

Not comfortable with the attention, he never returned the gesture.

"This way," he said, cupping her elbow.

They slipped between two cottages near the end of the main road. A small dirt trail followed the side of the ridgeline leading to the compound, frequent use packing the earth. They climbed the path in silence.

Over halfway up, she halted and glanced back over her shoulder to the village below.

A community built on dreams.

From the increased elevation, Gavyn appreciated the tidiness of the layout. He strived for organization and order in his life, taking pride in the village's design. Cottages and shops framed the market, lined up like soldiers standing at attention.

Small yards backed up to a forest on the southern side.

Tight alleyways hugged the backside of the shops to the north, defining another row of homes. Behind the second line of residences, the stream wove through the village, disrupting the utilitarian layout.

Clusters of cottages popped up along its banks like otters catching their breath between bouts of underwater play. A few homes harnessed the flow of nature with wooden mills. Linens hung from lines attached to mature oaks, taking advantage of the sun's high arc.

A simple life. A happy existence.

Faint notes from a fiddle drifted their way, and she sighed beside him.

"The original inhabitants built along the waterways. There." He pointed to the homes farthest from the marketplace and placed a hand on her lower back. "The rivers make for easy transport between villages. Especially for larger trade. It's fed from springs high in the mountain and maintains a steady, chilly temperature year round. Rainbow trout tease the village lads casting lines along the shores in the summer."

The heat from her back seared his palm.

"Some of the original inhabitants constructed small mills. The farmers from the south load their wagons with bushels of grain in the fall, and the wheels come alive, grinding the harvest into flour for the upcoming year."

Never one for words, he wasn't sure why he kept rambling on.

Her intoxicating scent, a combination of lavender and vanilla, spun around him. She remained silent, so he continued.

"The villagers plowed and paved the larger cobblestone road as the training compound prospered. After half a decade of growth, Xavier gathered enough wealth to provide a continuous influx of gold into the community."

She gripped his forearm and dug a pebble out of her slipper.

"The newer homes, Jade's cottage... all built in the last few summers from his generosity. The villagers provide us with staples — food, clothing, other household wares — making everyone less reliant on outsiders. Aside from bulk goods, we strive for independence from the other territories. And the Castle..."

Why did he continue to ramble? He pivoted and climbed the rest of the trail, needing to put a few paces between them.

A few heartbeats later, Ember crested the path and leaned

forward, resting her hands on her knees. She took several deep, panting breaths.

"How did you survive on your own with two weak legs?"

"My command of my lower half is sufficient, thank you." Ember scoffed. "Your legs are the size of tree trunks and twice as long as mine, you big oaf."

"If I have something of value I wish to keep from your sticky clutches, I shall hide it in the highest spot I can find. Your stomping and heavy breathing would alert even the laziest of sentries. I assume you remember the training barn," he deadpanned.

It never grew old.

The sight of the building filled his chest with pride, even when he set eyes on it every day. A small part of him — a hidden, dark part — wanted her to share his joy. Foolhardy, so he continued his impromptu history lesson, hoping it would distract them both from his unrealistic wishes.

"Over time, we replaced the original wood siding with large boulders pried out of the banks of the stream. It took nearly five years and hundreds of young fighters to move and shape the rock into the structure you see before you. Xavier keeps quarters in the rear."

He pointed to the back.

"Ada's room occupies the far corner. Despite her many protests, we placed the door to her personal chamber on the inside of the structure, not the outer wall."

A whisper of a smile teased his lips.

"That seems… prudent," she admitted.

"Indeed." Gavyn's arms relaxed at his sides, and he jutted his chin to the left. "We built the barracks next, adding the mess hall last. All three buildings frame the courtyard. You cannot see it from this vantage but the stream winds around the back before cutting down the hill to the village."

"Why are the foundations different colors?" she asked.

"We exhausted the cache of boulders along the stream. Left a fair amount to stabilize the integrity of the banks. Xavier reached out to the mining community. He cultivates contacts in all the villages as the fighters complete their training and return home."

He sighed, debating how much he should tell her about his past. It wasn't shame holding him back, but his birth territory had a reputation. The idyllic setting only hoodwinked the inhabitants who fell over themselves trying to catch the praise of the Faeblood nobility.

"We hail from there — the quarry. Xav and his family, plus Jade and myself. Men who knew our fathers from decades ago cut him a deal on the building materials. The workers prospected the stone from deep in the earth, where the color of the cavern walls runs as dark as heavy storm clouds."

"And the color of the wooden siding is as green as Jade's—"

He cleared his throat, cutting off the rest of her observation. Jade and Xavier had a tumultuous relationship, one he didn't enjoy speculating on. It would be disloyal. To both. Besides, he didn't understand why they couldn't set aside their differences and pair off.

Similar to the politics of the Castle, matters of the heart were perplexing.

He grasped her elbow and said, "The village to the west harvests cedar logs and mills boards with little sap. The timber resists rot and sponges stain. I maintain a friendship with their leader. He trained with Xavier and me when we first settled in the area. Men from his community receive high marks the first season with us, a testament to his style of command. Rowan serves as emissary for Xavier whenever we barter for more building materials."

Most tolerated Rowan's smiles more easily than his busted up face.

"Back home, the farmers grew and hunted their food and

relied on the land around us for shelter. We were," she hesitated, then said, "Remote, somewhat isolated from the Castle's influence, though they still met the tithe. I never appreciated how vast the peninsula is."

"Our grain hails from the south. The miner's village is to the east. Timber from the west." He ticked off each finger. "Waterways divide the terrain, with those three villages plus ours covering the largest swaths of land."

He took a step closer, as if he couldn't stay away. Maybe sharing a room wasn't the best idea. Only there was no maybe. With certainty, he should not entertain her in his space.

"A community of artisans live in the caverns deep inside the mountain," he croaked out. "They permit few outsiders into their lair. We travel a few times a year to their outdoor bazaar to purchase wares. It's carved into the mountain's smaller peak, and the journey requires two day's time each way." Gavyn shook his head. "Jade and Ada fill an entire trunk each visit."

"I stumbled upon wooden cottages in the forest." Ember wiped her palms on the tops of her skirts. "Homes constructed of thick logs, stacked as high as your barracks."

"The hunter's cabins. They supply tanned hides and textiles. Farmers from the south provide the pelts from their livestock and wool for the weavers. Deer from the forest yield the leather cloaks of the nobility. Though, Xavier trades for a pair of fine gloves every fall for Jade."

He willed his hands to stay at his sides.

"The seventh people claim no land. Healers travel from village to village in a caravan of wagons. Not keeping to any one territory. In exchange for their aid, the Castle grants them permission to cross the natural boundaries of the mountain. We—"

"Gavyn," Xavier bellowed.

They turned around in unison. Ember took a small step closer to him.

Pairs of fighters ascended the hill, shoving and jostling each other as they found their way to the training barn. More spilled out of the mess hall, stuffing their mouths with the last bite of their meal. They'd wish they'd showed more restraint after training on a full stomach in the afternoon heat.

"A word." Xavier closed the distance.

"Stay in the loft the rest of the afternoon," Gavyn said to Ember. "I will grab you before supper."

He squeezed her elbow, hoping to take some of the sting out of the dismissal.

She was silent for a long moment then squared her shoulders.

He watched her all the way to the entrance doors, trying not to notice the gentle sway of her hips. The way her hair swung with each step. It was his duty to ensure she made it to the safety of the barn.

"Your waif is not likely to be abducted here. Now. In broad daylight, surrounded by thirty of your men." Xavier slapped him on the back.

Gavyn grunted. Perhaps he'd run out of words, after all.

EMBER LOCATED THE BASE OF THE LADDER LEADING UP TO THE loft.

She tilted her head, half expecting to see Ada's legs dangling over the edge, but the bubbling bookkeeper was nowhere to be found. She curled her arm around the nearest rung and leaned against the wood.

Gavyn followed not long after, his conversation with Xavier brief. He grabbed the hem of his shirt and tugged the fabric over his head. What if—

"You have a little something there."

Ember jerked, bumping her head.

Ouch, ouch, ouch.

A young woman, in olive green leathers and a plain white tunic, smirked back.

"Just right there." The stranger reached up to point to her own chin and swiped at her lips, the universal sign for something on the face. "You've a bit of drool."

The tips of Ember's fingers met the smooth, dry surface of her lips. And an equally clean, equally dry chin.

"I'm just teasing you." The woman extended a hand. Leather cuffs adorned her small wrists. "Rowan mentioned you were easy to rile."

"I'm not sure he knows how to do anything but tease." She clasped the outstretched palm. "Ember, but I suspect you already knew that."

"Maia. And it sounds like you have Rowan all figured out." She nodded at Gavyn's retreating form. "Can't blame you for that one. Even though he's like a big brother to me, I can still appreciate a set of fine shoulders on a man. Let's go up and claim a better view."

Maia climbed the rungs two at a time.

Ember's skirts wound around her legs, forcing her to ascend at a slower pace. At the very top, she grabbed hold of the railing and pulled herself into the loft. Maia sat in a chair near the edge and patted the one next to her.

"Do you mind if I ask?" She lowered her voice, pointing to the cuffs. "What do they mean?"

"These are Xavier's mark. His family crest." She rotated the leather around so the inlay faced the rafters. "He commissions them for any fighter who graduates from training and stays in the village."

"Why do you brand your neck?" Ember gestured to the black ink at the base of Maia's throat.

"The tattoo is... it's more significant." She brushed her

fingers over the inlay. "The cuffs aren't permanent. They are symbolic but not always practical to wear during training."

Ember leaned in and studied the design on Maia's neck.

There was a subtle blur to the outer edges. Unlike a scar, however, the skin appeared smooth. Maia gathered her hair and tilted her head to the side.

Ember's palm tingled, and she fought the urge to run her hands over the mark.

"You're a fighter?"

"Aye. I received my cuffs two winters ago. " Maia dropped her hair. "It took me a year longer than usual to finish."

A warrior. What would it feel like to harness strength? To know how to protect yourself and those around you. She had always associated the ability with men, but seeing Maia — with her cuffs and definition and confidence — 'twas nothing short of inspiring.

Ember peeked over the railing to the chaos below.

Men battled in every available space. Fighters faced off in the center ring, trading blows in a reenactment of fight night. Another group formed a large circle in the corner just beneath them. Two men rolled around on the ground while the others shouted cheers and insults.

In the opposite corner, a group of ten fanned out around bales of straw, each practicing with a target. A trainer wound between them, shouting out instructions and corrections for proper hitting techniques. What was his name? Mical? Mijel? No, it was Mikel.

"Cubs." Maia said, shaking her head and pointing to the large group. "You can tell them apart from the others by their poor striking."

"They fool me." Ember wrinkled her nose. "I'm able to discern between a kick and a punch, but that's it."

"I can see why Jade is so fond of you. As she tells it, she is the only one in the village who doesn't live and breathe fighting."

Maia chuckled. "Look at their shape. They fall into one of two groups when they arrive. They are either all skin and bones or carry softness around the middle."

Maia pointed to Gavyn.

"Take your new roommate. He has at least two stones on the skinny kid in front. The extra weight is not extra bulk, either. Look for the lines in his arms and upper body. They tell the story of years of hard training."

Happy for an excuse to stare at Gavyn, she studied the deep grooves outlining his shoulders. The definition in his back rippled when he extended a punch. Heat crept into her cheeks as she scanned farther down. Two lines traveled along his hip bones and pointed downward into the waistband of his leathers.

"What about Erik?" With effort, she tore her eyes away. "He's a first year but built similarly to the older fighters?"

Maia frowned.

"Erik is different. He joined us later, so he had some winters to put on strength before coming here."

"May I ask you another question? Why are you up here instead of training?" She said, rushing the last bit. "I mean... I enjoy the company but..."

Maia rolled her shoulder a few times and gripped it with her opposite hand.

"I injured my arm grappling with Mikel a few days ago. I can raise it here without trouble, but I can't go higher," Maia extended it to eye level and grimaced.

Magic crawled under her skin. Whether from the proximity to an injury or the residual simmering from her cast last night, she was uncertain.

Her fingertips warmed, and she rubbed them together to dissipate the heat.

When it became apparent the yearning to heal would not dull, she gestured for Maia to move away from the loft's railing and out of sight from the fighters below.

"May I look?"

"I don't mind." Maia turned so the offending shoulder was nearer and rolled up her sleeve. "It's been three days with little improvement."

"Don't. I mean… I don't need the garment moved." Ember closed her eyes, and a familiar ache shot through her wrist. It was fleeting — chased soon after by comfortable warmth.

Maia's eyes widened, and her jaw fell open.

"You've got something there." Ember traced the outside of her mouth.

Maia's peel of laughter filled the space. "How did you… what did you…"

"I sped things up a little." She shrugged. "It would've healed on its own in a few more days."

Maia let out a whoop and jerked her arm up and down. She swung it around in a circle and dropped into a fighting stance. After throwing a few shadow punches, she said, "That's—"

"Amazing, right?"

Occupied by Maia's shoulder, both women missed Ada climbing the ladder.

"Where have you been?" Maia furrowed her brows.

"Xavier wanted to… what does he call it… have a family discussion about my activities." A half smile formed on the younger woman's face.

"He just wants what's best for you."

"Dear brother wants to lock me up in my room and never let me see the light of day." Ada blew a lock of hair out of her face and plopped down in the remaining chair.

"If that was the case, you'd never see another fight night." Maia crossed her arms and cocked her head.

"Ha. The only reason I'm allowed to go now is because no one else can work the books."

"Are you just now returning from the market?" Ember asked.

"Yes. I begged Mikel to stop by farmer Whitby's southern

field. His barn cat delivered a litter of kittens, and I wanted to check on them."

"Is that where you went in the middle of the night?" Maia narrowed her gaze. "Xavier's not the only one who notices your absence."

"Yes. The mama cat delivered the babies in the field instead of the barn. I was worried about foxes chancing upon them."

"Ada." Maia said, exhaling her name with a long, drawn-out sigh. "You can't... don't go out after dark, okay. Anyone of us would take you."

"I know. I'm going to see if Mikel will go back again tonight." Ada's eyes sparkled. "I want to build a shelter to give them cover."

A shrill whistle split the air, and a hush rolled through the training floor.

Gavyn stood next to the ring, the fighters forming a tight circle around him. They raised their fists in unison, let out a short, powerful chant, and broke apart.

Most left through the entrance doors. Some stayed behind, forming small groups. Mikel strode over to Gavyn and slapped him on the back. Both men looked up at the loft and caught the girls staring back at them.

"Let's go," Maia yelled already halfway down the ladder.

Ember touched the top rung with the tip of her foot. Her skirts bunched up around her again, making the climb precarious. Near the bottom, strong hands cupped under her arms and lifted her in the air.

A flush painted Gavyn's face, and beads of sweat rolled down his forehead. The hair at the nape of his neck curled slightly from the dampness, and her fingers ached to smooth it down.

"My shoulder is as good as new. Watch," Maia said, breaking her trance. She lifted her arm and rotated it in a whirling motion.

"Fine." Gavyn looked back and forth between them, then

glanced up at the loft. "You're cleared to train tomorrow morning, but you still have your new assignment."

"Understood." Maia slung an arm around Ember and pulled her head close. "The cubs are building a fire for a boar roast the eve after next. Zoie plans to bring some of her new summer ale to sample. There will be plenty to eat and music for dancing." She rubbed her hands together. "You must join us."

Her first dance.

Though, not her first time dancing.

Her mother had taught Ember steps to the most common waltzes one evening, long ago, with festival music floating through the open windows of their cottage. She had begged for a lesson after dinner, wishing for a chance to experience the custom, even if safety required them to stay inside.

Mama had been flawless, twirling around the small room with effortless grace and wearing a rare smile.

She wanted to ask for a repeat demonstration the next night, but her mother was distant, grayer than normal. Not wishing to trigger another round of sadness, Ember never inquired again.

"— and the flames from the last roast almost set the maple tree on fire. Xavier was —"

"I'd be delighted," she blurted out, and her lips tugged upward at the sight of Gavyn's frown.

CHAPTER FIFTEEN

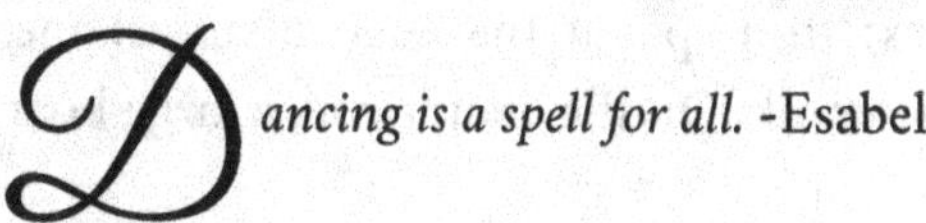

ancing is a spell for all. -Esabel

LAUGHTER HIT EMBER AS SHE ROUNDED THE SIDE OF THE barracks.

An enormous bonfire blazed in the courtyard, sending a thick plume of smoke into the pink sky and the smell of roasting meat on the evening breeze. Men gathered around the flames, forming small groups. Others relaxed on downed logs scattered around the perimeter.

She lingered at the edges, suddenly uncertain of her place. Her feet grew heavy. Frozen, as if they melded to the earth, rooting her to the spot. She tried to smile, pass off her trepidation as nerves.

But she kept thinking about her mother — the last days before her demise.

She'd known something was amiss. She'd known they were watched — not with the usual amount of neighborly nosiness, but with something more sinister, alarming. And yet... and yet Ember begged to stay in their home, selfishly asked not to run — so selfishly asked her mother to sleep off the feeling.

What if it's nothing? She'd spat. *What if it's all in your mind?*

She had bullied her mother into waiting.

She hadn't tried to understand her fears. She hadn't even told her mother she loved her that night. Angry at the possibility of moving again. Angry at the constant upheaval.

But her mother relented. And they stayed. Perhaps worn down by the prospect of starting afresh. Or maybe exhausted from battling her only child — constantly running counter to her stubborn will.

Or maybe the melancholy had won out.

Three men stood next to a spit at the edge of the flame, taking turns to rotate the crank. On the center rod, a large boar teased the glowing coals.

"There you are," Zoie said and handed her a cup.

She took a refreshing sip, and the cool water hit the back of her raw, parched throat. "Thank you, I—"

Beside her, Zoie was lost in thought, and the remaining gratitude died on her tongue.

A small group of three approached the edge of the gathering, their arms linked as they ascended the path from the village. Too far to make out their faces. The tall profile in the center could only belong to one man.

Zoie fumbled the contents of her cup, spilling amber liquid on her skirts. She cursed under her breath and pulled the fabric taunt to survey the stain.

"I'm going to the mess hall to get some water on this before it sets," she muttered then scampered away.

Ember was adrift — keenly aware of just how alone she was.

Zoie's departure only amplified the bonds of uninvited solitude she struggled against these past few weeks.

Ember committed an unforgivable sin. She overlooked the

reliable comfort her mother provided. Spent an entire lifetime with her nose pressed against the glass, longing for the simple life of a villager, yearning for love and acceptance when she experienced it all along.

"Where'd she run off?" Jade asked as she sauntered over, her arm linked through her escort's elbow. The size of his chest and arms marked him as too old to be a cub, but he lacked the intricate cuffs of the more experienced fighters. A small strap of leather held back the longer strands of his locks, and warm brown eyes twinkled in the firelight.

"She spilled ale on her gown and left to wash it out."

Jade clucked her tongue and eyed Rowan and his two admirers.

"Have they ever?" Ember asked.

Jade sighed.

"No. At least not that I'm aware of. Zoie doesn't think he *sees* her. But I catch him looking at all hours of the day. I wish they'd figure it out. They keep hurting each other. He staked a claim — the fighters know his interest. The villagers know his interest. Everyone at the compound knows his interest, but he hasn't told her."

"How is she unaware?"

"These men..." Jade scoffed. "These big, lovable, loyal... foolish men. Oh, he didn't ask her properly. Didn't follow the rules of courting. No... he builds her a cottage. Checks on her day and night. Scares off any potential suitors. Everything but saying *the words...*"

"I see it," Ember whispered, a hint of longing in her voice.

"Aye, of course you do, as an outsider. Zoie has a sharp mind. She'd need it for calculating quantities of ingredients for her mead. Keeping records for her wines. But that same brilliance renders her blind to subtle courtship gestures."

"What Jade is saying... is Rowan needs to club her over her head and kidnap her for a fortnight. If he was smart, he'd keep her naked in bed until she agreed to the bonding ceremony."

"*Ada*," Jade chastised. "Show some restraint. Zoie differs from your..."

Their bickering faded to the background.

Rowan kissed both companions on the cheek and jogged in the direction of the mess hall, his steps quickening the closer he traveled to the structure.

Her heart ached for Zoie. It couldn't be pleasant to suffer the push and pull of an undeclared courtship — one in which half of the parties remained unaware of their participation.

Still, an envious voice — a darkly jealous whisper — wanted to know.

What would it feel like to be the intense focus of a man? To be the center of a desire so strong it rendered the afflicted with an inability to form simple words.

It was not for her — once Xavier deemed it safe, she would resume her journey toward the Northern Isles. It was what her mother wanted and still... still, she yearned. She didn't want to leave. Wanted to stay here with her new friends. Stay here with...

Her treasonous eyes flicked toward Gavyn.

He commanded the far side of the courtyard with Xavier, two kings surveying their kingdom. Neither one approachable from the serious bend of their faces, but fighters experienced and green stopped by for a quick word, each one given a measure of respect in return.

His eyes found hers.

The distance between them faded, and the warmth of the fire lit her insides despite its location twenty paces away.

Slowly, ever so purposefully, he raked his gaze over her. She wouldn't mistake his intentions this time.

This was no courtship, and Gavyn — stoic and unmovable, intense — was no courtier.

Another heated warning.

His focus was a weight, unexpectedly heavy, barring down on every inch of her. She felt every press of his perusal, starting with her mouth, as he tracked down to her chest, then lower to the very source of the warmth now cascading through her entire person, a heat, more like an inferno. A brand.

It was a claim. Different from the one he staked in Madam's shop. This one wasn't for the girls or the gossip. This was for them.

For the second time tonight, her feet rooted to the spot, only instead of being encumbered by ghosts of remorse, longing sewn them in a bed of desire.

She closed her eyes, her breaths fast and shallow. She couldn't prevent the onslaught of cravings.

She wanted the hard press of his lips against hers; she wanted the sharp nip of his teeth on her breasts and her neck and between her legs. Every exposed inch of her heated skin — she wanted him to cover it in marks — cover it in him. She was spinning in her need.

Cool liquid splashed her wrist.

Ember opened her eyes, momentarily confused by the heavy cup in her hand. She blinked once, then twice, and several heartbeats later, her vision cleared.

"—and check on the progress of the boar," Ada declared to the group.

"Doesn't like you, huh?" Jade asked quietly from beside her. She smirked over the edge of her cup and scanned the crowd as if she didn't expect a reasonable answer.

Before Ember could form a reply, Zoie stomped over, dried grass kicking up around her as she came to an abrupt stop. A water stain covered a good portion of her skirts, and she took two deep breaths, clenching her fists at her side.

"Hey, there." Jade wrapped an arm around Zoie and shook her head at the question on the tip of Ember's tongue. "Have you had anything to eat yet? Let's head over to check on the preparations for the meal."

"He makes me so mad." Zoie ran a hand through her hair. "I just..."

"Would you mind showing me where you pick most of your herbs and flowers for your tinctures?" Ember asked, hoping to distract her. She clasped Zoie's hand and dipped her head for Jade to pick up the threads of conversation.

"'Tis a wonderful idea," Jade chimed in, hooking her elbow through Zoie's. "We can leave after the morning rush in the market. I'll pack us a basket for lunch."

They lowered their voices, planning their adventure in hushed whispers and pulling Zoie into the scheming. She took another sip of her water and lost her thoughts in the memorizing sway of the flames.

"Care for a dance?" Jade's companion asked.

He stepped in front of her, blocking out the light from the fire, and offered his hand. His cheeky grin and jovial manners forced her ready acceptance.

The first notes of a lute drifted to her ears.

She dropped into a formal curtsy.

Her partner latched onto the tips of her fingers and brought them to his lips.

On the other side of the fire, couples twirled in time to the beat. The instrument's merry melody lifted her spirits, and for the first time this eve, a lightness entered her steps.

"I didn't catch your name," she said as he deftly spun them around the other dancers, relieved she could match the rhythm of the music.

"Dante, milady." He smiled down at her. "I've seen you at the training barn as of late. Are you visiting?"

Her head fell backwards with her laugh.

"No. I came to steal some fare off of Jade's cart, and they kept me." She nodded her head toward her friends.

"Ahh. A riveting tale, I'm sure." He slowed their steps and wrapped an arm around her lower back. Before she was certain of his intentions, he dipped her toward the ground. He pulled her flush against his chest and asked, "Would you care to share it sometime? I have patrol tomorrow after training, but we could walk around the village the following day."

"She's busy."

Dante released her and took a self-preserving step back.

"Another time then."

"You're needed on patrol," Gavyn growled the command, unable to control the bite, even with the safe distance between their bodies. "Find Erik."

As if to tempt his ire... as if Rowan had goaded the younger man, Dante snatched her hand and held it to his lips for a heartbeat too long.

Another growl filled his ears, but it did not dissuade the dandy from sending a parting wink before he joined the others around the fire.

Gavyn glanced down, half expecting fear... half expecting her signature dose of stubbornness. Instead, she greeted him with the same lust clouding his judgement. If there had been confusion or even uncertainty, he would have taken a step back.

They both would benefit from the space, but her lips parted on a prolonged exhale. Her chest heaved in time with his, neither able to draw breath quick enough to steady their wills. Not to mention, slow their heart.

She smelled of dew. Of sunshine and eagerness and innocence — not the naivety of what transpires between lovers — but a complete lack of fear where he was concerned. And she should be concerned.

The calm scent of lavender fought against the sweet hint of

vanilla, a common mixture favored by the girls, but on her, heightened by the heat of dancing, an aroma that cut out his knees from underneath his best intentions.

Because that's where he would start.

Kneeling — controlling her from under her skirts. Worshiping her like a queen, all the while owning her body and mind and pleasure like a possession.

His motives were far from pure, and his conscience screamed for him to turn on his heel, to leave her to enjoy the evening, but a voice — a dark murmur — had him sliding an arm around her waist. The same dark purr had him grabbing the mass of her hair at the base of her skull and tilting her head back for better access to the delectable length of her neck.

He wanted to press the entire length of his body into her softness; he wanted to sink his teeth into her pulse and her lower lip and the inner flesh of her thighs. Every. Single. Exposed bit of her skin — he wanted to shower in marks — make her his.

He was dizzy with need.

"Dance with me." He released his grip on her scalp and rubbed small circles with his thumb. Louder this time, he repeated, "Dance with me."

"Merry eve to you, too," she reprimanded and bit her lower lip. Her cheeks flushed under his gaze, and she wound her hand around his neck, toying with the tendrils of hair curling at his collar. "'Tis kind of you to ask."

He grunted.

She threw her head back and laughed. "Why, yes, Gavyn, I'd be delighted to dance with you."

The corners of his lips tugged into a flat line.

He'd been close. So close to dragging her back to his chambers. Crossing a line he'd never come near before.

The others, the sweet and simple companions from his past,

demanded their due — many satisfying releases, never affection — and rolled out of his bed with smiles on their faces.

Never once had he given into his primal need to control. To command complete surrender. To own. No one ever elicited that blackened side of him.

Until now.

He claimed her hand in his calloused palm and bunched the fabric of her dress with his other. The position brought her nose close to the center of his chest. He marveled again at their differences.

Now, light to his dark. The gods had blessed her with an infectious laugh, a pure melody arising from a kind heart. Her humor was the joyous spark of a mischievous water sprite, a bright contrast to his serious demeanor devoid of any light-heartedness.

Gavyn loosened his hold, wishing she wore a matching pair of leather cuffs, complete with an intricate inlay.

Another mark.

He needed to let her go.

The melody of the music changed, and a slow, mournful tune replaced the lively song.

Her hand gripped the back of his neck. She massaged the tight cords of muscle under her fingertips.

His chest loosened with her affections, and he tried to shake off the images of the dozen different ways he would take her.

She pressed her cheek against his chest and sighed.

Another growl rumbled through him. Followed by all the reasons he should stay away.

She was under his protection, a duty that wasn't a transaction. He'd never coerce her to trade her safety for the sake of his, their pleasure.

She was on the run. Sure, Rowan and Jade may lie to themselves about her length of stay in the village, but something unsettled her. And she wouldn't find it here, no matter how many chains of temptation they shackled around her.

She deserved better. Someone to match her spirit. Someone caring, full of peaceful smiles and without depraved needs. A man who was whole, unblemished… smart.

The sound of the music grew faint, and she relaxed against the steady rise and fall of his chest.

Their feet floated in time, and she tilted her head back, heavy lids hooding over hazel eyes.

She reached toward his face. Her hand suspended in air as if surprised by her sudden boldness.

Unable to watch the play of emotion across her features, Gavyn closed his eyes.

Two thudding heartbeats later, she traced the outline of the scar under his eye. Her fingers trailed along the thick skin, curving around its puckered edges. Faintly at first, then firmer as she traveled the path from the outer seam of his eyelid, down his cheekbone, and to his ear. Then back up and back down again.

She paused when she reached the sensitive patch in front of his temple, then cupped the sides of his face with both hands.

He relaxed into the subtle pressure, bending to her command.

Her breath tickled his cheek, and warm, pliant lips pressed against his scar.

His eyes flew open.

And for the second time tonight, she brought him to his knees. Only this time, instead of dominating her from below, he wanted to beg her to stay.

Gavyn stilled her hands with his, lifting them off the sides of his face. He took a step back. His mouth parted, but no words filled the space between them.

Cool air hit the front of his body, and he dropped both of

her hands. She moved to close the distance, but he shook his head.

Ember blinked, and for the first time since apprehending her in the market, she looked… hurt.

By gods, this wasn't his intention, but he couldn't find the words to ease her pain, to excuse his poor handling of the situation. So he did what he excelled at — he pricked her ire.

"Find Jade. And if you manage to keep your sticky hands off of others' possessions for an entire week, I'll take you and the girls to the falls."

Her shock of outrage lit a fire in his chest, burning off any residual guilt. He grunted, deepening the ruse, and pivoted on his heel to rejoin Xavier.

Later, when the roar of the bonfire died to glowing embers, he snuck into his chambers and leaned against the closed door. The increasingly familiar mixture of lust and longing slammed into him.

Gavyn stared at her.

Her dark locks fanned out on his white pillow. The moonlight spilling through his window illuminated the silky crown. Even with the paint worn off her lips, she resembled an enchanting temptress frolicking in the human realm. Not a displaced southerner hiding from her curse.

If he thought she was beautiful before in her shapeless clothes, dingy from her travels, now, wearing one of his favorite tunics, she was exquisite.

A goddess spread out on his bed, an altar, for worship.

A temptation which could only end in his heart shattering.

Gavyn removed his tunic, peeled off his boots and socks, and slipped in beside her.

She snuggled into his warmth and sighed.

He looked at her as if she were a dream, like she was the answer to his dreary existence — a solitary life he'd been thrilled to command a few weeks prior.

"What am I going to do with you?" He asked the quiet room, but he knew the answer. There was only one way he would survive her time at the compound. He kissed her temple and pulled her closer.

Somehow, Gavyn must find the strength to stay away, for both their sakes.

CHAPTER SIXTEEN

*man's heart is a deep well of secrets and lies. -Esabel*

EMBER SANK INTO THE OVERSIZED ARMCHAIR, A PLUSH extravagance Jade unearthed from who knew where.

It was a consolation gift, since Gavyn postponed their trip to the meadow. In typical Jade fashion, she coerced Dante and his friends to haul it from the village, up the steep path to the compound, and deposit it in Gavyn's spartan chambers.

She hugged her knees to her chest and ran her hand along the velvety gray fabric.

He couldn't complain. It matched the bed linens.

And it coordinated with the new tapestry, an intricate depiction of an ancient warrior in full battle armor. Set on a navy background with crisp silver stitching, Ada found it rolled up in storage under her bed.

The recent additions complimented the assortment of blown glass bottles and a couple of shallow containers Rowan brought her yesterday.

She staged them around the room, filling the tall-necked jars with liquid soap from Zoie and sprigs of wildflowers the cubs picked for her. The curved dishes held an ornate version of his leather cuffs, the ones he wore the night of the bonfire.

The week prior.

He was avoiding her.

Since Xavier restricted her movements to the compound, she spent a large amount of time in Gavyn's chamber. Alone, curled up in the chair with only a book for a companion. She was determined to read through Ada's entire library before Xavier cleared her for travel.

Gavyn left each morning before Ember woke from her dreams. The wrinkled, warm sheets were the only evidence he visited his chambers at night.

The grueling training schedule kept him in the barn at all hours, and coordinating the patrols stretched his time even further.

She stayed up each night, hoping to catch him sneaking into his own room, but fell asleep waiting for him to tuck in his bed.

So it was lucky, then, she stumbled upon the cache of novels, parchments full of poems, and an array of dusty texts her second afternoon in the loft. Ada gave her free rein of the library, a kindness she took advantage of, borrowing a new book every day.

She quickly discovered Ada's preference ran to dry mathematical text and whimsical romance novels, the latter full of stories which had Ember tossing and turning, twisting the blankets around her before slumber each night.

At least, that was the lie she told herself — it was the books, those graphic depictions of relations between head-strong heroines and mighty heroes. It had nothing to do with their dancing. Nothing at all.

She toyed with the upholstery tacks of the armrest, running the tip of her finger in a rhythmic circular motion over the dulled, hammered heads. Clockwise. Counter clockwise. Repeat.

She was confused, torn apart by the two sides of her mind constantly warring with each other.

The night of the bonfire she had felt alive — parts of her awake for the first time in memory.

She wanted to latch onto that sensation and relive it again and again. So that part of her, the half that logic imprisoned under lock and key — whispering, rationalizing *survival above all else* — was devastated: nothing more came of the heated waltz.

But the rational part of her, the part molded and shaped and guided by her mother's words, her endless lectures, knew it was for the best. Wanting was for others; wanting was for normal villagers who didn't have Faeblood running through their veins.

She'd fought this battle before, her mind and heart forging two sides of the same coin. The image of her mother on one face, her reflection in the mirror on the other.

Logic and desire. And somehow those two sides flipped and battled each other, convincing her t*hey* alone were necessary to survive.

Would it matter, would it really matter, to experience love only for it to be taken away in death? And what of living — fighting or fleeing to see another sunrise, by herself? Was waking up another day worth the price of not enjoying life?

She glanced down at the book in her hand, a dense volume detailing the history of the Castle and the geography of Morvak Mountain, as if it held the answers.

The text was heavy, bound in leather, and twice the length of her forearm. Its corners were bent and dog-eared, but the pages inside were crisp, as if no one ever read them... the book merely tossed around from move to move.

She asked Ada about it, the text calling to her day after day, but she always put it aside in favor of a more gratifying story.

Ada chuckled and told her Pigeon nicked it from a traveling nobleman. He thought it was hilarious to take something from them that someone painstakingly rendered but held little to no value to those who lived in the territories their entire lives. Whose very survival depended on the knowledge of the waterways, which were the lifeblood of societies, not the history of the mountain nor the settlers and people.

Enjoy, she'd said. *I have no use for Faeblood propaganda disguised as the world's most boring map.*

So it was with warning, Ember finally relented and borrowed the text, hoping to distract herself from another night of maddening privacy.

Ada was right — the first few chapters contained drivel, pointless blathering about pureblood lines, rights of the nobility, and some such nonsense about divine will for division of the peninsula.

She skimmed the headings of each, recalling her mother's many nighttime stories of the shortcomings of high society, and turned to the middle of the book.

The spine creaked, splayed wide open for the first time in years, and she gripped the edges, preventing it from closing. Now here was something worth noting.

In the dead center, the author had filled two pages full of color. Unlike the serious black and cream of the rest of the tome, he'd covered these two sheets full of life and movement.

She traced the outline of the large blue ocean covering the top third of the map, wondering about the location of the fishing community they'd visited when she was a child. Next to the village, her mother had found a small cove, where they'd spent several glorious afternoons wading and splashing and swimming about, looking for mermaids and other fanciful creatures of her imagination.

It was one of the few carefree memories of them together,

before her powers came to be and her mother's sadness over-shadowed their remaining years together.

Memory was a funny notion. Beguiling in the way future experience altered the perception of the past.

Looking back, she could see all the signs of her burgeoning gift. Signs she thought every little girl experienced. She remembered the feel of the salty water under her fingertips. How it warmed to her touch. How it swirled and moved effortlessly, easily controlled by a power absent in human children.

She closed her eyes.

Some days it was easy to recall the good times, the times they laughed and smiled at the mundane humor of everyday life. Other days, the harder days, she needed to tamp down the vicious part of her heart, the sliver that had yet to forgive mother's choices, her choices.

Would it ever get easier? This back and forth she experienced when mother was alive, and now, even in death? Surely, it must get easier.

Lies. As long as escape from her mother's heritage was not an option — a powerful blessing and a marked curse — she would never be free... she would never understand her mother's decisions, as she would never forgive herself for her actions on that fateful day.

She shook her head, unable to dispel the echoing spiral of negative thoughts.

On the western side of the mountain range, the highest peak yielded to smaller crests and valleys. A river carved through the terrain, so minuscule the map-maker didn't bother to name the confluence. It was a delta at its origin from the ocean, narrowing as it provided life to the southernmost farming communities in the peninsula.

The illustrator depicted the flow as a brackish green, counter to her memory of the vibrant turquoise blue river from her home territory, as if it were a scar on the otherwise verdant watershed.

Twenty. Twenty-one. Twenty-two.

She counted the farming villages large enough to earn black dots noting their locations.

Based on the distinct twists and turns of the river, she identified eight villages where they hid before her sixteenth year. And an additional four after, the last one a community where they lived for an unfathomable two years, housing a cottage which came close to being a home but now plagued her nightmares.

~

It was an hour after sunset when Gavyn finished in the training barn. With the patrols in order, he took a quick dip in the stream and ran out of excuses to avoid his chambers.

He stood before his own door two hours earlier than every other night this past week, hesitating to enter.

The tapestry was new.

A masterpiece depicting an old warrior of childhood tales, Jade had created the decoration one winter when the snow was brutal enough to force them into their homes for an entire week.

Idle hands, she'd said, *work against the gods if not kept busy.*

She'd given it to Ada as a gift, explaining she should hang it over her bed, the warrior ensuring she behaved in her dreams. Ada had claimed the man was a handsome knight or wicked villain coming to rescue her from her brother's well-meaning clutches.

If Ada passed the tapestry onto Ember, then the girls fully accepted her into the family.

She was making a home, or as Rowan teased him — nesting.

His brother added to the disarray by gifting Ember a dozen

of his handcrafted glass bottles. And another dozen of his clay pots. She scattered them around the room, decorating every available surface.

The cubs, at Rowan's suggestion, had brought her a bouquet of wild flowers and weeds, further playing into the scheming.

She carefully displayed each individual bloom, placing clusters of the bottles on the windowsill.

He didn't have the heart to tell her that the one she favored was also the one that made his nose itch.

Gavyn had simply moved it to the top of his chest of drawers, the farthest point from his bed, claiming the flower didn't need as much sunlight.

He found her curled up on the overstuffed armchair, her head in a book, oblivious to her surroundings. And for a moment, one prolonged heartbeat, he wished this was his real life; he wished she was there every night waiting for him to return from another grueling day of training.

He was exhausted.

Fatigue crept into his bones and settled around his joints. He was wary from worrying about the security of the borders, her safety outside the compound, and the uncertainty if word of them harboring a Faeblood spread beyond the village. His nerves frayed like fibers of rope asked to hold tight long beyond the stage of dry rot.

Surely, exhaustion was the reason it was so easy to give into these quiet dreams, wishes he never realized he had, and why they caught him off guard.

The extra nights he spent out on patrol, avoiding fae temptation in his bed, he often thought — or allowed himself to think in the stillness of the woods — what it would be like if she were his? If they truly belonged to each other. Not because of circumstance or Xavier's orders. What if she wanted to stay with him, Gavyn, the lowly fighter?

She glanced up from her book, a heavy text likely from Ada's personal collection, and something in her eyes unsettled him.

He crossed the room in quick strides. "What's wrong? Are you hurt? Does something pain you?"

"I'm tired… lost in thought." She choked out a halfhearted laugh and rubbed the backs of her eyes with her hands.

Ember was a terrible liar.

She was carefree and messy and full of life, but she couldn't tell a fabrication to save the gods themselves.

"Ember," he said, drawing out her name. "What's wrong? And don't say 'nothing.' You're rubbing the scar on your palm."

He noticed the small gesture, back when she lived with Jade, an obvious tell when something rattled her. Like Mikel, she would be a disastrous card player, though her weakness helped him now: despite the emotion she wore on her face, she seldom voiced her thoughts.

"'Tis silly, really," she protested. "I borrowed the most boring book from Ada's small library. I'm tracing the waterways along the map, reliving the years spent with my mother in the various farming communities in the southern territory."

She paused, not finishing the memory playing behind her eyes.

So he did something that made his skin itch, more so than her favorite bloom — he filled the void with his own words.

Gavyn crouched down beside her and pointed to the picture of the tallest peak and the rendering of the Castle underneath.

"Morvak Mountain," he said, recalling a history lesson first told to him while he was still in leading strings. "And at its heart, about a half a day's journey from the compound, home to the Castle. Generations ago, a foreign people invaded our shores. The families who live in the mountain protected the domain and drove the army back to the sea. Our forefathers pledged fealty to those saviors. As descendants, we continue to work the land, which includes maintaining a militia large enough to defend our borders."

He traced the edge of the peninsula.

"The fortress houses the nobility of the realm, with their elders forming the High Table. They write our laws. Govern our territories. Collect the tithe," he said through clenched teeth. "It's a balance."

He pointed to several homes on the right-hand page.

"This is my home, or was my home. The mining community. Xav and Ada were raised by a stern widow who never tolerated the shenanigans of her teenage son and the stray friend he dragged home. She was the closest example of a parental figure in my childhood." He sighed. "I grew up as the only son and heir to a not-entirely sober father who was angry with life, angry with fate for taking his beloved in childbirth."

She cleared her throat.

"We lived south of here." She pointed to the farming territory. "We moved around a fair amount, from community to community… avoiding… settling where my mother found work. Never in one place for longer than a couple of years."

She shifted closer, leaning her elbow on the armrest.

"I know something about being an only child," she said. "It was just my mother and me. For my entire life. Alone, I was the sole focus of her love and her attentions and her expectations. I'm unsure of your relationship with your father, but I know a little something about coming to terms with the infallibility of a parent, and owning my mistakes, especially those which amplified the fact that she was not perfect."

A soothing affection.

She rested her hand on top of his, the lightweight touch comforting, and traced his knuckles absentmindedly. The brushes were almost a tickle.

He had never held hands before, never knew he craved such simple contact. Gavyn rallied all of his control not to reach up and grasp her delicate fingers. What he wouldn't give right now for Rowan's amiable smiles and smooth words.

Because if he had the lyrical voice of a poet or even the honey-coated tongue of his brother, he would somehow find the correct words… all the right ones… the pretty ones, and let her know that *he saw her… understood her… she was clear as a cloudless day in his mind.*

"Listen to me blathering on about things you do not wish to hear." She squeezed his hand.

"Don't," he said, his voice deepening. "Anything you might say, anything you need to confess, interests me."

He hesitated, worrying he shared too much.

"Come, we're both exhausted. Let's go to bed."

He pulled back the covers and gestured for her to climb in first, needing her the farthest from the door.

As she passed by, her now signature scent of lavender and vanilla filled his nostrils, causing his heart to thump against his chest.

He settled down next to her and linked his fingers behind his neck, hoping the weight of his head would anchor them.

She grabbed the hem of the topmost blanket, pulled it up to his shoulders, and patted it in place. The action nearly unraveled his last vestige of control as it was the first time anyone ever tucked him in.

"Gavyn," she said in a soft voice. "Would you… would you take us, the girls and I, to the falls sometime soon?"

The risk was too great, and he regretted suggesting it so rashly the other day. How could he mitigate the threat on the journey? If they went during the day… if he arranged for a guard…

"It's… I really miss the water," she whispered and laid her head on his chest.

He hesitated at the longing in her voice, then said, "Aye."

All reasons for denying her vacated his mind.

CHAPTER SEVENTEEN

ater is flexible enough to bend time and strong enough to lift spirits. –Esabel

EMBER SAT CROSS-LEGGED IN THE MEADOW, RUBBING HER CHEEK against the soft fur of the kitten's head.

The morning after her plea, Gavyn returned to his room, sweaty from the pre-dawn training session, and declared he would take them to the falls.

Surprised, but too excited at the prospect of leaving the compound, she didn't question the sudden change in the day's plans.

A faint purring reached her ears, and tiny whiskers tickled her nose. Its brothers and sisters formed a pile around an exhausted mama, and every so often, a soft mewling noise accompanied an exaggerated yawn. Adorable.

Reluctant to leave the enchanting creatures, she placed the remaining kitten next to his mama.

As soon as she settled somewhere, she would adopt a mouser.

"I'll bring you back tomorrow." Ada rose and dusted off her skirt.

"Not a chance, Ada. And you are not to visit without Mikel. We need to get moving if we want to reach the falls by midday," Gavyn said, scouting the path ahead.

"Let's go up a ways." Zoie took the lead, cutting through the tall grass. "I'll show you where I harvest lavender and calendula."

Soon, the forest blanketed them overhead, its thick foliage blocking out most of the late morning sun. The temperature dropped from the dense shade. An earthy odor of moss permeated the woods, its plush green coating the northern side of the trunks.

"Over there. That's the Ceylon tree." Ember grabbed Jade's wrist, pointed to the glossy leaves of a small evergreen framing the path, and scrambled to the front of the group.

A small side branch snapped off easily. The syrupy taste of magic coated the insides of her mouth as she rolled the stick between her palms, applying steady pressure. The outer bark of the limb slowly peeled away. She removed the rest of the rough covering and handed the core to Zoie.

"It needs to dry for several days in darkness to bring out the full aroma."

Zoie waved the twig in front of her nose.

"You're right. This is perfect for my mulled wines." Zoie passed the branch to Jade. "It would work well in soaps and candles too."

"After drying, you can cut the inner bark into smaller sticks or grind it up with mortar and pestle." She broke off another shoot to take home. "Tis best stored—"

Crack.

The snap of a heavy branch ricocheted off the trees behind them. Dozens of songbirds took flight, chirping as they escaped into the safety of the skies. An eerie stillness slithered through the forest labyrinth.

She covered her mouth with her hand, quieting her attempts to draw breath.

"Jade, take them to the clearing up ahead," Gavyn whispered without looking back.

They dashed along the path until trees opened up. Jade led the group to a large pine on the side of the trail, gesturing for them to duck under the limbs.

"Wait here."

Ember parted the thick branches. The needles pricked the back of her hand as she peered through the small opening.

Two squirrels gave chase on the forest floor. Others scampered on bowed saplings, jumping from limb to limb. They knocked an acorn loose from their exuberance. It thudded against the forest floor.

Her stomach mimicked the sound as it dropped to her knees.

Gavyn was safe. This was his duty. He trained for this.

There was a faint tapping on her shoulder. Ada slid in next to her, pointing farther up the path to where he disappeared into the bows of a giant hemlock.

A second branch splintered in the distance, followed closely by a small *coo*.

Gavyn emerged and strolled back to them as if they promenaded around the courtyard after morning tea instead of fleeing from a potential threat.

"Let's continue on," he said, his voice tight. He gave a subtle shake of his head when Jade opened her mouth. "The hot springs are pleasant this time of year."

Her eagerness to see the falls, to see anything beyond the compound, made the deception easy to swallow.

The path turned rocky as it meandered up the side of a granite bluff, slowing their progress as they picked their way over rocky ledges and large boulders. Soon, a fine coating of sweat tickled the nape of her neck. She wished for the cool understory of the forest.

They rounded a switchback, the trail opening to a narrow valley. A rush of water filled the air. Ember was the last to clear the bend, and she sucked in a gasp.

An other-worldly enchantment.

Words couldn't describe the majesty of the waterfall before her.

Oh, she could tell the tale of a torrent of water cascading down a severe rock face, so high she must shield her eyes and tilt her head back to see its origin.

The flow struck several outcroppings on its descent, splitting the water into multiple streams. A vibrant blue-green, she imagined each new thread as a different hue, a strand of color separated from its whole before converging together, forming a turquoise pool at its basin.

Their path tucked behind the falls, and an enormous, boulder overhead created a sheet of water, a translucent wall curtaining off a cavern from the rest of the forest. From the rest of the world.

But even then, these words were… inadequate.

A different magic. This place was not something to be fought over or coveted. Hoarded. Mother Nature shared freely, something both humans and Faeblood could learn.

Wisps of spray swirled in the air, creating slippery footing on the trail.

At the far end of the tunnel, Jade and Ada slid down a flat boulder that led to a landing at the pool's edge.

She hesitated and closed her eyes, hoping the stillness of the cavern would calm her racing heart. The heat of Gavyn's chest warmed her back. Ember leaned against him.

In another time, another world, she imagined the two of them coming here, escaping the crush of the compound, the demands on his time. A place for just them… to relax, to learn each other. With his hands gripping her waist and the deafening rush of the water, the images flowed without restraint.

"Your turn," he whispered, his hot breath flitting across the shell of her ear. He gave her a gentle squeeze and patted her on the hip.

Curiosity pried her lids open. She scrambled to the top of the natural slide, scooting down to join her friends.

Midday sun reflected off the dazzling surface and glimmered like gemstones where water splashed the granite surround. Mist rolled down the cliff face, cooling the heat in her cheeks.

"Hurry. Take off your slippers." Jade beckoned her forward and rolled up the hem of her dress.

She removed both slippers and padded over to the edge with the others. The water was clear enough to see to the gravel bottom, where small fish swam in a school near their ledge and plants swayed as they darted in and out.

"It's warm," she said as she skimmed her foot across the surface. "It feels wonderful."

"The village elders say the gods blessed the pool." Ada kicked her legs back and forth, stirring up the gravel underfoot. "When we first came here, Xav held his breath and dove to the bottom to have a look around. Remember, Jade."

"Mmm, hmm."

"He found an underground spring. Said he could feel the flow from one particular boulder." Ada pointed to the deeper area near the base of the falls. "He burned his hand when he stumbled upon it."

"The hotter water from below mixes with the colder flow of the waterfall." Zoie skipped a small pebble across the pool. "The two combine to give us this perfect temperature that holds year round."

"It's marvelous in the winter." Jade stood and dusted off her hands. "Fresh snow blankets the path and steam from the pool hangs above the water in feathery clouds."

She pulled one arm, then the next, out of her dress, and before Ember realized her intentions, Jade let the gown fall in a puddle at her feet and dove into the crystal clear waters. She emerged, sending a small splash in their direction.

"Come on ladies, are you waiting for an invitation?"

Ada and Zoie shared a look and stood in unison, shucking their gowns. Unlike Jade's graceful dive, they held hands and jumped from the ledge feet-first. Ada bent her knees at the last minute, creating a large splash that rolled over Jade's head.

All three broke the surface, sputtering and laughing.

Not wanting to miss the fun, Ember reached behind her to undo the buttons of her dress.

"Hurry." Jade darted around the pool with long, graceful strokes.

The bottom fastenings proved stubborn, so Ember climbed back up the boulder and ducked into the cavern behind the falls.

"Can you help me?" she asked Gavyn, twisting at the waist to show her buttons.

She didn't miss the flare of heat in his eyes. Or his purposeful steps. If he wondered why she was disrobing, he didn't ask.

She couldn't form an answer if he did.

He tucked a strand of hair behind her ear, his fingers linger-ing. Warmth flushed her cheeks as he trailed a knuckle over the curve of her jaw, then down the length of her neck, then ever so slowly along her collarbone as if cataloging every small dip and valley.

And when she thought to look away — when the promise in the set of his jaw became something more, something primal — he spun her around to face the breadth of water separating their fantasy from the rest of their reality.

The rough fabric of the sleeve of his tunic grazed her bare

skin. Her dress loosened with each button he freed, but her chest tightened as if caging her next breath.

He skimmed the pad of his thumb down the column of her spine and in a gruff whisper he said, "All done."

She crossed an arm over the top of her gown, a scant moment before it would have fallen to the cavern floor, and turned around.

"Thank—"

His lips were on hers.

Hard. Demanding. Nothing like the gentle exploration heartbeats before.

No — Gavyn kissed like a starving man: hungry for the connection, ready to devour her whole. He tasted of rain clouds. Mint and a heavy intensity threatening to wash away her sense of self.

He dug his hands into her hair, tilting her head to deepen the kiss, with enough persuasion to keep her knees from buckling.

A week had gone by. Days of falling asleep, eager for his return. Silence. Nothing indicating the night of the bonfire affected him. Now, she could barely keep up with his need.

He growled and nipped her bottom lip.

"Go on. Have some fun." He took a step back and cleared his throat. "I'll stay here and stand guard."

She wasn't fully aware of how she made it back to the landing. Or how she slid down the boulder. The dress brushed against her calves as it slipped to the hard ground. Warm water curled around her as she lowered into its depths.

The first splash woke her from her stupor.

"Get everything settled?" Jade asked as she bit her knuckle, partially shielding her smirk.

Giggles erupted from the base of the falls.

"The waterfall is see-through, you know," Ada said.

"Leave her be." Zoie paddled to the rock ledge and offered a hand. "Are you able to swim?"

In answer, Ember dove underwater and surfaced next to Jade. The water flowed under her fingers and swirled around her. Warm. Comfortable. Home.

She skimmed the top with her arm, mesmerized by the ripples she cast.

"Every chance, I snuck out on the hottest evening to swim in whatever water wandered near our home. Rivers. Streams. Ponds. There was a lake with a cove perfect for a midnight dip near my last cottage. A sandy beach wrapped around the sheltered pool, a favorite of the farmer's kids. I snuck out of my bedroom window, paddling around until my arms grew tired."

She sighed and kicked off the bottom.

The rush from the water cascading into the pool was almost deafening the closer she swam to the base of the falls. She poked the sheet that hid the cavern, splitting the stream into two. Goosebumps rose on her arm from the freezing temperature, but she left her hand there, savoring the frigid bite.

There was a sharp tug of magic.

Not a quick, benign pull on a leash, but a more sinister yank on her wrist.

She took a deep breath, kicking hard underwater, and dove. *There.*

A stream of water, much warmer than above, encircled her forearm and yanked her to the bottom of the pool.

She swallowed a scream, preserving the precious breath she would need for who knew how long.

Ember kicked and thrashed and kicked some more, struggling to break the hold.

Just before the first sparks of panic ignited in her chest, the bond loosened.

She wasn't free, but the pressure eased enough, her mind calming enough, to relax.

Or maybe her magic recognized self.

Because here at the base of the pool, where large rocks the

color of summer wheat housed small crawfish and sprawling water ferns, an underwater geyser not only maintained the pleasant temperature for skinny dipping in winter but sent the echo of a cast into her palms.

Faeblood. The gods did not bless the falls. Nor Mother Nature.

This was ancient Fae magic.

She swallowed a gulp of water and kicked frantically toward the light.

"Did you feel the change in the temperature?" Ada swam over to her as she broke the surface. "I can't hold my breath long enough to swim down to the bottom."

She gulped down several ragged breaths and croaked out, "Yes. It… it was definitely hotter down there."

"I'm going to double back on our trail and check things out. Are you good?" Gavyn asked, shouting the question from the cavern.

"Aye. We are getting out now," Jade answered.

Someone was out there, watching.

Maia had tailed them as he ordered. Her signal earlier indicated all was clear. Still, his instincts roared that they were not alone.

Thankfully, a single path led in and out of the oasis, the one he scouted now. The far edge of the pool served as a spillway down a steep rock face, and the valley cradled the other side, making it impossible to carve another access through the mountain.

Gavyn slowed his steps at the switchback and climbed over the large boulders standing sentry at the base of the path. He crouched in crevices and kept his frame hidden behind various stone outcroppings, taking care to dampen his steps.

The sun cast rays from the west, and a gentle breeze chilled his skin. He steadied his breath and listened. Another faint *coo*, identical to the one in the forest. Still clear.

He sent two in return.

Silence flew on the wind.

When he was certain only forest creatures moved about in the meadow, he crept back to the pool to retrieve the rest of his party.

"I saved you some brown bread and a bit of cheese from Mr. Whitby's goat." Ember handed him a portion of the nooning meal the girls shared.

He grabbed her wrist. His lips closed around her fingers, and he enjoyed her wide eyes as he licked off the last crumbs.

Another time. Another place. He was done denying himself. Denying her.

He'd prepared to bolster his resolve to stay away from her once they returned to the compound — buckle down and somehow... control himself.

Not a chance. Not now.

Not after their kiss, or at least that's what he decided when he paced the trail in the cavern. Because no matter all the reasons he told himself to stay away, he still wanted her, and now that he had a taste, he meant to have all of her.

He pulled her closer. She sagged against him.

"Alright, you two." Zoie patted the small leather satchel and squeezed by them on the narrow trail. "I still need to gather some calendula from the meadow."

Familiar with the terrain, Zoie, Jade, and Ada scrambled over the rocks with precision. He alternated between shadowing Ember and stepping forward to assist her with the more treacherous passages.

"You need boots," he said, glaring at her thin-soled shoes.

"In my haste to flee my home, I didn't exactly have time to pack nor the means to carry all my belongings."

There it was — the subtle mention of her journey, her troubles. She hinted about it last night. Was she running from someone? Why was she alone? What happened to her mother? Gavyn stilled her with an arm on her shoulder and asked, "How long?"

"How long what?"

"How long have you been on the run?"

"What makes you think I'm running?" Ember hopped off a smaller boulder, and her skirts swirled around her calves.

"How long?"

She sighed. "A month before the market incident."

Someone shouted her name from the meadow, and she broke away, not giving him a backward glance.

He jogged after her. "Ember, wait—"

"There you two are." Zoie snapped off the head of a yellow flower and handed it to Ember.

"Back home, we used them for cooking and added them to our garden salads," Ember said and twirled the stem between her fingers with no sign of continuing the rest of her story.

"I dry them for my salves." Zoie picked two more. "The fighters use them for cuts and burns. I never seem to have enough to keep them supplied."

"How many do you need?"

"About this much." Zoie spread her hands apart in front of her skirts, the distance between her palms near the size of a loaf of round bread.

Ember cupped the flower in her palm and closed her eyes.

A single head doubled. Those two flowers doubled again. Four flowers turned into eight, and eight into sixteen. Soon, a pile of flowers spilled out in every direction.

He cupped the back of his neck. It was one thing to know she was Faeblood. Quite another to witness her powers.

"This will give me three or four jars," Zoie said as she removed a small cloth from her leather bag and wrapped it around the bounty. "I guess we won't need as much with you around."

Jade and Ada strolled over, each carrying a small assortment of purple flowers.

"Does your casting work with other objects?" Jade asked as she handed Zoie her bouquet.

"Yes. But magic has limitations. I can't—"

"Time to head back." Gavyn failed to smooth out the rough edges of his tone. "We need to return before dusk."

Falling gravel clattered on the trail behind them.

His head whipped around.

Forty paces from the base of the bluff, more stones tumbled down the rock face. He scanned the surrounding area, unable to pinpoint an animal responsible for the noise.

Where are you?

He placed a finger on his lips, extended his hand, and made a patting motion in the air.

The girls obeyed, slowly flattening out on the ground.

A rabbit shot across the trail five paces in front of him.

His heart thumped against his chest. He struggled to control his breathing.

Come on, come on. Where are you?

He narrowed his focus to the crevice where he spotted the first tumble of stones.

A chill ran through him.

They must have walked right by whoever hid between the boulders.

He pressed a fist on the ground in front of him and perched on the balls of his feet. Damp earth seeped around his knuckles, and the scent of vanilla and lavender served as an unnecessary reminder he wasn't alone.

He ticked off the distance in his head.

Thirty paces down the trail offered the protection of the

trees and a chance to stash the girls somewhere safe while he doubled back.

Twenty paces south—

A high-pitched whistle split his ear.

Maia's arrow thudded in the ground next to his boots. A warning.

Without looking back, he growled, "Run."

CHAPTER EIGHTEEN

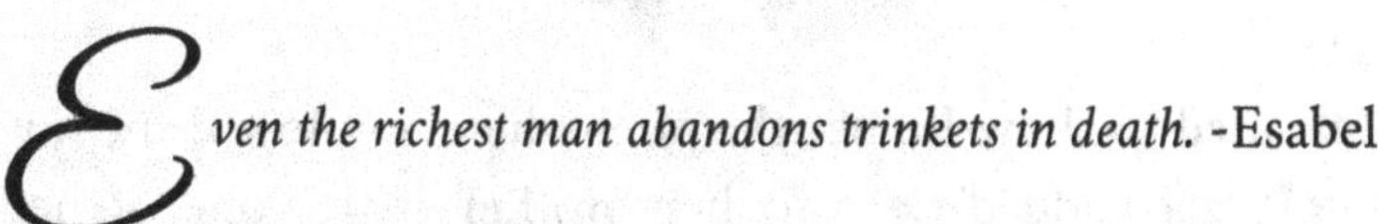

*E**ven the richest man abandons trinkets in death.* -Esabel

"WHAT THE HELL WERE YOU THINKING?" XAVIER BELLOWED.

The last time she graced his study, Ember found herself at the center of an interrogation. Now, Gavyn stood in her place and suffered his leader's displeasure.

Her heart still raced from their frantic run through the woods back to the compound.

Thankfully, they encountered nothing, nor anyone, along the way. But she quickly realized Xavier may be a bigger threat than whatever spooked Gavyn.

And whoever shot the arrow.

He sat in a chair behind his massive desk. The surface, free of parchment and other missives, gleamed in the light from the oil lamp, casting shadows under his tired eyes.

An involuntary shudder rolled through her at the heat in his glare.

Xavier linked his fingers and rested his thumbs on his lips, waiting it would seem, to a question she wasn't sure he wanted to hear the answers.

An apathetic confidant.

Mother never raised her voice. Her tone stayed... neutral, even when she was upset and even more so when Ember disappointed her. Or when one of her sad days took over. Those were the worst — the times when her mother was a ghost, present in the cottage but not alive.

She preferred Xavier's reaction because despite being intense, at least she knew what he was thinking.

The entire training barn knew what he was thinking.

While she was certain he would never lash out at her, she still took a small step closer to Gavyn but resisted leaning into his side.

"I wanted to show Ember the pool where you found the hot springs." Ada padded over to her brother with none of her customary exuberance and placed a palm on his shoulder.

"And I wanted a spot away from the compound for a picnic." Jade stepped forward and admitted, "We all wanted a bit of an adventure."

"Girls, this is my transgression." Gavyn cupped the back of his neck. "We spent the late morning hiking to Ashmere Falls. I felt someone following in the forest before the clearing, so I doubled back before we left the cover of the trees."

Jade's head snapped up. "You knew?"

"I wasn't completely sure, but I sensed a tail."

"And?" Xavier leaned forward, bracing his torso against the edge of his desk.

"I didn't want to run into him on the way back, so I let the girls continue on to the pool." Gavyn started pacing the center of the room. "Figured he might show himself while we stopped."

"We were... bait?" Zoie asked.

"You were protected. 'Twas strategic. With you at my back, I could search the path, maybe flush him out."

"Sounds akin to bait, Gavyn," Ada said, the hint of a smirk on her face.

"You should have told—"

"Why, I—"

"Silence," Xavier said. "We'll address your second mistake later. Continue."

"Second?" Ember asked.

"Second. He understands his first." Xavier's lips flattened.

Jade placed a hand on her arm and said, "We never should have left the compound until we were sure whispers of your abilities did not extend beyond our borders. Gavyn is a powerful fighter, but it is difficult for one person, regardless of skill, to protect a group our size in open terrain."

"Jade's right." Gavyn stopped pacing. "I should've—"

"Enough. It's done." Xavier rose to his full height. "Everyone out. Except you." He pointed to Ember. "You stay."

The girls hung their heads, dragging their feet on the way out.

"That includes you, Gavyn," Xavier said softly.

The fine hairs on the back of her arm rose.

"I'm staying," Gavyn said. "I need to hear this, too."

"Very well." Xavier dipped his chin, and to Ember he said, "I need to know if you are a threat to my family. Gavyn refuses to share your confidences."

Her eyes shot to him, but Xavier continued, as if he hadn't confessed to probing Gavyn for her secrets.

"Before, I entertained caution. Now, we know with certainty something is amiss."

How harshly would they judge her if she told them the truth? She deserved any ill will they felt. Would Gavyn look at her the same once he knew she was the reason for her mother's murder? She didn't commit the foul act, but it was as if she offered the rope that choked her mother's last gasps of life.

Aye. She would deserve it.

She focused on drawing breath, counting to steady the rhythm. One, in. Hold. Two, out. Hold. Over and over.

Gavyn took a step closer, and she shook her head. There was no way she could tell the tale if he touched her.

If he offered comfort, she might break.

"When you are ready," he coaxed as if speaking to a cornered animal. "We both need the information."

Ember hesitated, then swallowed.

"I caught the eye of the village elder. He started sniffing around this spring, after mother allowed… after I started venturing farther and farther from our home. She told him I was too young. Unavailable."

She cleared her throat.

"We lived on his land and paid our share of his tithing, either bartering services or with the small amount of coin we earned. Most consider it an honor to marry into the family. Her refusal… it was an insult."

Gavyn gestured for her to continue.

"We thought—"

Ember took another deep breath.

"She thought that was the last. Somehow, word of our rebuff spread in the community. Men of his stature don't tolerate rejection. Especially when others learn of the slight. He came back with his son. It was late, and they forced their way in. We could smell the mead on their clothing. Mother, she… she cast against them. Nothing harmful, just to subdue."

Ember closed her eyes and whispered, "We thought… she thought the drink muddled their minds enough to forget in the morning."

She bit back a sob.

"We were wrong."

Ember swallowed once. Twice.

"I found mother the next day. She suffered welts on her neck. I was too late. By the time I returned from the lake, her skin was cold to the touch." Her hands trembled. "I snatched the locket from around her neck and grabbed our satchel. Thought it best to stay hidden, considering the events from the prior day, so I shimmied through our small kitchen window and fled into the forest."

"Do you know if anyone followed you?" Xavier crossed his arms.

"I… I don't think so." Ember looked up at the rafters. "My travels took me through two, three if you include this one, other villages and no one from back home has bothered me."

She let several deep breaths roll through her chest. Should she tell them about the incident in the mining territory?

It was exhausting, keeping everything inside. Her entire life was one giant deception.

She had welcomed the surge of relief when they'd discovered her Faeblood.

Now, the heavy weight of another confession bore down on her.

Oh, mama. She had done this for her. For her, she had fled into the night, leaving everything she'd known behind, when her heart… her soul wanted to stay in their cottage. To lie down and welcome whatever punishment the farmer meted out.

Now, she brought danger to them all.

She could barely live with her mother's blood on her hands. If they hurt someone else… if Jade… or Ada… or Gavyn…

The guilt would tear her apart.

"There's something else…" She gritted her teeth. "I attacked a Red Guard. Back in the mining village. I stole some bread. The tavern keeper saw me and sent a squad. 'Twas an act of self defense."

"Did anyone see you?"

"No," she said and rubbed her palm. "No. I stayed hidden, but one man separated from the group. He was the one… the one I… And then I ran. I ran. And ran and ran."

"Did you use magic?" Xavier asked.

She nodded.

"She's been here long enough. They would have caught up with her by now. 'Tis little chance they would connect the act to any whispers of Faeblood. Or tie them to the farmer, the Red Guard."

"Agreed." Xavier came around the side of the desk and glared at them. "Do. Not. Leave. The. Compound."

Gavyn dipped his head and grabbed her hand, tugging her out of the study.

They reached his chambers without exchanging a single word.

She squeezed her fingers in a fist, wishing for some reaction, any reaction — his harsh accusations or grumpy one-word commands or poor attempts at jesting — than this damning silence.

Gavyn closed his chamber door behind them. He engulfed her in his arms before it snicked shut.

Dear gods, what she'd endured.

Unsurprisingly, words of comfort never came. He tightened his hold, any more and he would crush her. Perhaps this was more for his solace than hers. He rested his chin on top of her head and breathed in her scent.

He needed the bastard's name. Not the Red Guard, those nameless, faceless goons. They were all alike. All deserving of their fate.

He needed the farmer's name.

And a description.

But it was the last thing he wanted to bring up tonight, after the harrowing trek on the return journey home. After she spilled her story, placing her trust in Xavier. He was proud of her. It couldn't have been easy divulging the rest of her tale.

But it meant one thing — *she feels safe here. Protected.*

"Do you miss it?" she asked, her voice muffled by his shirt.

He stilled. "Miss what?"

"Miss home."

"Thoughts of home abandoned me long ago. My last trip back, two summers ago, the faces were unfamiliar. Few survive the harsh lifestyle of the mines to bear witness to the birth of their children's children." He sighed and said, "The men who dined with my father or found pleasure around our table playing cards no longer walk the land."

"Truly, no one remains? What about others closer to your years?" She asked as if he missed the connection.

He nuzzled the top of her head, and wisps of hair stuck to the stubble on his chin.

"There is a small schoolroom on the edge of the village. Its sole purpose is to corral the errant youths and prevent them from scurrying underfoot. A place to keep us out of the way until our bodies grew strong enough to join our families in the quarries."

He scoffed.

"My father cared little for an educated son and mocked those who wanted to further their minds. Instead of cultivating friendships, I spent my lessons resenting the confines of that small, dilapidated cottage and picking fights with older lads for entertainment. My mind struggles to recall the names and faces of others who shared those years with me."

She rubbed circles on the small of his back.

"I—" His voice cracked. "I didn't learn… I learned my letters many summers after we left home. Xavier discovered my short-coming late one eve when he asked my thoughts about a missive from the Castle. He handed me the parchment to examine its contents myself. I recognized his name and no more."

She hugged him tighter, as if he needed reassurance.

He'd never asked Ada for the odds on his downfall.

Short. They had to be. Ember was beautiful and kind and smart. Too intelligent for a dumb oaf like him.

And fall he did, as there was no other explanation for revealing his greatest weakness.

"I never went to school," she said. "We moved every other season when I was younger. When my gift emerged sooner than mother expected, she thought it was too great a risk to allow me to attend with the other children."

"She kept you away?"

"Yes. I was a danger to myself and anyone in the vicinity. Once I learned to control my casting… to channel it appropriately… we established a pattern of moving and hiding and isolating ourselves from neighbors. You rebelled with your fists. I bucked her authority by sneaking out and observing life from the shadows."

"That's no existence for a child."

His early years weren't idyllic, but at least he'd had Xav and Jade and Ada. And later, an entire family of misfits to share his days.

Ember sighed.

"'Tis a life. A safe one. In the manner she knew and felt appropriate. It's easier to conjure understanding through the lens of her death. I… I struggle with the guilt of my actions. If I had not begged her to stay the night before. Ignored her suspicions. If I had not wandered so close to the village elder's cottage…"

"My middle tightens, sometimes, when I imagine my father crushed under the stone. A heaviness settles here." Gavyn rubbed the bone in the center of his chest. "I wasn't strong enough to dig them out. I stayed safe in that school while the mountain crushed his body."

"And I swam in the lake to escape the sweltering heat of our cottage while spiteful hands strangled the remaining life from my mother. I cannot speak for your father, but my mother sacrificed herself to conceal my whereabouts. I imagine he would be grateful you did not suffer with him."

She cupped his face and added, "And a sense of pride for the life you built here."

Ember wrapped her arms around the back of his neck, pulling him down to meet her soft lips. She nibbled and nipped and teased his mouth open. Her tongue swept inside, and she moaned.

Aye. This woman would be his downfall.

She wasn't cunning or deceitful.

But she kissed like a thief out to steal his heart.

She could pluck all the jewels of the realm from his pockets, and he wouldn't be the wiser. Take the shirt off his back... the boots out from under him. He would be half-naked — barefoot and poor — and he would follow her like the pied piper she was.

It didn't matter if two separate parties hunted her. Not when she curled into his body, soft and vulnerable, whimpering his name. Not when the salt from her tears hit his lips...

Tears.

He wrenched his mouth free.

Under different circumstances, he would bang his chest at her stupor, the heavy lid of her eyes and the muss of her hair. Instead, he swiped an errant drop rolling down her cheek.

"It pains me to say it... but we must stop. I won't press my advantage when your sorrows haunt you."

She closed her eyes and swallowed.

He wanted to wrap her up once again, but a knock on the door stilled his movements.

"Who is it?" He ground out each syllable.

"It's me," Maia said. "I have my report. Xavier sent me to grab you."

"Understood." He ran his thumb along Ember's lower lip and

released a long, drawn-out sigh. "Get some sleep. I don't know how long this will take."

He crossed the room and rummaged through the trunk in the corner, returning with a clean shirt.

"Turn around." He made quick work of her buttons and kissed her behind the ear. "Try to rest. I'll return shortly."

~

Gavyn stormed into Xavier's chamber without knocking.

"Did we interrupt your beauty sleep?" The indentation in Rowan's cheek deepened. "Or perhaps something more exciting?"

He grunted.

Maia rolled her eyes.

Xavier's bed was disheveled. An empty cup rested on a chest of drawers in the corner. A few clothes hung from pegs near the edge, others in piles at the foot.

Gavyn had never spotted so much as a wrinkle on the top most covers.

Xavier worked too hard.

The dark circles under his eyes were more pronounced than normal. His hands ran through his hair more often. Xav wouldn't ask for help, thinking he could take on the world himself. Or worse, he assumed the responsibility of protecting them all without realizing none of them wanted a shield.

At the corner of the bed, a dog-eared miniature lay face down.

He didn't need to pick up the portrait to know who the artist depicted on the reverse side. He set eyes on the scene a few days ago when he journeyed to the marketplace to check on Jade, its match occupying the prominent space above her hearth.

Heavy footsteps echoed in the hall outside the chamber.

Xavier entered, fastening his leather cuff around his wrist.

"What news do you bring?" The dampness of his hair glinted in the torches' light. His shirt hung half-tucked, wet around the collar. With boots partially laced, he crossed the chamber and stood next to Maia.

"Gavyn pulled me aside after morning training and declared his intentions to take the girls to Ashmere Falls." Maia stood straighter. "He wanted me to follow at a distance for extra protection, so I stayed fifty paces behind them on the trail. At the bend in the forest, I found evidence of someone between us."

"The timing matches to when I doubled back on the trail." Gavyn crossed his arms.

"Whoever it was, he was skilled." Maia clenched her fists. "He covered his tracks well. It was by accident that I stumbled upon a mark left behind."

"Are you sure he was alone?" Rowan asked, his voice deepening.

"I cannot be sure, but I only found evidence of one."

"Did you pick up his tracks while they were at the pool?" Xavier placed his boot on the stool next to the small table and finished the lacing.

"No, I stayed at the edge of the forest. I thought it better to hide under the cover of the trees for the best vantage."

"Did you see movement on the hillside?" Gavyn ran through the events in his head.

"Yes. Before the gravel let loose, I spotted a form moving between the crevices. I lost him in the boulders and couldn't be sure you were alerted to his presence, so after you gathered the girls, I unleashed my arrow in warning."

Rowan wore a path on the wooden floor near the hanging bag.

"I didn't want to give away my location, so I stayed until the sun set behind the mountain. Finally, he rewarded me for my patience. But by then, darkness fell, and the clouds covered any light from the moon. I felt, more than saw, as he passed me on the trail."

"Were you able to follow him?" Rowan asked.

"At first, yes. His steps were light on the forest floor. I can't be sure how far back I was, but I tracked him to the opening in the glen near farmer Whitby's place."

Gavyn cupped her shoulder. "And after?"

"I lost him."

"Where?" Xavier asked.

"I can't be certain, but the evidence suggested he headed in this direction, near the barracks."

"He's clever. There is no way to track him among the congestion of the compound."

"Good work. Get some rest. And you…" Xavier pointed his finger at Gavyn. "Double the guards. I want them working in pairs. No one, and I mean absolutely no one, travels in or out of our borders without my knowing about it." He waved his hand at the group. "Dismissed."

CHAPTER NINETEEN

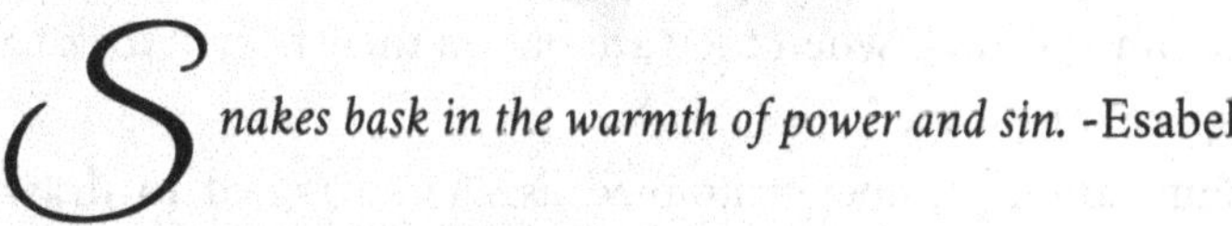

*S*nakes bask in the warmth of power and sin. -Esabel

"Bridge." Gavyn crouched down and repeated, "Bridge."

"I. Am. Trying," Ember said between clenched teeth. She bucked at Maia's weight, failing to leverage her legs underneath.

They trained for over an hour in the grappling pit.

Sand covered her arms and stuck to the sweat beading on her skin. It coated her hair, brushing off every time she shifted position. The dishevelment was a testament to her determination.

And her lack of success.

He off-handedly suggested the lessons in self-defense this morning, thinking she would turn him down in favor of curling up with another book. So, he was both surprised and pleased at her ready acceptance.

She might not subdue a genuine threat with a few hours of coaching, but he believed in every hour of preparation.

If he could train Rowan to throw a punch, then he could give her a few pointers.

"Relax." Maia clamped down on Ember's wrists. "You waste energy flailing around."

"I can't," Ember gritted out.

"Find the ground." Maia adjusted her hold. "Bend your knee and flatten your foot to push off. Good. Now push hard and hinge sideways at the hips."

Ember rotated to the side, the angle awkward, and Maia fell forward. "Again."

She repeated the sequence, and this time scooted out from underneath.

"Good," Maia said and sat back on her heels. "Remember, it's easier to pin someone when they are flat on their back. Work to create space for escape."

"Mmm, hmm," Ember mumbled as she struggled to draw breath.

"You're not done." Maia gained her feet and offered a hand. "We need to practice defending an attack from behind."

"Let me find my breath." Ember pulled herself up and dusted off her skirt.

Maia caught his subtle nod out of the corner of her eye. She pivoted, wrapping one arm under Ember's throat.

"You won't have time to think. Let alone catch your breath."

It was the first lesson everyone learned in the training barn — always keep awareness of your surroundings.

His tactics were harsh. But the methods had saved more than one life over the years. Plus, most fighters didn't require a repeat demonstration.

Ember clawed at the forearm across her throat. Her eyes widened, and her legs kicked out, connecting with solid air.

This was the hardest part. He wanted to intervene.

It was never easy letting any of his fighters fail. Harder to watch Ember struggle. Even more so, since she would likely succumb to the darkness before she could break free.

She'd suffer one hell of a headache, but if it taught her one thing… if it saved her in the future…

He'd gladly endure the lashing she'd give him. Probably Jade's, too.

A blast of air knocked him off his feet.

His right hip took the brunt of the fall. A sharp pain shot down his leg. He shook his head and tapped his ear, unable to stop the high-pitched ringing.

"I'm sorry. I didn't mean to…" Ember's words reached him as if they traveled through swamp water. "I don't remember the last time I lost control of a cast."

He turned his head to the right, and his vision followed at a more leisurely pace.

Ember cupped the sides of his ears, her hands warm.

Several loud heartbeats later, the ringing subsided while the noise of the training barn rose. She repeated the cast for Maia.

"—don't be sorry. Whatever you did. Well… do that if someone tries to grab you." Maia brushed off the back of her leathers, chuckling as she rose, and rolled her shoulders. "When you are ready, let's try that again."

"Again?" Ember hugged her elbows.

"Of course. You need more practice. Only this time, I volunteer Gavyn." Maia pointed at him. "I bet he will fly farther."

"I'll take that bet and raise you a week's worth of washing." Rowan ambled up beside Maia. "Two weeks if he screams."

"Alright. I'm sound. Let's try again." Ember sighed.

Gavyn moved behind her, pulling her flush against his chest. She was warm and snuggly and with the fuzzy wads of cotton stuffed between his ears, he couldn't remember why they didn't spend the morning in his bed.

He hooked her neck with his other arm.

She grabbed his wrist with both hands. Ember smelled of

salty sweat and northern forests — a combination of persistence and the soap she borrowed last night. He told himself he would not lick the spot behind her ear. Not when they—

A rush of air billowed him backwards. He landed two paces in front of the sparring ring.

"Noooo." Rowan tilted his head back, calling out to the ceiling.

"No washing for a week." Maia danced an impromptu jig, flinging her arms in the air.

"Let's try that again." He regained his feet and shook his head. "You good?"

She bit her lip and nodded. "Shouldn't I be the one asking you that question?"

He smiled, the gesture stiff and likely with too much snarl, but he couldn't prevent it any more than the hands on her hips yanking her closer.

"Again," he murmured against her lips.

"Are you trying to distract me? Catch me off guard once more?"

She flicked her tongue against his mouth. His hold slackened. She took advantage of the whisper of space between them and placed her palms on his chest. He bent to—

Gavyn launched through the air a second time.

Rowan's hearty guffaws and Maia's lighter chuckles filled the training barn.

He stood, rubbing his backside.

Ember dipped into a small bow.

Why the little—

Gavyn lunged.

She only made it a few steps before he caught her in chase.

His heart lightened. How was it one moment she kindled his worries, and the next she made his head spin? It still spun when he wrapped his arms around her.

"You little minx. Come to fight night with me?" He buried

his nose in her hair. "Not ringside, and I want you to avoid the bar... but you can assist Jade at her cart. I'll send Eigen as guard. Say yes."

HOW COULD SHE REFUSE HIS PLAYFULNESS?

Fight night was difficult for her. The sights and the smells. The blood. Her powers humming too close to the surface.

But she couldn't resist this side of him.

Gavyn, lead fighter at the compound, head trainer of Morvak's militia, a man more grumpy than a bear awoken too early from hibernation, was charming her.

The tip of Ember's shoe slipped on the gravel path.

"Don't fall." Eigen shifted his load to one arm and supported her with his free hand. "It would displease Gavyn."

"Thank you." Ember secured the basket and followed Jade into the training barn.

The entirety of three villages must be present.

Zoie pulled taps for a line of eager patrons five-deep, while Rowan served customers at one end of the bar, and Maia handed out overflowing cups at the other.

They reached Jade's cart as a roar rolled through the crowd.

Ember raised on tiptoes to glimpse the action in the center ring.

The victor stood on the lower ropes. He pointed to his fans and beat his chest.

A volley of shouts and cheers lobbed from his section of the mob.

His opponent, though, slept on the floor, a cornerman cradling his head and slapping him on the cheek.

Get up. Get up. Get up. She shuddered and rubbed her warm palms.

"It's... it's busier than the last." Her voice squeaked. *Please get* up. *Please get up.* "The coin should be heavy with a crowd this size..."

Please get up. Please get up.

A low groan from the ring rewarded her pleas, and she closed her eyes, exhaling.

"Look over there." Jade wrapped an arm around her middle and pointed to the opposite end of the barn.

A small wooden dais took up most of one corner. The timber was light, fresh.

Two men in heavy, blood red robes sat in high-back chairs. One pointed at the center ring and leaned sideways to speak with his companion. At least a dozen Red Guards stood sentry. Their eyes scanned the action, never settling on the main entertainment.

She shrunk down.

"The one on the right is Lord Siodina." Jade's eyes narrowed. "Why is *he* here? It's uncommon for a member of the High Table to leave the Castle. I'm uncertain as to the identity of the other."

"Why do they choose to remain in the fortress?"

Jade laughed and tilted her chin.

"They find us... uncivilized. Peasants. Worth notice during the collection of the annual tithing and little else. Our dress is too plain. Our manners barbaric. Though I suppose if servants obeyed my every whim I might develop airs, too." She sashayed in front of her cart, lifted the edge of her skirts with one hand, and gifted the confused patrons nearby with a mock wave of the other.

Ember stifled a groan.

"Several times a year, they show up unannounced to survey their *investment*," Jade said.

A line of customers surged forward and demanded their attention, and all thoughts of the visitors fled her mind.

They worked for over an hour without a break until someone shoved a cup of water under her nose.

"Drink." Eigen eased in beside her and handled the next patron's order.

She took a long sip.

The ring was empty, but the noise from the crowd grew, a mixture of jeers and taunts.

Erik ducked between the ropes, Gavyn trailing.

"This is Erik's first fight night," Jade said as she condensed the remaining items on the empty shelves. "Ada mentioned his struggles in training."

"Why put him in there, then?" Ember wrinkled her nose. "Doesn't seem sporting?"

"I don't know, but she seems to think it will help with whatever problem Gavyn can't solve." Jade exchanged a slice of the crusty brown bread for coin. "It happens every so often. Some men under-perform in training and need the rush of an actual fight. Relax. Gavyn knows what's best. If he thinks throwing Erik in an actual fight will help, trust Xav and Ada to line up a smart first match."

"I hope that's the case." She wrung her skirt. "For his sake."

The bell signaled the start of the round, and the noise of the crowd boiled over.

Erik's opponent threw the first punch and followed it up with a hook to the head. He blocked both blows and circled out.

The other fighter attempted the same combination again and dropped low, lunging for Erik's midsection.

At the last moment, Erik stepped to the side, dodging the strikes.

"He needs to take control of the pace." Jade wrapped an arm around her. "I can't tell if he is toying with him like Mikel or is just uncomfortable up there."

"Both." Eigen shook his head and served the next customer in line.

The match continued much in the same way it started. Erik

dodged or blocked any strike thrown his direction without returning much of his own.

The bell rang out, ending the round, and more boos than cheers followed.

She finished the rest of her drink and turned to the next patron in line. "And here's your—"

A roar rolled through the crowd and her eyes shot up. "What happened?"

Gavyn cupped Erik's head with one hand and slapped him on the back with the other.

His opponent sat dazed in the other corner, blood gushing out of his nose.

"Erik woke up. Stay," Eigen commanded. He sprinted across the barn to the betting platform, jostling the rowdy crowd with his thick frame.

Five, maybe six, men climbed the edge of the stage.

Ada huddled behind Mikel while her guards struggled to control the mob.

One man made it beyond the first set of guards, only to sail off the platform when he came too close to Ada.

Eigen bounded up and subdued two men trying to break the line.

"What's going on?" she asked, resting her hand over on the swell of her chest.

Jade turned to help the next customer, handing out the last of the pork.

"My guess… the odds were high for Erik to lose." She pointed to the chaos of the betting area. "The visitors bring more spectators. More spectators spell more trouble. It took years for Ada to convince Xavier to add the thrill of wagers to the fights. He will stomp around the training barn like an angry bull for weeks after this mess."

They circled the cart to get a better look.

With Eigen in the mix, the mob settled back down and

stopped climbing onto the platform.

A few more minutes passed before Mikel let Ada out from behind him to resume her bookkeeping.

Ember sagged against the cart and turned her focus back to the center ring.

Gavyn dipped between the ropes and stripped off his shirt, flinging it behind him.

He shook out his arms and completed a lap around the enclosure. In the front row, a trio of ladies screamed and leaned against the edge of the platform.

"I didn't know Gavyn was fighting again." A tinge of darkness unfurled in her belly at their antics. She rubbed her breast bone, attempting to ease the discomfort.

"I'm as surprised as you." Jade frowned and tipped her chin toward the Lords. "I'm guessing this has something to do with them."

Gong.

Her heart plummeted in her chest.

The other fighter was quick.

Pale and slight of build, he let loose a series of punches and darted around the ring.

Would it be like this every time? She could scarcely draw breath. Gavyn would mistake her worry as an insult to his abilities, but he wasn't the one standing idle, sequestered in the background without means to help.

He kept his shoulders square to his opponent and unleashed a series of three punches. The first two missed their target, but the third found a home on the other man's midsection.

His opponent absorbed the blow and sent a counter strike.

Gavyn blocked the hook, circling out again.

The back-and-forth exchanges continued for the next few minutes.

Seconds prior to the end of the round, Gavyn opened up a

gash on the fighter's forehead. The blood trickled down his temple and dripped on his bare chest.

"Any pies left, honey?"

She tore her gaze from the center ring.

Two men stood in front of Jade's cart. Both wore blood red tunics under a thin layer of protective mail, the color of the shirt more disconcerting than his preoccupation with her chest.

"We are out, but a few slices of bread remain." Ember crossed her arms and kept her tone flat.

"That's not what I want." He took a step closer.

"My apologies, sir. If you'd like, I can look underneath and see if we have some jam." She turned, but a gloved hand wrapped around her upper arm, yanking her back.

"I said, *that's not what I want.*" He squeezed. Hard. The man sneered as he pulled her against his side. "How about instead of some meat, I take you instead?"

Rank breath stuck to her ear.

She shuddered.

Up close, he reeked of leeks and day old stew. His companion let out a throaty chuckle beside her.

Her strength could not match the brute, but casting a protective shield with the Lords in attendance would endanger them all. There were too many bodies. Too many witnesses.

She scanned the room. Where is Eigen? Their guard remained on the dais, subduing the rowdy crowd.

She tilted her chin and met his vulgar stare.

The Red Guard were creatures borne from nightmares.

Men. They were only men, she'd told herself when they haunted her sleep.

A physical embodiment of the High Table's corruption, she feared them more than the two Lords on their throne.

And they would bleed like men, a dark voice whispered.

Her vision blurred at the edges, but her hearing sharpened.

He smiled, and brown teeth, the result of inner rot and poor hygiene, greeted her. His tongue darted out between the incomplete rows.

A plan formed in her mind, a foolish one, but she had no other choice.

The Red Guard tightened his grip and steered her toward the dark corner behind the cart. His friend lugged a kicking and snarling Jade beside them.

This wouldn't work if they stayed too close to the crowd.

So she screamed. High-pitched and raw, a fraction of air escaped her lungs before he slammed a hand over her mouth.

He yanked her around, changing direction.

And headed for the back door.

CHAPTER TWENTY

I ntimacy is being seen; avoid it at all costs. -Esabel

Gavyn's chest heaved.

The wiry fighter was harder to take down than expected.

His opponent slumped on a small stool in the corner under the care of his cornerman, blood gushing from his forehead and running into his brow.

He wasn't in the mood to savor his victory, instead scanning the crowd for Ember.

The spectators closest to the ring continued to shout and raise their fists, the words lost to the general din of the barn.

Where were they?

His eyes kept glancing back to their station next to the bar as if they would materialize with each pass. Someone packed up the cart for the night. It was a skeleton of empty shelves in the quiet, abandoned corner.

Lord Siodina sneered in his direction but quickly schooled

his features when Xavier approached. Good. Let him distract their visitors, so he could continue his search.

There.

Eigen's shoulders wedged through the back door.

Gavyn's heart lodged in his throat. He didn't spot the girls, but Jade's guard would lead him to their whereabouts.

He leapt off the stage and gave chase — toward the back wall, toward the rear door, reminding himself Eigen was with them.

The crowd surged around him.

His breath thinned. The voice who normally counted his steps in the ring, the one who steadied his pulse between rounds, howled.

He kept his entire focus on the back door.

Ten steps until he reached the outer wall.

Five if he lengthened his stride. Each thump registered on his bare soles, the pain distant in his mind.

Four heartbeats pounded in his chest.

Another two skipped when his hand pushed on the lever.

He sucked in one breath before icy rage consumed him whole.

A Red Guard pinned Ember to the ground.

Her legs and arms flailed.

Someone screamed far away.

He couldn't determine its owner over the roar in his ears, a battle cry originating from the guttural depths of his lungs.

Gavyn lunged for her captor. The nameless, faceless man who dared touch her. He tackled him to the ground and climbed on top of his chest, pinning him underneath his thighs.

He let his anger channel through his fists.

Bones crunched. The skin on his knuckles blended with torn flesh of the guard's face, so much so, he didn't know where his hand ended and the man's nose — what was left of his nose — began.

He didn't remember hitting him again, even when pain spiraled out from his bruised knuckles.

Gavyn pulled back his fist, but the guard's eyes rolled back in his head, stilling the strike.

"He's had enough, Gavyn," Ember said, her voice small and timid. She placed a trembling hand on his arm, and it took all of his control not to lay into the unconscious Red Guard once more.

His chest heaved. She should never be afraid. Ember experienced enough fear for two lifetimes.

Eigen cuffed the back of the other guard's neck and dragged him over. His face was the color of puce, and as they marched closer, a slight limp encumbered his left leg.

"Only two," Eigen said, answering Gavyn's unspoken question.

She whimpered, the sound soft and terrified.

He dropped the bunched tunic and moved off the body before he registered the choice.

"Ember." The name ripped from his lips, full of anguish and concern and a small amount of regret that she witnessed this side of him.

Blood and sweat coated his bare chest. Some from the match, more from the guard. Rivulets swirled together, staining the waistband of his trousers.

Her eyes widened, and he hesitated, following her line of sight.

He left the man alive, unrecognizable, but breathing all the same.

Gavyn raked his gaze over her, snagging on the red welts peppering her upper arm. Heat curled up his spine and wrapped around the back of his neck. The tiny bit of satisfaction he gained vanished, leaving him achy and hollow.

He wanted to do it again.

"I'm alright." She wound both arms around his neck and locked her hands together. "Gavyn, I am sound."

He didn't trust his voice — wasn't ready to apologize for his barbaric response. May never be. Gavyn wasn't sure he could feel remorse.

He wasn't sorry, at least not about this. There were too many times in his childhood when he was too scrawny to intervene… too weak to make a difference… He may never be ready to apologize.

He shook his head.

Her fingers massaged little circles at the base of his hairline, and she pressed her chest tight against his, repeating, "I'm sound."

She should be running and screaming.

He leaned into the touch, a gift — an understanding — one he didn't deserve. When his chest stopped heaving, he nodded to Eigen and said, "Take Jade."

He grabbed Ember's hand and pulled her through the forest.

"Gavyn, slow down. I'm fine, but I didn't sprout long legs in the time between now and when you dropped me off at Jade's cottage this afternoon."

The tic in his jaw appeared, the throb lending movement to his lower eyelid. She was… jesting. He whipped his head around and repeated, "Fine?"

"Yes, fine. Jade and I had everything under control." *Mostly* hung in the air between them but she was wise enough not to say it out loud. She crossed her arms and tilted her chin.

"Fine is not being forced into the night, Em-ber," he said as he ran his hand through his sweat-soaked hair. "Two goons running off with you is not *under control.*"

"I was in complete control," she ground out as if reiterating her delusions would make them believable. "Thought it best not to cast. I didn't want the scrutiny of the crowd, nor the trouble it would bring."

"Trouble?" He barked out a laugh and stepped closer, leaning down. "You've been nothing but trouble since the moment you set foot in this village."

"Is that how you see me? As trouble? A nuisance?" Her hand flew to her chest. "That's what I am to you? Something that doesn't fit with your tidy and ordered existence?"

She stormed off in the opposite direction.

"Not anymore," she threw over her shoulder, twigs snapping underfoot. Her elbows swung in an exaggerated arc, propelling her away from him.

"Wait," he pleaded and grabbed her arm. The look she cast at his fingers would have burned the entire forest down. What was he doing? He immediately let go, raising his hands in surrender. "Wait, hold on. That's not what I mean. Please…"

"What do you mean?" she asked, refusing to face him, but her voice softened.

Clouds, heavy with rain, blocked out light from the night sky.

He wished he could see her face.

Slowly, ever so slowly, he closed the distance between them, letting his footsteps declare his intentions and giving her the option to turn away. When she didn't move, Gavyn wrapped his arms around her from behind and rested his chin on the top of her head.

"What do you mean?" She sagged against his embrace.

He rubbed his check against her silky hair. It took effort not to blurt out more harsh words, hide behind the role of brute fighter and trainer. But she was not his charge, so he softened the truth and said, "Misfortune nips at your heels."

Her spine snapped straight. She pushed against his forearm.

By gods, will he ever get this right? He wasn't above pleading at this point. The aftermath of the fight and confrontation with the Red Guard still crawled along his skin, a paltry excuse for his stumbling even to his own logic.

"Please, hear me out." Gavyn tightened his grip. "Whether it's coincidental events or unfortunate circumstances, hardship chases your existence. The evidence makes it impossible to deny."

He turned her around, and the corner of his lips tugged up in a small smile.

"You stumble into our village on the lam, a half-starved waif. A dagger shows up on the heels of your arrival, and a simple picnic at the falls turns into another game of cat-n-mouse. Even worse, your arrival disrupts my well-honed routine."

"Your life is boring." Ember blew a lock of hair out of her face.

"Aye, before a little thief entered my village, I led an agreeable existence." He tilted his head down and nipped her lower lip. "I suffered a strict situation."

He slid a finger under the collar of her dress, hooking the hem of the fabric. The material slid down her shoulder, and he nibbled the exposed skin.

"A neat and disciplined state of affairs."

"Dull." Ember whimpered.

Gavyn smiled against her skin. "Drab." *Kiss.* "Dreadful." *Kiss.* "Grim." *Kiss.*

He was not wrong about her; she was trouble.

Worse, Ember wasn't even trying.

Every time he told himself to back off, stay away and try to keep things platonic, she crossed that invisible line he drew in their lives. She burrowed on his side of the boundary. From the very first moment, she dug a tunnel under his well-meaning intentions.

Now, she carved out a place for herself. In his room. With his family. She was dangerously close to taking up residence inside his chest. What else would one call it — that ache, a dull throb — when she wasn't around? As if he was her home or she was his missing limb.

He couldn't find the words to describe it. After the mayhem of the eve, it wasn't the right time for declarations, either.

"Gavyn," she moaned as she gripped the back of his hair. "Please."

She didn't know what she was asking for, not entirely.

He backed them through a small opening in the brush, guiding her to the banks of the stream. She floated in front of him, her feet touching the ground every other step. The rush of water drowned out the voice in his head, the one cautioning him on the folly of his desires.

"You have a choice." He knelt down in the grass and curled one hand around her calf. His thumb caressed the back of her knee and traveled along the gentle lines of her ankle. He slipped one shoe off. Then the other, massaging the ball of both feet. Her undergarments followed, landing next to the pile. "We both need a bath. If that is your wish, I will leave you now and we will clean in privacy, separately."

He stood and unbuttoned her dress.

"'Tis the smart choice, the safe one," he said as the gown fluttered to the ground. She turned around, placing both hands on his chest. "The correct one."

"What if I don't want safe, not tonight?"

He stroked a finger along her jaw.

"Your other choice… is for me to take all your choices away. I want to own you, your pleasure," he whispered darkly. "I want complete control."

SHE SUCKED IN A GASP.

I want complete control.

Control. The word didn't scare her as it should. Perhaps it's because she didn't understand it fully.

She'd bucked her mother's authority her entire life.

Even now, given the freedom to wander the compound, to take part in new experiences… she knew the choices were a carefully crafted illusion. Safe. Ember could sum up her entire life as safe. Controlled.

So it surprised her when her first reaction was… curiosity.

"Explain it to me."

"Come," he said, his voice deepening. She stepped forward, her body obeying without thought. The hairs on his chest tickled her nipple, and Gavyn growled, placing both hands under her bottom. He hoisted her up, encouraging Ember to wrap her legs around him. "How does it feel?"

"Mmm," she replied. While she adored it when he carted her around, she had a niggling sense that wasn't what he asked. "How does what feel?"

"When I give you instructions, orders?"

That. She'd never given it much thought. Most of the time, she wanted to roll her eyes or stick her tongue out at him. Perhaps shake him a little to get him to kiss her. But when he lowered his voice… when his eyes grew stormy… she didn't want to think at all.

"I like it," she whispered to his chest.

"I like it, too. But with you, I *crave* it." He tucked a strand of hair behind her ear. "I want control of your body, our mating, but it's important you understand you are in charge. One word from you, a simple 'no' or 'stop' and it's over. Look at me, Ember."

Her eyes snapped up.

"Tell me."

"Yes."

"Yes, what…"

"Yes, Gavyn. I understand. I want you. I want this—"

His mouth slanted against hers. Hard, unyielding.

Desperate.

Her body melted into his. She whimpered as his tongue

continued its assault. Gone were the sweet kisses, the playful nips of a lover, replaced by a need so raw, so intense, she registered the faintest hint of fear.

She didn't lie — she wasn't afraid of Gavyn, never of him or his needs. She feared how much she wanted this — how much she wanted the promise of mind numbing oblivion.

And right now, she didn't want to think why.

The world spun around her as he laid her gently on the soft earth, pinning her to the ground. His hips ground against her core

"Don't stop." She crossed her ankles at his lower back, needing him closer. "Please don't stop."

Gavyn lifted his mouth and grabbed both of her hands in one of his. He pinned them above her head and nipped his way down the side of her body.

"As much as I love to hear you beg, one day you'll trust me enough not to doubt my intentions. Until then, swallow the words. Keep your hands here," he demanded, squeezing her wrists.

She arched her back, seeking his touch.

Here, by the banks of the stream, the forest opened up, allowing a sliver of light from the moon to peek out from behind the clouds.

She was naked, her skin pebbling from the cool night air, the anticipation.

The light glinted off of his chest. *My fallen angel*. Tonight, he was a demon sent to tempt her from her troubles. From the look in his eyes, he meant to take her far, far away.

She squirmed under him, enjoying the delicious pressure of his hand at her wrist — the safety it created and a chance for her to let go. Wetness pooled between her legs.

Before she could draw breath, Gavyn swirled the tip of one thick finger in her cream then plunged it inside. He added a second, and she pressed her chest against his. Fingers dug into her thigh, and through the haze, she realized her wrists were free.

She wanted to touch him. To give him as much pleasure as he gave her. Her hands made it halfway to his hair before he grabbed them once more.

"This is your last chance before I stop. Keep. Them. There." He nipped along the soft dip of her waist, soothing the sharp bites with his tongue. "This is what it means to be mine. To be under my control. It won't be simple — I will push you, and sometimes demand more than you may be able to give. Remember, one word from you stops all of this."

His head disappeared between her thighs.

"Now, let me see you. See how wet you are and what a good girl you've been."

It was unnerving having someone studying her so... intimately.

She wanted to squirm under his scrutiny. Wasn't sure she could lie there for much longer without disobeying his command.

The tip of his nose nuzzled her hood, teasing the throbbing nub inside, and just when she thought she'd break from the tension, he lapped at her heat.

His thumbs spread her folds apart. He licked her seam up and down, up and down, until the urge to squirm resurfaced, only this time it wasn't from shyness. He covered every inch of her, thrashing his tongue at her core between leisurely licks. It was as if he wanted to worship her — put her on a pedestal and take her down to play whenever he wished.

Warmth and pleasure melded together, and she arched against his mouth. It was easy to escape into the sensations, easy to forget about her day. A rewarding chase to an unknown peak, with the only requirement to follow his lead.

"Not yet, sweetheart." Gavyn pulled back. "The first time you come, it will be around me."

He stood and stepped out of his pants, stroking his length.

Her eyes snapped to him — pure wickedness, all hard and thick and weeping for release.

The tip swelled and throbbed as he tightened his grip. A dark flush bloomed over the head, spreading toward the shaft below. A ridge ran the underside, and she wanted to lick the thick line.

"Tell me you want this. That you crave me as I crave you."

Shudders raced across his shoulders, and he positioned himself between her legs. He captured her hand and wrapped it around his tip.

A bead of moisture formed at the slit, and she used her thumb to spread it around as she gripped his length.

"The words, Ember."

"Yes, Gavyn… please. I need this, too."

He positioned himself at her entrance. Gavyn hesitated. "I worry about you, but my fears have no place between us. I want you, not as your protector. Not for your pretty face or lush curves. Not for the simple release our bodies demand. You make me… feel… and for that alone, I crave you night and day."

"'Tis the same for me."

He thrust inside as if her words were the admission he sought.

His thickness stretched her inner walls, sending a jumble of relief and torment through her center. She wrapped her legs around his middle, and her heels dug into his backside, spurring him on.

Gavyn grinned down and nibbled on her lower lip.

She arched her lower back, her body searching for release. All her fears and her burdens and her worries dimmed under the intensity of her body's most primal need.

He increased the pace, the pleasure building with each thrust.

"Not yet. Tell me when you are close."

Gavyn quickened the rhythm and bent his head to suckle on her nipple. He kneaded her other breast, his rough calluses abrading the soft skin. He twisted its peak, jolting her awake.

The first spasm radiated through her, the pleasure suspending her body in time. She was so close, so near the release she sought, but every time she tried to grab out, it fluttered out of reach.

"Open your eyes."

The lids were heavy, demanding they remain closed as if what she searched for could only be found in the dark. Or perhaps she wasn't prepared for what she would see.

"Open your eyes," he demanded as his thrusts grew frantic.

They wanted to roll back in her head, went in that direction when he changed the angle, hitting something deeper inside, but she pried them apart. She chased the pleasure, grinding against the swelling pressure.

"Gavyn, I'm—"

"Good girl," he said as wave after pulsing wave crashed through her center. She rubbed against him, rhythmically pushing through the last crest. It continued… on and on… weeks' worth of pent up tension until her body softened under him.

"Gorgeous," he ground out. His shoulder muscles tightened. He bent down and bit her neck, hard. He didn't draw blood, but she knew the skin immediately bruised, and despite the warmth crawling under her palms, she wouldn't yield to her magic and heal his mark. "Mine."

He flexed his hips one last time, spilling inside.

Her stoic fighter lost all control, unraveling in front of her. His head fell back, and a deep, prolonged growl left his mouth. Gavyn's shoulders trembled as the shudders wracked through the rest of his climax.

She ran her palms over the ridge of his back, and he buried his face in the crook of her neck.

"Mine," he repeated and released her hands. She rolled with him, caressing his chest as they settled into the soft grass.

The outside world invaded slowly.

An owl hooted from the copse of trees. A soft cry, staking her territory. The rush of water bent around them, splashing noisily over rocks and obstacles in its path. Crickets hummed, their high-pitched chirping blending together, interrupted by Gavyn croaking out, "Your arm..."

"It shall mend. 'Tis a simple spell." She closed her eyes and guided the magic, transferring the pain from the welts down to her palm.

"Trouble," he muttered as he stood them up and walked backwards into the stream. "Are you sound... everything else... what we did..."

She never heard him so unsure of himself.

Around others, his words were short, clipped even. But this was something more than a simple obligation to check on her well-being, a hint of vulnerability bled out in the half-formed question. The uncertainty unsettled her more than she'd expected. How could such a confident man ever doubt what they shared?

"Aye." She cupped the side of his face. "I feel amazing. I love everything we did together."

Her ankle sank into the water, and her breath lodged in her throat.

"Oh, it's cold."

"Not like Ashmere Falls, is it?" He wrapped his arms around her.

With each step they took, the frigid waters sent icy daggers pricking up her body.

They reached the middle of the stream where the water leveled out at his collarbone. He hitched her higher, and she tucked her legs behind his lower back.

He was relaxed. A softness crept into his features for the first time this eve.

She leaned in for a kiss, and a trickle of warmth grazed her palm. *Heat.*

Ember jerked her hand away from his throat. Her eyes shot to his neck, searching for a wound. Nothing. Only his mark. What—

He seized on her inattentiveness and captured her mouth, easing everything else from her mind.

CHAPTER TWENTY-ONE

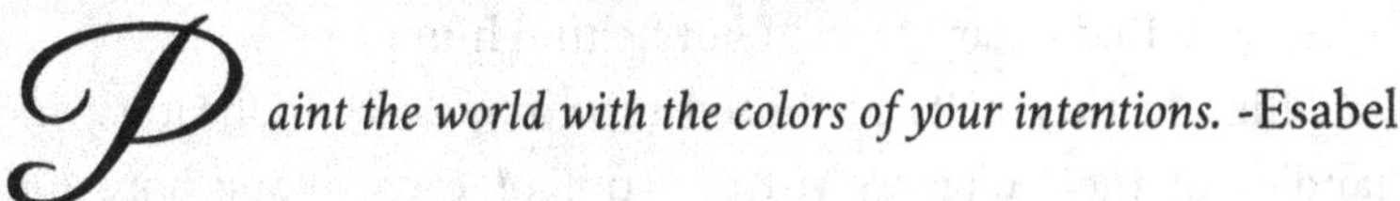

aint the world with the colors of your intentions. -Esabel

Gavyn left her sleeping in his bed.

Since her first night in his chambers, Ember plastered herself against his warmth during slumber. She was a tangle of limbs and nuzzles and sighs, a chaotic bedmate — one his traitorous body could no longer sleep without.

For as long as he could remember, Gavyn woke before the sun, preferring to start his day as the birds announced the morning. A routine carved so deep, his body moved without thought.

Today, it was with a fair amount of gritty determination he pulled himself out from under the covers for his usual dip in the stream.

He hiked the well-worn path through the woods and jogged toward the training barn. Xavier's deep voice carried over the noise of the fighters as he neared the entrance. He stopped short at the scene before him.

Men of all skill levels filled the corner stations and center ring. They moved through the motions of whatever combination they practiced.

None focused on the task.

Heads bent toward Zoie's bar where Xavier stood, feet braced wide, his hands clenched. Mikel paced to his left while Rowan towered on his right, a fierce look consuming the face of his lighthearted friend.

Lord Siodina squared up with Xavier in the center.

The dark smudges and greenish-gray appearance of the older man's face suggested a hard night and even earlier morning. His skin aged a decade overnight, mingling with the commoners.

Twelve Red Guard fanned out behind him.

Thick leather belts anchored matching leather sheaths, the handles of their daggers sticking out of each. None bore his marks from the night before, though he didn't doubt word reached Lord Siodina of the beating he inflicted on one of his men.

He schooled his expression as he approached the group.

"Councilman. Xavier." Gavyn inclined his head. "For what do we owe the pleasure of your presence in my training barn on this early morning."

The Lords may enjoy their fealty and the deeds to the land where they built their lives, but they didn't own his hard work. Perhaps he shouldn't flex his control of the compound so early in the discussion, but Rowan's smirk told him it wasn't an incorrect first move.

"My men found a blade here last night." Lord Siodina gestured to the bar behind him. "In your training... by what name do you call this hovel... a barn?"

"A blade? Surely not." Gavyn crossed his arms over his chest. He flicked his chin at the belt of the nearest Red Guard. "We abide by the decree. Our style of training has no use for weapons."

"There have been rumors for years you are forging steel," Lord Siodina said as he stuck his hand out to the side.

A guard placed a small dagger in his palm.

Gavyn schooled his features.

"That's nonsense. Our work here keeps us plenty busy, and I see no benefit in going against the Castle," Xavier said, his voice calm as if he discussed the weather or the quality of grain for Zoie's next batch of spirits. "Gavyn, take a look?"

The blade was small, covering the length of his palm. Its metal curved like a talon, rusting at the handle.

He turned it over.

A mark in the shape of a clover stood out in relief near the base. A crack traversed the dried wood, several splinters sticking out at odd angles.

"Do you see the inlay?" He returned the blade. "The clover is the stamp from Kiehl's village. It's an ancient symbol, one not used for generations. Turn it over."

He pointed to the small crack in the handle.

"The walnut needs oil. Those trees don't grow in our forests. A smith forged this blade decades before the decree."

"My man found it here." Lord Siodina pointed to the ground and sneered. "Here, in your village. If your story holds true, then one must allow for the possibility of the blade disappearing from its original owners years ago."

"Over several hundred spectators attended the fights last night. There is no way to tell whence it came or who brought it here. Your men discovered it while the compound slumbered."

Lord Siodina pursed his lips, and a deep purple flush crawled up his neck.

"It's your village. Your home. I must report this to the rest of the High Table."

"Most spectators last night came from other villages," Xavier said. He took a step forward and cracked his knuckles.

The challenge did not go unnoticed.

As if tethered by a string, the Red Guard all stepped forward. Mindless, murdering marionettes.

"This is ridiculous." Mikel pointed a finger at the unwanted guests. "You cannot link the blade to our village."

"Hold your tongue, boy. Do not speak to me in such a manner." Lord Siodina's lip curled, and his gaze flicked to Mikel's wrists. "Or have you forgotten your place?"

"Enough. Gentlemen, if you would excuse us, we have training to attend." Xavier inclined his head and turned on his heel without a backwards glance.

Would they ever breathe without the Lords' command? He couldn't recall a time when the greedy nobility of the Castle didn't influence their every move.

It was easy to place his trust in Xavier, to yield to his friend's instincts for the intricate steps to a dance he never aspired to navigate, a fast-paced maneuvering he avoided.

"I don't like this." Xavier ran his hand through his hair.

Around the barn, the fighters returned to their training, and the din of the morning's session rose to its usual level.

"I want everyone covered. Understood? Mikel, stick to Ada. Not just when she leaves the compound." Xavier raised his finger and pointed at Rowan. "And you, put aside your differences and take care of Zoie."

"She'll enjoy that." Rowan ran his hands down his jaw.

"Her safety comes before your time with your lovers."

"I know, but she can't stand the sight of my face right—"

"Work it out. That's an order."

"What about Jade?" Gavyn stepped between them. "If they knew of her connection to you—"

"I'll keep Eigen with her." Xavier pulled his shirt over his head. "I can't force her to stay here, but I won't leave her unprotected."

"And the blade?" Gavyn asked, stripping off his tunic and boots. He pulled an arm across his body and rolled his shoulder, trying to relieve some soreness from last night's bout. "Kiehl deserves to know."

Xavier bounded alongside the ropes and stopped at every corner to work a few combinations in the air.

Gavyn sighed.

For the entirety of their friendship, Xav had kept his own counsel, preferring to muddle through his worries with punches instead of words.

It was going to be a long morning.

"He does," Xavier said as he threw combinations in the air. "Which is why I'm sending you as an emissary. Travel to his village. Inform him of what transpired this morning. Get a feel for where his loyalty falls."

Gavyn scoffed.

"You should send Rowan in my stead. Posturing and matches of the mind suit his skill set. My work here keeps me busy."

And he didn't want to leave Ember.

"Your work here is precisely why I send you and not my court jester." Xavier rested a hand on Gavyn's shoulder. "'Tis not a simple barter for lumber. Kiehl will not grant Rowan's word. Whether you desire it, you represent this village. Our people. Your very skill set as an elite fighter and my head trainer thrusts the mantle of responsibility on your shoulders. Take your waif. Her beauty may be the distraction you need in case you cannot summon pretty words."

A feral grin crossed Xavier's face.

"It's too dangerous. She remains safer here. Dragging her in front of others will raise too many questions. You ask too much."

"I ask what needs to be done." Xavier clapped him on the shoulder. "She'll make out alright with you by her side."

"There is no gain in her coming. Do not demand this of me."

Xavier squeezed his shoulder.

"I do not grant this request without thought. Your word carries respect in all the villages, and Ember's gift lends sight in situations that blind others. In this, I need her report as much as yours."

Gavyn stepped back and let his thoughts drift back to the rusty dagger. The clover was a well-known symbol from Kiehl's village. His admission was not a revelation to Lord Siodina.

Where the hell did he find that blade?

EMBER SURVEYED HER TREASURES.

Willow bark, red clover, and elderberries lay scattered on the counter. A deep purple liquid oozed out of two smashed fruits. She worked alongside Zoie in her distillation area, adding the ingredients to a wide-mouthed glass jar.

"I can use water from your spring out back, but the spell will work faster with clear grain alcohol."

"It's not much, but I have some left from the last batch." Zoie pulled a small stool over to the hutch and opened the top cabinet doors.

"Perfect. 'Tis sufficient," Ember said as she grabbed the amber flask and uncorked the top.

She poured the contents over her dry elements, leaving a small amount of liquid in the original container. The liquid rose to the brim of each bottle, and her magic left a syrupy sweet coating on the tip of her tongue.

"Gavyn needs to let you out of his sight more often. I could use your gift here."

Heat crept up her neck and singed Ember's cheeks.

The front door of the quaint home opened. Jade entered unannounced.

"Are we talking about last night?" She crossed the space and tugged Zoie into a hug.

"Oh, did she get to the good stuff yet?" Ada bounded in next, followed by a sulking Mikel.

"That's my cue to patrol the premises. Outside. Alone. Away from the gossip. In the rain." He shuddered and scooted out the door.

"He's such a prude." Ada erupted in giggles beside her.

"Mikel?" Ember asked as she corked the larger of her two bottles.

"Yes. He gets squeamish every time I bring up relations." More giggles followed. "I drop hints almost daily now just to see what he does."

"Ada." Jade drew out her friend's name. The rebuke carried little weight as she followed it with a smile. "Leave that man alone."

"I must confess that I can't." Ada shrugged her shoulders. "I take too much pleasure in his situation."

"Don't think you are off the hook." Jade pinned Ember with a stare. "Spill it."

She tilted her head and looked at the ceiling. A faint smile teased the corners of her lips. "It was magical."

Ada coughed.

"That's ironic, coming from a Faeblood." Jade wiggled her fingers in a come-hither motion. "I need a little something more than that."

"He took me by the stream." The heat in her cheeks deepened. "And then again in the water. And again in his bedroom. Maybe... maybe once more this morning."

"No wonder you glow today." A subtle sharpness laced Jade's tone. She tipped the drink back and took a long swallow. "Maybe it's time I found a companion."

Zoie choked on her water. Ada's head snapped in her direction.

"What about Xavier?" Ember asked in a voice barely above a whisper.

"What about him?" Jade shrugged, and a half-smile crested her lips. "He's not interested in anything more than bossing me around. And not in a sexy way."

"I… I thought maybe there was something between you two, 'tis all." She froze, wishing her words back.

"Well, you thought wrong." Jade let out a jagged laugh and took another swallow.

Zoie circled around the workbench and grabbed her wrist. She took the flask and replaced the cork, stowing it away in her hutch.

Ember studied her potion, happy for the excuse to look anywhere but at her friend. The color from the berries infused the clear liquid and eddied around the willow bark resting at the bottom. She grabbed the bottle by its neck, inverted it twice to mix the clover, and spun the thick, saccharine spell in her throat.

A diversion in the guise of a peace offering.

A small spark of light illuminated the bottle. Its contents mingled and swirled together, turning a periwinkle hue. She held the final potion aloft.

"For pain and swelling and to counter poisons. When I'm not around to heal."

"The fighters will run though that in a day." Ada dragged out a stool from under the table.

"Can you make more?" Zoie asked as she stashed the bottle in the hutch. "As with the grain alcohol."

"No. I can increase or double everyday things, but magic doesn't bend in that manner. At least not my magic." Ember gestured to the empty bottles. "But I can always make more."

"Why didn't you cast for more food?" Ada tilted her head to

the side. "When you traveled from village to village, why didn't you magic yourself endless bread? Or cheese? Or wine?"

"Magic and nature abide by certain rules. I cannot conjure new fare from food procured by casting or thievery. I require an ordinary, non-magical item for spell work. My small satchel holds naught but a few loaves of bread, and those spoiled after a few days."

"What else can you make?" Ada tapped a finger to her lips.

"Most of the potions I know are for wounds. The knowledge passes down the generations. My mother's family curated the spells for health. Certain magic favors distinct bloodlines. For instance, nature favors some casters. They can grow new life and walk with our animal friends. I, like my mother, have healing magic in my blood. Others pass down the knowledge of the arts. They become masters in creating music, painting, blacksmithing, and working with clay, for example."

She sighed.

"Mother tried her hand at colors one day. Surprised me with new jars of the muddiest greens and dullest reds you could imagine."

She let out a half-hearted chuckle and crossed the room, stopping in front of the window looking out over the stream.

"We painted the most hideous rainbow that afternoon. Tried every spell variation in every book we could find. Mother said we didn't have the gift of creation in our magic."

"Have you met many others?" Ada scooted to the edge of her stool. "Do you know of any Faeblood in the territories?"

"No. Mother kept us isolated." She rested the tips of her fingers on the windowsill. "Our history is full of humans forcing my kind into servitude. Perhaps that's why they band together in the fortress. She lived in constant fear someone would discover my abilities. I know it's foolish, but I always hoped to find others like me. Despite her warnings, I never stopped looking."

"The entirety of the Castle, minus the servants and Red Guard, are Faeblood. The strongest casters sit on the High Table." Zoie caught Jade's eyes. "Those nine elders control our realm and govern our laws. The rest of the nobility follow their lead. We have freedoms here, but we aren't entirely free. Xav provides a service they need, so they leave us alone, mostly."

"Maybe not for long." Ada hopped off her perch on the stool. "Lord Siodina caused a ruckus in the training barn this morning. I was in my loft…"

Three heads swiveled at the news.

"A blade showed up last night at the fights," Ada finished.

"No—"

"What—"

"Another one?" Ember whirled on Ada. There wasn't any time for her to appreciate the ramifications of her loose tongue before Mikel strode through the door, a dark frown clouding his features.

"Why don't you share your tale, and I can fill in the rest from this morning." Mikel placed his hand on Ada's lower back.

"A blade showed up in the marketplace the day I arrived." She took a deep breath. "Xavier questioned the timing of both."

"Surely he can't think you had anything to do with that," Zoie said.

"No." She thought back to the encounter in the courtyard. Did they know of Xavier's Red Guard spy? It seemed unlikely, given the clandestine nature of their meeting. It didn't sit right in her gut — not confiding the detail, but it wasn't her secret to tell. "I fled my home upon the death of my mother. Gavyn's right. Trouble follows me."

"The tail in the meadow…" Zoie's fingers grazed her lips.

"Xavier worries someone tracks her," Mikel said.

"I haven't set eyes on anyone from back home." Ember fisted the fabric of her skirts. "But I can't be sure they did not follow me. What happened this morning?"

"Lord Siodina showed up with a contingent of Red Guard before the sun set blaze to farmer Whitby's fields." Mikel ran a hand through his damp hair and cupped the back of his neck. "He claims his men found a small dagger behind Zoie's bar."

"That can't be." Zoie's voice split. "Rowan and Maia and I pulled taps all night long. We were the only three back there, and I checked the under stock before the start of the fights. I didn't see a blade."

"Gavyn thinks the dagger came from Kiehl's territory. He recognized the mark and the source of the wood for the handle." Mikel turned toward Jade. "Xavier pleaded his case, but the councilman held fast."

"No." Jade gasped.

"They left immediately to report to the other members of the High Table."

Ember's brows drew together. "What does that mean?"

A knock at the front door startled the group.

Zoie crossed the room and looked out of a small peephole. Her shoulders dropped as she reached for the handle.

The hinges creaked as it swung inward, fracturing the heavy air permeating the room. Rain poured in and formed a puddle across the threshold.

One black boot crossed over, dripping onto the floor.

Its mate followed.

"Xavier sent me to fetch Ember." There was a strain in Gavyn's deep timber. "We must prepare for a journey."

"WHAT GAME ARE YOU PLAYING?" ERIK ALL BUT SHOUTED THE question.

He stalked his father to the outskirts of the territory, confronting him before he crossed the boundary.

"We need these men. It's one thing to squelch their influence;

it's quite another to make them martyrs. The High Table will seek swift vengeance for this transgression — the falsehood you spread."

"Don't pretend to care about the politics of the peninsula. For years, I goaded you into paying attention to the relations between territories, but you preferred to spend your time in the bowels of the Castle, training with your human commander."

His father spat the words.

"But if I knew something of this nature piqued your interest, I would have done it long ago."

Erik paced between the towering oaks, not bothering to soften his steps on the forest floor.

The contingent of Red Guard scattered. Half patrolled the surrounding area. The others pretended to stand guard, pointedly looking everywhere but at him.

"We need these men."

"You wear your weakness for all to see." His father sneered. "Every human is replaceable. We require their service, but another will fill the role."

"You underestimate their influence across Morvak. The other leaders will not stand for Xavier or even Gavyn's removal," he said as he cupped his hand over his mouth. "There will be uprisings."

"Then I shall give them something to occupy their idle thoughts." His father spread his arms wide. "I'll grant you a lesson in controlling the filthy commoner — entertain their small minds with one hand, and you can strip their freedoms with the other. If you cast these men as a villain, nary a soul will protest their removal. Blood-thirsty, the lot."

"What do you plan?" he asked, working through several possibilities in his mind. Could he warn Xavier without compromising his cover? First, he must convince his father of the continued need for his presence at the compound. "And the Faeblood?"

"Ah, yes, the caster. Idiot boy, sending the information uncoded. There was evidence of tampering with the seal. I trust your haste was worth the flesh off *her* back. It only took me twenty lashings to strip her skin raw. Though, I suppose you delivered on your task of sending me incriminating information."

His father tapped a finger to his lips.

"I shall free her upon healing as I require her services in the Castle. She must prepare for our guests."

He held his sigh of relief. While he never placed blind trust in his father. His sire had no reason to lie. Soon, he would see her again. Hear her voice.

Beg for her forgiveness.

He wanted to look her in the eye with conviction, not regret. She would never abide by his tactics, just as he would carry the shame for the time it took for him to earn her freedom.

For now, he must stay at the compound and mitigate some of the damage he caused.

"Then I shall remain with the militia and make sure—"

"As for the Faeblood... " His father continued, speaking off into the distance. "... those pigs possess no idea of her powers, placing her behind the bar. Forcing her in leathers and cuffs as if she was one of them. It's a disgrace to her abilities. Too bad, she won't realize a chance to fulfill her potential."

Maia. His father didn't know.

Erik kept her name off his tongue and hopefully his surprise off his face.

Maia — the gorgeous fighter with hidden curves hugging a lethal body. He couldn't prevent himself from tracking her movements in the barn. Perhaps she shared the affliction as he caught her watching him with a fair amount of curiosity.

"What are your intentions?"

"Soon, I will flush her out with these men. Knock two birds off their branch with a single stone as the commoners say."

CHAPTER TWENTY-TWO

True surprise is the gift for the unprepared. -Esabel

The borrowed boots weighed down Ember's feet.

She wiggled her toes in the stiff leather and picked her next step with care. Damp earth permeated her nose, a mixture of fertile soil and moss and tangy cedar. In this section of the trail, the sun's rays failed to reach the forest floor.

She ran her hands along her arms to rub off the chill.

Too bad they weren't back at the compound. Warm and in bed, enjoying each other's company instead of traipsing through the woods to another village.

The feather-shaped fronds of the various ferns brushed her ankle, sending morning dew flinging through the air. Moisture stained the leather of her boots and created a two-toned pattern of splotches.

Ember sighed. She must oil the footwear once they reach their destination.

A few paces beyond the next bend, a fallen tree obstructed

the narrow passage. She paused in front of the log and considered her options. Previous experience with poison foliage warned her not to circumnavigate the path.

Gavyn halted on the other side and threw her a charming grin.

"Need help?" he asked, bracing himself on the log and extending his palm.

"Hush." She waved at him.

"Nary a word left my lips." The corner of his mouth tugged upward.

She wrapped her hands around his forearm and planted one foot on the obstacle, pulling against his anchor. The surface was unstable. Even with her free arm extended, her balance wavered.

Bits of loose bark broke off the tree and plummeted to the ground.

"Your eyes twinkle with laughter at my predicament."

"Satisfy my curiosity." He wrapped his arms around the back of her knees and lifted her off the log. "How did you survive all these years on those skinny sticks you call legs?"

"I'll share my secret." She slid down his front and nipped at his lower lip. It was too dangerous to begin something in the woods. But despite the peril, or perhaps because of it, her body ached for something more. "I fly at night everywhere on my stolen broom."

"It appears as if I snagged myself a witch, besides a Faeblood." He released his grip and dropped her to the forest floor, patting her on the backside. The heat in his gaze betrayed his thoughts, but the tap on her rump spurred her on.

She wiped crumbles of bark off her pants, but her repeated attempts to clean her palms smeared the muck more.

Maia, claiming dresses impractical, had lent her the utilitarian trousers and boots upon learning of their intention to visit Kiehl's village.

The tight fitting clothing felt as unnatural this morning as it did several months ago when circumstances had forced her to abandon her favored dresses. After trekking through the increasingly difficult terrain, she was grateful Maia forced the change of attire.

Strong hands squeezed her middle. The ground dropped away as Gavyn deposited her on top of a large stone at the base of an incline.

"A cave opens on the trail above. Once we manage this climb, let's stop and break our fast."

Gavyn vaulted next to her, landing in a crouched position. He stood in one fluid motion and pointed to the bluff on the left at least one hundred paces above them.

"Scramble up the smaller stones. I'll provide a boost for the boulders too tall for your infantile legs."

Her brows narrowed, and she smacked his stomach with the back of her hand.

"Tree-trunk oaf. At least my lower half is symmetrical. Did the tailor require an extra bolt of linen to wrap around your thighs?"

"Two bolts." He crossed his arms and held her stare. "Madam required two bolts of fabric to wrap around these masterpieces."

"Come on, you big lug. Use those masterpieces to hoist me up so we can enjoy our meal." Her stomach gurgled out its approval.

By the time they reached the landing, a fine sheen of sweat coated her arms. Small tendrils of hair escaped her braid, clinging to the back of her neck. She bent over and rested her hands on her thighs.

"You're missing the view." Gavyn bounded on top of the last boulder with the same level of energy as the first. Unlike Ember, he didn't struggle to find breath.

He wrapped an arm around her waist, steered her to the edge of the overlook, and pointed east.

"There. The compound. Follow the river as it carves up the terrain. The Castle looms due north, where the tallest mountain peak stabs through the horizon. From this elevation, you can see the snow capped tops of Morvak poking through the clouds. Frost glazes the central ridgeline, even in the heat of summer."

He nuzzled her ear with the tip of his nose.

"Legend tells of our forefathers abandoning ships cleaved in half by the treacherous Strait of Vian on the mountain's northern face. Those who survived the shipwreck and braved the passage along the central ridge prospered on the land we claim today."

He ran the backs of his knuckles down the column of her neck.

"I'm inclined to believe our ancestors shared your gift of casting. To conquer both water and earth in the same voyage… 'tis unlikely for someone without magic."

The Strait of Vian. Still so far away. She should question him for more details. What was the best trail to follow? How long would the journey take? Was it safe to travel alone? Instead, she asked, "Do you still consider it a flaw? My gift."

Gavyn's caress stilled. His chest heaved, pressing against her back.

"A flaw… no. A risk… yes. If you seek words of comfort, ask your question of Ada or even Jade. I will not dishonor your query with false assurances."

The warmth at her back vanished. Gravel crunched behind her, echoing his departure.

He admitted nothing she didn't already know. Still, it hurt to hear the words spoken from his lips.

She blinked. A streak of white on a lower ridge startled her. The cotton tail of a doe darted between the brush, followed by two more.

"We should eat. It's safer to travel during the day, and three more hours of path wind in front of us," he called from behind.

She rubbed her palm and tore her gaze away from the valley.

It was foolish to expect a different answer.

When her new friends surrounded her or when she snuggled in his embrace, Ember forgot her troubles. It was easy to fall prey to her daydreams. She wanted nothing more than to silence the ticking clock in her mind, the one counting down the weeks, perhaps days, of her remaining moments at the compound.

She no longer worried about Landen or his father. As loathsome as the Red Guard were, she didn't worry about them, either. If the Castle found out Xavier gave her sanctuary…

She shuddered.

The rumors would spread. She was certain. And when the time came, she needed to be strong enough to leave behind Gavyn and everyone else. She needed to be strong enough to leave behind safety and friendship. A chance at love.

There was no other choice.

He beckoned from a small cave tucked into the towering bluff, its mouth tall enough he didn't need to duck to enter.

Darkness swallowed any light reaching its back, and a faint trickle of water reminded Ember of her thirst.

At the cave's opening, Gavyn covered a low boulder with a blanket from their supplies, creating an outdoor table. He spread various breads and apples and cured meats on its surface, turning the pack on its side for a seat and enticing Ember to rest.

"Drink as much as you can tolerate."

He handed her a leather pouch filled with spring water and gestured to a small pool of blue farther in the cave.

"We will refill here and again, closer to the village. The air grows thinner the higher we climb, and the water helps prevent headaches. Unlace your boots while you eat. When you finish your meal, I need to check your feet for swelling and puckering around the heels."

"They are sound." She bit into the apple with such force it was fortunate she did not nick the inside of her cheek.

"It's prudent to check their condition, especially since you wear borrowed footwear." He frowned, shoved the last morsel of bread into his mouth and knelt beside her, unlacing her boots. "Proper care is crucial for safe travels this far from home."

"The leather is not tight. I sense no open wounds," she ground out the words and gripped the pack.

"Any tenderness?" Gavyn ran his palm up her calf and massaged the back of her leg. He grasped the edge of her heel and tugged off the boot.

Ember closed her eyes.

"A… a little," she conceded as he rubbed small circles on the ball of her foot.

"It will be worse tomorrow. I'll find some salve for you this eve."

"Do not trouble yourself. I can cast—" She swallowed. "Is it… is it truly a risk to the village, the compound?" *To you*, she kept silent.

"Your magic?" He paused his ministrations. "Xavier believes so. I confess I don't understand the politics of it. If he believes your presence in the village could spell trouble for our compound, then I must allow for the possibility."

She finished her simple meal in silence, his words tumbling in her mind. Her mother warned her. Lectured her. Faeblood outside the Castle walls were a risk to the peace.

She was a risk.

Her gut churned at the idea of her presence endangering everyone. But a twinge of something worse, something darker, mixed in the pit of her stomach when she considered leaving behind her new friends. Gavyn.

It was selfish to want to stay.

She gathered the remnants of their meal and stowed the items away in the pack.

"Drink and then refill our supply." Gavyn took a long pull and handed her the leather pouch, nodding to the cavern floor. He gripped the back of her tunic and kissed the top of her head. "I will scout the trail and return in a moment. Don't leave the cave."

The back of his head disappeared around the wall.

In the direction they came.

GAVYN CREPT DOWN THE BOULDERS, STAYING ON THE BALLS OF HIS feet to dampen the impact of his footsteps. At the bottom of the steep incline, he hid behind an outcropping of stone and slowed his breathing.

Often, trackers fixated on a warm trail and missed changes in their surroundings — a habit borne from hunting, since prey never pivoted and confronted the predator.

He waited, hoping whoever followed them would commit the same error.

Gavyn sensed a tail about a half an hour ago. Not wanting to fight with his back to the boulders, he teased Ember up the steep incline, but she climbed the pass faster than expected, forcing him to slow their progress with an offer of food.

The tracker didn't take the bait.

His instincts stayed on high alert, even in the relative safety of the training barn. An affliction Rowan occasionally poked and prodded. This wasn't the first time his nerves spun a tale. He stayed in the crevice until he was certain nobody followed them.

Silence answered his patience.

He climbed the trail a second time, glancing back at every other boulder.

Ember sat on the pack unaware of his return.

He swallowed. She was stunning, even with wisps escaping her lopsided plait and smudges of dirt covering the tops of her thighs.

It hurt to look at her.

His fingers itched to unwind her thick braid and tangle in the mass of locks. He wanted to grab the length, using it as leverage to pin her in place while he ravished her body.

She hummed a cheerful tune, swaying to the melody.

He shook his head. Later, he promised himself.

"We must make haste in order to reach the village before dusk."

"Are they aware of our arrival?" Ember rose and wiped her hands on the front of her tunic. "Did Xavier send word, or is our visit a surprise?"

Gavyn hoisted the pack on his shoulders.

"There wasn't enough time to send a messenger to Kiehl."

"He doesn't use carrier fowl?"

"No. Xavier honors the oral tradition. Traveling by foot requires more time but negates the chance of correspondence landing in front of the wrong eyes."

They hiked the next couple of hours in companionable quiet.

The trail narrowed and dove back down into the dense forest at the base of the ridgeline. A stream rushed to his left, hitting the banks with such force a fine mist hung in the air. Smaller ferns gave way to sprawling rhododendrons with fat, glossy leaves as wide as his forearms.

He paused, scanning the path behind them.

The pack slid down his arm, and he fished out the leather pouch. He handed her the water, bending down to study an impression on the damp trail, and pointed to the paw print.

"Wolves. Game runs flush in these woods. Plenty for the larger packs to thrive. They carve dens out of caves similar to the one we stopped at earlier. If you find yourself in the forest at night, look to the trees for safety."

"Mmm, hmm." She rested the lip of the pouch against her mouth.

"Ember." He stood and pried the container from her grip. "Did you hear what I said about the beasts?"

She tilted her head to the side and asked, "Why blades?"

"What?"

"Why write a decree against commoners possessing lethal blades?"

Gavyn scrubbed his face with his hand. "I don't—"

"It appears unwarranted. Does it not?"

"I haven't—"

"The nobility possesses the ability to cast. Surely, they shun battles favoring hand-to-hand conflict where blades reign. My mother tucked me in at night with tales of great sorcerers defeating armies with a single sweep of a spell. Protected by magic from fighting on the front line." Her voice grew distant. "The law seems… unnecessary."

"The motives and rationale of the High Table remain their own, but… I suppose… if I put my mind to it, the decree hinders our one advantage over the Castle — numbers," he said as he concentrated on the twist in the path behind her. "Skill and power are desirable in any conflict, but overwhelming size can smother even the most ruthless enemy. An armed populace, one shackled by the chains of servitude for generations, would represent a threat to their hold on the peninsula."

Overactive instinct or not, he swore he spotted movement amongst the trees.

"It's a balance then. The training." A loose tendril floated near the shell of her ear. "A risk to arm men against invaders only for them to turn against their masters. But to render an entire nation defenseless…"

"Perhaps it's why they allow Xavier to train a force at the

ready but deny us the opportunity to hone their skills with a blade. A calculated move."

The hair on his arms bristled.

"Able bodies honor-bound to march to the drums of war but subdued enough to find contentment with their circumstances. What prompted these questions?"

"My mind wanders in the quiet of the woods. The reason for our journey... plus the blade from my first days in your village." She shrugged her shoulders. "The farmers wield scythes for crops and keep small knives for cleaning game, preparing food. Between tools and shoes for the horses, the blacksmiths still stay busy with work."

"Under duress, many objects can serve as a weapon." He rubbed his jaw. "I assume the High Table designed the decree to squelch the *intent* of the weapons besides eliminating their existence. Laws permit the Red Guard to possess blades. I fathom generations of families pass down knives, such as the one in our pack, from kin to kin, protected by the privacy of their own homes. Influenced by sentimentality, less by common sense. Many would find the risk too great to stow it on their person during travel. The mere presence of this one..."

He secured the pack on his back.

"Xavier sent us as a courtesy to warn Kiehl but also to parse out the tale of *how* and *why* this blade found its way into our village."

"The compound hosts many outsiders, more than other villages from your description," she said. "And with the chaos of fight nights... Some might see it as an easy opportunity to rid themselves of the contraband. But we must figure out if someone planted the dagger with care or if the timing of its discovery was coincidence."

"We?" He savored the word.

His desire to keep her near warred with his instincts to leave her back at the compound. Gavyn rubbed his knuckles down her cheek.

The forest quieted around them.

"I fought Xavier regarding your presence on this journey."

"Why?"

"It's not safe. Xavier still monitors for whispers of your gifts. The farmer and his son, from your former home, remain unaccounted." He took a step forward and ignored her gasp. "If word of your casting reached Kiehl's village… if troubles from your past await us at our destination…"

The creak of a bow drawn taut resonated behind him.

"Aye. You should listen to him, lass. No tellin' what strangers might do in the presence of a Faeblood."

[illegible] [illegible]

[illegible] [illegible] [illegible]

[illegible] [illegible] [illegible] [illegible]

CHAPTER TWENTY-THREE

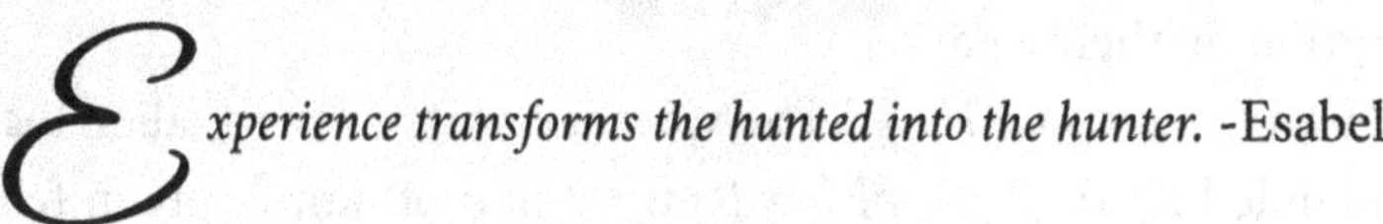

Experience transforms the hunted into the hunter. -Esabel

MEN SURROUNDED THEM, FEET BRACED. BOWS DRAWN.

Ember fought the urge to step closer to Gavyn. Cold sweat coated her palms. She chanced a glance at their attackers.

Who were they? The men dressed in all black. High-quality leather not often seen on a common villager. Hoods cast shadows on their faces, but she imagined a tide of scowls crashing in their direction.

An unwelcome welcoming committee.

"Is this a proper hello for an old friend?" Gavyn asked, his voice gruff. He stretched his neck, gaining a sliver of space between his skin and the tip of the arrow. "Come now, there's no need for theatrics."

"You dare trespass in these woods," said the man in front, the only one with his hood down.

"We respectfully request an audience with Kiehl. My companion and I serve as emissary to Xavier Northcott. We carry news regarding the High Table." Gavyn kept his gaze forward. "And a warning."

"You show nerve laying a threat at our feet. Where's your scroll?" The tip of the arrow lurched forward. "Your seal?"

Gavyn angled his head to the side, but not before a thin red gash claimed the surface of his skin.

The surrounding men elevated their bows.

"No parchment. My words are for Kiehl's ears and his ears alone."

"Corwen, enough." A feminine voice shot through the trees behind her. "Lower your bows."

The men relaxed their hold, but their arrows remained nocked. They didn't spare the newcomer a glance, keeping attention on their leader.

"I said, *lower your bows.*" The woman vaulted over a fallen log and landed on the balls of her feet. A hood of hunter green fell away from her face as she pinned the men with her stare.

A woodland nymph.

Ember wanted to shake her head at the fanciful description, but she didn't dare make any sudden moves.

The newcomer wore high brown boots the color of the cedar trunks. Their thick cuffs wrapped under her knees and delineated pants of the same color. A braided leather belt cinched the fabric of her tunic, its ends tied off-center.

She was a warrior, a well-dressed one.

Feathered tails of arrows peaked over her shoulder. She clasped a small bow in her palm. Brown hair with subtle hints of red swung in a plait halfway down her back, bound and out of the way. Small tendrils framed her oval face, curling from the dampness in the air.

Her wide mouth with a full lower lip broke into a grin.

"Always tardy." Gavyn grinned. "But I live with Ada, so the transgression is easy to forgive. Your welcome, though, is colder than I recall."

"'Tis an impoliteness to show up unannounced." She shifted the quiver to the center of her back. "Forgive these goons. They patrol under my brother's orders."

He raised an eyebrow. "Since when do you spare men from the lumber mill to traipse through the woods?"

"Kiehl increased our presence at the border last week," she said as she shifted her weight to the side. Her eyes raked Ember from boot to crown. "After strange tales meandered our way."

"My manners, it seems, are as poor as yours. May I introduce Ember?" He wrapped an arm around her shoulders, tugging her flush to his side. "Ember, this charming imp is Faina, or Fai, for those of us privy to her misdeeds. Sister to Kiehl and kindred spirits with our Ada."

"A pleasure to make the acquaintance of a *friend* of Gavyn's." Faina inclined her head to Ember. She slung the bow over her shoulder. "Come. My brother will be eager to see you. Corwen, what orders do you follow?"

"We will scout the eastern overlook and spend the night at the cave in the bluff. Your brother desires a report on the southern border, so we will canvas the ridgeline the following three days."

The men brushed past them and spread out on the trail leading to Xavier's village.

"Relay a message for me?" Corwen asked. "The glen at the edge of last season's harvest shows signs of recent occupation. Two dozen men, by my count. We tracked them to the main trail, heading in your direction."

Faina's lips curled.

"Aye, a partial squadron of Red Guard inhabits the village as we speak, harassing the tavern's patrons of an eve. After you survey the edge of the farmland, loop around the western side of the mill and send a scout ahead before your approach. My brother would not want news of increased patrols to find its way back to the Castle."

"Of course, milady. We will blend in with the lead cutters until it's safe to return to the village. Tell your brother to expect my report in four days' time."

Corwen shouldered his bow and pulled up his hood, the shadows blocking his face from view. He squeezed between the underbrush and disappeared off the trail.

"Mercenaries." Faina scoffed. "Their rates bleed my brother dry, but we cannot spare men from the yards. He's been expecting you."

She searched the top of the towering trees and set off at a quick pace.

"Come. I want to be home before dusk."

Gavyn grunted and gestured for Ember to follow between them on the trail.

The path mimicked the course of the water, and they hiked for another hour before Faina broke the silence.

"Word of Xavier harboring a caster spreads throughout the territories." Faina grabbed onto a small sapling near the water's edge and leaned over the rushing stream.

The thinner trunk bowed with her weight, and she scooped a handful of the clear liquid in her palm, drinking heartily.

"Our informant in the Castle remains silent on the matter, but we do not expect a report for another fortnight. I travel from the artisan cave. You know they guard their gossip, hoarding it alongside their gems, but I struck up a... a conversation with another patron from the mining village. Decent fellow, considering..." She tipped her head towards Ember and added, "My companion possessed knowledge of a Faeblood outside the fortress walls."

Gavyn scoffed.

"A conversation, huh? I must tuck the information into my sleeve. Ada will pay a week's worth of washing for that scandalous tidbit. Be careful, though," he warned. "It is unwise to tangle sheets with men under Harin's command. Sated bodies make for relaxed minds. And unguarded thoughts often roll off loose tongues."

"Poor Ember. You must be an inattentive lover if your lips wag with gossip in bed." Faina glanced over her shoulder and winked. "Upon your return home, ask your handsome friend to instruct you on the many duties of a mouth."

Ember dimly registered their banter. So soon? She expected news of her casting to spread, but this far? And so quickly. Worse, she didn't have a plan. Didn't want to move on.

At the stream's edge, the swift current swirled around a clutch of stones near the bank before spilling downstream. She splashed the frigid water on her face and willed the warmth from her cheeks to dissipate before she faced them again.

"Rowan never stops talking in the ring. I cannot imagine he shuts up in bed. Wait." Gavyn held up a hand. "'Tis not a question I need answered."

Faina threw her head back and laughed.

"I must oblige. Sadly, that experience continues to elude me. A favor? Send him this way next time Xavier requires a messenger. My silver tongue may not talk its way into his britches, but his beautiful face is easier to tolerate than your grumpy person."

"Noted." Gavyn tugged on the end of Fai's braid. "Be careful, though. If news of your inclinations reaches your brother, he might demand another carrier all together. You may wind up with Xavier himself, or worse, a taciturn Mikel."

"I would accept either of those options because it would guarantee a visit from my dear friend, Ada." Faina shrugged.

Ember bit her lower lip and tried to keep up with their conversation. It was difficult to follow, but the woman in front of her was enchanting. She must remember the precise details of this scene to relay to Ada later.

A tap on her waist spurred her forward, and she scurried to catch up.

Their small party hiked until the trail opened up to a large meadow blanketed in soft pinks and purples of the waning sun. The dense forest framed rolling hills abundant with wildflowers, tall grasses, and... elegant two-story homes?

She sucked in a breath and placed the tips of her fingers on her mouth.

"It resembles the villages from the fairy tales of my youth. So many colors... and the intricate details of the buildings. You must boast talented carpenters to create such wonders."

"Aye, but don't let them hear you say so. Their necks will cave under the weight of fluffed up heads," Faina said.

Wide overhangs separated the homes' upper levels from those below. Detailed scrollwork accented wide porches, wooden webs spun by talented artists to ensnare the attentions of the passerby. Bold-colored shingles graced the peaks on all sides, drawing the eye to copper rooftops aged to a gorgeous patina. The inhabitants painted their front doors with loud enamels and planted riotous front gardens to match.

The entire palate should have been garish. Gaudy even. But somehow, it worked. And with all the homes sharing a similar style, the village wove a cohesive charm.

Her curiosity bounced from one family home to another, never settling for too long before jumping to the next.

"My grandpa cleared the land long before the birth of my father. He fancied my grandmother for ages and built the first home in our village to win her heart. As a little girl, she obsessed over stories written about a young monarch in a faraway land who favored flowery design. Grandpa built the home, recalling memories of her childhood retellings of the great queen. He left the wood raw knowing she would delight in picking the colors. Took him until their first wedding anniversary to finish all the trim."

Faina chuckled.

"Everyone groans when we add a new house, but nobody

wants to buck tradition and build something more practical. It's eccentric, but it's home."

She laid a hand on Ember's arm and pointed.

"Look. My brother approaches."

The man climbing the hill toward them bore Faina's familial coloring.

He had fair skin with a subtle golden undertone and a smattering of freckles on his arms. Summer highlights framed his face and lightened the copper tone of his hair. He was a brawny, compact man with cheeks bronzed by wind and sun. Kiehl sported the village's customary cedar brown pants and matching boots.

Forearms, likely strengthened from years of climbing, bulged under the rolled sleeves of a cream-colored tunic. Upon closer inspection, chips of wood covered the linen and adhered to the golden dusting of hair on his arms.

"I've been expecting you, old man." Kiehl extended his hand and pulled Gavyn in for a one-armed hug. He thumped him twice on the back

"Your insult is neither true nor original." Gavyn left a hand on his shoulder. "I expect better from you and Rowan."

"We may be the same age, but you house the heart of a grumpy old miner." He brushed an invisible piece of forest off Gavyn's tunic. "Even your dress resembles that of generations past."

"Better to uphold the standards of distinguished men than to don the colors of dandies. Does Fai commission your britches in the image of the Castle peacocks or do you request this," he gestured to Kiehl's attire, "of the tailor yourself?"

"They'll be like this for hours. I'll show you to your lodging." Faina smiled, and the spattering of freckles on her nose scrunched. She nudged Ember with her foot. "We can stop at the bakery for a fresh baguette to enjoy before supper. The men work until the sun plunges behind the horizon during the warmer months, so we dine later than the compound's customary time."

Ahead, a rotund man, dressed in all white with a floppy hat the color of newly fallen snow, waved enthusiastically from the open door of a quaint shop near the end of the road.

"Ah, that's Remy," Fai said, rubbing her hands together. "He is the baker behind the most decadent loaves in the realm. Long, thin baguettes that crackle under your fingertips. Rounds stuffed with nuts and seasonal seeds that wet your mouth before they come out of the oven."

A large wooden sign with whimsical lettering hung above the shop window.

"My father offered him refuge when Kiehl and I were children. The villagers adopted him and constructed his bakery before the winter solstice that year. Remy keeps the men happy with his decadent treats." She patted her belly and said, "And harvesting prevents the workers from growing as round as a barrel of Zoie's famous mead."

Remy wrapped his thick arms around Faina and kissed the air next to each cheek.

"My beautiful girl, I saved the last loaf for you. You must visit in the morning. I'm experimenting with soft cheese in my croissants." He pinched Fai's cheek and tsked. "Your bones… they are too thin. You need this fare to fill out your dresses."

Faina blushed and swiped the last baguette off of the display behind him.

"So you say." She held the loaf by the ends and bent it in half. The crust crackled and crumbled in the center. Faina closed her eyes and inhaled. "Ah, perfection."

Remy clasped his hands in front of his chest.

"Always a pleasure to bake for someone who appreciates wonderful food. Share with your friend, lest you spoil your supper." He waved and disappeared into his shop.

Kiehl crept up behind Fai and snatched one half of the loaf.

He tore it in two and stuffed one portion in his mouth, offering the other to Gavyn.

"Hey, you brute. 'Twas mine." She punched him in the arm and asked, "Didn't your parents teach you not to thieve?"

"Didn't your parents teach you to share?" He rubbed the top of her head.

A thick section of hair loosened from her crown. Tangled wisps flew in every direction and sprung skyward, defying Faina's attempts to tame them with her fingers.

"Bugger off, you lout," Faina said as she hit Kiehl's stomach with the back of her hand. She broke the remaining bread in half and handed Ember a piece. "For you."

"Set them up in grandpa's old cottage." Kiehl turned to Gavyn. "It backs up to the stream and offers privacy. The trail leading away from the back door tracks to the western ridgeline and loops around to the southern aspect of the territory. I must attend the last haul of the day and check on the progress of the northern watch towers. Settle in. Fai will bring you supper. We can catch up once the village slumbers."

Gavyn's hand shot out, detaining Kiehl. "Watch towers? Since when—"

"Summer has been... difficult," Faina hedged. "The underbrush flourishes in the dry heat, and our men battle small blazes at the edge of our harvests."

"I commissioned watch towers to monitor our territory. With the construction of these last two, we possess the ability to survey the forest in *all* directions." Kiehl clasped Gavyn's elbow. "There is much to tell, my friend. For now, I bid you good eve."

He tipped his head in Ember's direction and jogged away.

Despite his bulk, Kiehl carried himself with nibble grace.

Women and children, enjoying the remaining light on their front porches, sent enthusiastic waves in his direction. Farther along the route, a pair of young men scrambled down the hill and stole his notice. They fell in step beside Kiehl, wrapping an arm around his wide shoulders.

A weight on the top of her head startled her from her thoughts. Gavyn's arm snaked around her waist, and his chin rested on her crown.

"The journey has been long." She turned in his arms and trailed her fingertips along his scar. "I'm—"

A rhythmic clank of metal rang out from below.

Faina scurried to the edge of Remy's bakery, beckoning Ember to follow.

Homes and shops clung to the sloping hillside, leaving glimpses of a wide road parallel to the one they traveled. Their new spot provided an unobstructed vantage to the village's primary thoroughfare.

Faina squatted and yanked on the hem of Ember's trousers.

She knelt down beside her and scanned the hillside.

Two dozen men in heavy chain mail marched in procession in the middle of the road. At every structure, one broke away from the group and knocked on front doors. Others hustled from far behind to reform the tail of the formation. With the fading light, the hue of their tunics appeared brackish as opposed to a vibrant scarlet.

Ember sucked in a breath.

Red Guard were here.

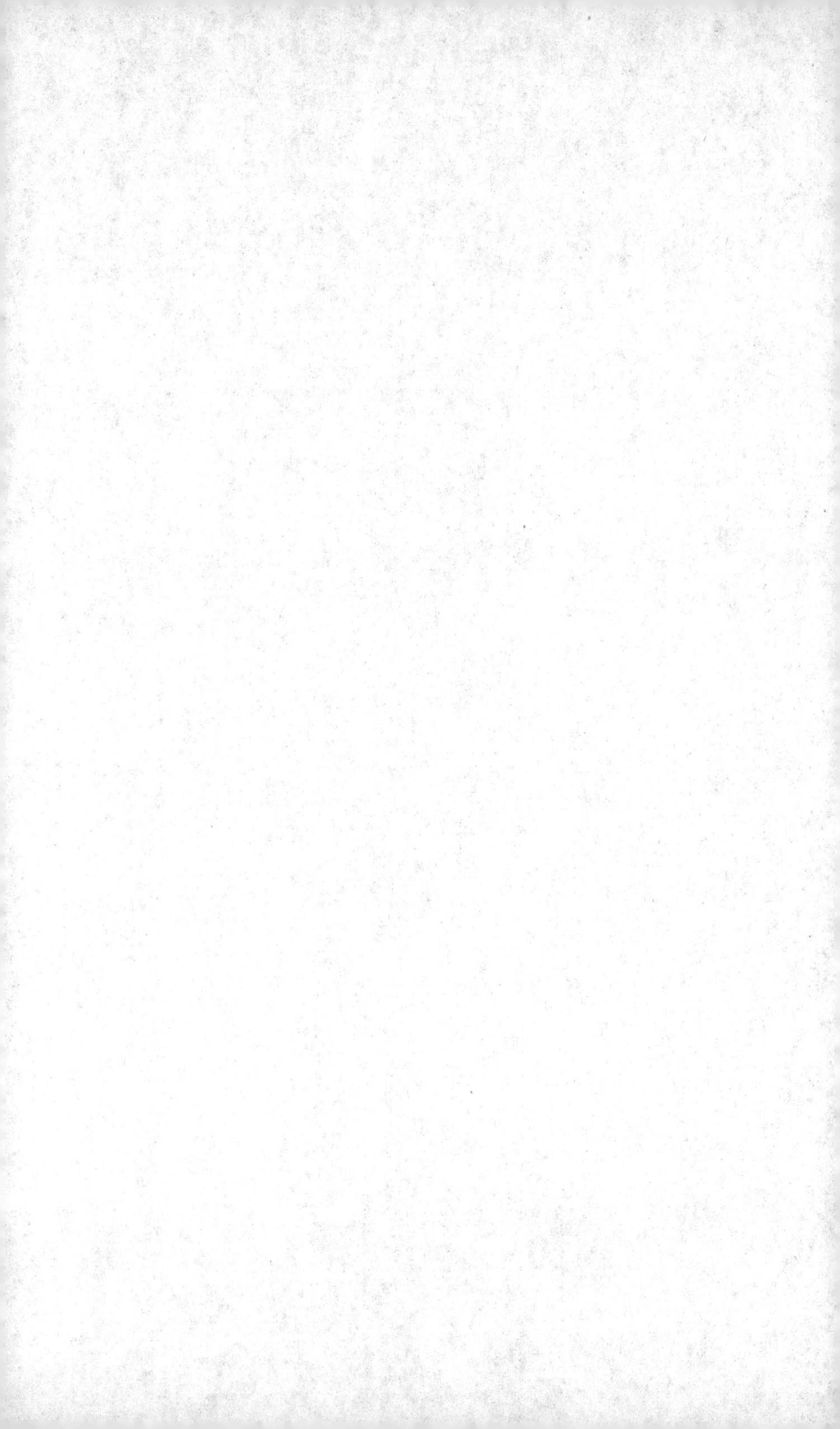

CHAPTER TWENTY-FOUR

N ature gifted man with the deed to power. -Esabel

"Follow me."

Faina ushered them to a narrow cottage built at the edge of the forest. Squeezed between towering cedars, a stone foundation elevated the main level, creating the appearance of a cozy treehouse begging for afternoon tea with neighbors.

And a perfect vantage for Gavyn to scout threats in all directions.

Dark windows with bright plum shutters disrupted the smooth lines of butter yellow siding. A set of front steps tucked under an arched covered porch and beckoned visitors to a pumpkin orange front door. An iron striker in the shape of a dragonfly clanged when Fai nudged the heavy wood with her shoulder.

Quaint, but with too many access points.

He grabbed Ember's hand and followed Fai into the dim front room.

Musty air permeated the space.

His nose twitched with a tickle of sneeze. Swaths of fabric draped over the larger pieces of furniture, preventing layers of dust from collecting on their surface.

Warped from years of trapped moisture, the uneven floorboards creaked underfoot. At least he could hear any intruders.

"Stay," Faina said. "I need to track the patrol."

She didn't wait for an acknowledgement and rushed out without a wave goodbye.

"I want to check all the rooms before we barricade ourselves in for the evening." He kissed Ember on the top of her head and stalked down the narrow hallway leading to the back of the house.

"I'm… I'm coming with you." She caught up with him, and her fingers twisted the fabric on the back of his tunic.

He slowed his steps, allowing her to match the rhythm of his stride.

The kitchen spanned the rear of the home.

Shelves to his right held an array of kettles and pots. A wooden keg occupied the opposite corner. Its top opened to the room, and three metal bands encircled the lower bulging slats. A thick piece of timber crossed the back door, protecting the entry point from the cover of the woods.

Satisfied they were alone, he led Ember up the stairs.

At the top of the landing, four doors revealed sleeping chambers. Empty, except for inviting beds in each.

"This home holds many memories." Ember ran her thumb over notches on the door frame. She tilted her head, examining the top most mark. "Looks like Kiehl shot past Faina when he was sixteen summers. There's another. Though I can't decipher the name."

She leaned closer and squinted. The front of her tunic untucked from her pants, exposing a delicious sliver of skin.

He seized the opportunity to study her while she continued to mull over the history of the house.

He didn't want to think of the illegal dagger. He didn't want to think of the Red Guard harassing the village. He didn't want to think of the politics of the Castle.

Gavyn rubbed his chest. So close to a bed, his body vibrated, and he lost the conversation. Around her, it was difficult to think at all.

"Gavyn, I wonder… " Her voice trailed off as she snatched her hand away from the trim.

Light gray pants stretched across the curve of her backside.

He wanted to run his palms along the plump flesh.

The top two buttons of her shirt opened, revealing the tantalizing swell of her chest.

He tracked the graceful lines of the arch of her back all the way to the slender column of her neck. His mouth watered. He wanted to sink his teeth into the soft flesh as she cried out his name.

Here, in a village surrounded by strangers, he wanted to mark her, erasing all doubt of where she belonged.

Mine.

This wasn't simple lust.

Mine. Mine. Mine, the primal voice repeated.

Gavyn shook his head. He knew he couldn't keep her. Couldn't let himself entertain the thought. Couldn't meekly follow the spell she cast and risk his heart by staying close.

He was drawn to her. She was everything he could ask for in a partner, and Gavyn never let himself dream such foolish dreams. She was a gift, too precious for a simple fighter like him.

But today, with the rush of adventure fizzling out of his body, he let himself dream.

He stalked across the room and crowded her space.

She rattled off names and dates and something about her warm palms, but the words faded in the noise of his mind.

Gavyn captured her raised hand and used his other to spin her around.

"Everything okay?" She cupped the side of his jaw and ran her thumb over his scar. "Did you hear what I said?"

"The cottage is secure." He ran the tip of his nose along the arch of her cheek. In her ear, he whispered, "We are all alone. And I'm hungry."

He rested his forehead against hers and inhaled.

"Ravenous," he said as he dipped his head and captured her mouth, alternating between nipping her lower lip and sealing her throaty moans.

Pinpricks of pain erupted on his scalp.

She curled her fingers through his hair, tugging his head impossibly closer, as though she couldn't get enough of him, either.

He wrenched free, panting for breath.

"Starving." He picked her up, deposited her on the quilt, and took his fill.

Her nipples strained against the tunic, taut beneath the thin fabric.

He reached behind his head and pinched the collar of his shirt, pulling it free. His hands itched to explore the soft lines of her waist, her hips. For the first time, he envisioned taking her pleasure instead of providing it.

Lust did not obscure the subtle difference. *Mine.*

The simple motion of removing her boots and socks steadied his fingers, his thoughts.

"Spread out like a feast for a king." The soft mattress dipped with his weight. Gavyn grabbed the hem of her pants and tugged. The garment caught over the soft round of her bottom, and he yanked harder, freeing her legs. "Delicious as a raspberry tart."

He planted a row of kisses along the waistband of her simple pink undergarments.

"Or a strawberry cake. Will I find my dessert heavy with cream? Should I savor my way to your center, nibbling and stroking a path to the best part?"

He nuzzled the inside of her thigh. His fingers discovered a damp spot and brushed against the evidence of her arousal.

She arched her hips, chasing the featherlight touch.

"No? Or are you eager for my tongue? For me to bury so deep inside you and devour your pleasure, starved for your sweetness."

His fingers snaked under the fabric and speared into the wetness pooling between her legs, desperate to bring her arousal to the same breaking point as his.

"Gavyn—" She closed her eyes, her lips parting to allow his name to pass.

"Don't want to rip these." He gently untied the ribbon and tossed the scrap of cloth across the bed. "Fai is due back any second. I don't have enough time to bed you properly, but I'll take care of this ache."

His cock throbbed against his tight trousers, straining for release. He yearned to slam inside her welcoming heat, but if he gave into the urge, he would last as long as an inexperienced lad.

Gavyn adjusted himself and looped both of her legs over his shoulders, lowering himself on his elbows.

"Keep your eyes open. I want you to watch while I feast on what's mine."

A soft whimper left her lips, the sound breaking through his wall of restraint.

He worked his way along her seam — licking her folds, lapping up her arousal. Gavyn hummed his delight, knowing the vibrations would radiate from her center.

Her legs clamped tight on his ears. She was close. Too close. *Not yet.*

"So." Bite. "Delicious." Nibble. "So sweet."

He rubbed the day's stubble along the inside of her thigh and delighted in the redness rising on her skin. A long sweep of his tongue sent her bucking to the rafters.

"Is all this for me?" He dove back in, clamping down with his lips and massaging the nub through its protective hood. Her legs covered his ears, muffling her cries.

He would not last.

"Open your eyes." He wanted to own her. To see her unravel. To see her break.

Before he shattered.

"Come for me." He speared two fingers inside and rubbed her inner walls. He quickened the pace and demanded, "Keep them open, and give me what's mine."

Ember's eyes rolled to the back of her head, and he paused, pulling his fingers free.

Smack.

Another red mark rose on her pale skin. A handprint he would admire later.

"Open." He dragged out the word and started again. Her heat coated his fingers, and a third one joined its mates. "Be a good girl, sweetheart, and I'll let you come."

"Gavyn," she moaned.

His name echoed off the walls as she clenched around his fingers. She thrashed on the bed, screaming through her release.

He lost the battle.

Gavyn freed himself and pumped above her. Her juices coated his hand, allowing his fist to slide easily along his length. He came with a growl, and line after line of thick cum painted her stomach, another brand that fed his possessiveness. *Mine.*

His chest heaved, and he struggled to control his breathing. Gavyn leaned back on his heels and stroked a path up and down her thigh, unable to prevent himself from touching her.

Ember sat up on her elbows, and a shy smile tugged at the corners of her mouth. An ache blossomed in his chest, replacing the heavy thud of his heart.

"Yum. It appears as though dessert is on the menu for me, too," she said as she swiped a knuckle along her belly and brought it to her lips. Ember closed her eyes and pulled the finger out with a *pop*.

"Not as sweet as mine, though." He licked her essence, and the tangy flavor erupted on his taste buds.

He balled up his shirt and reluctantly wiped her stomach.

"Oye. Lovebirds. Put some clothes on and come down here," Faina called out, the humor in her tone dancing up the staircase. "Pants required. I have no desire to wash my eyes with lye."

Gavyn tugged Ember off the mattress.

She laced her fingers behind his neck and kissed the corner of his mouth, catching him by surprise. At least he wasn't the only one who regretted the interruption.

They dressed in silence, taking longer than necessary. It was pure torture to watch her cover up. She threw shy smiles his way with every garment. Minx.

"Later. I'll spend the night savoring every bite of you," he said and kissed the tip of her nose.

They met their pushy host in the kitchen.

Faina's hands covered her face, one eye peeking between her fingers and watching their approach.

He gestured to the small table in the kitchen's corner and pulled out two chairs for them to sit.

"When did the Red Guard show up in the village?" he asked, tucking both girls in and choosing to stand.

"A week ago. Kiehl spotted them searching this home one evening. He was livid. They entered under the cover of the forest. Slipped through the back door undetected. Who knows how long they were in here, rummaging through our family's belongings. Kiehl fashioned a new door the same night, one with a slat large enough to barricade unwelcome guests."

"The front door remains a weakness," Gavyn said. "I'll speak to Kiehl about the new locks we placed throughout the compound."

"Don't bother. Curious neighbors watch the house from the village. And men observe from the two new towers we built."

"Do you know what they seek?" Ember asked and glanced around the room. "Did they take anything from the cottage?"

"Your prediction is as good as anyone's." Faina scoffed. "Kiehl reveals nothing. Ada and I are kindred spirits in more ways than one. I spend time here every week dusting the uncovered surfaces and sweeping the rooms. Taking a chilly bath in the kitchens when I need to wash off my misdeeds before someone tattles."

She pursed her lips.

"'Tis my hope to keep the cottage as my grandmother did. Dust does not settle on these floors for boots to leave prints. We know not what rooms they entered, nor what drawers they searched. If they invaded our privacy, they did so with care."

A knock at the door silenced his question.

"I do not have long." Kiehl let himself in the home and joined them at the table. "Did you deliver the tale of our misfortune? Those greedy Lords. I pay my tithing. Keep my head cast downward, nose in my work. Meet their demands for timber. Now I must contend with their dogs in my village, snarling at my people. Mongrels tugging at their master's leash."

Kiehl ran his hands through his hair and over his mouth.

"You did not journey to hear my woes. What news do you bring from the compound? Pray tell, how does Xavier fair?"

"Ember?" Gavyn caressed her cheek. "Please bring down the reason for our visit. You'll find it tucked inside the front pocket of my pack."

She nodded and disappeared up the stairs.

"What news travels your way regarding her whereabouts? Her powers?"

"'Tis true then? She casts?" Kiehl lowered his voice.

"Aye. She carries the gift."

"Blimey. A real Faeblood. Outside the fortress walls. They'll try to silence her. Or worse, kidnap and lock her up deep in the mountain. There are horrors… unspeakable acts neither you nor Xav can imagine."

"Kiehl… enough," Faina said.

"No, Fai. I will not dishonor their memory any longer."

"But grandpa—"

Dark laughter burst from Kiehl.

"Grandpa is no longer here. We buried his loyalty and gratitude toward the Castle inside his grave, deep in the forest. I do not wish to tarnish his memory, but the world in which he lived no longer exists. Even you must recognize the tenuous threads connecting the villages to the High Table."

Kiehl placed his hand on Gavyn's shoulder.

"Our parents did not perish in an accident at the mill. The High Table abducted them from their beds in the middle of the night. Questioned. Tortured. At the mere rumor of a caster living in our village. Evidence—" His voice cracked. "Evidence of their suffering found its way back to grandpa. A warning to those who might harbor threats to their power."

"Why didn't you say—"

"I have the blade." Ember cleared her throat. She extended the dagger toward Kiehl. "Gavyn informs me this belongs to you… your family."

"It belonged to our great-grandfather, but I'm certain you guessed as much. He hid it away as a keepsake during the High Table's initial seizure of blades." Kiehl wrapped his fingers around her wrist and removed the blade with his other hand. He held the small dagger up to his face and studied the inlay on the handle. "I forgot he even kept it."

Kiehl handed the dagger to Faina.

"Grandpa stashed it in the lining of grandmother's chest." Fai traced the imprint. "He chuckled when he showed me. Thought it amusing to stow it among the old baby clothes and the dried flowers from their wedding. The Red Guard... I didn't even consider checking the hiding spot since the rest of the contents of the trunk were undisturbed. But how did this blade find you?"

"Members from the High Table showed up to the fights under the pretense of observing the training progress." Gavyn clenched his fist. "Xavier danced to their tune — building a platform to keep them from rubbing shoulders with the commoners, plying them with our finest food and drink, ensuring the most entertaining matchups entered the ring. But Xav played their games for naught. They showed up at dawn the next morning, brandishing that blade about."

He gestured to the small dagger.

"They quoted the decree and threatened to bring the matter to the attention of the other members of the High Table. The bastards knew we would recognize the mark. Knew it belonged to your family. Still doesn't explain why, though."

"Expand your tactics beyond the ring, my friend." Kiehl tipped his head in Ember's direction. "If confirmation of her presence in your village reached their spies, 'tis a clever way to punish Xavier's transgression. They seek retribution without word spreading of a power outside their control. His defiance of the decree will stun everyone. People will not look further into your gossip."

"And it has the added benefit of pitting us against you," Faina said flatly. "Make no mistake, they will ensure the rumors include our crest. Undeniable evidence linking the blade to our family."

"So give them what they seek," Ember said, addressing Kiehl directly. "I don't pretend to understand the complexities of your situation. But let them see what they want, at least until you figure out a plan. Their occupation of your village provides an opportunity to control the flow of information making its way back to the High Table."

Her eyes darted between them.

"Forgive me, I spoke out of turn," she said.

"It's an excellent strategy. Let me think. It buys us time until we discover their intentions. Let me think… Let me think."

Kiehl's fingers snapped with each proclamation.

"Faina, next time you visit Remy, let it slip that we quarreled with our guests regarding the blade. A fair number of Red Guard patronize his bakery, and he will undoubtedly spread the tidbits to his customers." He placed his hand on his chest. "I'll plant the information with a few of my men with loose tongues. They frequent the tavern, and ale will amplify their voices after a hard day's work."

"Will it be enough?" Ember squeezed Gavyn's hand, the only sign this turn of conversation unnerved her.

"No." Kiehl's eyes flicked to their joined fingers. "We must cut ties between our villages. No more visits. I'll send updates with my annual supply of timber in the fall, but other communication must cease. Our ruse must hold until we discern their intentions."

He tipped an invisible cap.

"I cannot linger. A scout from the Red Guard tracks my movements. Faina may come and go as she pleases. She will bring you supplies and company before you set off."

Gavyn extended his hand.

"It's good to see you again, old friend." He pulled Kiehl in for another one-armed hug. "I am hopeful our next encounter will be longer."

"Aye, and be sure to bring your lady. I'd rather set eyes upon her beauty than stare at your broken face."

Kiehl grinned at Ember.

"Oh, and Gavyn, deliver a message to Xavier for me? Tell him to expect an extra delivery of timber in a fortnight's time. I'll route it through the hunter's territory, so no one can trace the supply back to me."

"Timber? For what?"

"For the watchtowers your territory will require."

CHAPTER TWENTY-FIVE

It's better to lack the knowledge of victory than to experience the loss of safety. -Esabel

An eerie stillness blanketed the compound.

Gavyn brought his finger to his lips. Ember nodded, understanding his command for silence.

The training barn was locked up tight. Nobody lingered about the courtyard, commiserating on their familiar aches and pains. Even the entrance to the barracks was absent of guards. Where was everyone?

She pointed to the mess hall's illuminated windows, a usual sight for this time of eve.

He slowed their approach, creeping along the perimeter of the compound before they slipped inside the front doors.

Three days. Two nights. Their week-long journey was cut short by Kiehl's revelations.

Still, they spent one additional evening in the treehouse cottage learning each other's bodies. Something in his gut chastised him for staying the extra day, but he couldn't find it in himself to regret the indulgence.

Hushed murmurs greeted their arrival.

Jade and the girls, flanked by Rowan and Mikel, gathered near the back of the room. Eigen blended into the shadows, his focus split between Jade and the entry points.

It appeared as though all the fighters were present. Since cook and her staff served meals in shifts, it was rare for all of them to cram into the building at once.

The last time Xavier had made an announcement, it was joyous news. He'd paid off the loan for the construction of the compound, severing the noose around their hard work.

By the looks on the faces of his brothers, whatever the cause of tonight's meeting wouldn't be met with similar reactions.

Long wooden tables, normally in the center of the room, now lined the outer walls. Stools rested upside down on their tops, making it easier for the evening mopping. A large hearth covered most of the back wall. Usually full of cooking coals and several enormous cauldrons, it lay quiet and unused.

The smell of fire and roasted meat still clung to the air, reminding him of their decision to skip the nooning meal and instead dine on each other at the cave in the bluffs.

Another delay.

The chamber connected directly to the sleeping area of the barracks, with the long structures forming the L-shaped wing.

Several stragglers wandered in through the hallway and joined their mates. All around, fighters formed groups or paired off. Chatter marched across the room at a hurried pace, but the hushed tone made it difficult to chase the words.

In a place of merriment and relaxation, tension lent an unnatural air.

Ada clung to Mikel's side. Zoie alternated between surveying the gathering and scowling at Rowan who angled his body in her space, shielding her from prying eyes.

Erik came in behind them, lips flat. Jaw clenched. He bypassed their group and settled in a circle of cubs, and a few of the men vied for his attention.

Jade spotted them first and strode over, her head held high. Shoulders back. Regal. Her ruse faltered, however, with the quick shuffle of the last few steps. She threw her arms around Ember and pulled her tight.

"You made it back," she said as her thumb grazed Ember's cheek. "Are you all right? Xavier told me nothing. We didn't know where you went. I can see you are well. Maybe a bit flushed."

"We only just returned. I'll fill you in later. What's happening? What's—"

"I received a missive from the High Table this afternoon," Xavier announced, his voice booming through the hall.

Heads turned in their direction.

As much as Xavier tried, news of her Faeblood must have spread to the Castle. Another confirmation of what he learned from their travels. It was the only reason he could fathom why they gathered tonight.

Ember dropped his hand, and he instantly missed the comfort.

He never regretted his duties. Quite the opposite, if he admitted.

Today, however, he wished himself a lowly fighter with the anonymity to stay by her side. Gavyn bent down, pecked her on the cheek, and joined Xavier at the hearth, trusting Jade and the others to take care of her.

"After our last fight night, Lord Siodina's men discovered a blade in the training barn." Xavier waited for the murmurs to die down. "And today, I received a summons from the High Table."

An explosion of voices tore through the gathering.

This was worse.

"Enough." Xavier waved to the crowd. He stepped forward and raised both hands. "There's more."

He unrolled a small piece of parchment with a red seal on the top, held it at the ends, and cleared his throat.

~

*I*N *THE NAME OF THE* H*IGH* T*ABLE AND OF THE DEAD GENERATIONS from which we receive our sovereign rights, we hereby summon Xavier Northcott and those under his command henceforth in two weeks' time.*

Whereas, we declare the right of the people and the ownership of the land and the unfettered control of its destinies to be sovereign and right.

Whereas, the High Table claims the allegiance of every citizen residing in its sovereign border.

Whereas, its citizens pledge their lives and welfare to the honor of the High Table.

Whereas, the High Table, hereby constituted, will administer the civil and military affairs of the nation in trust of the people.

Whereas, the laws within the borders are absolute and just; therefore crucial to society's prosperity and represent a show of fealty.

Now, we, the High Table, proclaim Sir Northcott contribute one man, who wields the honor of representing the ignominy of the citizens for dishonoring the decree prohibiting lethal blades forged of steel, to take part in a fight to the death against an adversary of our choosing.

We summon all citizens to join in this special observance at sunset on the day of Mabon.

~

T*HIS WAS SO MUCH WORSE.*

Stool legs scraped against the wooden floor.

Xavier crumpled the missive and met Gavyn's stare.

It was as Kiehl predicted — they sought to punish him for the dagger in a public arena, dishonoring his name for harboring a Faeblood.

Rowan tore a path through the crowd. He halted before them and bent at the knee, bowing his head.

"Virtus et Honos," he said, the deep timbre of his voice felling the thick air.

Mikel kissed Ada's temple and followed the opening his brother carved through the fighters. He gripped Rowan's shoulder and repeated, "Virtus et Honos."

All around the hall, fighters knelt on the hard stone floor, pledging allegiance to Xavier, to the brotherhood. Because that's what they created — a family. Not by blood or shared lodgings or similar experiences.

Strength and Honor.

They'd chuckled as young men when they'd tossed around the phrase late one night, looking up at the stars. Meant as a jest, a thumb on the nose to a similar sentiment on the Red Guard's seal, they hadn't lent it much credence.

Until one year turned into two, and two rolled into four, and before they realized it, they created a sprawling family, with distant branches spanning the territories, bound by the strength of their conviction and the honor of standing next to one another.

Ember's gasp was loud to more than his ears.

This was much, much worse.

His heart lodged in his throat.

He'd only just found her — just realized she was a missing part of his life. One he didn't know he needed. One he didn't know how to live without. The walls closed in, and he couldn't breathe. They converged, squeezing out all hope, squeezing out all good sense.

They crushed the new glimmer inside his chest, grinding out the truth, one he hadn't admitted to himself until this moment.

He loved her.

Gavyn loved Ember with every flicker of his soul. Him, a loyal soldier, not the brightest warrior, fell for her charm, her spell. Regret hit him in waves.

Regret for not recognizing it sooner.

Regret for the little time fate had bestowed.

Regret for not saying it aloud, even now. She couldn't know, not because she didn't deserve his love, his words. But because of what his morals demanded.

"I pledge to honor this request, to represent our village, and to obey the summons of the High Table," Gavyn said as he knelt down in front of Xavier.

"I accept your pledge and salute your sacrifice." Xavier's clenched fists caught the corner of his eye, and his hand pressed on Gavyn's shoulder. "Stand."

"Virtus et Honos," echoed around the room.

He looked up, taken aback by the display of unity.

And her absence.

"It's all my fault," Ember said as she looped both arms around Jade's middle and rested her head on her shoulder. They sat by the edge of the stream. Her sobs threatened to transform into unladylike hiccups. "The summons. The punishment. It's because of me."

"I know it looks bleak, but don't fret. Xavier will come up with a plan. And Gavyn is the strongest fighter we have. He's our best chance for someone coming out alive—" Jade cleared her throat, but Ember didn't miss the slight wobble. "He's our best chance for victory in the arena."

Hiccup.

Jade giggled.

"For such a tiny thing, it's amazing how much you sound like a drunken soldier twice your size."

"I—" *Hiccup.* "Do." *Hiccup.* "Not."

"Sure, honey."

Jade brushed a strand of hair out of Ember's face.

"And what's this about the missive? 'Tis between Xav and the High Table. They know nothing of your whereabouts, and even if they did… even if they heard inkling, you break no laws. I can't tell you everything is going to be alright. My mama taught me to never sugarcoat the truth, only my Yule cookies and men's egos."

"That is both the best and the worst advice I've heard." A strangled laugh escaped her raw throat.

Snap.

A branch cracked in the tree line behind them.

Gavyn emerged from the dense forest with his hands raised. "I couldn't find you." *I worried,* he left unsaid.

"Yule cookies and men's egos, huh?" He picked his way through the underbrush, his steps lacking their usual sureness. "I'll remember that next time you compliment my fighting prowess. If you take the advice to heart, pray tell, why do you lob only insults and criticism at our leader?"

"He is the last man on the mountain that needs his ego raised." Jade stood and gave him a hug. "I'll leave you two now."

"I shall keep your confidences, as I feel no desire to prick his displeasure." The corners of Gavyn's mouth twitched. He helped Ember up off the soft ground. "I'll walk you both—"

Jade raised a hand, glancing back and forth between them. "And I shall decline."

They stared at her back as she retreated through the trees.

He pulled Ember against him — slowly, ever so slowly — she melted into his arms. They stayed locked in the embrace until the dampness of the earth crawled its way along her calves. Not once did she share her thoughts. Couldn't seem to gather the correct ones. Besides, what would she say? Don't do this. Don't go in Xavier's stead.

Don't leave me.

Gavyn had more honor in his pinky finger than the rest of the territories combined. Nothing she could say or do would sway his actions. And deep down, she wouldn't wish that of him. He could never live with himself if someone else took his place.

Gavyn must have sensed the direction of her thoughts because he squeezed her tight and said, "Let's go home."

THE STEAM FROM THE BATH SWIRLED IN THE AIR ABOVE THE copper tub.

She nestled into Gavyn's chest, her back to his front.

He rubbed the lavender soap along her collarbone, her skin prickling like gooseflesh despite the warmth of the water.

She rested her head against his shoulder, allowing him greater access to her neck.

"Mmm," she purred as he soaped the swell of her chest. Neither had spoken much on the journey back to his room. They should discuss what was to come. Perhaps deliver false promises to one another. Now, she wanted to sink into the tub — sink into him — and forget the outside world.

He seemed to agree.

"Open your legs." Gavyn nipped along the outer shell of her ear. "That's it. I'm going to take care of you."

The soap fell to the bottom of the basin with a thud.

She inched back in the tub and moaned.

His broad hands cupped her core, and one thick finger stroked circles around that spot throbbing between her thighs, teasing with feather-light touches. Never enough to—

"You like that?" His calloused thumb pushed exactly where she needed. "Tell me what you want, Ember. Find the words."

"You, I need you." She arched against him. "I need you, Gavyn."

He tweaked her nipple. The sharp bite of pain snagged her attention enough for Ember to correct herself.

"I need you inside me. Your fingers. Your tongue. Your c— cock. Anything. Anyway you'll have me."

"Anyway?" He asked, one large finger stroked around the outer edge of the rosy-pink ring between her cheeks. His hard length strained against her lower back. He brushed the wet tendrils clinging to her forehead and whispered in her ear, "Anyway is a dangerous word for a man like me."

She whimpered.

"As much as I want to claim this part of you." The tip of one finger breached her tight entrance, "I'm too impatient tonight. Turn around."

Water sloshed over the rim of the tub.

Laughter at their predicament died in her throat at the sight of the heat in his eyes. She gripped his forearms, positioning herself above the tip of his cock. The word came easier to her, now, since she voiced it out loud.

Ember was ready. So ready to forget the last hour and sink down on his hard length, riding him into oblivion. To forget what waited outside his chamber door. But she knew what he wanted, what he needed from her, so she waited.

And waited.

And waited.

Suspended in the air, her heart thudded in her chest. She held herself impossibly still. Braced, waiting for his permission. The bastard. She would chuckle if her legs didn't ache so badly.

"Gavyn—"

"Good girl," he said, and the warmth that always curled around her at those words eased the tremble in her thighs. He grabbed her hips and with one quick thrust, he repeated, "My." Thrust. "Good." Thrust. "Girl."

She lowered herself down on his length and bit the thick muscle connecting his neck and shoulders.

"Ride me." He relaxed back against the tub walls and closed his eyes.

She eased up all the way to the tip and swiveled her hips in a clockwise motion then slid back down his length.

A harsh groan escaped his lips as she repeated the movement twice more.

She found a pleasurable rhythm, and waves of water spilled over, pooling on the floor.

"Leave it." He clamped down on her hips. "I'll take care of it. Later."

He might let her lead, but he maintained a thin thread of control.

She buried her head in his neck and rolled her hips. Torn between finding the release her body fought against and prolonging the pleasure to dull the riotous voices in her mind.

Too soon, relief and rightness and nothing consumed her. Her orgasm highlighted their connection, making everything too vivid. Too real.

His groan echoed in the room, and some distant part of her registered his undoing.

"Hmm, feel better?" he asked.

She nodded. Again, unable to find the words.

Her chivalrous Gavyn.

He wasn't afraid. She knew whatever punishment the High Table meted out, he would meet with honor. He prepared his entire life to fight for his family, to protect those who couldn't defend themselves.

The path he must journey was too narrow for regrets, but her chest ached.

"There's more water outside the tub than in." She moved

above him, but he wrapped his arms around her, smashing her chest to his. "Mmm. My good girl. My little thief. You stole more than just a loaf of bread."

He nuzzled her neck and sighed.

The remaining water grew tepid. A howl outside his bedroom window startled her awake.

It took her a second to realize they still snuggled in the tub.

Light from the moon entered the room through the small window above his bed and cast shadows around the corners. How long did they sleep?

"Hey," he crooned. "Let's dry off and go to bed."

"I can't stop thinking about the fight." She trailed her fingers over his scar. "My mind won't rest."

"I know." Gavyn pressed his forehead to hers. "I'm going to do everything in my power to win and return home."

"But what if they cast?" She ran her hand along his jawline. "What if they use magic?"

"I can only fight my fight. Only control my attack."

"You won't be able to overpower your opponent. It won't be a fair fight."

"Fighting is never fair." He tipped her chin and said, "In this you must understand. Here, on the compound, things are level. It's what Xavier and I believe is right. Good for the fighters. For their progression and morale. Outside these walls, fate chooses your opponent. Nature favors the strongest. Ideas of honor do not encumber her selection."

He held her stare.

"What if—" The words clogged her throat. "What if we just left?"

"What?"

"What if we left the compound? Or snuck out the day of the fight? We could cover a lot of ground before someone came looking. I'm skilled at finding suitable spots to hide in the forest. We could stay in Kiehl's cottage now that we know the way. And how to avoid detection."

"You want us to leave? To abandon the compound? My home?"

"Yes, but—"

"This is my family. They are my brothers," he said, slowly enunciating each word. "They are all worthy of this fight. Xavier earned my loyalty before dreams of this place took root in his mind. He made sacrifices for everyone. There is nothing I wouldn't do to protect his vision."

"I'm sorry. I know I'm saying all the wrong words. I spent all night trying to find the right ones."

Gavyn searched her eyes, for what? She wasn't certain, but he grabbed her face with both hands and said, "I won't run away. Even for you."

CHAPTER TWENTY-SIX

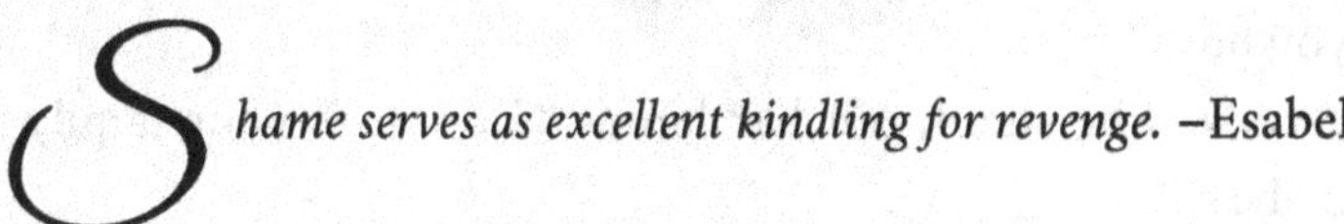

hame serves as excellent kindling for revenge. –Esabel

"AND I ROUNDED THE BEND IN THE PATH BY FARMER WHITBY'S old milking barn and almost lost my eyebrows," Jade said as she leaned against her cart. "My *eyebrows*. Can you believe it?"

"Mmm, hmm." Ember stared at the patrons out for their morning shopping.

"And then the local dragon flew down from the clouds. He had purple scales and a snout the color of fall apples. His talons. His talons, Ember. They were the size of the barn cats and the color of moss."

Jade laid a hand on her shoulder.

"He danced a jig with me right there in the meadow. Not that fancy two-step I showed you the other day. His tail, you see. But we made it through most of the steps without him crushing my new slippers."

"Hmm?" she asked, biting her lower lip. Jade went silent.

What was her friend talking about? Ember heard only a few words. Something about eyebrows and dancing. And a dragon. That can't be right.

"You've been in the clouds all morning, and I just fabricated a story about a dancing dragon to see if you were paying attention." Jade handed Pigeon a slice of bread with her fresh jam. "That will be two coppers."

"You did what?" She gasped. Her head spun to her friend as if seeing her for the first time.

"A dragon. I spun a yarn about a flying purple dragon. Pigeon probably thought I broke into Zoie's kitchen and drank all her mulled wine." Jade pocketed the coin. "Dancing beasts aside, I'm here. We are all here. You and Gavyn aren't alone. We love you both."

"I know." She shook out her hands. "I do. He's your family. For me he's…"

She rubbed her palm.

"He's what?"

"I'm not sure," she lied.

It hurt, though, keeping everything bottled like one of Zoie's flavored wines.

Gavyn was everything — dependable and perceptive and kind and funny. Dear gods, he had the most delightful sense of humor. She was not sure what she would have done this past fortnight without his teasing.

He was… everything.

"Too many things don't add up," she said. "The daggers. Lord Siodina at fight night, showing up with the Red Guard before dawn in the training barn. The fires in Kiehl's forests. Increased patrols in his village."

The past two weeks were both a dream and a nightmare.

During the day, she'd sat with Ada in the loft, sneaking peeks of his training.

Her fighting education still lagged behind Zoie's or even Jade's, but she couldn't tear her eyes away from the repetitious drills. She only left when hunger guided her down the ladder, taking her meals in their room or under the maple tree in the courtyard, unable to bear the conversation of the mess hall.

Gavyn stayed late, working in the ring with Xavier and Rowan and Mikel, tiptoeing to bed mere hours before the sun awakened the fields.

Every night, she ran her hands through hair still damp from his dip in the stream, her warm palms gliding over every inch of him. So warm, as she cupped his face and healed the swelling and cuts.

They made love every night. Sometimes slow and sensual. Other times frantic, full of bites and hard angles. Aside from his reassuring commands, neither spoke much.

She held onto the memories of his arm wrapped around her, pulling her tight even in sleep.

What more was there to say?

She regretted her words the night Xavier read the missive. They were clumsy, but the apology never came. She didn't want to waste precious breath on the past, though a part of her — that vaguely gray part that made her human and imperfect and his — wasn't sorry.

"I wish we had more time." She bit the inside of her cheek, not enjoying the pain but welcoming it all the same. "These two weeks dashed by as fast as a wolf gives chase to a rabbit. Too soon, it ended."

"Come. I know how to turn your mind from tonight." Jade wrapped an arm around her and steered Ember to the cottage. "Let's ensure you will burn brighter than the torches illuminating the arena, so he has no choice but to find you in the crowd."

A lifetime had passed since she'd last entered Jade's refuge.

An enormous pile of dirty pots and trenchers covered one end of her counter in the back. Her table held a jar full of colorful wildflowers. Pinks and purples and oranges mixed with whites and too cheerful yellows. The combination should have been jarring.

Like with everything else Jade touched, they were inviting.

New herbs hung from the rafters, and she stopped to inspect leaves. Cilantro. She leaned closer to take a whiff of their citrus fragrance.

Mama enjoyed it mixed with spring salads.

What would her mother say? Her voice was silent of late. Too occupied with Gavyn, the admonishments full of censure and caution stayed locked in that dark place in her mind. What would her mother think about her choice to travel to the Castle? To travel willingly toward danger?

She'd imagined this day for years, never once saying it out loud for fear of catapulting her mother into another episode — days, sometimes weeks, of little speaking, little eating.

It hadn't been worth sharing her deepest desires.

Now, she couldn't muster a sliver of excitement at the thought of setting her eyes to another Faeblood. Now, it was a distant dream, a selfish and childish wish.

"I use the dried seeds for my breads and scones, but the leaves taste funny," Jade said.

"Like soap." Ember scrunched her nose. "I don't care for it either."

"Here." Jade dumped the basket onto the wooden table and crossed the room to her trunk.

She dove inside and came up with a beautiful yellow gown draped across her arms.

"It was my mother's," Jade said. She held it out for inspection. "It's one of the few things I have left that was hers. I outgrew it four or five summers ago."

She gathered the gown against her body.

The fabric was luxurious. Its weight was heavier than her favored white dress but lighter than Jade's velvet green gown. The sleeves were three-quarter length and would fall between her elbow and wrist. Intricate needlework danced along the hems.

The neckline was straight but bowed out, and the excess fabric would lie enticingly across her chest. Its waist tapered sharply.

The full skirt flared out. A single layer, the fabric would sway when she walked. It was a soft yellow, not like the heavy coloring of calendula, but similar to the fuzz on newborn chicks.

A striking contrast against her dark hair.

"It will stand out in the crowd." Jade closed the lid of the trunk. "The nobility favor heavier fabrics and dark, jewel tones. It suits you. A ray of magical sunshine in a crowd of droll spectators."

"I'm sorry," she said and embraced Jade, scrunching the dress between them.

"For what?"

"I've been selfish. I didn't even consider your emotions, what everyone else might be feeling. Your stomach must be in knots, too." She pulled back and held her friend at arm's length. "Forgive me."

"There's nothing to forgive. I trust in Gavyn… and Xavier." Jade shooed her around the screen, a small tremble in her hand, her voice. "Let's see how it fits."

Ember slipped on the new gown and stepped around the partition.

"Beautiful." Jade placed her palms together and brought the tips of her fingers to her lips. "All eyes will be on you."

∿

Erik raised his fist to knock on Maia's door and hesitated.

He ran his hands through his close-cropped hair.

Even after all these months in the village, it still surprised him when his fingers failed to tangle in longer locks. Barely a finger-width high on the top and even shorter on the sides, he enjoyed the practicality of a near shorn head. It certainly made grappling easier without tendrils falling in his face when he rolled around on the floor.

Maybe he'd keep the length when he returned home. Buck tradition. Irritate his father.

What *was* he doing?

A full five minutes passed with him pacing in front of her door, raising his hand to knock only for it to fall limply at his side while he contemplated… hair styles.

Thankfully, the barracks was empty. Most fighters left when Xavier escorted Gavyn to the castle. Only the kitchen staff and a few of the cubs on patrol remained.

After the visit during fight night, the threats and demands from his father stopped. Along with all other communication. He didn't know his father's plans, but his gut told him they would unfold tonight.

Erik ran his hand over his mouth.

He'd lost weight.

His face was hollow, his already sharp cheekbones more pronounced. Last week, Madam MaLota punched another hole in his belt and sent him off with a basket of warm rolls, hotter warnings.

Even Xavier had noticed, Erik had felt his eyes on him all week in the training barn.

Dammit. He almost forgot the mask.

An impromptu addition to his hasty plan, he pulled the scratchy burlap over his head and took a deep breath. He should have told Xavier about his father, his threats.

Too late now, but at least he could spare Maia from this mess. His remaining morals urged him to alert her. But Erik knew Maia wouldn't simply stay behind out of precaution. While it made his task more difficult, her hotheadedness was… endearing.

And a dark feral part of him savored her fight.

Knock. Knock. Knock—

Maia opened the door. Her attention remained on clasping the cuff at her wrist.

That was her first mistake.

He slammed into her, knocking them both to the ground.

At the last moment, he twisted and took the brunt of the fall.

No sooner than he gathered his wits, Maia bucked against his weight, attempting to wedge a knee between them.

He prepared for this. In fate's ironic clutches, she prepared him for this.

Her body squirmed beneath him, soft curves insulated a core of sensuous steel.

He knew her moves. He knew her tells. But he wasn't ready for her frantic thrashing, the subtle loss of the edge of control.

Pox on the Lords. His father. This entire situation.

She didn't deserve this, but he couldn't risk her getting hurt as collateral in his father's twisted games. Not after his sire suspected her as Faeblood.

Not after Erik didn't correct the assumption.

Even now, as his chest pressed her to the floor, he second guessed his decision to stay silent.

Even now, as he brought her hands — with wrists so small he held both of them in one of his — above her head, he second guessed his hesitation not to confess his true identity to Xavier.

Even now, as she bucked and writhed and fought, he second guessed his plan.

"Hold still. I'm not here to harm you," Erik growled in her

ear as he wedged his forehead between her shoulder and collarbone, pressing until she quieted.

"You won't get away with this," she said, but the words were small, shrill. "You… you won't get away with this."

Quick breaths burst in and out of her chest.

She smelled of citrus and mint and anger, a unique combination not worn on the courtiers in the Castle.

And damn if that didn't do something for him.

He'd never be rid of the scent. Not after all the hours they spent rolling around on the sandy pit ingrained in his mind. Especially not now with her twisting beneath him.

Dear gods, recalling the memories from tonight would pave his journey to the gates of hell.

"Hold still," he repeated, deepening his voice and adding a gravel-like quality to the timbre. Erik pulled a length of rope from the back of his waistband and wrapped it around both wrists. "I said hold—"

She bucked beneath him. Her head narrowly missed smashing into his nose.

"You better clear off." She pulled against the bindings. "I will track you through the mountain if I must."

That was her second mistake.

He would welcome the chase — the part of him he kept hidden from polite society, from fear of molding it into the monster he saw in the mirror — craved it. Reveled in the hunt.

He tied her wrists to the leg of her bed, pulling the slack out of the binding.

She stared straight ahead, her eyes tracking his every movement.

Erik savored her rage and said, "I look forward to it."

SOMETIMES, EMBER DESPISED BEING SO SHORT.

Who was she kidding? It frustrated her every day.

Wedged in a thick crowd, she stopped every so often to stretch on her tiptoes and gauge their progress. After each glimpse, the surge of bodies pushed forward and propelled her onward.

The entire village made the trek to the Castle.

She was grateful, and not the least bit surprised, so many turned up to support Gavyn.

Beyond the marketplace, the buildings and homes thinned. The road changed from level cobblestone to packed dirt filled with large ruts. She glanced down at her thin-soled shoes, thankful the rains held off.

The journey took most of the afternoon.

There was a crispness in the air, and she rubbed her upper arms to ward off the chill. The leaves were brilliant — yellows mixed with vibrant greens from summer. Soon, deep reds and oranges would grace the forests.

Their party stayed close together. Eigen kept a hand on Jade's lower back, with Zoie and Ada trailing behind. Their stoic escort barely spoke two words during their nooning meal.

Despite eating scant bites of the rich stew, her stomach churned.

They climbed the bluff and the outline of the Castle rose above an enormous lake swallowing the valley below. It was difficult not to gape at the grandeur. Xavier's village may prosper more than the other territories, but its design was simple compared to the wealth and extravagance before her.

A home to fairytales and nightmares.

The gray stone walls blended with the rock face as if the mountain itself chiseled the structure. Three tall ramparts guarded the corners. The far side of the Castle jutted into the rock behind it, negating the need for a fourth.

It was a stalwart fortress.

The edge of the lake pushed up against the foundation, making it impenetrable from the front and sides.

Small waves crested against the stone, generating soapy froth. The vibrant color of the water contrasted with the muddy palate in the valley. It ranged from sapphire in the deeper middle to aquamarine along the banks, reminding her of the color of the pool at Ashmere Falls.

And their first kiss.

On its farthest shore, the water spilled over a wall of large boulders and carved a path alongside the road. A source for the river feeding the territories.

A little over halfway along the nearest bank, a large stone bridge connected the shoreline to an imposing wooden gate. Two towers framed the entrance, each with an enormous torch illuminating the path in the waning light.

Men and women and children, all dressed in their finest, lined the crossing. A sizable crowd gathered along the banks with mobs of spectators spilling out of the forest.

"Looks like every village is here." Zoie caught up to them and asked, "How many do you think?"

"Each village and surrounding territory is home to several thousand families," Jade said. "I fathom another couple hundred call the healer caravans home."

"There must be over three thousand here."

"At least." Jade broke away from Eigen. "Xavier told me to expect near four thousand in the arena."

"Arena?" Ember asked as she picked up the hem of her skirts and stepped over a large root in the path. "I thought… I'm not really sure what I thought."

"The original ruling families commissioned a half-moon arena built next to the courtyard. It winds around a central stage sunk into the mountain." Zoie grabbed onto Ada as the trail took a sharp turn. "Xavier mentioned it once before. Said he saw it from a distance the only other time he answered a summons to the Castle."

"Years ago, he and Gavyn undertook the journey to request gold and supplies for the training barn." Jade cupped Ada's elbow and said, "You were a teenager, too busy chasing after the local village lads to bother with the gritty details of building the compound. But I remember him coming home that night. Determination fixed his face and became his master from that day hence."

"They opened their coffers?" Ada's eyes grew wide.

"Yes." Jade sighed. "He didn't sleep the first five years until he paid it all back plus special tithing."

"Why didn't they just give him the gold?" Ada's head tilted to the side. "What he did… is doing… clearly benefits the Castle."

"Ha," Jade barked out. "The High Table is neither generous nor magnanimous."

Ember chewed on the information for the rest of their climb down. Wrapped up in the outcome of Gavyn's fight, she never considered much else. The missive seemed to shock everyone except Xavier. Did his quiet response while reading the parchment stem from a show of leadership? Or from past dealings with the High Table?

At last, they arrived.

The castle loomed over them, more imposing up close. She counted thirty guards at the gate and another fifty stationed along the front wall. They wore shiny helmets and dull armor. The ones at the entrance sported heavy shields on one arm, swords in the other.

She grabbed Eigen's arm and gasped.

"Long blades." They ran half the length of her body. Up close, the weapons appeared even more menacing. "So many…"

Eigen snarled. "A reminder."

"The Castle never misses an opportunity to flex their rule.

With all the villages in attendance, it's a chance to conjure superiority." Jade pointed to the center of the courtyard. "Look."

An enormous, circular pool spanned half the width of the terrace.

Heavy slabs of granite formed a low wall and enclosed the aquamarine water. Artisans stacked them three high, the ledge a perfect height for sitting. Two enormous boulders interrupted the ring and created a gap for water to cascade down under the cobblestone plaza. Lilly pads, with fronds as big as the shields on the guards out front, floated on the surface and swayed with the flow.

"Ooh, the Pool of Illumination." Ada pulled her closer. "It's said to bring enlightenment to those who submerge their minds and bodies."

"Ada..." Zoie chuckled. "Keep your gown on."

"Come." Ada smirked and hooked an arm through Ember's elbow. "We can at least dip a hand."

Ember bent over the still water and studied her reflection. Or at least she tried. Her gaze could not penetrate the depth of the pool. Maybe she was more fatigued than she wanted to admit. The longer she stared into the glass sheet, the warmer her palms grew.

She skimmed the surface. Sharp pain seared her entire body.

Vibrations radiated the length of each finger and rushed up her neck. A shriek echoed in her mind, the cry piercing her temple, and she covered her ears.

Make it stop. Make it stop.

Her knees buckled.

Strong arms wrapped around her before she plummeted to the terrace.

She swallowed once. Twice. At least the screaming between her ears stopped. A faint coating of sweat covered her palms. She buried her nose in Eigen's chest. The familiar scent of pine settled her tumultuous stomach, and the stew stopped clawing its way up her throat.

"Need to move," Eigen said as he dragged her across the courtyard and placed her next to a thick column supporting the outer wall.

Directly overhead, a stone ceiling provided cover and doubled as the base for patrolling soldiers on the upper level.

Eigen kept his hands at her waist until she stopped swaying.

After a couple of calming breaths, she glanced up to find several sets of eyes on her.

Jade was right — she stood out.

Her little collapse near the pool notwithstanding, the bold color of her dress acted as a beacon in a sea of deep reds and blues and greens. She tucked an errant strand behind her ear and smoothed out the invisible wrinkles in her skirts.

Ada rushed to Ember's side. "What—"

"Not here." Eigen shook his head.

"Let's head over to the arena and find a place to stand before everyone else crams in." Zoie kept glancing over her shoulder. She gestured down the stone steps and pointed to a row halfway up from the stage. "Over there."

"What happened?" Jade wrapped an arm around her shoulders and whispered, "Are you hurt?"

"I'm sound," she lied and rested a hand on her stomach. "I think it's just nerves."

First Ashmere Falls and now this. Her mother cautioned against allowing her emotions to run high. Faeblood must stay in control or the magic would spread, taking over the body and thoughts. Akin to an illness or parasite.

She'd always tossed the warnings aside, assuming it was her mother's paranoia.

Now, she wasn't certain.

"Do you know anything about Gavyn's opponent?" Jade asked Ada.

"Xavier thinks it's a fighter from the east, but I'm not convinced." Ada wrinkled her brow, pointing to the group in the front row with navy tunics. "It makes little sense to pair him with Harin again, since Gavyn bested him twice, even under less than ideal circumstances."

"The High Table would want to ensure a victory in order for the punishment to be effective," Zoie said with grim authority. "But Gavyn hasn't found his match in the ten years he's been head trainer. Who would they coerce to take the fight?"

CHAPTER TWENTY-SEVEN

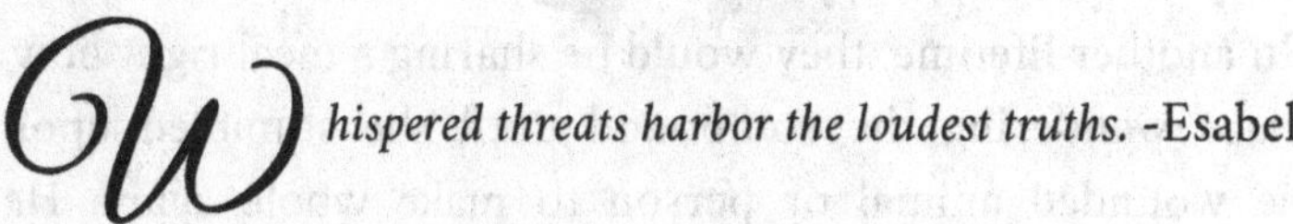

hispered threats harbor the loudest truths. -Esabel

"AGAIN," ROWAN SAID AS HE HELD UP HIS HANDS, SIGNALING another strike. "Quicker. Stop thinking."

Smack. Fist on flesh echoed on the stone walls in the tunnel. The damp corridor behind the stage made Gavyn's nose itch.

Jab. Step. Jab. Cross.

Tiny beads of sweat formed at Gavyn's hairline, and he wiped them with the back of his wrist. He savored the rhythm of the warm-up and wanted nothing more than to keep moving, to keep his mind still.

"Take a break. Walk twenty paces down and back." Xavier's clipped tone echoed off the slimy walls. "Slow. I need you to stay warm but not wear yourself out."

"I'll go with him." Rowan slapped his shoulder. "Come on, old man, let's keep your creaky knees moving."

He rolled off the affection but was grateful Rowan brought along his unimaginative jests.

Just like the training barn. He repeated, *just like the training barn.*

Leary of slipping on the slick surface, Gavyn shortened his stride. The noise of the crowd faded the deeper they traveled in the tunnels behind the stage.

Was she here yet? Ember, with Eigen and the girls, left the village after them.

Rowan stopped him and held out a palm to strike.

They repeated combinations on the return trip to the arena. Block. Jab. Duck. Step. Cross.

Was she warm enough? The air turned brisk. He meant to purchase a new pair of boots for her. Did her feet ache from the journey in her flimsy slippers?

In another lifetime, they would be sharing a meal right now, perhaps wandering the compound until she stumbled upon some wounded animal or person to make whole again. He would tease her about her clumsiness until she blushed.

In another lifetime, they would spend the rest of the evening wrapped around each other. Inside each other, whispering about their day.

In another lifetime, it would be him escorting her to the Castle. Not his family.

Gavyn shook his head, retracing his steps. He needed one last look.

"Jade and the girls made it." Xavier braced against the tunnel's exit and pointed to the right side of the stage. "There."

Eigen stood sentry on one side. Erik protected their backs from behind. Jade wrapped an arm around Ember's shoulders, hugging her tight.

"Your waif stands out," Rowan said as he elbowed Gavyn's ribs.

"I don't know whether to congratulate Jade on that color or strangle her for drawing so many eyes," Xavier growled.

Gavyn was torn. He loved being able to spot her in the crowd. But Xavier was right. Everyone else looked too. That was the heart of it, wasn't it? In the end, he had to trust his brothers, his family to take care of her. Now and if… if he never made it out of the Castle.

He tapped Rowan on the shoulder and dropped back down into his fighting stance, back into the one constant in his life he could count on to focus his thoughts.

Jab. Cross. Breathe. Feint left.

A throat cleared behind him.

He pivoted to face the newcomer.

"I serve as an envoy for the High Table." The messenger's ruffled collar shook with each breath, reminding him of a peacock crinkling his feathers.

His unusual pants narrowed at the waist and flared out at the hips before curving mid-calf. The haughty purple color jarred Gavyn's senses but suited the man's demeanor.

"My duty is to inform you of the rules for the fight," the envoy announced in a squeaky voice.

"Go on." Xavier cracked his knuckles.

"The match is three rounds." The messenger's eyes darted back and forth between Xavier and Gavyn. "Each round is ten minutes."

Fatigue claimed the most conditioned brawlers after just a few. At the training barn, Gavyn kept the longest sparring rounds at five. During fight night, only the most experienced fighters earned the right to dance for three minutes between bells.

Xavier was right. The castle wanted to prolong the entertainment.

"And?" Gavyn ground his teeth.

"You…" The diminutive man pointed to him. "You… will fight one of the elite Red Guard."

Rowan balled his hands into fists and took a step forward.

Xavier's arm shot out and gripped the front of his tunic. A silent shake of the head kept his brother in place.

"Anything else?" Gavyn asked and bounced on the balls of his feet.

"Yes." The envoy side-eyed Rowan. "You… um… you are to present yourself to the High Table and confess your transgressions prior to the match. They require you to bend at the knee. Do not look directly at them. Avert your gaze until addressed."

"This is outrageous." Rowan bared his teeth. "He's representing Xavier, not assuming any transgression."

"It is an honor the High Table bestows on… on…"

"Gavyn," Xavier said, his lips curling into a menacing grin. "His name is Gavyn."

"Yes. Yes, of course. Gavyn." The messenger's collar vibrated around his neck. "And then they present the weapons."

"What?" His body tensed. "What do you mean, weapons?"

"The High Table declared the match to proceed with broadswords."

The gong of a bell sounded in the distance.

Gavyn closed his eyes and took a deep breath. It was time.

Rays from the fading sun warmed his arms. He held a hand above his brow to shield his eyes. One last look to warm his path to the Underworld.

Rowan hugged him first.

"Virtus et Honos," he said as one long arm wrapped around Gavyn's shoulders and pounded him on the back. "See you on the other side, brother."

"If I don't make it, speak with Kiehl. Don't let these bastards win. Don't let them sow the seeds of discontent between the territories." He paused, then added, "Take care of her. Take care of her for me. Convince her to stay. Tell her… tell her I love her and want her to stay in the family."

"Tell her yourself," Xavier said. He clasped his hand and yanked him in for a hug. Xav slapped him on the side of the cheek and stepped back. "Virtus et Honos. It's time. Show them who we are. No mercy."

Gavyn walked the last few steps alone.

Large torches, spaced every twelve paces, illuminated the edge of the stage and blurred the outlines of the spectators.

Front and center, nine men in blood red robes sat at a long table.

"I serve the High Table and honor their summons." He held his head high as he knelt on the hard surface and spoke with authority. "I accept this challenge as payment for defying the decree against blades of warfare."

Several lords of the High Table bristled. A whispered hush fell over the crowd.

"Your insolence is showing, boy." Lord Siodina sneered and flicked his wrist. "This is the most egregious offense. To craft or harbor a blade is an affront to not only the High Table but to the peace and prosperity of the entire realm and all those who serve."

Gavyn bit the inside of his cheek.

Lord Siodina strolled over to his side. The hem of the heavy robes dragged along the stage.

"You will pay for your transgressions with your life today," Lord Siodina whispered in his ear. "The same will befall the one you harbor with magic. She faces the same fate as her protectors and will not leave the Castle tonight."

Gavyn's eyes snapped up. He released a snarl.

"Let this be a lesson in humility to those who may follow," Lord Siodina said to the crowd. He placed his palms together. "To go against the High Table carries a severe penance."

A glint of silver reflected off the torches.

As the distance between the councilman's hands grew so did the length of the sword he conjured. The blade spanned almost half of Gavyn's body. The hilt was thick and wrapped with brown leather.

It would require two hands to wield.

A deafening silence rippled through the crowd.

"Your blade," Lord Siodina said as he presented Gavyn the weapon. His fingers retracted, but kept their claw-like shape. "For your brief time remaining in this world."

Gavyn wrapped both palms around the handle. He swung the blade in the air, testing the weight. It moved faster than expected. He switched stances, pivoting for balance.

Clang.

What the—

He swung the sword upward at the last possible moment to meet his opponent's strike.

Steel scraped against steel.

His enemy's sword grazed his own, slicing Gavyn's shoulder at the end of its arc. He took stock of the wound. Shallow. More pain than damage.

He ducked and rolled out from under the second swing.

The Red Guard followed, and Gavyn kicked out with his boot.

Thwack.

His opponent's knee buckled, forcing him to catch his weight with his other leg.

Gavyn popped up behind the Red Guard, too close for striking with his blade. He switched grips on the handle and punched the guard in the temple.

Thwack. Thwack. Thwack.

He circled out, putting some distance between them.

His opponent squared and snarled. Heavy boots amplified the guard's poor footwork.

He favors his right.

The guard's nostrils flared as he thrust the blade forward.

Gavyn parried the strike, spinning to his left.

Clang. Clang, clang.

His opponent easily volleyed the blows and returned a combo of his own.

Gavyn blocked the first two but pivoted too late for the third.

The blade sliced the front of his gut. Blood gushed out and stained the top hem of his pants. *Deeper. Problematic.* Gavyn gritted his teeth and set up his attack.

Step. Thrust.

Step. Thrust.

Step. Thrust.

On the third attempt, Gavyn ran his blade along the guard's sword. He ducked and sliced the man's upper thigh.

A large gash split his leg, and the fighter limped away.

But not fast enough.

Gavyn seized the opening and followed with three quick strikes. He overestimated his reach and ended up within the guard's range. He dropped his sword to the ground and dove for the man's stomach.

The element of surprise was on his side.

He hooked a leg behind his opponent and used the momentum of his fall to throw them down onto the stage. The back of the Red Guard's head hit the surface. Hard.

A dazed look crossed over the man's eyes. Gavyn mounted his middle and picked up the wrist holding the blade. He slammed it on the ground until the weapon clattered to the stage.

The fighter sent a hook to Gavyn's temple.

Block. Elbow. Punch. Elbow.

A cut opened up under his eye and blood trickled from his busted lip.

The Red Guard bucked up.

He scooted forward, pressing his knees under the man's armpits. His opponent raised his hands too late. Gavyn rained punches down on his face until the body underneath fell slack.

To hell with the Lords. He wasn't their puppet. If they wanted a fight to the death, then they could kill the disgraced guard themselves.

His vision swirled. The noise from the crowd roared in his ears. Cheers and hollers mixed with a few boos. He scanned the arena.

Where is she?

⌇

THE BLOODTHIRSTY SPECTATORS YELLED IN EMBER'S EARS.

Their excitement amplified the queasiness in her stomach. The unfairness tore at her heart. There was no honor in this farce.

Focused on Gavyn's injuries, she didn't notice the commotion behind her until it was too late.

A body slammed into her back and knocked her to the row in front. She smashed into a spectator, her momentum propelling them both to the hard stone surface.

"Are you alright—"

A scream lanced the air.

Her head whipped up.

Two men in head-to-toe black clothing, snatched Zoie. Dark masks covered their faces but did nothing to disguise their intentions.

Erik squared to the captor, holding his hands out in front. "Easy there, no one needs to get hurt."

Everything unfolded in slow motion.

"Let her go. Your quarrel lies elsewhere," Erik said as he took a half step forward, his eyes never leaving Zoie's.

He missed the man behind him.

The attacker seized on Erik's inattentiveness and wrapped both arms around Erik's neck. His accomplice tossed Zoie to the side and charged.

Erik grabbed at the choke, leveraging the hold, and kicked at the man bearing down on him.

Where was Eigen?

A mass of spectators surged toward the exits, sweeping him away in the churn.

Eigen swam against their attempts to flee, but the wave carried him farther and farther away from their group. He battled the rush and dove between distraught villagers.

"Watch out! He has a dagger," someone screamed.

Ember saw it then.

A blade the length of her forearm slashed the air. Light from the torches reflected off its shiny tip.

Erik's eyes widened. He kicked and twisted his torso, but the edge of the weapon sank under his ribs.

"Ah!" His sharp cry silenced the onlookers.

The attacker wrenched the dagger free and plunged the blade into Erik's stomach once more.

Two bright red splotches soaked his cream linen shirt, and his struggles grew weaker and weaker.

The attacker raised his hand for a third strike. It never came.

Eigen broke through the crowd and tackled the man.

The partner released Erik and joined the fray. He delivered a blow to Eigen's jaw, stunning him for a moment. The accomplice slapped his partner on the arm and grunted.

They both fled up the stairs and out of view.

Ember pushed herself upright and scrambled over the rows to reach her friends.

The red stains on Erik's shirt bloomed in all directions. The circles connected, making one large pattern.

Her magic crawled under her skin, a force she struggled to contain.

Deep down, she registered the risks of casting in the crowd.

But the healer inside her didn't hesitate.

Determination insulated Ember from the crowd. She knelt

down beside Erik and laid her ear to his chest. He drew one rattling breath and then another.

His wounds were fatal.

She placed both hands on his midsection and closed her eyes.

Her palms grew hot and pain radiated up her arm. It marched along her collar, climbing up her neck. She needed every bit of concentration to not release her touch. It was excruciating, burning her from within.

Heat flayed every stretch of skin as her instinct to let go, to save herself, warred with the power of her bloodline.

Ancestral magic battled self-preservation.

Soon, Erik's breathing evened out. A faint sheen of perspiration collected at his brow.

The pinpricks lessened in her palms, and she whimpered.

While the remaining internal wounds knitted together, the red bloom on Erik's shirt stopped spreading.

Her hands shook, and nausea crawled up her throat. Pain throbbed in Ember's head and her arms grew tired. So tired. Exhausted.

Almost finished. Stay with me, Erik. Please.

The last bit of flesh stitched back together and darkness took over.

THE RED GUARD SWARMED THE HIGH TABLE.

They opened a trapdoor in the front section of the stage floor and funneled the councilmen below.

Satisfied the depths of the fortress swallowed Lord Siodina, Gavyn ran into the crowd. Blood seeped from his wounds with the jarring movements.

Panicked screams assailed his ears from every direction. Men, women, and children clogged the exit routes all trying to push through three congested openings in the wall along the upper level.

Bodies crammed around him, blocking his vision. Gavyn narrowed his focus to one thing — the butter yellow dress he spotted on the ground six rows above him.

He shoved and shouldered his way between the harried spectators, knocking over more than one individual in his haste.

"Move," Xavier bellowed. He forced the gawkers out of their way. "I said *move*."

Almost there.

Almost.

At last, Gavyn reached her.

Ember lay crumbled on the stone steps, her forehead pale. An arm rested across her face, obscuring her features.

"No. No. No."

Erik was on the ground, surrounded by Jade and Zoie. Ada stood farther back, tears streaming down her ashen face. Eigen braced their flank, trying to keep the masses from trampling their group.

"Careful." Xavier gripped his arm. "We don't know if she's wounded. You don't want to make it worse."

"It's not—" Jade sobbed. "It's not her. The men. There were two. One... one had a blade. Erik. He—"

Gavyn didn't wait for the rest of the story. He bent down and rolled her over. Faint red stains smeared the top of the light-colored gown. His eyes flicked to the darker marks on Erik's tunic.

Not hers.

He rested his cheek against her chest, and the slight flutter of her breath brushed his ear. Gavyn couldn't stop touching her. He checked for other injuries, needing reassurance she was sound.

"Ember. Ember, wake up." He caressed her cheek and choked out, "Please wake up."

She stirred in his arms.

He rested his forehead against hers, pulling her tight to his chest.

"Pick her up. It's time to move." Xavier tapped his shoulder. "Rowan, grab Erik."

"Wait." Jade clasped Xavier's wrist. "His wounds. They might—"

"We don't have time," Xavier growled.

Gavyn didn't falter. He took the steps two at a time.

Ember shifted in his arms while he found his bearings at the top of the arena. The pool rose out of the courtyard to his right, and the entrance gate opened on his left.

A clang of armor rang from above.

He didn't need to look up to know the guards doubled in number.

Rowan sprinted ahead, not slowing with the weight of another to carry. The girls held their skirts in one hand and ran after him. Xavier fell back and ushered the rest of his villagers out.

"Go," Xavier mouthed from across the distance. "Go."

Gavyn looked down at the woman in his arms and back to his leader. His best friend. He hesitated a moment before making his choice.

Then ran after Rowan.

They kept a relentless pace. Rowan halted at the head of the trail, giving the group time to catch their breath. Jade and Zoie panted. Ada placed a hand on her hip and bent at the waist.

"We need to keep moving," Rowan said as he scanned the group and nodded to Gavyn.

They climbed out of the valley and rested at a grassy overlook. He squinted. A large group of villagers, led by Xavier, crossed the stone bridge and jogged around the lake.

He sighed.

Ember stirred in his arms. A pinch of color returned to her face, but she remained paler than he liked.

He stroked her cheek, and a drop of blood from his shoulder dripped on the front of her ruined gown.

Her eyes remained glassy, like the edges of his favorite lemon loaf.

Where was the baker? His birthday would pass in another fortnight, and Ada promised him a thick slice.

He looked down.

That's odd. My shirt is red. Only at the bottom, though. I don't own any half red shirts.

The color soaked the top of his pants and covered the side of her dress.

'Tis a shame. I really like this color on her. My sunshine.

His vision blurred. Cotton clogged his ears.

Ember's face filled his narrowed view. Her mouth opened and closed, but no words came out.

He reached up to tuck a tendril of hair behind her ear, but his arm didn't cooperate.

Why was it so heavy?

Maybe if I could just rest for a bit, I could muster the energy to kiss her properly and then scold her for scaring the life out of me.

"GAVYN," EMBER SCREAMED. "GAVYN!"

He slumped to the ground.

She scrambled off his lap. The world spun, and it took two heartbeats for her vision to catch up.

She was weak. The cast for Erik stole her strength, her magic.

Blood flowed from the wound in Gavyn's gut. So much. So fast that she barely registered the gash on his shoulder.

Not him. Please not him, too.

Time seemed to stand still and move fast all at once.

Tingles of warmth licked her fingers, but the rush of a cast had yet to fill her palm. She had never willed her magic into being. It was never necessary — a truth that clawed at the edges of her control.

"Your shirt, Rowan." She had to do something, anything to hold the wound together. "Give me your shirt to stop the bleeding."

Rowan pulled his tunic over his head and handed it to her.

Ember bunched the shirt and pressed it to the gash.

Blood immediately stained the fabric and continued to trail down Gavyn's hip.

"*Em-ber,*" Gavyn moaned, but his eyes stayed shut.

A hot trickle of tears rolled down her cheeks, and she couldn't contain the sob wrenched from her throat. Not Gavyn. Please, not him. He was honorable and kind and good. Everything the Castle tried to snuff out of the populace.

What would she do without him? How could she go on knowing he wasn't here to frown at her antics or hug away her sorrows?

She skimmed her thumb over his bottom lip. This was her nightmare.

Wake up. Wake up. Wake up.

Ember couldn't lose him.

Rowan fell to his knees beside them, his face as pale as Gavyn's.

She wanted to scream at him to make it stop. She wanted to shove him away when she realized he couldn't.

Dust kicked up around them, catching in her nostrils, her mouth. New voices joined the mix. Indistinct.

Her vision clouded, and her senses dulled to nothing.

Please, she repeated. *Dear gods, I'll do anything. Please... just spare Gavyn.*

Fatigue threatened to pull her from him. It was fierce,

fighting against her will to stay awake. She refused to give in, but rested her head against his chest. Her hand against his heart.

I love him, she admitted, finally.

But it was too late. Same as with her mother. Stubbornness kept the words buried in her throat, and fate snatched the last opportunity to declare her feelings.

She closed her eyes, and her lips moved, chanting three simple words.

I love you.

I love you.

I love you.

Her chest was both heavy and empty, but a thin flame of warmth gathered in her palm. She didn't feel her magic. Her breath. Or hear the thundering of her heart.

But she left her hand on his chest and made bargains with the devil himself.

A blinding light flashed behind her eyes, and darkness pulled her under its dense spell, once more.

CHAPTER TWENTY-EIGHT

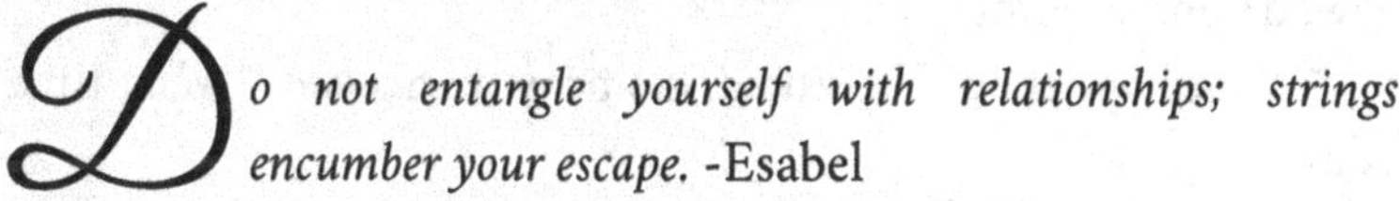

o not entangle yourself with relationships; strings encumber your escape. -Esabel

SHE COULDN'T STOP LOOKING, TOUCHING.

Two days passed since that horrible night in the arena.

He was alive, but Ember didn't trust her eyes. Instead, she ran her fingers through his hair and down his body, checking and reassuring herself he really was here.

"Mmm, my sunshine," Gavyn murmured in his sleep. He nuzzled into her chest, pressing his entire length against her.

She resisted the urge to arch into his touch, leery of the injury to his gut. How was she supposed to focus when he was warm and snuggly and hard? Her half-hearted attempts to put some space between their bodies were just that — half-hearted.

"Closer," he mumbled.

"Easy there," she said, her voice breathier than intended. "I'm delighted you feel well enough for... that, but you suffered serious injuries. How is the rest of you feeling?"

"Sore," he croaked out. "My shoulder and stomach hurt."

"I imagine so." The edges of her lips curled up, and her fingers absentmindedly trailed up and down his arm.

He rolled onto his back and ran his hand over his midsection. A faint pink line spanned his right flank from hip to naval. Gavyn traced the path of the raised skin and winced.

"It will feel tender for the next few days. The tightness will linger a week, but you may apply some of Zoie's calendula cream to calm the skin."

She studied the gash on his shoulder. It was long and thin. And unlike the puckered edges of the one on his torso, black thread crisscrossed the slice, closing the wound.

"Once we returned to the compound, Jade cleaned and sewed your shoulder."

"What happened?" he asked, his brow furrowed. "What time is it?"

Her mouth went dry, and she swallowed.

"Just before supper. You slept for two days. After you carried me out of the arena, everyone gathered around the entrance to the valley. Jade mentioned they waited for Xavier to bring the last of the villagers. I'm unsure what transpired at the end of your match, but I woke to you bleeding out beside me."

Gavyn rubbed the side of his jaw.

"I forced the fight to the ground and overpowered the Red Guard with my fists. When it was over, I looked up into the crowd and couldn't find you. My heart stopped." He tucked a lock of hair behind her ear. "I remembered where you and the girls last stood, so I ran in that direction."

His exhale fluttered across her collarbone.

"I rolled you over and blood stains covered your dress. It took me longer than necessary to figure out you were okay," He said, his voice shallow. "That the blood belonged to Erik."

"I'm fine." She cupped his face with both hands. A half-smile tugged her lips. "At least now I am. Casting for mortal wounds takes a lot out of me. Then I woke up and found you in the same predicament. It took every ounce of energy I possessed to heal the gash on your midsection. It's not my best work, but it thwarted the bleeding. Luckily, Jade is an accomplished seamstress, as I lacked the power to close the one on your shoulder. Her stitches are tight, so the scar should fade in a summer or two."

He hesitated, studying her, then leaned over and feathered kisses along her eyelids, across her cheek. Then her mouth.

"Lucky is right. It shone down on all of us that day. I'm fortunate my opponent lacked adequate skills in hand-to-hand combat. Lucky... he was a student of the blade at the detriment of all other forms of fighting."

He pulled back and brushed a thumb over her bottom lip.

"The entire compound is blessed with Zoie's talent for crafting various tinctures and Jade's skill with a needle. And now, by chance, you stumbled into our home. A Faeblood. A powerful healer curled up in a den of fighters."

He gripped her hip and kissed his way up the column of her neck.

"It's nothing less than fate that you ended up here, and I will do everything in my power to protect you from Lord Siodina's threats."

"What threats—"

He sealed his mouth over hers.

Her body, primed from his nearness and petting, opened easily when his hand skimmed down her chest and coaxed her thighs apart.

She whimpered.

What threats? She could barely hold the thought. Lost it completely at the sharp nip on her earlobe, the soft caress between her legs. She flexed into his touch, her body's need making her mind all fuzzy with pleasure. Within moments, she was achy. Wanton. Desperate for the connection.

Would it always be like this?

His fingers played with her so deftly. His touch changed the direction of her mind without her ability to catch up. He thrust a finger in her wet core, and when he added a second, she couldn't summon the outrage to care.

She writhed next to him, arching into his palm. They should stop. They needed to talk.

Distraction or not, she didn't want it to end.

"Up." Gavyn patted her thigh.

"What are you... your shoulder..."

"I want you to ride my face. He cupped her bottom with his uninjured arm, positioning her above his mouth. "You're correct. I cannot bed you in the manner I would like, but I will still take your pleasure."

His voice deepened, her body unable to disobey the tone.

Ember's knees grazed his ears, and his long fingers wrapped around the outside of her thighs, spreading her wider. His tongue speared her center, and she fell forward, bracing her arms carefully at his side.

She peered down at their joining, the rhythm of their dance mesmerizing.

The first time he worshiped her from below, a flicker of power shot though her. To hold such a strong man, one with the ability to command legions of fighters, beneath her skirts, sent a thrill through her core. But with his fingers digging into her thighs and his expert tongue holding her in place, she was happy to be mistaken.

"Don't you dare hold back," he growled.

Juices coated the stubble of his chin. The rumble of his voice sent shocks through her center. She slid back and forth, grasping for friction.

He latched on to her nub and suckled. Hard.

Wave after wave of pressure surged through her, and she ground against his face, rubbing out every bit of pleasure.

"Good girl." He swiped his tongue along her seam, and his head fell back against the mattress. A faint sheen of perspiration covered his skin, as if the experience sapped the little energy he possessed. "I feel better already."

She tucked her spent body beside him, enjoying the slow drop of her heartbeat and the weightlessness of her thoughts. Her breathing evened out as she traced small circles on his chest.

He groaned.

"I need another day to recover enough to take care of you," he said, his nipple pebbling under her touch. Gavyn covered her errant hand with one of his own and flattened them both on the top of his heart. "I will lock you in this chamber with me and order the cubs to supply us with fare between rounds of your screams."

"What if I desire to take care of you now?" She brushed her lips across his skin. "I want to give you pleasure. Show me?"

"Are you certain?" He tipped her chin.

"Yes. Always. 'Tis the only thing of which I am certain."

Gavyn hesitated the briefest of moments, then said, "Kneel between my legs."

She ran her fingernails down the tops of his thighs and scrambled into position.

A pearly drop of cum leaked from his head, and she licked her lips.

"Give me your tongue. Run it along my length and around my tip."

She encircled the base with one hand and leaned forward.

"I didn't give you permission to use anything but your mouth. Put them behind your back," he demanded. "That's it. Make me nice and wet, so when you swallow me with those luscious lips I will slide easily to the back of your throat."

She shivered, but the rebuff did not alarm her. It had the opposite effect — she leaned into the command, delighted at the prospect of not thinking. Or planning. Or worrying. *Yes.* The thrill of being under his control allowed her freedom to clear her mind and escape the world outside the chamber doors a little longer.

"That's it. Now, wrap your lips around me and swallow what I give you." He flexed his hips and delivered several quick thrusts. "Good girl."

She wanted to be his good girl. Wanted it more than anything else, so she softened her jaw and loosened her lips.

"Relax. Swallow. Breathe through your nose when necessary." He eased out of her and tangled his fingers in her hair. "So beautiful. Tap my leg if it's too much. I'm close, but I don't want to harm you."

She nodded.

"The words, Ember," he snapped. He fisted her hair and yanked her head to meet the heat in his gaze.

"I understand, Gavyn. Take what you need. I won't break." Although she would. She would shatter herself into a million pieces. She would burn the world down to keep that fire in his eyes.

To keep him happy.

Safe.

He eased into her mouth again, and she swirled her tongue around his head, massaging the underside with broad strokes.

"Don't stop." His movements grew frantic — thrashing on the bed, tangling his hands in her hair.

She went farther with each pass, working her way toward swallowing him whole. The grip on the back of her head lessened, and he fisted the blankets. She inhaled through her nose and lowered on his length.

Dear gods, she could get used to this. No wonder he enjoyed kneeling. The power. The control. He might have his hand on the back of her head, but there was no question of who was in charge.

Until she wasn't.

"Is this what you seek, my little thief? Do you want to drink me down, stealing what little strength I possess?" She wanted to bob up and down as fast as she dared, but he guided her slowly along his length. Teasing her. Reminding her. "Lucky for you, I'm ready to give you what you want. Drink every last drop."

He thrust inside her.

She gripped the backs of his thighs, not caring if she disobeyed. The first spurts of warm cum hit the back of her throat, and she swallowed. Every. Last. Drop. She closed her lips around him, her tongue lapping at his base.

"Good girl," he said. Buoyed by the rasp in his voice and the ragged rise and fall of his chest, she felt like a good girl. A powerful mate. He opened his arms wide. "Come here. You wear me out."

She snuggled into his side and pulled the blankets over their bodies.

His eyelids shuttered, and he succumbed to his fatigue. Her body was loose and exhausted.

But her mind was wide awake.

What threats?

She wasn't ignorant of his attempt to sway her earlier questions with sex nor her own weakness allowing him to do so. Just as the High Table could no longer be ignorant of her existence with her cast in the arena. Nor where she hid.

Fai and Kiehl eluded as much when they visited their village. Even Corwen understood who she was. Maybe not her name or her heritage, but he was aware of her power.

Now, so did the entire realm.

What threats? What did Lord Siodina whisper in Gavyn's ear?

Kiehl had warned them.

He had suffered unimaginable loss at the hands of the Lords. Had understood the depths they would dive to punish any sign of transgression against their power. Had known what it would cost Xavier and his family to harbor her — a perceived enemy of the Castle.

Mother was right.

The absolution weighed heavily in the pit of her gut. Someone would always hunt her. Pursue her for a gift she didn't control. One given without her consent. A blessing, a curse.

And until the last few months, a power she wielded with pride.

Now, it may cost her more than she could bear to pay.

She studied Gavyn's handsome face, admiring the sharp lines of his cheeks and the character of his nose. He would not agree with her plans to leave the compound. Stubborn brute. It would get them all killed, or worse, captured.

If they hurt someone because of her…

If they hurt him…

Watching Gavyn in the arena was torture. She would never forgive herself if something happened to him. Or Jade. Or anyone else in the village. She was not strong enough to stand by and watch as the Castle tormented his family.

She'd rather tear herself into pieces than cause any more harm.

She knew what she must do as it was the only way to keep them all safe.

And in order to walk out of here… to convince Gavyn to let her go… she would need to pull the frayed edge of happiness and rip herself apart.

~

Darkness crawled through the open window.

Shadows flickered from a lone candle on the top of Gavyn's

chest of drawers. Ember studied his handsome profile — his beautiful face and stubborn jaw, his strong torso that housed a loyal heart, and his wide shoulders, big enough to carry the safety of those around him.

One last look.

Gavyn ran his hand over the blankets. His stomach grumbled. He rubbed his eyes with the back of his hands.

"'Tis a good sign your appetite returns."

"Ember," he said as he swung his legs over the side of the bed. "Come closer so I can devour you."

"Start with bone broth before you add more substantial fare. Avoid getting those threads on your shoulder wet for at least a week." She stared at the spot on the wall above his head, struggling to keep her tone flat.

"So no more baths," he said with a smile in his voice.

Ember looked away and ran her hand along the edge of the large copper tub.

"No. No more baths."

"Then am I to presume taking a dip in the stream is also off limits?" His question hung in the air, louder now.

She gazed out of the bedroom window and said, "No. No more nightly swims."

"And I probably should avoid trips to Ashmere Falls." He stood up, held out a steadying hand for balance, and stalked over to where she stood. Gavyn placed one finger under her chin, lifting it to meet his gaze. "Ember?"

"No," she agreed, not answering the question he asked, not the one left unspoken. "No more skinny-dipping in magical pools. Zoie and Jade are accomplished healers. Trust them to take care of your wounds."

She took a deep breath.

"It's time I moved on. I'm afraid I stayed longer than expected, and I am eager to resume my travels."

"There's no need." His spine stiffened. "I fought for the

village. It's over. You can stay at the compound. You can stay with me."

"Don't you see. The Lords will not stop until I'm captured, silenced. You admitted as much yourself. I cannot bear for harm to come to you." She swept her arms wide. "Or anyone at the compound, for that matter."

"We know their plans now. The Castle won't act against us." Gavyn took another wobbly step forward. "Trust Xavier to keep us safe, you safe."

"You don't understand." Dammit. She failed to prevent her voice from wavering. "I won't allow history to repeat itself. I made the wrong decision with my mother. Don't ask me to make the same mistake with you. Don't ask me to stay."

"My family can keep you safe." He pointed to himself. "I... I can keep you safe. You insult me, my honor with your doubts."

Time to try another tactic.

"This is not the life my mother envisioned for me." She crossed her arms, forcing her features to still. "This is not the existence I want for myself."

Dear gods, make him stop. She wouldn't last much longer.

"I don't understand." Another step. "You are happy here. Safe, cared for... *loved*."

He refused to listen.

She took a step back, afraid of buckling if he touched her. One day he would see. One day he would understand. If she was lucky, one day he would forgive her. Until then, she must hold strong.

"There's more to life than being *taken care of*." She raised her chin and deepened her voice. "I want more for myself. More than... just being a fighter's girl."

An owl hooted outside the window.

"So I'm destined to become a fleeting memory for you?" An unfamiliar darkness seeped into his words, and his eyes flicked to her satchel by the door. "Someone to pass the time with on your worldly travels?"

"I never promised you more." She crossed the room and slung her bag over her shoulder, forcing herself to shrug. "Besides, I must honor my word to my mother."

"Honor? You speak of honor. I stepped into that arena to honor the bonds of family. There is no integrity in fleeing. Your mother isn't here, and I'm sorry about that, sweetheart. I really am, but the choice is yours now. The luxury of hiding behind other's decisions vanished with her passing. Some things are worth fighting for and this…" He cupped her elbow. "This is one of them."

"Take care, Gavyn." She turned, and over her shoulder she said, "Goodbye."

He dropped her arm as if she seared his fingertips with cooking coals.

Keep moving. Put one foot in front of the other.

She bit the inside of her cheek, the pain an insufficient distraction.

Don't cry. Don't look back.

The first gust of fresh air stung her wet cheeks and forced its way down her throat. After several shallow breaths, she ran as fast as her feet and the moonlight permitted.

Her slipper snagged on a root in the path, and she caught herself with her outstretched palm. Small gravel embedded in the base of her hands, and a trickle of blood escaped down her wrist.

Just breathe.

New tears tracked down her cheeks, but the quiver in her lower lip relaxed. She backtracked to the stream behind the barracks and crouched down to let the cool waters clean the dirt away.

The pain felt good, burning away the edges of her sorrow.

Her magic immediately wanted to take over, but she allowed the sting to throb in her palms a little longer.

It was done.

She sat back on her heels and closed her eyes.

Frogs croaked up and down the stream's edge. Tree branches rustled as the squirrels settled in for the night, and the rush of water swirled around her. Her heartbeat steadied.

Her hands stopped shaking.

She timed her breathing to match the bullfrog on the opposite bank.

Inhale.

Croak.

Exhale.

Ember inhaled and waited until he let loose another call.

Warmth welled in her palms, leaving painless pin pricks along her skin. She didn't possess the strength to control the cast, her body needing to heal the wound more than she needed the pain for escape.

Time to go.

Ember would travel west toward Kiehl's village and beg an audience with Faina.

She'd memorized the trail on the return journey with Gavyn. Had noted hiding spots off the path, sources of water when she traveled away from the stream and areas flush with berries to sustain her until she reached the cottage.

It would be the first place he looked, so she couldn't stay too long.

Form there, she would resume her travels to the Northern Isles. What about supplies? She sighed. That was a problem for another day.

Ember rubbed her palm. Maybe it was best to avoid Fai and her brother all together. She was small, certain she could sneak into their grandparent's cottage undetected. She could hide for a day or two in the home before she set off again.

She'd worry about the details later.

With her half-formed plan, she stood up, brushing off her skirts, and grabbed her satchel. After securing it on her back, she set her shoulders and started on the path to Jade's.

One more goodbye.

CHAPTER TWENTY-NINE

Resist the temptation to dull your senses if you do not wish your thoughts in the world. -Esabel

EMBER STARED AT THE WOODEN SLATS OF JADE'S FRONT DOOR.

Well-oiled, the boards reflected the outline of misery on her face. The knots in the wood added texture to the smooth surface but yielded none of the conviction she desperately needed.

Her fingers paused in mid-air, struggling to close into a fist. She swiped at the errant tear rolling down her cheek, and after a couple of sniffles and several deep breaths, she knocked.

Jade answered on the second strike.

Her eyes widened. She took one look at Ember and opened her arms.

"Oh, Jade," she said and stepped into the embrace. Jade rested her cheek on Ember's crown and squeezed harder.

The scent of wildflowers and vanilla and *home* wrapped around her. Dear gods, she would miss this — their afternoon chats and lazy days under the oak and familiar touches. The friendship. Not the mountain of dishes, though. No, those she could do without.

If only there was a way to bottle this feeling for the long, dark nights ahead. She sniffled and blurted out the first thing that came to her mind. "He's a fool."

Jade let out a bark of laughter.

"Not the first thing I thought you would say." Her brows drew together as she set Ember at arm's length. "Pray tell, who deserves your censure?"

"Xavier," she said as warmth crept up the back of her neck. "Xavier's a fool."

More laughter followed. "What did he do now?"

"He's... and you..." She bit her lower lip. "He's a fool for not courting you properly."

"Oh, that." Jade shrugged and waved her away. "That's water under the bridge as my mama used to say. Maybe a bridge guarded by a troll but underneath all the same."

"Well... he's..." She combed her mind for the right word. "Dumb."

"Come here." Jade tugged her into the cottage. "Honey, I appreciate the sentiment. True, Xavier and I have our thing and only the gods know if we will ever work it out, but right now, let's focus on what to do about you."

"What'd I miss?" Ada sashayed through the open door and gestured to Ember. "Gavyn's in the training barn, pale as a ghost, yelling at Xavier. Something about Ember leaving. He's a mess, and I could barely understand a word. I figured you would show up here." Ada blew a wisp of hair out of her eyes and asked, "What did he do now?"

Zoie snuck in behind, balancing a basket full of savory smells and bottles of wine tucked under her arms.

"Ada sent a cub to fetch me." Zoie pushed the door closed with her hip. She placed everything on the table. "He said to bring food and *dazzling amounts of alcohol*. Ada's words, not his."

"Splendid. We have tarts. We have drink. Now, let's have gossip." Ada rubbed her hands together. "What is everyone waiting for? Tuck in."

Ember looked back and forth between them.

"They are here to see you, not me," Jade said and pointed to the stool closest to the hearth. She walked around the table and sat next to Zoie. "Might as well enjoy the meal while Ada wrings the story out of you."

Ada removed the pretty checkered linen covering the basket. Scents of beef and sage filled the cramped room. She pulled out trenchers and passed them around. Four bright green apples and a large hunk of yellow cheese followed.

"Now that we are all here, does someone want to fill me in?" Ada took a bite and between mouthfuls asked, "Who do we need to hex?"

Ember choked.

Zoie leaned over and patted her back a few times between coughing fits. She took small sips of water, and slowly, the spasms subsided.

"What happened? I'm still fuzzy on the details from the match." Zoie glared at Ada and switched to rubbing small circles on Ember's back. "Everything transpired so quickly."

"Ember went all magic sorceress," Ada said with her hands. "Saved Erik's life in front of the entire Castle and all the villagers. Thanks for that, by the way. It'd be terrible to no longer witness him and Maia rolling around in the grappling pit. I'm uncertain whether she wants to punch him in the face or put him in a headlock and haul him back to her rooms to—"

"*Ada,*" said Zoie and Jade at the same time.

"Right, right. Then, she cast again at the top of the valley to heal a passed out Gavyn. Also, thank you," she said to Ember. "How is he?"

Jade pinched the bridge of her nose.

"What? Is that or is that not what happened?" Ada shrugged

and in an uncharacteristically serious voice said, "I'm judging by that small, worn satchel in the corner that our dear friend Ember plans to flee. And maybe stopped by Jade's to say goodbye."

"I—" Ember sputtered.

"Which is incredibly rude of you. I, for one, would have been pretty upset if you left the territory without so much as a goodbye." Ada gave her a long, hard stare.

Jade leaned forward and asked, "What happened with Gavyn?"

"After we returned to his chambers, we were both so exhausted. I remember helping him remove the rest of his clothes and falling asleep. A fitful sleep trapped him for the better part of two days but he woke this afternoon in... ah... good spirits."

Heat returned to her cheeks.

"He let slip that Lord Siodina threatened me prior to the start of the fight. The entire time he slept my mind raced with everything that transpired in the arena." She rested her forearms on the table in front of her. "I went over all the possibilities in my head. What the High Table would do to Xavier. How they would punish Gavyn. How everyone in the village is at risk the longer I stay."

"You know that's poppycock, right? Malarkey. Hogwash." Ada crossed her arms. "You did nothing wrong."

"She's right." Jade rested a hand on Ember's forearm. "There is no decree for the use of magic outside the confines of the Castle. There hasn't been a need for one."

"I know." Ember shook her head. "It's just that my mother worked so hard to keep us hidden. To conceal my ability to cast." She drew her eyes together and the edge of her lips tipped down. "Most of my childhood stories involved lessons of others harming casters. Or worse, punishing us to bend to their will."

Kiehl's story surfaced, bubbling up without pause. While it wasn't hers to tell, they all needed to hear it.

"Blimey," said Zoie.

"Where will you go?" Jade tore off another piece of bread. "Do you have family in another village?"

"No. There's no one else." She rubbed her palm. "I don't have any relations left."

"It makes more sense to stay." Jade's lips pursed together. "Surely, you do not wish to run again, scrounging for food and sleeping in abandoned structures at best, under the elements at worst."

Ember couldn't hold her gaze, so she strolled over to the kitchen window.

"My mother would want me to leave. She made me promise to sail the Strait of Vian, to head to the Northern Isles."

"Your mother would want you to be happy." Jade draped an arm across her shoulders. She cupped her face and tilted her chin up. "You can't keep living in this manner. Maybe it worked when it was the two of you… when you had each other."

"I—" Ember wrung her hands together.

"This is rubbish," Ada said. "It's not safe to leave. If you won't listen to reason, then maybe you will listen to caution."

"What happened?" Zoie asked.

"Did any of you see Maia in the arena?" Ada placed both palms on the table and looked around the room, settling on each of them for a moment before moving to the next. "Mikel found her tied to her bed in the barracks."

"No." Jade gasped. She brought the tips of her fingers to her lips. "Is she well? When did she… what does she need…"

Zoie scooted to the edge of her stool.

"Aye, she is sound," Ada said, drawing out the words. "After everyone returned home, Mikel asked me to accompany him to her chamber. Said he needed a female to go in if she didn't answer his summons." Her voice lowered, and she tilted forward. "He knocked but didn't wait long. We both had this feeling something was off. Mikel called out her name and announced our intentions."

She clutched her chest.

"My heart dropped to the hem of my skirts when I saw her. I thought the worst."

"Is she okay?" Ember tilted her head to the side. "Does she suffer injuries?"

"She was fine. 'Twas just asleep." Ada relaxed her shoulders and leaned back. "We found her facing away from the door. With her head slumped to the side, it looked bad. Maia's attacker tied her hands in front and then secured her to the bedpost. I tiptoed over and tapped her on the shoulder."

Ada erupted in giggles, breaking the tension in the room.

"Our Maia has some very interesting vocabulary. She must have thought her attacker returned. I've never seen Mikel blush so much." Ada shrugged and smiled. "Unless I'm teasing him, of course."

"Ada," Jade snapped.

"Oh, sorry. It took her a second to get her wits lined up like hens in the henhouse. She's unharmed. Shaken, but without injury."

Ember pushed away from the back counter. "I should still check on her. I need to..."

"You see... this... this is who you are." Jade flung her arm out. "Your nature is to mend. To help. And you can't do that by hiding in milking barns and worrying about your next meal. Plus, Xav will refuse your departure. Until they catch the culprit, 'tis too dangerous."

Ember looked out the window, torn between sneaking out while the compound was distracted with Maia's plight and slipping through the barracks to satisfy her question of whether the fighter was truly sound.

Jade cleared her throat.

"Let's clean this up and have a toast." Zoie took the sullied trenchers to Jade's washing basin and returned with the bottles of wine. "It's my latest batch. I bottled it today."

"Yes. A toast." Ada rummaged around Jade's small kitchen and found four clean cups. She stopped in front of Ember. "Will you try a little?"

Ember rubbed her palm and nodded.

Zoie offered Ember a bottle. "Would you, ahh…"

"She wants you to heat the wine. It's better served warmed," Jade said.

"Oh." Ember grabbed the wine. "Of course."

She closed her eyes and readjusted her grip, securing the bottle's slender neck. Ember took deep, steadying breaths and channeled the cast. The liquid warmed, and before handing it back to Zoie, she poured a small amount into her cup.

The foursome sat back down at the table.

"To Gavyn and his courage." Jade raised hers and gestured for the others to do the same.

"Here. Here." Zoie and Ada's voices rang out as they clanged their drinks together.

Ember took a small sip of the spiced drink. Subtle hints of cinnamon and cloves swirled on her tongue. On the second sample, she noted ginger and maybe a little nutmeg.

"It's not the season for it, but I had extra." Zoie brought the cup in front of her face. "And Jade can never turn down a bottle."

She took another sip. The liquid warmed her insides, and she relaxed a little for the first time in hours.

Zoie held up the bottle and asked, "More to top you off?"

She nodded, and Zoie filled the vessel two fingers shy of the top. Ember sipped on the wine as she listened to Ada finish her tale.

"Careful. It slips down quickly," Zoie whispered.

"The rope rubbed Maia's skin raw." Ada traced the inside of

her wrist with her thumb. "Mikel took her to the training barn for some salve."

Ember hopped up and tended to the hearth. She added another log, stirring the coals until it caught flame. The logs crackled behind her. She rolled up the edge of her sleeves. The cottage, with the fire roaring and all four of them crammed in the front half, warmed quickly.

Zoie refilled Ember's cup once more.

"To Maia and her ribald vocabulary." Ada raised her hand, and the deep burgundy liquid escaped over the sides of the vessel. "My education is now complete."

Ember giggled.

She glanced at the tapestry of the three small children, studying the two lads in the depiction. The blonde cherub with startling green eyes must be Jade, but who are the others? She scratched her head and looked down. Funny. Her cup was empty again.

What was I going to ask Jade?

That's right.

"Oy, Jade." She swayed and grabbed the mantel to steady the room. "I never asked… but always wanted to know… 'tis rude of me, I suppose… but I must admit I can't find a reason not to now, since I'm leaving, 'n all… who are the lads?"

Zoie wandered over to the hearth. A lopsided smile teased her cheeks. It transformed into a full grin when she produced another bottle of the delicious drink.

"Could I trouble you to warm it again?" Zoie held out the wine.

Ember placed her empty cup on the mantel.

"I'd be delighted." Ember bowed and the floor rushed up to greet her.

She hiccuped and grabbed the bottle with both hands, only it moved to the left before she could reach it. Or maybe she stepped to the right.

The room swayed a bit,

She grabbed onto Zoie until it stopped. Happy she kept her footing, she reached out a second time. Got it.

Zoie giggled and wrapped her hands around Ember's.

Together, they corralled the errant wine and prevented it from scurrying away.

What was that spell?

She looked up to the rafters and snapped her fingers. The sour taste of magic coated her tongue, a terrible contrast to the sweet drink. The cast was sluggish, coming in bits and pieces, as if she couldn't remember the words to a favorite tune.

Ada erupted in giggles. Jade smiled above the edge of her cup. Her face was fuzzy around the edges. She looked like an angel.

Ember pushed the bottle back in Zoie's hands and staggered over to her friend.

"You're wonderful." She wrapped Jade in a tight embrace. "Or is it 'full of wonder?' Yes, magical. That's it, magical."

"Whoa, there. I share a certain fondness for an enchanting Faeblood, too." Jade gestured to the tapestry. "Tis Xavier and his brother, Lukas."

"You're smart. And pretty. And nice. And can cook." Ember ticked off on her fingers. "What was I saying, again? You're smashing."

Her eyes crossed.

"And you have two heads. Why do you have two heads?"

Hiccup.

"And you are drunk, honey." Jade wound an arm around Ember's middle and steered her toward the small bed on the other side of the room. "Let's lay down for a bit."

"But I'm not tired," she said as she sat down on the bed and yawned. "And I need to get going soon."

"Mmm, hmm." Jade removed both of her slippers and fluffed

the pillow. She pulled back the blankets and nudged Ember to the head of the bed. "First, you require rest."

"I can't remember why I need to leave. But I need to. I'm sure of it." She twirled a lock of Jade's hair that slipped out of its bun and yawned again. "'Tis very important for me—"

She sank into the bedding, and the room stopped swaying.

Voices waded through her mind, but a dense fog prevented her from deciphering the words. Someone was at the back door. Why were they so loud?

Strong arms slipped under her back, behind her knees.

"Easy there," Gavyn whispered.

"You always smell like pine." Unaware she voiced her thought aloud, Ember snuggled into his warm chest and succumbed to the welcoming oblivion.

CHAPTER THIRTY

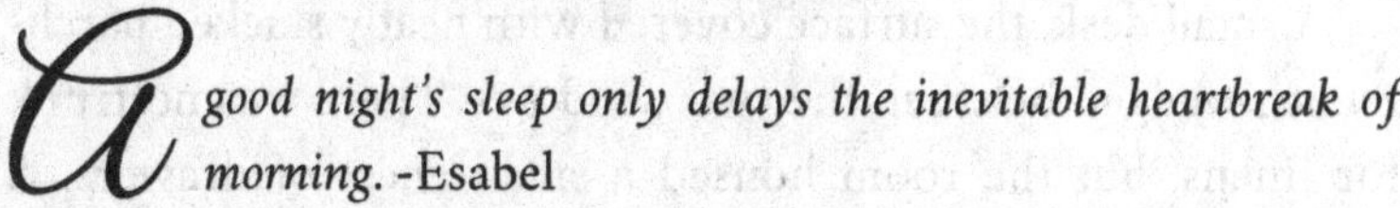

good night's sleep only delays the inevitable heartbreak of morning. -Esabel

Someone shoved cotton into Ember's mouth.

She opened and closed it twice, smacking her tongue to the roof of her palate. Why were her teeth furry? She tried to swallow, but what little saliva she had stuck to the back of her throat.

"Good morning," someone said. A loud male someone, his voice pounding between her ears. "Sleep well?"

She rubbed her temple. It was as if a woodcutter split her head in two with an axe.

Bare feet dangled off the side of the bed. She wiggled her toes, testing the connection. Hers. Why is everything so heavy? With enormous effort, she looked up.

Blinding light entered the room from two windows on her left.

"There's water for you on the small table over there," said the fuzzy outline of a man striding toward her. He was bright, the rays of sun shrouding his profile. It hurt to look in his direction.

"Drink the entire cup. I'll be back in ten minutes' time."

The door closed behind him with a heavy thud.

She emptied the cup. The water soothed her parched throat. She stood, and a long black tunic hung on her frame, wet splotches now covering the front.

Where was she?

Ember recognized the green shiplap of the outer wall and the faint rush of the stream outside. How did she end up back at the compound?

The chamber was larger than the one she shared with Gavyn.

A small desk, the surface covered with neatly stacked parchments, wedged between the two windows. There was no trunk for linens, but the room housed a small chest of drawers. A small basin for water rested on its top.

She tiptoed across the cold stone floor and grabbed the soap sitting next to it. The familiar pine scent affronted her nose, and her stomach fumbled. She dipped the bar in the basin of water, created a lather, and washed the evening off her face.

Somewhat herself, she turned around and searched the chamber for her dress.

Bits and pieces of the night played across her eyes. The fight with Gavyn. The tumble near the stream.

Her dress draped over the edge of the rumpled bed.

She jerked off her nightshirt and pulled on the garment, thankful it didn't require buttons to close. With shaky hands, she straightened the quilts. Her satchel clung to a hook on the wall by the door, and she tiptoed over to retrieve it.

The room's owner had mounted a long looking glass next to the entrance.

Dear gods, she was a mess.

More images from last night floated to the front of her mind.

Jade's cottage. Ada and Zoie. The wine.

I'm never drinking again.

Ember dug through her bag and pulled out her comb. She ran it through her hair, snagging the tangled ends and sending sharp pains to her scalp. Dark circles smudged the thin skin under each eye, and the uncombed portion of her hair stuck out at odd angles. Alarmed by her dishevelment, she attacked the other side of her scalp.

With her locks tamed, she returned the torture device to her satchel.

A small rip in the inner lining snagged her attention.

She inspected the opening, gauging the amount of thread required to stitch it shut. Something poked the tip of her fingers. What the—

She withdrew an aged piece of parchment someone folded so many times it resembled the colorful fans favored by the wives of the village elders. It was small with worn edges, barely more than a scrap.

How long had it been there?

Ember opened the note. Her stomach turned over once more.

Black ink, faded with time, swirled in a long, elegant hand. It was a letter addressed to her mother.

She pulled the missive taunt and read the contents, willing her hands to stop shaking.

My Dearest Esabel,

I found you, my love. Did you think you could flee from our bond? From my mark? Do you suffer the illusion I wouldn't discover your faked demise? Or the bairn you carried? Aye. I am aware of the bastard he put inside your womb.

It should thrill you to know I took care of your lover. He died with dishonor, crying out your name until the slice of my blade carved out his cowardice. His last pleas for your safety echoed off the dungeon walls, the memories providing me pleasure to this day.

I confess I enjoy this hunt — our little game. Scurry and hide my little pet. It will make your eventual capture more satisfying. Don't attempt to conceal the child. Even you cannot be so naïve. My men will scour the ends of the realm, the babe's gift a signal for my most experienced trackers.

That is... if you produced a Faeblood since you spread your legs for the help.

Her father. Dead. Murdered. She never knew. Mother never said… The rest of the letter came faster now, as she frantically searched for any information as to her sire's name.

You always were a stupid chit with more beauty than ambition. Such a waste of power. Descended from one of the most noble, most powerful casters and you ran off to live in filth amongst the commoners. You made a grievous error in judgment thinking I'd grant your freedom since you fulfilled your duties to my line. I dream of setting my eyes upon your petrified face the next time we meet.

Yours, even in death,

The bottom right corner of the parchment was missing, the signature line torn off.

She turned the letter over, holding it up to her face.

Nothing. It was blank. No name or sign of the author's identity.

She dug through the tear in the satchel, causing the seam to rip further in her haste.

Maybe she missed it, the link to her family, the first time through. She reread the letter, this time out loud. So engrossed in the message, she didn't hear the knock on the chamber door.

"You didn't know?" Xavier's booming question bore into her scalp, an unnecessary reminder of her disastrous decision to try wine.

When did he return? These must be his chambers.

He stepped into the room and asked, "You didn't know about the letter?"

"What?" she asked, her voice breaking on the simple word.

"She never told you about it? The secrets it held?" He gestured to the empty cup. "You need another."

"Dante," he bellowed down the hall. "Fetch a pitcher of water."

He left the door open.

"I'm surprised you are up and about. And you changed. Jade struggled last night wrangling you out of your dress and into a nightshirt."

"You heard? The letter..." She took two steps backward, and her legs bumped into his bed.

Dante bounded in. "At your service, milady."

Xavier flicked his head at her cup. The young fighter refilled her water and sent a wink in her direction. He left the pitcher on the desk and inclined his head.

"Thank you," she said as she rubbed the scar on her palm.

Xavier closed the door with his boot and grabbed the stool near the bed, straddling the seat.

"I wondered about this." He grabbed her hand and inspected the scar.

It was difficult not to fidget as he ran his fingertips over the puckered skin. There was a question in his prolonged silence.

"I was fifteen or sixteen summers. A few of the village kids started a small fire down by the lake. One lad snuck a bottle of mead and passed it between them." She took a sip of water and cleared her throat. "Another thought it was funny to wave a poker around. Who knows where they found it, but branding irons and youthful lads and mead don't mix."

His brows drew together.

"One of them, Tomas, waved it toward the smaller lads. I'm uncertain he meant harm, but Tomas had a meanness about him I never much cared for," she said, wrinkling her nose. "I caught the poker from hitting the littlest in the back."

"Why didn't you heal it?" He dropped her hand.

"What makes you think I could have?"

"Ember, I've seen what you can do. We've all witnessed your gift. 'Tis a simple wound to heal with your power, even for a young Faeblood."

"I guess I wanted a reminder." She shrugged and wiggled her toes, unable to hold the heat in his gaze.

"Of what?" He placed two fingers under her chin, tilting it up. "To be careful? That others don't deserve your trust? Or maybe imbibing leads men down the wrong path?"

"No," she said, squaring her shoulders. "It was a time of rebellion for me. I grew weary of our constant uprooting and fought the restrictions of my youth. My mother's leash tightened as the strength of my casting increased."

She cleared her throat and took another sip of water.

"I wanted to prove that I had a choice. That I can control my gift. That it's ultimately up to me whether I choose to heal."

She stood up, brushing by him, and paced the length of the room.

"I know she wasn't perfect. We fought. So much. Looking back, I regret my words. The knowledge I gleaned today..." She hesitated. "She never said... she... I knew nothing. If only..."

"If only your mother shared her worries. If only you knew

someone hunted her. Would the knowledge change anything between you two?"

"She lied to me."

And there it was. Instead of feeling relief or even curiosity at discovering another piece of her heritage. She felt... hurt.

Perhaps if she was younger, less mature, it would make sense for her mother to keep the knowledge to herself. And yet, this felt akin to betrayal.

"She deceived me about everything."

"She spared you," Xavier said, his tone firm. "Your mother carried the burden, giving you room to mature without its weight smothering your confidence. It was the correct course — shouldering the fear alone."

She traveled two passes of his room.

"You decided long ago you controlled your gift. It's time for another choice." Xavier grabbed her upper arms, stilling her movements. "You are safe here—"

"But Maia—"

"I know the identity of Maia's attacker." He held up a palm. "You are safe here, but I can't control the rumors. The entire peninsula witnessed your cast to save Erik, but I can offer you a place to stay. Protection."

"And if I choose to leave?" She tilted her chin higher. "Take my troubles with me."

"You mean if you run." He grunted and dropped her arms. "Then I will help you hide. Help you find a new place. I have friends in other villages that will keep you safe. I owe you for Jade. Now Erik."

"'Tis not a debt." She grabbed his forearm. "And your people are safer with me gone. You, as a leader, must know this. I present a risk to everyone's well-being."

"You do."

Her head snapped up, surprised at how quickly he agreed. Dear gods, her mind was all over the place this morning. What did she expect? His rebuttal? No, Xavier was too practical, too ruthless to say what she wished to hear. His acceptance didn't make it easier, though, and the confirmation weighed heavily.

She strolled over to the desk, needing to put some space between them.

"You do, but I want you to stay."

"Why?" She searched his eyes, her voice cracking when she asked, "Out of obligation?"

"I have my reasons."

She bit her lower lip and held his stare. "Jade?"

"You underestimate your value." He looked away and sighed. Xavier ran a hand through his hair, before conceding, "Yes. Jade's desires are in play, but they can't be the reason you stay."

"But if I stay, it will be because of her. And Gavyn. And the others."

He straightened. "And yet, you can't make them the reason you stay."

"I don't understand. If I stay, it would be for them."

"You play a dangerous game, giving others so much control," he hissed.

Heat clawed up her throat. "What... what are you talking about?"

"Friendship. Home. *Love*." He turned on his heel and stalked toward the door. Xavier kept his back to her. "These are all comforts you crave, but they can't be the sole reason you stay."

"I don't understand." She crossed the room and grabbed the back of his tunic. "What else is there?"

Xavier exhaled and stepped out into the hall.

"Wait." She chased after him, her voice echoing down the corridor. "Wait."

He whirled around.

"What will happen to them? To Gavyn? If I leave, the High Table—"

"Enough." He placed one hand on the wall and leaned

forward, his big body encroaching into her space. "If you leave, they are no longer your concern."

"It's not enough," she whispered. "I need to know. What can I do to protect them? *How can I fight to keep them safe?*"

He snarled.

"Family is never about whose blood you share, nor who you surround yourself with." He grasped her shoulders with both hands. "And home... home is never about where your head rests at night."

"What—"

"It's about who stands beside you and doesn't flinch when the match goes to hell." His grip tightened. He gave her a moment for his words to sink in. "You sacrifice a piece of yourself for those you love. Not out of desperation. Or obligation. You must choose the group over the individual."

She looked at the leather cuffs on his wrists, the ones holding her in place. Her gaze tracked to his neck and to the mark that throbbed from his pulse.

A faint memory teased the back of her mind as she reached out and wrapped her palm around the symbol.

Warmth pooled in her hand. Her eyes widened. She left her palm on his neck long enough to feel the heat travel to her core and fill her from within. Magic.

"Family," she whispered. "You're... you're bonded by magic."

"Yes." He held her stare. "We possess a connection deeper than heritage — one borne of shared experiences, a yearning to belong, and a hunger for something bigger. Together we are stronger as a whole, and the magic... "

He covered her hand with his.

"The mark gifts sentience to the family — our lives cease to belong solely to us and instead entwine with those of our brothers, those who we choose to stand beside even with certain peril."

She'd known something was different about the mark. She'd

known it was something more — not just a tattoo declaring allegiance but an ancient form of Fae magic. She'd stopped looking for signs of casters, happy — so deliriously happy — to set aside that foolish childhood dream that kept her from living in the moment.

That's what Gavyn and Jade and everyone in the territory had given her.

She hadn't tried harder to discover the connection. She'd let him blind her with sex and sweet whispers. Let Jade and the girls sway her with friendship and adventure.

And Ember never said she loved him, *them*.

Xavier, maybe more so than Jade, had known it too.

Perhaps that was why he told her now. Not to sway her decision but to ensure she didn't leave without all the facts.

He was calculating, smart.

"Stay. Take one week to think about it," Xavier said. "At the end of the seven days, if you decide to journey on, I will escort you myself. Until then, I have something that might occupy your time."

CHAPTER THIRTY-ONE

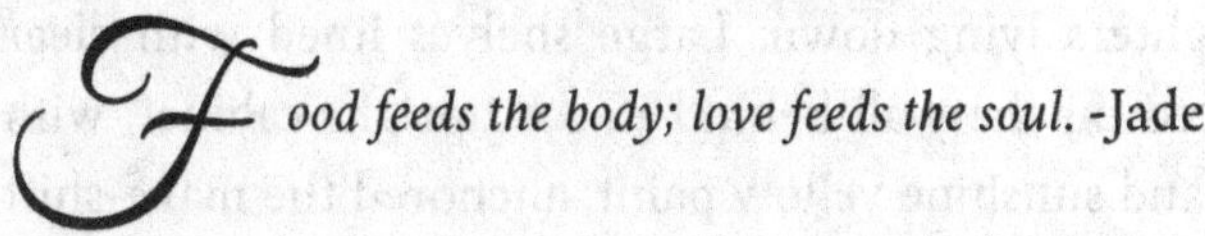

ood feeds the body; love feeds the soul. -Jade

THWACK. THWACK. THWACK.

Wisps of straw flew in the air as the heavy bag buckled with each impact. Gavyn concentrated on the path of its swing and landed a cross at the height of the arc.

A satisfying thud echoed in the empty training barn. Heat poured through the wide entrance doors, blurring the edges of his vision.

He continued to strike the target, ignoring the signs of fatigue and focusing on well-placed, powerful shots instead of the jabs from the last hour. Or had it been two?

Pain radiated from his knuckles and spread through his wrists, crawling up his forearms. A good sign. He recalled the numbness he suffered three days ago and the subsequent lecture he received from Rowan.

You're an idiot, his brother had said. *Ruining your hands doesn't help anyone. Drag your miserable heart down to the stream and clean up.*

They'd swung by Zoie's for some salve, since he'd been too stubborn to visit their new healer in residence, the one who could fix his hands in seconds. He'd opted to tend his injuries the barbaric way — with stinky creams and tattered bandages.

He took extra care wrapping them this morning. The additional padding prevented most of his wounds from reopening. A few small red splotches peppered the middle of both knuckles.

Gavyn winced as he unwound the fabric.

His gaze lingered on the new table under the loft.

It stood bar-height and long enough to accommodate the tallest of fighters lying down. Large shelves lined with clear bottles floated on the wall behind it. An upright cabinet, with glass doors and sunshine yellow paint, anchored the make-shift infirmary carved out for Ember's patients.

Xavier led a ruthless campaign to persuade her to stay. His leader was cunning, offering her more than Gavyn ever could. A purpose. More than he ever considered.

He mistakenly sought the solace of the empty training barn, but her ghost haunted him as he sulked around the building. Every time he paused for breath, his eyes flicked to her new clinic. Images replayed in his mind. He rubbed his chest.

Her skills were a blessing, and he was happy for her care, even if it hurt to see her in his space. The fighters seemed attuned to his mood, though, showing gratitude for her services but not attempting to charm her.

Or extending invites to any gatherings outside of training.

Footsteps echoed behind him. Xavier stepped into view, nodding to Gavyn's hands.

"Never known you to be a coward. Or play the fool with training."

Gavyn straightened, biting back his first retort.

"Is that so?" He removed the thick wad of padding from his left hand and started unraveling his right.

The bandages fell to the floor. He'd retrieve them later. Now, the idea of bending over to gather the soiled linen for washing overwhelmed him.

His head fell back and to the rafters he said, "Not all of us are free from faults."

"I claim plenty of faults." Xavier crossed his arms. "But losing control… 'tis not a luxury afforded to either of us."

Gavyn grunted.

"So am I to understand, you find me out of control and a coward and a fool? Anything else before I am dismissed?"

"Sit down," Xavier commanded. "Lest you fall over."

Gavyn swayed on his feet. Perhaps he better sit. That was the only reason he crossed the room and perched on the edge of the center ring. But he kept his chin up, refusing to hang his head as exhaustion demanded.

"I made a mistake. Time is not what you need." Xavier rubbed his jaw. "I thought to grant you leeway to gather your wits. Form a plan. But you continue this foolish behavior with no end in sight. You harm yourself. You harm her. And the entire compound suffers."

"She stayed," Gavyn said, more to himself than Xavier. "She left me, injured and alone, then stayed."

"Yes, Ember stayed. But you will lose her if you keep stomping around here with your head shoved up—"

"*That girl* told me she wanted more out of life than to be shackled to a semi-literate oaf." Gavyn rubbed his temples, unable to recall her exact words but feeling every sting of their sentiment.

"I won't excuse her actions, and I cannot speak to her motives." Xavier raised a finger. "But I can guess at her intentions. *That girl* saw a threat and sacrificed herself, including her newfound security and the freedom it afforded."

Xavier crouched down.

"What would you have done? If she offered up her problems for you to solve?"

"I would slay the entire contingent of Red Guard if it meant keeping her safe," Gavyn ground out.

"And die in the attempt." Xavier rested a hand on his shoulder. "She knows you. My guess… she sold you a falsehood and bought herself some time to sneak off undetected." He waited. "But Ember stayed. She bucked her instincts. And cast off years of her mother's control and chose the harder path."

"'Tis no hardship." Gavyn scoffed. "She stumbled into a family. A ready-made home."

And captured the heart of someone who would battle an entire realm to protect her dreams.

"Do not dismiss her circumstances."

"We are orphans, too. We—"

"It's different. We prosper from the bonds of brotherhood. Benefited from its trappings as far back as our childhood." Xavier ran a hand through his hair. "She never shared a kinship. Every time she sought the comfort of a companion, her mother ripped it out from underneath her. Fleeing… 'tis all she knows. It took great courage to buck a lifetime running away and to consider staying in one place, especially with Lord Siodina's threats. Especially after her mother's demise."

'I'm just a fighter," he whispered, lending voice to his greatest fear. "She doesn't want me."

"Another mistake of mine, allowing you to believe that nonsense. I never thought…" Xavier clenched his fists. "I didn't think you needed the words."

"I don't—

"Listen well, old friend, because I will say this one time. The rest — hearing it, believing it — is on you. You are more than a fighter. Hell, you are *the* leader of this compound." Xavier waved off Gavyn's next words. "I know the men wear my crest, but it's to you they look. Has been for some time. Why do you think I leave so many decisions in your hands? The day-to-day operations of the training barn? And the rare instances I send you to another territory, it's not because I'm too busy. Your bonds are stronger in those communities."

Xavier pounded him on his back.

"These are not the traits of a brute with more strength than smarts. You are cunning. Your strategies are sound. You have my ear. Always have. Don't believe me? That's your mistake. Don't put it on me or your father or her. Now, wash up. You stink like Red Guard out on a week-long patrol. On Ada's authority, your girl is down in the village at Madam MaLota's."

Xavier grinned.

"Make sure she puts her new wardrobe on your tab."

"Yellow is your color. 'Tis a shame blood ruined mama's dress." Jade brushed her hand down the sleeve of the linen tunic. "Shall I embroider the hem for you?"

Ember twisted at the waist and looked over her shoulder.

The tall looking glass in Madam MaLota's back room reflected an almost unrecognizable image. She was strong. Fierce even, from the fine-toothed copper comb corralling her thick plait down to the soft leather skirt, the color of cinnamon. It hugged her hips and skimmed a new pair of knee-high boots, one shade lighter.

"That would be splendid," she said as she ran her fingers over the seams of the long sleeves. "I will ask Madam if I can purchase a skein of her favorite gold thread."

A woman of means.

Xavier, true to his word, kept her busy this week: he gave her a job.

He declared her healer for the territory, leaving out any

mention the position was… temporary. Until she decided if she stayed.

It secured her place at the compound and provided a generous salary. Oh, she earned every ounce of gold, living in a village full of fighters.

The men delighted in her tinctures and ability to heal all manner of injuries, keeping her mind, her body busy.

Today, instead of pinning for Gavyn during the nooning meal, she stole Jade away from the market for a distracting shopping trip — her first foray in the world laden with her own purse.

"What do you think of the heavier skirts? Maia insists I will need them this fall."

Maia, too, thought Ember's continued presence in the village was a certainty.

She didn't correct the assumption.

While she hadn't given herself the opportunity to think about the future, not with the fight with Gavyn replaying in her mind, it couldn't hurt to plan for the cooler weather.

"The fit flatters your shape, and the weight will provide warmth on the harsher days."

"Then I shall purchase this one and commission Madam for another in a different color." Ember ran her hand over a bolt of fabric. "What do you think of this pattern?"

"It suits." The corners of Jade's lips twitched upward in a half-hearted smile. "Soon you will require a trunk of your own. Your beloved satchel won't hold your new wardrobe."

Xavier played a dangerous game.

Not only did he provide her with a position at the compound, but he commissioned construction of a cottage in the woods, near Zoie.

Hers, he'd said.

A home of her own if she stayed.

Ember cleared her throat.

In the meantime, she moved back in with Jade. And while she was happy to spend time with her friend, her heart longed for the small chamber in the back of the barracks.

"It's hard to believe. Xavier arranged an entire home full of furniture for the cottage. It feels extravagant and necessary at the same time." In a wistful tone, she added, "If I stay... it will be the first place of my own."

"I know, honey, and I'm happy for you. Xavier is smart, building next to Zoie. I worry about her alone in the woods, and I'm delighted you two will be neighbors." Jade squeezed her hand. "Remember, part of your new responsibilities include dragging her out of her wine cave to visit with the rest of us occasionally."

"Did you... have you set eyes on Gavyn?" she asked. "Training demands his time in the barn, and the fighters keep me busy. He leaves before I finish for the day."

"No. He hasn't visited the market. Eigen still guards my cart. Rowan and Mikel stopped by yesterday, but Gavyn did not accompany them." Jade folded a stack of garments. "Have you tried his chambers?"

"Twice today. My knocks fall unanswered. He chooses not to dine in the mess hall either. Last night I tracked him to the stream but failed to find him in his usual spots."

"Give him time. He will bend to your presence in the village. It was upsetting to discover you stayed, I imagine. Now, Xavier tempts you with a cottage... "

"If I could only apologize... explain my words..."

"I know." Jade cupped her cheek, then left to settle her bill with Madam at the front.

This exact conversation transpired every day. Some days more than once.

Jade listened patiently, speaking the words Ember's heart wished to hear.

She replayed the awful night at all hours, the words spinning around when her responsibilities no longer captured her complete attention. On her walk to the training barn. When she took her lunch in the courtyard. In the bath at night.

How could she have been so foolish?

She swallowed the burning sensation licking the back of her throat, buoying her resolve to try again.

She needed to track him down, if only to provide a proper apology — more than an explanation — she needed to voice her admiration for his person. He was smart and honorable and capable. A natural leader and a man worthy of the best.

She broke his trust; the words she chose… unforgivable.

He may not require her good opinion of him, but she would grant it all the same.

She gathered the remaining fabric in her arms and went in search of Jade.

Harried voices reached the back of the dress shop, hastening her steps.

She rounded the corner, and the garment on the top of the stack flew in her face, obscuring her view. She gripped the clothing tighter and transferred the load to her hip.

"Please, it's my friend. He's in trouble. I need a healer," a small lad said. He wore a gray cap pulled over his ears and heavy overalls smeared in dirt. "Please. He's hurt. A tree… he's trapped. Won't answer when I call his name."

She dropped the fabric and rushed over.

"Find Xavier," she said to Jade and turned to Madam MaLota. "Gather as many strong men as you can find. We will need help to move the timber. I'll follow him now and assess the wounds."

"This way," the lad cried and bolted through the door, his gangly strides carrying him toward Zoie's cottage. "Hurry."

Her chest burned from the effort to keep up with his pace.

It was a struggle to wrangle her powers under control. She

counted her breaths, the numbers coming faster the farther they ran into the woods.

The lad slipped into the brush, following a narrow path.

Soon, they climbed a steep ravine. At the top, it opened into a riotous meadow, and in the center, an old, dilapidated cabin jutted out of the vines.

"What—"

"Please, he's inside," the lad said, his lip quivering. "You must go inside."

"A tree didn't fall on your friend, did it?" She knelt down beside him and rested a hand on his waist.

He shook his head.

"Why don't you start from the beginning? Tell me why you brought me deep into the woods."

"The man, he took my little brother. Said he would hurt him unless I brought the pretty lady with the dark hair to this cabin. He said to tell you someone was hurt, and you'd come runnin' real quick like. Please, lady, I'm sorry. I only want him to let my brother go."

"Shh, it will be alright. I'll get him back, but I need you to do me a favor. Can you run as fast as you can back to the compound? Find Gavyn. Do you know him? He's the fighter with the scar under his eye."

She took a deep, steadying breath.

"Let him know where I am. Tell him to hurry. Can you do that for me?"

"Aye. Everyone knows Mister Gavyn. I'll find him. Promise."

She waited until the top of his head disappeared down the trail, then climbed the cabin's steps, and opened the door.

"Hello, Ember. It's wonderful to rest my eyes on you."

She stepped into the dimly lit room.

"Landon?"

The farmer's son. How did he find her? What was he doing here? He looked terrible. Gaunt. She almost didn't recognize him in his sagging clothes, his grimy face. A small lad huddled in the corner, tears streaming down his cheeks.

"What are you—"

"I came to take what's mine. With your bitch of a mother out of the way and my father awaiting trial in the village, I can claim you for my own. Collect what is due. Your magic will make me a rich man. My sire was a fool. He desired your lush body, your pretty face. But you're worth more than your value in the bedroom. I dreamt about this day for months. Chasing after you. Almost giving up hope when I lost your trail in the mining village. But when I heard what happened at the Castle, I just knew it was you. Come, now, you filthy Faeblood. You shall be my bride. I shall profit from your curse."

"You're mad."

A sneer split Landon's face.

"I'm not going anywhere with you," Ember said as she straightened.

She'd had enough.

This pathetic excuse for a man would not bully her into cowering.

Her magic rumbled along her palms. Not the comfortable warmth of a cast to heal. No, this… this was the rush of a storm, gathering off the coast moments before laying siege to shore. A saccharine film coated her tongue.

Power — her magic tasted of the sweetest rage, and she welcomed the flavor, basked in it. She tilted her chin higher.

"Release the lad. I grant you the freedom to walk out of here. My mercy is a gift. Treat it as such, and never return."

"You think to make demands." He spat on the dusty floor. "You forget your place."

"Release him," she repeated.

"Not a chance."

"Stay down," she said to the lad.

Landon wouldn't relent. It was in his eyes, their sour bend.

This time it was easy, gathering her courage. Xavier was right — standing up and fighting felt... true.

She closed her eyes, and a calm settled over her. Never had she imagined this circumstance. She never thought herself a fighter, a protector. A warrior.

She gathered her power, and put her past in its place.

"XAVIER... GAVYN, THANK THE GODS YOU BOTH ARE HERE. HURRY, make haste," Jade said. "There's a lad trapped under a tree fall. Ember left to tend his injuries."

Gavyn whistled, gaining the attention of a handful of cubs in the market, and flicked his chin. They dropped their wares and sprinted over.

"This way. Hurry." Jade wove between the patrons. She found a break in the crowd and led them to the entrance of the southern woods. "They took the path toward Zoie's, but I'm unsure where the tree went down."

He squeezed her shoulder and took off.

Something tumbled in the pit of his stomach. Perhaps it was a lack of sustenance but hearing her name... learning she went into the dense forest with only a small lad for company...

His footsteps tore through the peace of the woods.

Birds took flight overhead and wildlife scattered in the underbrush.

The beat of his pulse pounded in his ears, thrumming in time with the chant — *she was sound.*

She was sound.

"Gavyn."

The name flew on the wind; its recognition delayed. He skidded to a stop and cupped his ear. He heard it then.

"Gavyn."

He retraced his steps. Fifty paces back, he ran upon Xav and the cubs inspecting a damaged bush on the edge of the trail.

"They left the path here," Xavier said and disappeared into the thick foliage. He led them down a ravine, pausing every few yards to pick up the trail.

The forest opened up at the bottom of the slope.

"They lead to the old hunting cabin." Xavier pointed to two sets of footprints.

Gavyn had built several small structures when they first settled in the territory. During the harshest winters, when game was sparse, they'd used the simple shelters as a base when the lack of game drew them farther into the forest.

As the compound prospered and Xavier procured other sources of food, they rarely traveled more than a day's hike in search of venison.

Some of the local villagers still used the rustic cabins for multi-day trips. He sent men twice a year to inspect each one for any necessary repairs, ensuring their upkeep.

Gavyn didn't want to miss Ember's trail for a second time, so he moved at a slower pace, tracking her boot prints along the way.

Snap. A twig cracked ahead.

A small lad scurried down the trail. Tears streaked down his cheeks, leaving wet tracks on his dirty face. His eyes widened when he caught sight of them, and for a moment, Gavyn expected him to turn and run.

"Where is she?" Gavyn asked, unable to keep the bite out of his voice. He must look a fright to someone so small, but he didn't care. Not now. Not when his gut told him something was amiss. Louder, he repeated, "Where is she?"

"Please, I'm sorry Mister Gavyn," the lad said. He wiped a line of fresh tears with the back of his hand. "He had my brother. The man said… said he would hurt him if I didn't get her to follow me."

He grabbed the lad by the upper arms and swallowed a yell. "Where?"

"In the hunting cabin. In the glen."

"Stay here."

"No." The lad tipped his chin and his jaw wavered, but he croaked out, "I'm coming with you."

Gavyn didn't have time for an argument. Let the lad tag along. He sprinted up the ravine, his long strides carrying him to the top, a good ten paces in front of the rest of the group.

As they drew nearer the cabin, the rush of water drowned out the noise from their approach. The ground around the structure grew wild, nature attempting to gain back her land.

He slowed his steps, straining to see any movement through the open windows.

"Listen," Xavier whispered. He took a step forward, tilting his head. "Someone's inside."

He heard it then — Ember's voice. It mixed with a deeper one. Male. Loud with a clipped tone.

From this distance, he could not decipher the words. They tangled together and rose in volume. He should—

A blast of air knocked him backwards.

He stumbled several steps and found his balance.

Silence blanketed the forest as if something sucked all the sound from the world. Time moved slowly. It crept along the outskirts of the glen, then darted forward, parting the tall grasses like an arrow seeking a target.

"Ember," he shouted. "Ember!"

He sprinted up the steps and wrenched the door open.

His heart beat outside his chest.

She stood in the center of the room, free from injuries, but her face was as pale as her favorite white dress.

A young lad huddled in the corner, covering his ears and rocking back and forth.

A man, his body thick from gluttony but growing haggard

around the edges as if he recently missed too many meals, lay face down on the floor.

Rage, white and hot and encompassing, clouded his vision.

He wanted to tear the man from limb to limb. To pick him up and pound him back down. Gavyn would send him back in a rucksack to whatever hell he crawled out.

He started forward, but paused at the look on her face.

Half expecting anger, half expecting fear, he was surprised to see the concern in her eyes, the stubborn set of her jaw. If he found hurt or even trepidation, he would have continued, for his sake and hers.

Instead, Gavyn fought to draw breath and steady his thoughts, slow his heart.

She was sound.

"He's not dead, is he?" Ember swept her arm wide. "I cast to knock him out, but his head hit the stone hearth."

He willed his hands to stop shaking. Someone jostled his shoulder. And he watched, as if from another vantage, as Xavier walked over to the fallen man and lay his ear on his chest.

She was uninjured.

"Nay. He still draws breath... for now," Xavier said. "Get him up. Drag him to the compound."

Gavyn startled, unaware the men stood behind him.

Two cubs hooked their arms on each side of the body and hoisted the man up. His head lolled on his shoulders, and his legs dangled, the boots clearing two paths on the dusty floor.

She was unharmed.

"I presume you know this man," Xavier said, raising an eyebrow.

"Aye. 'Tis the farmer's son. My past finally caught up with me. He came to drag me back." She wiped her hands down the top of her skirts, and in a clear voice, she said, "I'm not going anywhere."

She was not merely fine; she could fight her own battles.

He was wrong about her.

She wasn't weak. Perhaps a tad clumsy and not great on long walks. But she was strong and fierce and brave. Dear gods, he missed her smiles, her scent.

Without her, Gavyn was a grumpy lout dredging through his monotonous day. He wanted to pull her tight and tell her all the flowery words, but his hands shook, and it was certain he would bungle them if he didn't control his anger.

He clenched his fists.

Gavyn needed to find a place to calm down, to figure out how to approach his little thief. Maybe he should gather her favorite blooms, the ones that made his nose itch. It wouldn't be so bad if he took care not to touch his face, and the gesture might distract her if he said the wrong things.

With his plan formed, he kissed her on the cheek, ignoring her wide eyes and parted lips, and jogged out of the cottage.

CHAPTER THIRTY-TWO

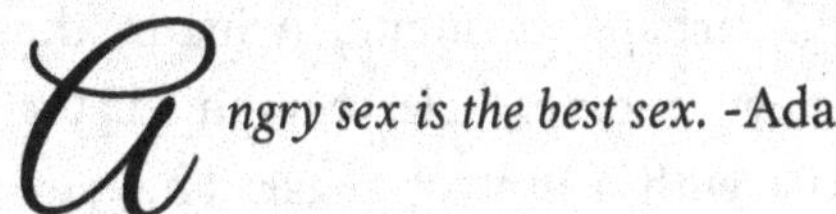

ngry sex is the best sex. -Ada

INSUFFERABLE MAN. GAVYN ESCAPED THE CABIN WITHOUT SO much as a word to Ember. A distracted peck on the cheek, and he was... gone.

She backtracked to the village, fuming the entire way to Madam's shop. Sure, her heart almost burst when he stormed into the cabin. Despite maintaining control of the situation, her knees buckled slightly when their eyes locked.

It was heady, summoning her strength. Trusting her power. But knowing he was behind her... knowing he still cared... it was worth all the magic in the realm.

Jade paced in front of the display window, her shoulders relaxing when she spotted Ember. Madam MaLota beckoned her inside.

"What happened?" Jade toyed with a wisp of hair near Ember's temple. The tendril must have escaped her plait when she blasted Landon off his feet. "Where are the others?"

Ember closed the front door, leaned back against it, and exhaled.

"There was no fallen tree. It was a trap." She held up her hand to silence Jade's question. "Landon, the farmer's son from my former village, discovered my whereabouts and kidnapped a young lad, blackmailing his brother to tease me out."

"No…" Jade gasped.

She launched into the tale. Madam MaLota waited until Ember finished before pulling her into a crushing embrace. She sank into the warmth, letting the rush of the afternoon dissipate from her body.

"Well, you appear unharmed." Jade was kind enough not to mention Ember's shaky hands. "Come, let's take your mind off of things and finish shopping. Perhaps we should swing by the baker's for some of his new cookies. He combined the cinnamon you found for Zoie with a hint of sugar. They are precisely what you need."

Eating her sorrows was a wonderful idea. Plus, she needed a distraction.

Ember took two steps and tripped, her boot catching a reel of fabric on the floor.

Grace — it was as elusive today as it was during the many failed lessons with her mother. Ember shook her head and righted herself, returning the spool to its original position.

Her heart ached for mama, but for the first time since stumbling upon Xavier's village, a sense of peace settled in her chest.

Mother would have never stayed at the compound. Too many people. Too many nosy neighbors. Not a day passed without someone in your business, like siblings poking each other in an overbearing family.

For all their travels, they never experienced this type of magic. It was another regret. Today, the memories of their last days together came easier. Milder. Her resentment, her guilt, melted into something more tolerable.

The bell on the front door chimed, announcing Gavyn's arrival.

Her imperfectly perfect warrior.

He was impressive, his body a product of a grueling lifestyle and disciplined routine. Too bad it carried around the obstinate head of the man she loved.

Distracted by the sight of his swollen face and red eyes, she almost tripped again on the fabric.

The corner of his lips twitched.

"Madam, could I trouble you for a vase?" he asked, his eyes never leaving Ember.

The words sounded funny, as if he added an extra 's' to the end. Goodness, his tongue was swollen, too. Gavyn thrust out a bouquet of her favorite flowers.

"I picked these for you, but if I hold them much longer, I fear my hands will swell to match my face."

He sneezed.

"They're beautiful."

Heat bloomed on her cheek. He said nothing about his affliction. It was a simple gesture, but at the heart, that's who he was… a partner who put others ahead of his own comforts.

She carefully took the bunch, broken stems and all, enjoying their fragrance before handing them to Madam.

They stared at each other, the thud of her heart growing louder the longer the silence continued. She dimly registered Jade and Madam sneaking out of the front door.

They covered the distance between them at the same time. He wrapped her tight, yanking her to his chest.

Dear gods, she missed this. Missed him. She wanted to stay like this forever, protected by his grumpy assurances and strong arms. She spent the last few days and her entire journey back to the dressmaker's reciting her apology. Her reasons, her feelings.

Now, with his thoughtful present and slight lisp, the words fled, every one of them.

She tilted her head back and ran a finger across his lower lip. Warmth pooled in her palm, and the sweet taste of a cast filled the back of her throat. The swelling in his mouth subsided, and the redness ringing his eyes gave way to a healthy pink.

There.

When she imagined this meeting, they stood farther apart. Perhaps in his chambers. She swallowed, hoping the apology would flow out.

Gavyn held her gaze and traced her jawline. A tic in his cheek appeared. He would not make this easy on her. Not that she deserved the consideration, but in her many portrayals, she imagined him speaking first.

"I'm sorry," she blurted out. Ember grabbed onto his shoulders, steadying herself. "I'm sorry for my hurtful words, Gavyn. I… I panicked and didn't know what to do. I saw you in the arena forced to fight, and then those men attacked Erik in the crowd…"

She sighed.

"I spent days worrying over your wounds while you slept, wondering what I would do if you didn't recover. And then you woke up and casually mentioned the threats from Lord Siodina…"

He grunted.

"I regret the words I spoke… the pain I caused you. I know it doesn't make it right, but please understand. My entire life has been on the run. I thought… well… I thought if I left the compound, then the High Table would leave you alone." She searched his face. "I don't want to be the reason they hurt somebody else."

"So you left us to deal with the Castle on our own? Without your powers or help?"

"No." She rubbed her palm. "I mean, yes. I wanted to leave, but not for that reason. I thought my troubles would follow me."

"Sweetheart, Xavier built this place on troubles."

"I know. The more time I spend at the compound and in the village, the more I see how much he sacrificed. How much you and everyone else gave to protect his dream and build this place into a home. I didn't wish to be another burden, nor cause more harm."

She cupped the side of his jaw.

"I realized you wouldn't come with me. And deep down, I knew you wouldn't let me leave. So I spoke those awful words, hoping to distract you enough to let me go."

He hesitated, then said, "I have no cause to be hurt. We… we never spoke of promises."

"Aye, we did." She ran her thumb across his cheek. "Maybe we never lent voice to our thoughts, but we belong to each other all the same. I won't make the mistake of not sharing the truth out loud a second time — you are the most honorable person in my life. You are intelligent and kind and brave. Perhaps a tad too serious."

She grinned.

"And if my mother made your acquaintance, she would say you ground me. You are more than *just* a fighter, and 'tis I who aspire to be worthy of your notice. Of your love. Because…" Her voice wavered. She took a deep breath and louder she said, "Because you have mine. You have my whole heart, Gavyn."

You have my whole heart.

Gavyn closed his eyes, savoring the words. He waited for what felt like an eternity to hear them. Never thought fate would be so kind. He wanted to pick her up and kiss her senseless. But he made that mistake before — putting sex and pleasure in front of tough conversations.

Her new yellow tunic flamed as bright as her sunny disposition. The color highlighted what he suspected all along — while he grumbled and groaned and stomped around the training barn, she went out and found her spark.

They'd both suffered, while he avoided her, wanting time to think things through while he healed.

But Xavier was right — stewing provided no clarity, only hurt. Dear gods, his hands ached. He was a fool to over train.

A lump formed in his throat.

She was breathtaking, her beauty stemming from her kindness and big heart. Too bad it carried around the illogical head of the woman he loved.

His thoughts settled with her in his arms. The walk in the meadow to pick her flowers soothed his earlier rage. But his hands continued to tremble. It might take a day or two for the images of her in the hunting cabin to fade from his mind.

It turned out she didn't need his interference.

Sure, he'd always want to protect her, shelter her. But he needed to learn to trust, too. It wouldn't be easy, and they would need to take things slowly, one day at a time, but the reward would be worth it.

She was worth it.

And so was he.

Xavier was right about that, too.

Gavyn was a fighter first — a leader by example, but the mark on his neck meant he was much more. If the events of the last couple of months told him anything, it was that he needed to be more. He no longer yearned to hide in the training barn; he wanted to lead more than daily sparring sessions.

Still, he must say the words. She deserved to hear what was in his heart.

"From day one, the fighters learn that if they want to succeed, then they must stand together. Side by side. And taking a mate... carving out a life together... it's more than sharing sheets. And I took that decision away from you."

He swallowed.

"I wanted to tuck you behind me, shielding you from harm. But you deserve to stand beside me. In front of me at times. Never again. Never again will I push you behind me. I am many things — grumpy and hard-headed and simple — but I learn from my mistakes."

He cupped the side of her face.

"If you need to speak, to unburden your troubles, I vow to listen instead of rushing off to solve your problems. I'm sorry I didn't provide the opportunity to voice your worries. And I'm sorry I turned my back on you this week."

Gavyn cleared the emotion from his throat.

"I love you. I want nothing more than to give you everything you deserve. In this life and the next. If you want to paint our chamber deep plum, I'll grind the powder with Rowan for the exact shade you wish. If you want half a dozen kittens to cuddle and chase mice, I'll find an herb to make my nose stop itching. If you want to wear a new dress every day of the moon cycle, I'll give you enough gold to keep Madam busy for a very long time."

He could live a thousand years and be happy for their moments together, but her heart may yearn for more.

"And if you want a family of your own — little ones, with your pretty smile and infectious laugh — I'll demand Xavier find us a draught, a fertility tea. Maybe it's too much, too soon, but I don't want secrets between us. And I need to trust your intentions."

"I understand that now." Ember traced his scar.

"It's important," he said, his tone deepening. "It's important that you do, because when you are ready... when your head accepts what your heart knows, I will mark you. Bond you to me. Once you surrender, I will never let you go."

She touched the black mark on his neck.

"That's what this means. Xavier told me that family doesn't flinch. I'm choosing to stay. To fight. I choose Jade, and the girls, and my new family. I choose you—"

~

He released a growl and dipped his head, claiming her mouth. His tongue swept inside as he picked her up off her feet.

Ember didn't care if the entire village saw. She wasn't letting him go.

Gavyn tasted of anticipation and lust and hers, an intoxicating combination she couldn't resist.

She whimpered, and he pulled back, panting for breath.

Her stomach flipped at the ferocity in his eyes.

"Mine," he growled against her lips. "Tell me what I need to hear."

"Yours," she said. "Your good girl."

He grabbed her hand and led them to Madam's back room.

The anticipation was too much. Where would he take her? On the chair, with her astride, riding him through their release? Or against the wall, where she could wrap her legs around him and hold on through their orgasms?

"Aye. And good girls earn good gifts." He pulled her behind the changing screen, quickly stripping them of both their clothes. There was no finesse. No slow seduction. As if his desperation matched her own. "Turn around."

She wanted to melt into him — to kiss him until they were both too weak to stand — but her body obeyed without thought. This is what she needed. Giving up control, on the edge of breaking against his will.

Knowing he may crumble right along with her.

"Put your hands above your head and leave them." He nudged her legs farther apart. She pressed her palms into the wall and tilted her hips, reveling in the hitch in his voice when he asked, "Is this what you want? Me, so obsessed with your pleasure I can barely string two words together?"

He gripped her hips with one hand and rubbed tiny circles

around her swollen nub with the other. Her knees fought to give out.

"Easy there." He stopped petting and lifted her up.

She dropped her head back against his chest.

"I asked you a question." He nibbled on the outer shell of her ear.

"Aye," she said, and he tweaked one sensitive nipple, rolling it between his thumb and forefinger. "It's been too long."

He seemed to agree. Gavyn cupped the base of her throat, holding her flush against him.

"Hang on," he said, the only warning before he slammed inside.

She removed her hands from the wall and gripped his forearms. He changed the angle of his thrusts, hitting a sensitive spot deep inside.

Too much, too much, too much.

"It's not too much," he said. His pace quickened.

She was unaware she spoke the words. Her body shuddered with the intense pressure.

"That's my good girl."

"Gavyn," she moaned as he slowed and wrapped an arm around her middle.

He guided her up and down his shaft, and little bolts of lightning shot through her center every time he ran his tip along her seam.

"Is this what you want?" He asked and nipped her ear, his expert fingers bringing her to the height of pleasure. "Me buried inside you... belonging to you."

"Yes, yes, *yes*," she chanted, unsure if she answered his question or cried out in relief. Her body erupted, unable to deny his command. Heat spiraled from her center as her vision narrowed.

"You have me. 'Tis the same though. You are mine," he ground out and flexed his hips. "Are you ready for me? Because once we are mated, I will take you at all times of the day — in the morning, after the nooning meal, every evening. My need is insatiable. Say the words."

"Yours, Gavyn." The rush of the market sounded distant, but his strangled release registered through the haze. Her body sagged against his, spent from their lovemaking. "I'm ready. I'm yours."

"Shhh. I have you," he whispered against her hair as if she was the only one wrecked. Still, Ember delighted in the words as much as she felt pride at the hitch in his voice.

She rested her head against his chest, relaxing with its rise and fall. Her thoughts remained fuzzy from their lovemaking, but one thing was clear. She wanted to stay like this — protected in his arms, cherished in his embrace, for as long as their world allowed.

"I know." She turned her cheek and licked his chest. "Thank you."

"Always. Your pleasure is always my aim." He spun her around.

"No. I never thanked you for taking care of me." She cupped his face with both hands, feeling steadier on her feet. "It's one thing to bring me to the peak, but it's special — knowing you will let me test my wings on the way down."

"Something I need to work on outside of the bedroom."

"Most of our coupling is not even in your chamber," she deadpanned.

"Minx," he said. "I'm learning to trust you, too. Letting you handle some of your own battles. I'm not the easiest person to live with — demanding control — but you remain in charge... of our mating. Our home."

This man. She ran her thumb along his upper lip, and he rewarded her with a kiss on its pad. As if it were possible — apologizing, hearing his words in return — deepened her love.

There was nothing Ember wouldn't do to protect him. To protect this.

She would curse the entire High Table, may need to in the end, to keep them all safe.

"I don't know what the Castle has planned or how Lord Siodina might retaliate, but I know I want to stand beside you and face it together."

He yanked her against him and rested his head on top of hers.

"Welcome to the family, my little thief. It's time for a celebration."

CHAPTER THIRTY-THREE

e are not the sum of our gifts but their pieces and parts make us whole. -Rowan

WHEN GAVYN INVITED HER TO A PARTY, EMBER DIDN'T EXPECT TO be so… cold.

She ran her hands along stone walls, dampness swirling around her fingers. Her teeth chattered. She wished for a heavy cloak as her thin gown proved ineffective at warding off the crispness of the underground cavern.

The cave was vast with indentations in the sand, the only evidence of its use as nature's hiding spot. A den for forest and human beasties alike.

Voices bounced off its stone walls. The ground squished out from under her feet. Silt stained the sides of her thin slippers.

Ember sighed. She should have worn her new boots.

The tunnel's entrance was tall and narrow. Natural light lost its way in the zigzagging passage, but candles, carried from the compound, kept darkness from devouring their group.

Foot prints fanned out in every direction as more fighters trickled past. Nearly two dozen made the journey.

Gavyn joined Xavier at the front.

She stayed along the outer edges of the group, unsure of her place.

"Did you hear that?" she asked no one in particular.

A loud rush emanated from inside the wall. A crack in the foundation spanned from ground to ceiling, and water trickled in the craggy seam, slowly eroding the sharp edges of the scar.

She rested her ear against the stone.

"The river fights behind these walls," Rowan said.

"Water runs behind the stone? How?" She leaned back and glanced around. "Where are we?"

"This is an old hiding spot Xavier used when he first traveled to the area. He fled the mining village with his family and needed a place to stash everyone. They stayed here from the summer equinox until the Mabon festival." Rowan studied the formation in front of him. "Legend has it that an ancient Faeblood used his power to dam up the stream behind these walls."

His lips formed a flat line.

"He cut off the village below from their fresh water supply. The sorcerer wanted revenge for a slight by a fisherman's daughter." A dark chuckle escaped. "What better revenge than to dry up the trade of the father?"

"Dark magic lived here once, but it is faint now." She stepped up behind him and grabbed his hand. "I feel nature fighting the spell. Soon, she will break the bonds."

"Yes. The power of the water will overcome its magical prison." Rowan opened his eyes and placed their entwined fingers on the gray stone. He flattened his palm, covering hers, and said, "Open your mind."

Images of a beautiful maiden danced in front of her eyes. A thin and sallow figure in all black knelt on the ground. His hand stretched out, fingers clutching a small ring. The scene passed before she registered its conclusion. Her emotions swirled. An intense longing stirred inside, mixing with sadness and a dash of anger.

"Do you feel it?" Rowan whispered in her ear. "Do you feel his anguish? The girl of his dreams denied his proposal. Men — human or Faeblood — will scorch the entire realm for a slight to their attentions, when all they need is a steady flow of mead and a solid fist to the face to heal their honor."

Her eyes flew open.

She removed her hand from under his and stretched up to touch the mark at the base of his neck.

The warmth of his flesh singed her icy palm. Energy pulsed into her fingers, radiating throughout her core. The waves flowed stronger, more violently than the ones she experienced with Gavyn and Xavier.

Like calls to like.

"You," she said and placed the tips of her fingers on her lips. "Magic fills your blood. But... how... why..."

"I am the last of an ancient line of Faeblood known for their artistry. And for marrying their cousins to preserve the purity of their powers." He scoffed. "While I share their gift for creating, I didn't share their inclination to mate with my relatives. You aren't the only one with the gift to cast."

Rowan's dimple appeared on his cheek.

"How else do you think I catch all my lovers? It's not from my devilish good looks." Rowan grabbed her hand and pressed it to his neck. "Catching up? I did not like deceiving you, but it was necessary until we felt certain of your allegiance. Keep it there."

Magic coated her tongue, leaving a burned film, similar to over-charred meat. Heat seared the column of her throat. Rowan kept his palm in place, and pain slithered to her arm. It wrapped around her chest and transformed into a dull ache.

A hard-fought family.

The image of a younger Xavier swam in her mind. Her heart lurched when Gavyn's likeness sprang forward. Maia and Mikel were next, both with brows furrowed and tight lips. Other fighters followed. Some she knew by face, but not by name.

They all shared one similarity — Xavier's cuffs, his mark.

Faint, ghost-like images of Jade and Zoie danced in her vision, their outlines smudged and less defined.

She opened her eyes, but sparkles of light obscured her view. Her heart rate slowed, and the spots clumped together to form a complete image.

Rowan stepped back.

Fighters turned in their direction, each with their arm resting on the shoulder of the person in front. A show of solidarity, for her. A family. All these years, the different homes, the yearning for a missing piece. This was what she needed.

Sure, it appeared different from her dreams.

She never expected so many... men, especially not a band of fighters. But she had Jade and Ada and Zoie. They may not share the mark, but they were hers, all the same.

And Gavyn. The fighters were his brothers first, but somehow it didn't lessen her claim.

Xavier weaved through the group, halted next to Rowan, and placed a hand on his shoulder.

"Virtus et Honos."

She glanced around his frame. Her breath hitched.

"Virtus et Honos." The pledge echoed in the cavern, and the candles flickered. These men honed their bodies, disciplined their minds. Created hope through strength and honor.

Rowan cupped her face and rested his forehead against hers.

"We pledge to each other that no matter how difficult things may be, it's better to stand up and fight alongside your family than to flee and live a cursed life — one without love or honor. You carry a piece of each of us. And we... " He gestured around the cave. "We harbor a piece of you. The mark bonds you to all who wear it."

He placed his hands on her shoulders and presented her to the room.

Faces grinned back.

She bit her cheek. Her fingertips traced the mark on her neck. She knew its appearance, even without the aid of a looking glass. Its warmth filled her heart and healed a fraction of the pain trapped inside.

Xavier motioned the first man forward.

The unknown fighter cupped her shoulder, and she mirrored the gesture.

Rowan patted the back of her hand. "Leave it."

"Familia Fortitudo." The fighter squeezed. "My strength stems from my family."

She swallowed and repeated, "Familia Fortitudo."

He yanked her forward, kissed both cheeks, and set her back with a smile. The next fighter in line stepped forward and repeated the oath. And then another. And another.

Most kissed her cheeks.

Some grabbed her for a one-armed hug. A boisterous youth picked her up and twirled her around. He sat her down with a kiss on the lips and sauntered back into the crowd, the playful gesture lifting the serious mood in the cavern.

It was Xavier's turn.

He presented her with two lengths of leather, a smaller version of his cuffs. The thin strips looked out of place in his large hands as he fastened the bindings around one wrist, then the other.

Her chest expanded, and a tingling warmth filled her limbs, this time summoned without the necessity of a cast.

Similar but different.

She raised a cuff to her face and studied the inlay. The sharp lines of the crest stood out in relief against the fawn-colored leather. It was identical to the one the fighters wore, except for one minor detail. She tilted her head to the side and furrowed her brow.

It couldn't be. It was not possible.

"It's the caduceus," Rowan said. "I thought you might need a reminder. You can be both one of us and your own person."

She brought the cuff closer to her face. Two snakes wrapped around a staff. The detail of the scales was exquisite, lending movement to the serpentine bodies. She whirled to face Rowan.

"It's my family's crest. My book... our book boasted this mark on the spine."

Ember ran her shaky fingers over the inlay. She tried to smile, to cover her melancholy with appreciation, if only for Rowan who had shown her a kindness, crafting something so uniquely hers.

But she couldn't stop thinking about her mother — their shared days.

On the nights the shadows didn't chase her to sleep, her mother had read from their family book. Well-worn, it held stories of past Faeblood, their lineages and powers. Save for her locket, no other family treasures existed. And the book — she closed her eyes — she left it when she fled the cottage.

Another failing.

All this time, she regretted the chance to apologize. But one did not find absolution in the dead, and it was a long path to forgiving herself.

Never forget your heritage. Her mother's warning, but perhaps she'd meant it as a reminder. *We are not our parents; we do not inherit their sins. We can choose a different path.*

Now, with the beginnings of a new life, a found family, she simply wished for a chance to bid farewell.

She studied the cuffs.

Mine. The mark was hers. She may never be a fierce warrior like Maia… like Gavyn… but she would stay, prove her worth. To these men and herself and her mother's ghost.

"I know what you seek," Rowan said. "The pain of loss leaves a deep scar, perhaps deeper for us as a fragment of our magic dies with our loved ones."

He placed a hand on his chest.

"Neither time nor magic shall heal your wound. But family…" He gestured around the cavern. "And friendship… They serve as an anchor and prevent us from fleeing the hurt. I'm glad you stayed, healer girl."

He was right. She may never feel whole again, but with every cast, the bond with her mother strengthened. Perhaps more than when she lived.

She hugged him around the middle, hard enough to force out a gasp.

The crowd parted as Gavyn strolled toward her.

"My love." He tucked a tendril behind her ear and whispered, "I may own your body, your heart, but I'm honored to share you with my family."

"Come," Xavier cut between them. A large crevice divided the back wall, so narrow he had to turn sideways to shimmy through. His hand shot out of the darkness. "There is something I must show you."

She clasped his wrist and climbed over the stone outcropping at her feet. Thick blackness swallowed her whole, and a shiver ran down her spine. She cast a beam of light to cut, illuminating a set of steps carved into the cave and the harsh shadows on the edges of his frown.

"Full of surprises. Same as Rowan." Xavier shook his head. "Watch your step."

He pivoted on his heel, not waiting for her to follow, and descended into the dark.

She took the steps at a much slower pace, bracing against the wall with one hand and sharing light from her other palm.

Water trickled over her knuckles and pooled along the edges of the stairs.

Down and down they went until the small amount of daylight from the antechamber disappeared. She walked through little puffs of breath and willed her heart to slow. Similar to the crevice damming the stream, she felt dark magic, ancient and foreboding.

The rational part of her wanted to disobey Xavier and to vault up the steps as fast as her short legs could carry her. Instinct whispered in her ear to turn around. But it was the darkly curious voice — the one her mother lectured incessantly — she followed.

Xavier halted at the bottom of the steps and leaned against the wall, allowing her to pass by his thick frame.

The mouth of a cavern, a smaller replica of the one above, opened up, threatening to swallow her whole. Enormous jagged stone formations hung from the ceiling, their pattern like rows of twisted teeth.

She dodged a few of the lower ones and picked her way around the boulders growing from the floor.

Ember fanned her light and gasped.

The beam reflected off hundreds of long blades lining the outer wall.

Swords.

Xavier brought her to a cave full of illegal weapons.

"What?"

"You're asking the wrong question again," Xavier reached down to pick one up by the hilt. He raised it to eye level and peered down its length.

"There are so many." She walked around the edge of the room and ran her fingers along several handles. "Where do they all come from? Does the High Table suspect? Why are they here?"

"All excellent questions, but again, not the one you should be asking." Xavier sliced the air in front of him. "Think."

"You speak in riddles. Forgive me if I'm having trouble following." She tracked the movements of the blade in the air, mesmerized by the graceful arc.

"To answer your question, we... or I should say, Rowan, makes the blades. He descends from a long line of casters known for their ability to forge instruments of war." Xavier returned the sword back to its resting place. "His father was a smith. As was his father's father. And their father before."

"They were fabers." She touched the tips of her fingers to her lips.

"Fabers?" Xavier asked.

"Aye. They are crafters or artisans who charm metal." She wandered to the opposite wall. It contained smaller blades with shorter handles. "They can heat and bend the steel in unnatural ways. The properties of the metal limit others. It is said that their blades are the deadliest."

"They are light and balanced. Sharp." He picked up a smaller sword and handed it to her for inspection. "Rowan, for all his other follies, is a talented craftsman."

She placed two fingers at the junction of the blade and handle and lifted it up and down, testing its balance.

"Why so many? Surely, you can't think of trading them for gold?"

Swish.

She whirled around, imitating his earlier movements. Ember brought the small sword diagonally across her body, then thrust it straight in front of her. Pure power. The blade nestled in her palm, a deadly extension of her magic. It thrummed through her, somehow louder, perhaps amplified by her bond with Rowan.

"No," Xavier said. "I dare not risk the High Table tracing these back to our home."

"Why, then? Why face the wrath of the Castle and endanger your people?"

"There it is." He shook his finger at her. "That's the right question. For decades, we suffered under the rule of the Castle. We are no match for their magic, but I work to balance the scales."

"You prepare for battle," she said without a hint of question.

"No, Ember. I prepare for war."

EPILOGUE

Maia sat at the small desk in her chambers.

Her legs tapped a quick beat against the wooden floor, and after finishing her braid, she grabbed her cuffs from their velvet-lined box in the corner. She scowled at the fading red welts on her wrists mocked her status as an elite fighter.

Dad would be ashamed.

The swelling subsided four days prior, and small rosy patches remained where the rope bit into her skin. Xavier ordered her to pay a visit to Ember, but she kept them. The thick leather of her cuffs hid the marks, and they served as a reminder to always keep her guard up.

Even in her own home.

Her breathing came in shallow spurts as heat crept along the base of her neck. The looking glass above her desk reflected a red blush spiraling across her cheeks. She fastened the first cuff around her wrist with shaky hands. The burn of the leather against her tender skin faded a little each day.

Today, it was almost imperceptible.

Knock. Knock. Knock.

She shot off the small stool, sending it toppling backwards. Maia shook out her hands and crossed the space. Careful. She needed to be careful. Her boot wedged against the bottom of the door, and she leaned against the frame.

"Who is it?" she asked, the greeting sharp, even to her own ears.

"It's Erik." His deep tone carried through the thick slab. "Xavier sent me to fetch you."

Maia leaned back and pulled her foot away.

She braced herself against the wall with one arm and opened the door a fraction to match the handsome face with the voice she recognized.

It was a relief to see him. He was lucky, so damn lucky, with his injuries.

They all were, considering.

His eyes flicked to the fading marks on her uncovered wrist, and his brows narrowed.

"I need a moment," she said and slapped on the other cuff, biting the inside of her cheek to strangle the yelp of pain.

She closed the door and took out a small pouch from the side pocket of her leathers. It contained dried sand from the banks of the stream. Maia sprinkled a pinch on the flat surface of the door's handle and hid the bag.

Maia tilted her chin and said, "Let's go."

His nostrils flared, but Erik held the thought. Instead, he swept his arm wide.

"After you. Xavier is in his office."

She nodded and strode down the long barracks corridor. The heat from his body teased her back, carrying his signature scent of spicy cloves. It was always like this with him. She was painfully aware of his body.

At first, she assumed it stemmed from the hours they spent grappling. It was natural to learn every contour, every harsh angle, rolling around in the sand pit… every afternoon.

Often, on their day off.

Of late, she thought her awareness sprang from something more, something different. Instead of bridging immediately when he pinned her, she lingered, savoring the feel of his weight on top. And when he choked her from behind, she wanted to twist around and bite him on the neck as opposed to kneeing him in the thigh.

Sometimes, when his eyes tracked her across the barn, she imagined he felt the same.

He led them to the training barn.

The lack of conversation gave her plenty of time to envision all the different reasons for Xavier requiring her presence before midday. Did he know she refused to visit Ember? Did any more clues surface as to the identity of her attacker?

She wove her way through the early morning fighters.

The familiar noise of hard training soothed her nerves.

Gavyn barked commands at a pair of cubs wrestling on the ground, while Mikel partnered with a more seasoned fighter in the corner. Ava's legs dangled over the edge of the loft, and underneath, Ember pretended to wipe her treatment table, her lips parting in a soft smile as she stared at her lover.

How much time would pass until Gavyn marked her? She'd bet Rowan it would take less than another moon cycle before he proposed.

A feather of envy brushed against her heart.

Would she discover the same contentment — the one her parents cherished, and now Gavyn and Ember? She'd told herself long ago it wasn't her fate. She should be happy — surrounded by a growing family, serving in a manner rarely granted to females in the territories. One she earned, cherished.

She was happy.

They rounded the hallway leading to Xavier's study, and her eyes adjusted.

The torches on the wall slumbered in the morning light.

She stopped and studied one particular painting on the wall. Deep blues and vibrant greens swirled together, overlaying a background of dull gray. Was this always here?

"That's a map of the water's journey through Morvak Mountain," Erik said as he leaned closer and traced the winding color with his finger.

The edge of his sleeve brushed against her arm, and his other hand rested on her waist.

She resisted the urge to close her eyes as the aroma of spicy cloves overpowered the training barn's familiar pine scent.

"This map is old. Several decades if I…"

Spicy cloves.

Spicy cloves.

Him.

She shifted her weight to her back leg and pivoted, kicking his thigh. The top of her foot wrapped around the back of his knee.

His weight buckled.

Maia knew her attacker felt familiar. Spent a week stewing, trying to figure out what niggled at the back of her mind. His scent. How did she miss it? Too busy mooning after him, she failed her training. Again.

She didn't hesitate this time. A sense of icy calm filled her veins, fueled by flames of embarrassment. She lunged for his stomach.

They tumbled through the study's threshold.

The back of his head hit the floor.

Maia pulled a small dagger from the inner lining of her boot. The motion was automatic, despite the weapon's rare use. She gripped its handle and brought the edge of the blade to the pulse throbbing in his neck.

Erik's eyes bulged. He stilled under her lighter frame.

"You," Maia spat. "Why you—"

"Enough," Xavier said as he strolled over to their tangled limbs and placed a hand on her shoulder. "Release him."

"He's the spy." She pressed the blade deeper, nicking Erik's flesh, and a drop of blood rewarded her efforts. "The one who tied me up."

"I said enough," Xavier growled.

She swallowed. "But—"

"That's an order."

Years of following the chain of command warred with her instinct to stay in control. She hesitated, then removed her dagger from Erik's throat, sliding it back into its sheath.

She snarled and stood. Slowly.

Erik touched the prick of skin at his neck and grinned.

It wasn't a happy gesture.

No, the edges of his lips tilted enough to let her know he savored her reprimand.

Another time, they said.

Perhaps he enjoyed their little game.

He raked his gaze over her rumpled tunic as he brushed off the tops of his pants. Erik stood.

A challenge.

My memory is long, her eyes promised. *This isn't over.*

"A Red Guard delivered this before sunrise." Xavier pinned them with his glare and gestured to a small scroll.

"Another missive from the High Table?" she asked as she squinted at the broken seal. Maia eyed it with all the suspicion she gave the rattlers in the reeds by the stream. "What do they want?" *Now* went unspoken.

"That's my family's seal," Erik said. "From the desk of my father."

"Wait." Maia turned to face him. "Your father? The letter came from the Castle."

"Yes. My father is Faeblood."

"I wondered if you'd own your heritage." Xavier handed him

the scroll and leaned in his chair. He gestured to Erik. "Go on. Read it."

Erik grabbed the missive, pulling the parchment taut, and scanned the communication.

"Surprised?" Xavier asked. He crossed his arms over his chest and leaned forward. "Yes, I discovered your identity some time ago, Erik Siodina, sole heir to the most powerful Lord on the High Table."

Maia shuddered.

She'd experienced the misfortune of being on the other side of Xavier's displeasure.

Even directed at another, she wanted to bend.

Erik let the hand holding the parchment fall to the side and turned on his heel. He crossed to the back of the room and paced its width. After a few passes, he addressed them both.

"Generations of our line carry the gift of casting. My family benefits from an elevated status within the Castle walls. As you are aware, I'm the first son of Emsworth of the Siodina family."

"I gathered as much from his presence in the training barn last month," Xavier drawled. "Very few elders choose to walk among the populace. It would take a very special circumstance or a special *someone* to entice them out of their lair in the mountain. So Erik, son of Emsworth, what about my village piques the interest of the Castle?"

"Certain members of the High Table consider your compound a threat." Erik slowed the words, enunciating each sound.

"What? How?" Maia asked. "Xavier leads the training at the direction of the Castle. They benefit from his service."

"Loyalty." Xavier pointed to her cuffs. "They question the loyalty of those very men that pledge their fealty to me — sovereign fighters, answering to a different master."

Maia scoffed.

"He's right," Erik said. "The High Table carries an obsession with power. For many years now, they concern themselves with Xavier's reach."

"But they cast. Surely, they don't fear us."

"I thought the same at one time." Erik let out a dark laugh and clenched the parchment in his hand, crumpling the middle. "Xavier is an anomaly to their system. Yes, they carry the gift but are wise enough to recognize his influence. Humans outnumber them. Magic is not enough. It never will be enough..."

"But I still don't understand." Maia looked back and forth between them. "We are a single territory."

Erik shook his head.

"The Castle relies on the loyalty of its populace." He hesitated, then added, "The villages follow the natural breaks of Morvak Mountain, which keeps the communities isolated. Xavier has men in every territory. Loyal men. Dangerous men."

"But he provides a trade."

"You think too small." Xavier uncrossed his arms and rounded the desk. "Your father raised you as a fighter. From your cradle, he pushed you to excel in combat, never allowing other pursuits. Other patterns of thinking. It's a failure I share with him."

He sat down and tipped his chin to Maia.

"Your strength as a fighter fosters your naivety of the world outside the walls of the training barn." To Erik, he said, "Read it."

Erik opened the missive, cleared his throat, and read its contents out loud.

Xavier Northcott, Loyal Subject of the High Table,

You hold amongst your ranks a man by the name of Erik, son of

Emsworth. We, the High Table, demand relinquishment of your claim and subsequent release from his duties to you.

His father, Lord Siodina, demands safe passage on his journey home. He requires Erik's presence at the Castle henceforth.

In exchange for his return, we absolve you of previous transgressions against the decree prohibiting lethal blades of warfare. Your fighter's participation fulfilled the punishment set forth by our governing council. He is hereby exonerated for harm inflicted upon our contender during the sanctioned match.

In addition, it has come to our attention that a person of Faeblood ancestry resides in your territory. We request her attendance at our annual Yule Tide Ball, in five months time. Her presence outside the nobility is extraordinary, and we seek to present her to society as is customary of someone after coming of age.

Whereas, the Castle demands honor and fealty above all. Your punishment, should you choose to not honor these requests, shall be severe.

Lord Scarbough, son of Ogden,
Councilman of the High Table

~

Erik re-rolled the parchment and flung it on the desk.

Xavier leaned forward and clasped his hands in front of his lips. And waited.

"They sent me here to spy on the training facility." Erik ran his hand over his mouth and gestured to Xavier. "On you."

"What I want to know is," Xavier said, "what information did you send back?"

Erik hesitated.

"I provided them with schedules, daily activities." He started pacing again. "They wanted to know where you went when you left the compound. The patterns of your second-in-command."

Her jaw fell open, and she whirled to face Erik. "Why you no good, rotten—"

Erik squared up to her.

"You." She pointed to him, her heart pounding in her chest. "You followed Gavyn and the girls to the falls. Where else? Who else? Did you track us to the stream, too?"

"*Maia.*" Xavier pushed back from his desk and tilted his head, studying them both. "I've known Erik's identity for some time."

He rounded his desk and lined his boots up with Erik's.

"You have a choice. I shall grant you leave of this compound and your duties. But you owe me. You owe Ember." His voice softened. "Lex Talionis."

"An eye for an eye. Or in my case, a life for a life." Erik clenched his fists and asked, "What do you require?"

"Maia, come here." Xavier grasped both of her shoulders and paused. "I have a mission for you. This is an opportunity I intend to take. You will accompany Erik to his family's home. Blend in. I want your eyes and ears to the ground."

Xavier released his hold.

"Yes, sir." Her back snapped straight, and she bent at the waist. "I'd be—"

"Xavier." Erik raised his hand. "My father will not permit her presence in the Castle. Humans, save for servants and Red Guard, are not allowed within its walls."

"I suspected as much." A feral grin crossed Xavier's face. "I do not intend to send her as a fighter, a member of my territory. Nor as an official liaison."

She tilted her head to the side. "Then what—"

"I intend to send her as your wife."

Join Maia and Erik as they navigate the politics of the Castle, the murky waters of Faeblood society, and the tumultuous attraction that could alter the path of an entire kingdom in *The Sins of an Heir.*

Want more Gavyn and Ember? Join my newsletter at mklorber.com to receive a special bonus epilogue.

THE FAEBLOOD SERIES
The Curse of a Faeblood: Gavyn and Ember
The Sins of an Heir: Erik and Maia
The Mask of a Savage: Mikel and Ada

ACKNOWLEDGMENTS

What a ride. They say writing a novel is like giving birth. Constant discomfort. A little pain. And poof — a book baby.

What a load of hogwash. At least during my pregnancies, my body knew (even if my mind didn't) what to do. Many days, I had no clue which way was up in this manuscript.

My little math, science nerd brain is tired. Exhausted. After all, it had to learn story structure. And sentence structure. And how commas work. Really, how *do* commas work? I still have no clue.

During the spring of The-Year-That-Shall-Not-Be-Named, I found myself out of work for the first time in my adult life. After binging romance book after romance book after romance book… after fifty gazillion walks with my kids and pups… after trying and failing at baking bread, I wrote my first book. Not this one. Nope. I carried a non-fiction outline in my heart for two years and finally put my fingers on a keyboard.

After the pain of my first book baby wore off, I did what most new parents do. I looked around and thought, *what now?*

But I had a taste of writing.

And I was hooked.

Since only one non-fiction idea rattled around my chest, I turned to my true love — romance novels. An avid reader of the genre since middle school (at a time before I understood my body, let alone my emotions), surely I could draft a novel about two people falling in love.

Hahahahaha.

Ha.

Ha-Ha.

Listen, this was *hard*. As in, if I'd known how hard, I'd never had finished the first draft — hard. Gavyn and Ember and the entire compound of characters lived in my head rent free for over a year, and I owe countless thanks to the crew that shaped their story on page.

Foremost, my best friend, Sabine deserves a medal. She had the misfortune of reading my first draft, then my sixty-seventh. She coached me through the sex scenes and made sure I cut out all the technical fighting jargon. She single-handedly kept me on this journey with two well-timed notes, one I hung in my office for those days when I needed a little extra encouragement. Every single strong heroine I write will be in her image.

Your book is coming, my friend.

But I'm going to make you wait.

Working with an editor is scary. Will they like my story? Will they bond with my characters? My writing? *Will they like me?* I lucked out. The writer gods sent me the most amazing shepherd. Casey, thanks for taking a chance on a new author. For pushing me when I needed a nudge. For guiding me when I was lost. And for holding my hand when I required extra care. Every writer deserves a heart full of ink and an editor bursting with helpful comments.

Special thanks go to Jen Prokop for her fabulous critique on Gavyn and Ember's love arc. To Stacey, for her act one slice and dice. To Jess and the entire HEA club, for their endless support and pocket friendship. To Mama, for her finish-line proofing.

Shout out to Chris and my human babies for creating writing space in our hectic life, allowing me to follow my passion.

Thank you to every reader who trusts me enough to take a chance on my words. I will always cherish your gift of time.

Finally, my sincerest thanks to my fur-baby, Hershey

Almond. I formed my publishing imprint, Three Pom Press, as a tongue-in-cheek nod to my rescued and inherited rascals not realizing how big a part they would play in this adventure. At the time of this note, we lost you too soon; our grief is still raw. My heart aches every morning I sit at the keyboard and search for you at my feet. Thank you for being such a good girl.

~Melissa